IT IS RISEN

Jessica Christ, Book 5

H. CLAIRE TAYLOR

ISBN: 978-0-9996050-4-2 (H. Claire Taylor)

FFS Media, LLC

contact@hclairetaylor.com

For the man upstairs

whose bedsprings I hear when I'm trying to sleep.

Bravo, sir.

Contents

Chapter One

Chris scooted closer to Jessica on their Tempur-Pedic sex pallet afloat in the middle of the Pacific. Earlier that day, she'd watched a documentary on the vanishing wildlife of Samoa, but now didn't seem like the time to tell her boyfriend about that.

He brushed a hand up and down the exposed flesh of her waist between the thin fabric of her bikini bottom and the tie holding on her top. "I love it when we do it in your mind," he whispered. "Always so exotic."

"It's not *entirely* in my mind. Clearly you contribute to it."

He stared hungrily into her eyes. "No, babe, this is all you."

She shook her head, "Ehh ... no, I don't think so. I wouldn't invite the Avengers to watch."

Chris's eyes darted over to another mattress raft bobbing gently up and down fifty yards away. He waved enthusiastically to the passengers aboard it then turned back to Jessica. "First, that's the Justice League. Second, can't you see how jealous they are of you? I mean, *me*?"

She decided to ignore it. It wasn't real anyway, so who cared? She pressed a finger to his lips. "Let's stop talking about it."

He nodded emphatically then put on his game face. "You're right. Less talking, more doing."

She rolled her eyes, but couldn't keep from smiling as he pressed himself up against her and they kissed, the mattress rocking gently on the placid ocean waves, the Justice League looking on disinterestedly. He made quick work of untying her suit in the back, but before he could detach himself from her mouth long enough to free her from the top completely, the sound of a throat clearing stole her attention away from the sexy task at hand.

She held the cups of her bathing suit in place, knowing instinctually who she would find hovering over the mattress oh-so judgmentally. She didn't know much about the Justice League, but she was certain *this* guy wasn't part of it.

Jesus's hair and robe billowed slightly in the ocean breeze as the waves lapped around his sandals.

"Oh hey, bro," Chris said casually.

"Heavenly Father's blessings to you, Christopher," Jesus replied, beaming.

"You catch the Roma-Juventus match the other day?" Chris said.

Jessica's head whipped around to him. Wait a second.

They were talking sports. But it wasn't football, as far as she could tell.

"Oh yes." Jesus nodded enthusiastically. "What a game. Dear old Dad even spoiled it for me, and I still enjoyed it."

"Fernando was on fire. That hat trick?"

Jesus chuckled. "We call those holy trinities up there." His eyes darted skyward, and Jessica was officially confused; was Heaven physically above them? She thought that was just a metaphor or a simplistic crutch for the human mind. "Just a little angelic humor." Jesus's laugh sent giddy chills through Jessica's body.

She shook them off. "As much as I love that my boyfriend and family get along, I'd love it even more if you'd get to the point of why you're here, Jesus, so we can get back to what we were doing."

Jesus's smile faded. "You mean sex outside of marriage?"

"Sex outside of reality," Jessica corrected, not appreciating his tone one bit, "and it's got God's stamp of approval, so save the lecture."

"I'll save *that* lecture," he said sassily, bracing his hands on his hips and kicking one foot out to the side, sending a spray of salt water onto the corner of their mattress. "But obviously I'm here with a specific purpose, otherwise I would not make the effort to crash your sin fest."

Jessica groaned. "It's not— Okay, fine. Change is hard; I know. Now get to the point."

"You're dragging your feet again, sis."

"I'm not dragging my feet. I can't start a business with a snap of my fingers"—she squinted at him, arching her brows—"*can* I?" Jesus shook his head quickly. "Damn. Then I need time. I haven't even perfected my recipes yet. No point in building a bakery if no one wants to eat what I have."

Jesus sighed and gestured down at the mattress. "Do you mind if I sit?" Jessica and Chris scooted over and Jesus made himself comfortable. "You're stalling, dear sister. You can improve your recipes while you go through the process of opening the bakery. And besides, that's not the only thing you're avoiding."

Jessica looked to Chris for backup, but he simply nodded along with whatever Jesus said.

"He's right, you know," Chris added.

Chris was no help. Noted. "I don't even know what you're talking—"

"The *book*," said Jesus. "You haven't even cracked the cover. Don't you want to know what propaganda and egomaniacal lies are being spread to the masses?"

Of course she *wanted* to know that. "But God said I shouldn't read the Bible until the second edition came out."

Jesus waved that off and blew a raspberry. "No, not *that* book. Jimmy's book. Come on now. How have you not even started it? I just— I don't understand. I mean, I read the New Testament as soon as it was released, and let me tell you, there were some major inconsistencies despite it being well-intentioned. One might have an easier time connecting plot points between Michael Keaton's Batman and the Dark Knight trilogy." He chuckled.

"I *knew* Jesus was a DC guy!" Chris held his hand in the air, and Jesus flinched.

"No," Chris mumbled from the corner of his mouth. "I'm not gonna strike you. You just hit my hand with your hand."

Jesus stared at Christopher's palm. "Oh! Ha! Like they do in sports!"

"Yeah!"

They high-fived, but Jesus's boyish elation faded from his face quickly as soon as he returned his attention to his sister. "I encourage you to at least know what Jimmy claims you've said. You might also learn a little about him that could help you." Jesus stood. "Also, maybe read the Bible a little, too. Sheesh, I can't believe you're not even curious about it. I mean, not to toot my own horn, but I sort of hand it to the Pharisees ... a bunch of times. Well, except for that last bit." He shrugged a shoulder. "Can't win them all, I guess ...

"Aaanyway, I'll let you two resume getting to know each other in an unholy way. And I definitely don't want to be here for that."

"We don't want you here for that either," Jessica said. "That should go without saying."

Jesus tilted his head, squinting dubiously at her. "Should it? It seems you two like an audience." He hitched a thumb at the nearby raft, where Wonder Woman and Batman were trying to snatch fish out of the water.

"Okay," Jessica said, "first of all, it wasn't my idea to invite the entire Justice League to—"

"Please," Chris said, "*that's* not the entire Justice League. Aquaman isn't even there and"—a splash a few yards away pulled Chris's attention—"Oh, there he is. Well. Even still, that's not the entire Justice League."

"You know, Jesus," Jessica said, "if you don't approve of our admittedly weird sex life, you could just stop showing up."

Jesus groaned exasperatedly. "No, because then how would I make sure you kept on with your journey?"

Jessica threw her arms into the air. "How should I know? Listen, you have a little sway up in Heaven, right?"

Jesus bent slightly at the waist, his interest piqued.

"Then why don't you ask for the rules to be changed? If I can convince our Father to make some tweaks, so can you. I mean, really, Jesus, do something for yourself for once. If you're not going to look out for you, who will?"

Nodding slowly at first, then more enthusiastically, Jesus said, "Yeah ... Good point! Thanks, sis." Then turned on his heels, causing ocean spray to fly out around him, and stomped off across the water.

She turned back to her boyfriend. "Where were we?"

And as Superman flew in lazy, idle circles overhead, Chris reminded her just where they'd left off ...

Chapter Two

Jess rolled to her side on the massive, luxurious mattress, and her eyes immediately fell on the boxes she hadn't yet unpacked since her move from San Marcos to Austin. She decided to cut herself some slack, considering she'd only been in this condo for a week. Add that to the shock of living alone and the exhaustion of daily life in a big city, and she had a fairly strong excuse for the lack of progress.

But on the other hand, she hadn't really done anything else all week, except watch TV on the leather sofa, stare out of the picture windows that overlooked downtown, and try not to think too much about how all of this was likely one huge mistake.

Forcing herself to crawl out of the exquisitely comfortable bed, the lucid dream still fresh in her mind, Jessica knew Jesus was right. She needed to get to work. As it was, she was living on borrowed time, borrowed money, and in a borrowed condo.

The latter was a bit of a mystery, but it was one that her subconscious could further chip away at *after* a few cups of coffee.

She padded across the chilly floor, cursing whoever thought concrete was better than carpet, and flipped on the pendant lighting over the kitchen island to avoid tripping over her own feet or a yet-to-be-unpacked box.

Wendy Peterman was to thank for this sophisticated dwelling, which Jessica still didn't feel like she deserved. The publicist claimed it belonged to a client who was wealthier than was useful for any human being and who preferred not to bother with renting it out, opting instead to house Jessica for free, on the off chance that it could amount to a tax write-off down the road—as if Jessica were a walking $501(c)(3)$.

Jessica's instincts told her not to accept such a generous gift. However, with Wendy as a liaison, Jessica decided to override her gut and go with her head because Wendy was also a terrifyingly dogged vetter; if Jessica's messy public life *did* eventually ruin Wendy's career, the woman could probably make a good living as a private investigator. And besides, Wendy proved time and again that she possessed better judgment in matters like this than Jessica. If this setup could later hurt Jessica's image in any way, Wendy wouldn't let her touch it with a twenty-foot pole.

And it was a sweet condo. While Jess wouldn't admit it aloud, that factor played in heavily to the decision to accept the offer. Outside of an identical situation to this one, it was unlikely Jessica would *ever* be able to afford somewhere this nice. Especially when she was without a job and virtually broke.

Though not *penniless*.

She passed the jar of pennies on the way to the Keurig, dropped in a K-cup, then wandered to the fridge to see if she still had any yogurt.

She did not.

It's probably better that I don't eat anyway. My morning plans are not necessarily conducive to a full stomach.

Once the Keurig beeped at her, and grabbed the cup and headed over to the breakfast nook, which was really just a designated corner of the open great room. She set down her mug and sighed, staring at the floor in the far corner where a book lay open but facedown, right where it'd slid to a stop when she chucked it across the room a week before. But only *after* Wendy had handed it to her, assigned it as her homework, and then left.

Rising from her chair and tiptoeing over, she bent and picked up *Railed to the Cross*, shut it, and stared at the cover where her name was still branded across the front.

With a foreword by Jessica Christ stared back at her like a challenge.

Probably because it was. Jimmy had a plan, but what that plan was, God only knew.

What kind of shit are you pulling, Jimmy?

GREAT QUESTION. I HAVE MY SUSPICIONS, BUT IT'S STILL ANYONE'S GUESS.

So maybe even God didn't know.

Can't you just jump into his head and figure it out?

READ THAT BOOK THEN YOU TELL ME IF **YOU** WOULD WANT TO JUMP INTO JIMMY'S HEAD.

Ugh. There was no getting around it. She would have to read the book.

But wait.

Have you read the book?

OF COURSE.

Can you sum it up for me?

THE LORD AND CREATOR OF ALL THINGS HOLY IS NOT YOUR SPARKNOTES.

That's not what you said when I asked you to sum up Heart of Darkness *two years ago.*

THAT WAS A ONE-TIME THING BECAUSE I AM A MERCIFUL GOD.

And summing up Jimmy's bullshit isn't a mercy?

NO. IT WOULD BE A DISSERVICE.

Whatever that means.

Once she was seated and had adequately scalded her tongue on the unnecessarily hot cup of coffee, she cracked open the cover, flipped to the table of contents, and stopped when her eyes landed on *Foreword by Jessica Christ.*

Below it were the chapter titles, but she would get to those later. One crap heap at a time.

She flipped forward and began reading what she'd supposedly written.

When I first received the call from Reverend Dean, or as I like to think of him, "Uncle John," with the request to write a foreword to his life story, I didn't know what to say.

Truth be told, I was a little overcome by the gesture.

"Oh for fuck's sake!"

YEAH, IT DOES NOT GET ANY BETTER.

"Uncle John? What the hell is that anyway? His name's Jimmy! Why would I call him Uncle John?"

THE ANSWERS YOU SEEK ARE ALL IN THE BOOK.

Ugh. Fine.

She continued reading.

After all, who reading this right now can't remember an instance of me publicly calling out Jimmy as a fraud? I've done it time and time again, often going to the heart of his ministry and trying to destroy the faith of those most loyal to him.

In short, he and I haven't always seen eye to eye.

"Well, that's true enough."

THOU SHALT STOP PAUSING SO OFTEN. THIS IS GOING TO TAKE FOREVER.

You're exaggerating, but fine.

This has been mostly my fault.

"Come on!"

I was just a kid. I grew up in such close proximity to Uncle John that I saw the man and not the messenger. But I still remember with fondness the times I spent with him as a young girl. He would drive all the way to my home in Mooretown and take me out for ice cream. I could talk about anything with him, like my best friend whose name was probably Miriam, or the boy Crispin I had a crush on. Even as those friends faded into the oblivion of time, Jimmy stood by me.

His faith in me is breathtaking, and I've returned it in kind when I could. As Jesus resurrected Lazarus to show others the power of God, so did I breathe life into Jimmy in front of the White Light Church congregation and hundreds of millions of YouTube viewers. Every bit of that was real and actually happened. Anyone who tries to deny the hard facts of it denies God Himself and shall unfortunately burn in hell for all eternity. His rules, not mine.

She shut the book. *I think I need a break.*

IS THIS NOT WHAT YOU EXPECTED?

No, this is exactly what I expected. Except lazier, surprisingly. Did he really not bother to remember Chris's and Miranda's names? He's had multiple encounters with them. Chris even called him last year to come down to campus and try to ruin my life.

She pushed the memory from her mind. It had been

the catalyst for their transition from taking a break to broken up. Those were dark days she didn't care to relive (Mason who?). Besides, nobody won when her buried hatchets resurfaced. Grudges tended to appear in her shared dreams with Chris, and when they did, her subconscious could be a little vindictive with the setting. For instance, after Chris was a half-hour late picking her up for a date, their nightly rendezvous had landed them in Chris's mother's bedroom, and nothing either of them tried altered the location or the disturbing amount of detail that Jessica's mind had retained from the few brief visits to Bethany Riley's room.

AH YES. JIMMY DOES POSSESS A SHARP RECOLLECTION OF YOUR COLLEGE CAREER, THOUGH. READ ON, CHILD.

> *And yet, I still strayed, despite Jimmy's loyalty to me.*
>
> *A college campus is a dangerous, godless wasteland for anyone, and for me, the devil's temptation proved too potent, and I succumbed to drinking and drugs and deviant sexual indulgences time after time until, with the loving guidance of Uncle John, I returned to my Father's side, the Prodigal Daughter of the Almighty, or as I've come to know him in recent days, Deus Aper.*
>
> *My hope is that my failure will serve as a reminder that mankind is naught more than pigs, each and every one, but God gives second chances, and we must not squander them.*
>
> *I was lucky enough to preview this book before*

publication, and I can tell you, you're in for a real blessing. I haven't read anything this profound since Biblio Deus Aper (available at all major retailers for $17.99). The Reverend Dean's life is a story about redemption, about discovering the power of faith, however misguided or unfounded it may seem. It's about following God's path toward salvation, and ultimately, about not causing God's fiery wrath to rain down upon us all.

Most of you likely bought this book because you know of Reverend Dean, the one who God visited as a hog and sent on a mission to let the world know about His daughter. But there's so much more to him than that. Before that fateful night, he was a completely different person, and while God was preparing him for his purpose, he didn't know that.

Some may have picked up this book with the intent to ridicule. To those, I have only this to say: be careful. You may start out with evil in your heart, but as you read about the boy who grew up into the great man, you will start to see some of yourself in him. In fact, I'd go so far as to say you might begin rooting for him, despite your original intent. I hope that you'll let your heart be changed by his incredible story as you come to understand the truth of Jimmy's mission and the purity of his actions that not a single human swine on this entire planet actually deserves.

Blessings,

Jessica Christ

"Wow. Wooow. Ho-ly—"

WHERE DOES ONE EVEN START, RIGHT?

You almost sound like you're enjoying this.

OF COURSE NOT. BUT YOU HAVE TO ADMIRE THE NERVE.

Uh, no. No, I don't. Maybe you find this funny because he's not making things up and claiming you said them.

DO NOT WALK THAT PATH WITH ME, CHILD. DO YOU KNOW HOW MANY MILLIONS OF TIMES OVER THOUSANDS OF YEARS PEOPLE HAVE WRITTEN WORDS AND THEN CLAIMED, "SO SAYETH THE LORD"? IT'S CONSTANT. IN FACT, IT'S HAPPENING RIGHT NOW. IN THIS VERY INSTANT.

Okay, so you kind of know what this feels like. Fine. But what now?

THAT IS A PATH YOU MUST DISCOVER ON YOUR OWN.

You're not coming with me?

OF COURSE I'LL CHECK IN, BUT I DO NOT WALK PATHS. I HATH NO FEET. OR LEGS.

What about that poem Maddie had on her wall, the one about footprints in the sand? Rumor has it, you walk with lots of people.

FIRSTLY, AND I CANNOT BELIEVE I HAVE TO

SAY THIS AGAIN, THAT WAS JESUS. HE AND I ARE NOT ONE AND THE SAME.

Jessica walked to the bedroom, grabbed her phone and texted Chris. Surely he would be more sympathetic to her situation than God.

"Read the foreword to Jimmy's book. As bad as I thought."

By the time she made it back to her coffee, Chris had responded. *"Go back to sleep and I'll take your mind off it."*

So Chris was no real help either. She considered ranting to Miranda, except that would require admitting to Miranda that she's only just started the book and hardly made it through the introduction. Chris could commiserate with not wanting to read—in general—but Miranda wouldn't show the same sympathy. And Miranda would be right in this, as she usually was. Jessica should just suck it up and read the damn book.

Well, it's early. I have all day to plug away at it.

The condo was silent. She couldn't even hear the AC running, though she could feel it. Stupid energy efficient systems. Where was the cranking and grinding she was used to? This whole city was too damn efficient.

Although ... she could probably use more efficiency in her life, if she were being honest. She hadn't been efficient at anything in a long time, and especially not since moving to Austin the week before.

I should stop resisting and let the city take me along for the eco-friendly ride.

She dressed, threw the book, her wallet, and a handful

of pennies from her penny jar into her Nu Alpha Omega tote bag, and left her luxury home.

Her front door fed into a long indoor hallway with glazed concrete walls and floors, and recessed lighting. As she walked down the single flight of stairs toward the condominium foyer, she spotted her across-the-hall neighbor, a not unattractive man who looked to be in his midthirties but who, for some reason she couldn't pinpoint, she suspected was really in his midforties.

He grinned at her as he approached, heading toward his front door. "Good morning, Jessica!"

"Morning, Jeremy!"

"Where you headed to this early?" He tucked his leather portfolio under his armpit, freeing up his hand that he slipped into his back pocket. A jingle of metal announced he'd found his keys.

"Not sure. A coffee shop somewhere. You have any recommendations?"

His eyes popped open excitedly. "Do I!" As he rattled off his favorites nearby, Jess nodded along and let the list run its course. She hadn't learned a lot about city life, but she had learned that when asking someone for a food or drink recommendation, one should expect a list of every related establishment the person knew, along with a brief assessment of it.

"... And then there's Hill of Beans, which isn't bad but the baristas there are divas," he finished before taking a deep breath.

"Okay, cool. So which one's closest?"

He paused, thought about it, then shrugged. "I guess Starbucks. But they're socialists, and not the cool kind. So you probably want to go to Bat-Ass Brew. Just a block east of here on the north side of the street."

"Will do. Thanks."

What he did next would take some getting used to. He said, "No problem. Take care," and ended the interaction like a normal person would do to another normal person.

She loved Jeremy platonically. They'd addressed the messiah-in-the-room when they'd first met, back when Wendy showed her the place that was soon to be her home. But Jeremy made it clear her particular situation was neither here nor there to him. Jeremy was just her neighbor who didn't give a damn what she did in her private life. In short, he was the kind of neighbor one *could* love.

Jessica slipped on her big sunglasses and a Texas Rangers baseball cap—a trick Wendy had taught her that worked remarkably well to avoid notice—and stepped out into the hot July sun.

It wasn't that Jessica didn't appreciate a good walk—stretching her legs after spending the week alone indoors was actually quite pleasant, even with the heat radiating from above and below making her feel like a baked ham. Her reason for picking the closest location was less related to her own energy, and more related to her limited supply of pennies.

"God is coming to smite the earth!" shouted the homeless flavor of the week who'd camped out along her short route. Despite his inaccurate belief, she tossed a couple pennies into the Styrofoam Whataburger cup that shook in his unsteady hands. While Jessica preferred when the homeless used glass or metal cups—the sound of the pennies falling was much more satisfying that way—she did feel a slight sense of gratification in helping the man, even though he called her a whore immediately following her charity.

Yet another of Wendy's rules of conduct, Jessica had started to warm to it (especially when metal or glass cups were involved): always give to the homeless, but not a lot and always change.

It was a publicity move, to be sure, but it made sense. Jess knew the kind of luck she had, even if God insisted luck wasn't a thing. If Jess walked past a panhandler without giving him a single glance would be the one time some freelance amateur paparazzi snapped a good picture and made a million dollars selling it to some faux news entertainment site, most likely Eugene Thornton's. The headline would be something like Stingy Attention Whore Supports Murdering Homeless Veterans.

The AC at Bat-Ass Brew swept over her like a refreshing waterfall as she escaped the sticky July air. She paused on the front mat and looked around. The cafe had a nice ambiance—small, strange trance music in the background, mostly young business people with earbuds in, chatting quietly with their Macbook screens. Best of all, no one was staring at her.

She pulled off her hat and sunglasses, shoving them into her tote.

Still, no one was staring at her.

She approached the counter hesitantly, trying to remember what tagline Jeremy had included with this place. Was it "slow service" or "has great smoothies but so-so coffee" or "failed health inspection because of rats"?

"Hey, fellow human. Welcome to Bat-Ass Brew. How's life?" The tall guy behind the counter looked higher than she'd ever been, and she wasn't sure if she felt jealous or judgmental. Either way, she wasn't here to talk about life. Not with—she looked at his name tag—Rebel.

Stupid name. Probably not even his real one. He's probably Francis or Jerry.

"Life's fine." She looked up at the menu hanging on the wall behind him, and realized she might need a minute. Why couldn't any of the menu items just be called what they were? There was no "coffee" or "Americano" or "mocha latte." At the very least, why hadn't whoever made the sign had the common decency to include the ingredients below each item? It wasn't that she didn't *get* what they were going for with the names, she found the theme entirely unhelpful and useless. This wasn't some kind of theme park, it was a coffee shop, for whoever's sake!

She decided there was no point in guessing. "Uh, what's in the Mocha Guano?"

Rebel was slow to verbalize his response, nodding slowly with squinty eyes a few times first. "That's a good one. Free trade pistachio coffee, coconut milk, and cocoa ethically harvested from Amazonia. I can add whipped cream if you want."

That sounded like a lot of stuff that didn't need to be in coffee. She turned her eyes back up to the menu, randomly selecting another possibility. "What about the Milwaukee Protocol?"

"It's just an iced coffee."

"Okay. I'll do that."

Rebel approved with a drawn-out bob of his head. "You want that with rabies?"

"What."

"It's just an extra shot of espresso."

She'd come to Bat-Ass Brew with a mission, and that was to read some of Jimmy's awful book. Her hope had been to save up energy, and indeed replenish it, through the thoughtful use of stimulants. However, getting said stimulants was sapping all her mental and emotional reserves. So, to get things moving, and because she now needed a little extra pop, she said, "Okay, sure. Yeah. Give me rabies."

"Cool." But he didn't enter anything into the tablet in front of him. "You look a little tired. One of those days, huh? You got something big coming up?"

"Just reading to do." She focused down at the tablet, hoping he would take the hint.

"Oh nice. You a student here?"

"Nope." She tapped her fingertips on the counter, hoping the sound drew his eyes and he remembered the last crucial part of the transaction: payment.

"Yeah, you're too beautiful to be a student here."

"That's not a thing."

"So what do you do?"

Oh for her father's sake. "I'm the messiah."

A stupid openmouthed grin spread across his face. "Nice. Milwaukee Protocol with rabies, you said?"

"I guess so."

Finally, he entered it into the tablet and headed away from the counter to make her drink. Meanwhile, she turned to take in the rest of the space. Rebel's annoying existence aside, she instantly liked the place. The energy was good. Most everyone kept their eyes to themselves, focusing on a screen or a book or a stack of papers. *Could I recreate this for a bakery?* Though Bat-Ass Brew had a small glass case with muffins and cookies, almost no one seemed to be there to snack. Coffee then, that was the unifying factor.

It was settled. Whenever she opened her bakery, she would make sure there was a good coffee selection. And just like that, her mind began painting in small bits of the previously fuzzy vision of her future bakery. She was starting to dream in detail, something she wasn't sure she had the ability to do, outside of the lucid dreams she shared with Chris.

Rebel's voice cut through her pleasant imaginings. "How long you been in Austin?"

She turned toward the counter again, trying not to let her irritation sweep away the pleasure her imagination had just conjured. "About a week."

He grinned like an idiot. "Well, welcome to Austin. Man, it sure has changed."

"Yeah? You been here long?" She jabbed her credit card at him.

He nodded and swiped her card. "Going on two years. Came down here from Denver with nothing but the clothes on my back."

"That's great." She didn't bother returning her card to her wallet before darting off to find an open table.

A spot by the window called her name, and she settled in with her bag and drink before pulling out the book and staring down at it like it might jump at her at any moment.

She couldn't keep putting it off, though. She was here, and it was time to grit her teeth and read whatever drivel Jimmy was pitching as his life story.

It occurred to her that she didn't actually know anything about Jimmy. Where had he come from? Who was he before she was born? What had caused him to be such a massive pain in the ass?

It was just enough of a draw for her to flip to chapter one and start reading ...

Special, gifted, valuable, blessing—all words we use to describe our children in these modern times. No heed is given to whether these terms apply, and most often they do not. We assume, and wrongly so, that we are helping children when we attach such sycophantic adjectives to the fruit of our loins. In all but a few cases, the attempt at good parenting—no doubt born more out of a parent's egotistical need to believe they themselves can produce something great and of value than out of genuine objective observation—simply muddies the waters as children become teens and teens adults, each one then facing disappointment after disappointment when the world does not recognize the innate greatness they have been raised to believe exists somewhere within their stale, sin-stained soul. So few individuals are actually born with that special something inside them, that seed that can be sowed for the betterment of many, and the cacophony of entitlement wafting up from the masses as they shout, "What about me? Recognize me!" threatens to drown out those few who actually matter in God's plan.

My mother never called me special or gifted or valuable, and whenever she mentioned blessings she usually referred to the moments when I was away or had otherwise left her alone. There was no inflation of my ego growing up, that much is certain. If there were a currency-manipulation going on, it was in devaluing my existence. On the few occasions when I hinted at a future outside of Hawthorne, Alabama, my mother found the nearest long object and struck me on the back of the neck with it. Sometimes twice. Three times if I dared dream of such things on the Lord's day.

She peeled her eyes from the page, sat up straight, and stared at the student artwork on the wall facing her. What was this strange thing she was feeling? Could it actually be ... ?

No. That was crazy. She would never feel sympathy

for Jimmy. *If* his mother actually beat him, he probably did something awful to her to earn it, like ...

Again, no. There wasn't anything she could think of that would earn a kid a beating.

So maybe he was just flat out lying about it.

NOPE. JIMMY'S MOTHER REGULARLY BEAT HIM FOR JUST THAT OFFENSE.

Am I supposed to feel bad for him?

YES. THAT'S HOW EMOTIONS WORK.

But he's such a dick now!

THE LORD DOES NOT DENY THAT EITHER.

So what, I'm just supposed to forgive him for being literally the worst thing that's ever happened to me because his mother beat him? Just call him up and ask to be friends?

OH NO. THOU SHALT NOT DO THAT.

Then what do I do with this?

FEEL TWO EMOTIONS AT ONCE.

But that sucks.

THAT IS ACCEPTABLE. LIFE MAY SUCKETH.

She glanced down at the page, reading the last sentence over again to pick up where she left off, when two women around her age sat down at the table across from her, talking about their personal lives. While she wasn't immediately certain *what* they were saying about their personal lives, the unnecessary volume with which they chatted made her certain of the general topic.

She stuck her fingers in her ears as nonchalantly as was possible, and started reading again. The tone started to feel much more like Jimmy.

So I stopped speaking of it. But I always felt it. Always. My intuition wasn't drowned out by a chorus of others feeling the same thing, which is how I knew it to be true. I was different from my cross-eyed and webbed-toed peers. Those destined for greatness understand it, that feeling in your bones, the electricity in your muscles that starts to tingle when you brush up against your own potential. It sets your hair on end and engorges even the humblest servant of the Lord in undeniable ways.

An unshakeable faith in my own grand potential kept me going through the school-yard bullying in those first six years before I finally dropped out to help my mother full-time. It comforted through the nights where, after a week without running water, my own stank kept me awake, and the bodily chaffing was a slow torture. It even sustained me through the many beatings from my mother and her string of sinner boyfriends, each encapsulating one of God's deadliest seven sins.

"And I was like, 'My body my rules, bitch!' He didn't like that, but who cares? Not my fault he didn't know how to pull out."

Jessica glanced up at the woman. She was toned, wore yoga pants and a shirt that Jessica assumed was created in an African village, though even as she assumed it, she knew it was a bit of a logical leap. The girl had her blonde hair pulled up into a high bun and leaned across the table toward her friend—like one might do when one *didn't* want the entire cafe to hear—as she loudly explained the situation. Her golden-skinned friend looked on with mild interest.

"So then Craig's like, 'it's my baby, too,' and I was like, 'duh, why do you think I'm asking you to go halvsies with me on the procedure?'"

"Craig's such a caveman," said the friend.

"God, right? Like, where can I find a woke man in this town?"

They were using words she knew, but following along with the attached meanings was a different skill entirely. She went back to the book.

I marvel at my resilience at such a young age, and I don't believe I would be the man I am now had I been persuaded by an external source to believe I was special, blessed. I suspect I would have become deaf to my inner voice, the one that endures even to this day and doesn't speak in trite pleasantries, but shows me through sensual means that I am, indeed, a crucial element in the dawn of a new age.

I weathered those swine-like men, for I knew in my heart that this was the test the Lord had sent for me, this was what He required I endure to ensure that I was strong enough to carry out His work later on.

And I know now that I passed His trials. Each and every one of them, though I may have faltered temporarily along the way.

The first of Deus Aper's many trials was Dale. Dale was Greed. He moved into our ramshackle home, hardly more than a shanty, when I was but one year old, yet weaned off the breast of a reluctant madonna. Dale was on disability. The war had done him in, he said. My mother was on permanent disability after my biological father shot her through chest, pellets from the shotgun permanently damaging her right lung, causing her sighs to sound like the wind pushing open an old rusty gate at the end of a quiet country road.

"We're gonna be late for the march," announced the blonde, standing abruptly and yanking Jessica's attention back to her.

"Fine," said the golden-skinned friend, "but I need to grab some food for the road. You want anything?"

The blonde hedged, nibbling her lip as she thought about it. "Nah. They don't have any good vegan stuff here."

"Oh yeah, I forgot you do that now. Well, I'll meet you out by the bikes."

My mother was on permanent disability after my biological father shot her through chest, pellets from the shotgun permanently damaging her right lung, causing her sighs to sound like the wind pushing open an old rusty gate at the end of a quiet country road.

Shit! It just didn't make any sense! Jessica didn't feel strongly one way or another on what women did with their bodies, and she was no expert on the self-sacrificing lifestyle of vegans, but from what she *did* know, they definitely shouldn't be getting abortions, right? The illogic was numbing and irritating at once.

... permanently damaging her right lung, causing her sighs to sound like the wind pushing open an old rusty gate at the end of a quiet country road.

Seriously, though, how could a person object to eating a chicken's unfertilized egg but then go and remove their own fertilized egg without any moral objection?

Stop being judgmental.

I'm not being judgmental. I'm just trying to be logical.

"Shit." Jessica closed the book. She'd thought she had a little momentum, but now it was ruined and she was more frustrated than before.

KEEP READING, CHILD.

I can't focus.

YES, YOU CAN. YOU JUST DON'T WANT TO FOCUS.

Is any of this even true?

YES. STRANGELY, MOST OF IT IS FACTUAL. AT LEAST THE EARLY CHILDHOOD.

So, it's a lie later on?

PARTLY. BUT SO ARE MOST MEMOIRS. JUST WAIT TILL YOU GET TO HIS TIME IN CARLSBAD.

What happened in Carlsbad?

NO SPOILERS.

Oh, now you're all holier than thou about spoilers.

NEWS FLASH. I AM ALWAYS HOLIER THAN THOU.

How is he allowed to lie so much and get away with it?

HUMANS ARE GENERALLY ALLOWED TO DO WHATEVER OTHER HUMANS DO NOT STOP THEM FROM DOING.

Point taken. I'm going to do something about it.

I SUGGEST YOU RUN WITH ENDURANCE THE RACE THAT IS—

You know I hate running.

She packed up her things, shoved a handful of pennies into her pockets for the trip, and headed back to the condo.

It was time she gave Wendy Peterman a call ...

"You have to know a lawyer," Jessica insisted, staring down at her laptop screen from the moderate comfort of her sleek living room couch.

Wendy's I-don't-have-time-for-this expression stared back from her corner office in downtown Dallas. "Of course I do. If you must know, I'm dating two lawyers at the moment."

"Oh wow. I didn't need to know that, but good for you, I guess."

"*Very* good, Jessica. Very good. But you're still not suing Jimmy Dean. Not yet."

Jessica flopped back on the couch. "Why not? This is an open and shut case."

Wendy pressed her lips together. "Clearly, TV dramas have not done you good, Jessica. In real life, there's no such thing as an open and shut case. The legal system is built so all a person can hope for is an open and maybe two years later settled out of court with shared fault case. Plus, you think Jimmy would commit such obvious libel without expecting you to sue? Have we met the same conniving narcissist? He's baiting you. He wants you to sue."

"Really?"

Wendy sighed. "Well, maybe. I honestly don't know what he wants you to do yet. But trust me, I'm trying to get to the bottom of it. It's not easy dating two lawyers, so I'm in as big a hurry as you are."

Jessica nodded, then paused. "Wait. Are you just dating them to get legal counsel on this?"

"Duh. You think I'd pay the insane hourly rates for advice on a pro bono case?"

Jessica wasn't sure what to say. "Thanks for taking one for the team, I guess."

"It's fine. They're both skilled lovers. Although Devon is just a little too ... I don't know, clingy? So he'll be the first to go. Listen, I have a meeting in five, so I gotta wrap this up. Here's the plan. You've been neglecting Twitter and Instagram lately, so two birds with one stone: those are your platforms to dispute Jimmy's claims. He can't speak for you there; only you can. Your followers are hungry for word from you, and you'll be able to cut off the rumors at the pass, since none of those people read books anyway. They've probably heard rumors and commentary at this point, but they haven't heard directly from Jimmy through his book. You might still have time to set the record straight. Get them on your side."

"But the trolls—"

"Trolls are like HPV, Jess. Everyone who's lived a life worth living has them. They may flare up here and there, but the vast majority of them never amount to anything worth worrying about. Just ignore it and keep tweeting."

Wendy's office phone buzzed beside her, and she glanced down at it. "Gotta go. Just do what I say, okay?"

"Of course. Good luck with your—"

Wendy's face disappeared, replaced by black, before Jessica could finish.

Okay, if Wendy was willing to date two lawyers to help the cause, Jessica could be better about social media.

She snapped a picture of the book cover with her phone, drew the word "lies" over the image with her fingertip—that seemed like a very social media thing to do —and then started typing the caption: *This foreword is 100% not by me. I'd never work with Jimmy. What a loser. Sad.*

She read it a couple times. It didn't sound like anything she'd actually say, especially that last bit, but she'd been an apt pupil of Twitter and Instagram lately, and she'd learned to code switch, so ...

She checked again for typos, then posted.

The comments flowed in immediately. She checked Instagram first, hoping it could give her the support she needed to venture into darker social platforms ...

Baeatthebay *I knew it! So happy rn.*

DrewskiBrewski512 *Proud of you. Hope you're doing okay.*

NativeTexaCali *You go girl! Sue him for all he's worth!*

claireorwhatevs *I believe you.*

The support was nice. She'd take it, soak it in.
Okay. Onto the next.

She opened Twitter and already her notifications were in the dozens from people liking and RT-ing and replying to her post. She braced herself, trying to recall the Instagram love. *Let it give me strength.* Then she read the comments.

Abortion Kween *@FemDem97*
> *Replying to @therealmccloud*
> *when u kinda feel for a religious zealot bc she a victim of co-opted feminism*

Southern Fride *@2fast3furious*
> *Replying to @therealmccloud*
> *only sad thing here is you bitch*

Christians 4 Jesus *@stopmuslimists*

Replying to @therealmccloud
quit ruining our country America is for Christains

Jimmy4Prez *@whitelightfight1o*
Replying to @therealmccloud
sumus omnes porcos u fat whoremunger pig oink oink!

Ur New Daddy *@crimsontablet*
Replying to @therealmccloud
go fix me a sanwish

She tossed her phone onto the couch beside her.
Yep, she thought.
Wendy was right. I guess I have HPV.

Chapter Three

Despite Miranda's past insistence that the lighting in Jessica's condo was perfect for this type of thing, it was proving impossible to get a shot of the damn cupcake that didn't make it look like a big, mushy turd.

She stepped back from the kitchen island where she'd staged her photo studio and reassessed.

Maybe it wasn't the lighting that was making this Instagram undertaking such a pain in the ass. She squinted at her creation.

The cupcake looked remarkably like a brown turd.

That's what she got for trying to add chocolate on the inside.

I should definitely learn how to bake.

Didn't matter. She'd mastered the art of a warm, moist chocolate chip cookie, so she grabbed one of those from the cooling rack, switched out her subjects, played around with the angles a bit, then snapped a series of photos.

These were sure to garner plenty of social approval when paired with the hashtag #diditallforthecookie, though she wasn't entirely sure why that should be amusing. Was there a double meaning she was missing?

God, in all His finite wisdom, had suggested the hashtag that morning during His daily motivational lecture. She figured that listening to him on this one rare occasion—not about His intended topic of safe food handling, but about the hashtag—was easier than trying to think of something clever for herself.

Staring at the picture on her phone, she wished for the thousandth time that her personal branding wasn't so literal. Her browned face stared back at her from the top of the cookie, winking in a way she might expect from a man at a bar thirty seconds before he slipped something in her drink.

She selected a filter and posted the photo, and the notifications came flowing in immediately.

With great effort, she set her phone facedown on the counter and ignored the feedback.

The timer beeped and she walked over to the oven, pulling out a small sheet of warm yeast rolls.

While she let them cool, she returned to her phone and, her impulse control failing her completely, scrolled through the comments, despite knowing it was a terrible idea. Even on Instagram, a mean one would crop up every dozen or so comments. There was no safe place.

The first few were encouraging, though, saying the cookie looked good and Jessica's image looked beautiful on it. One even posted a crying emoji that Miranda had previously explained meant someone was laughing so hard they were crying, and not that Jessica had actually made someone cry. Her hashtag even got some love, which she knew pleaseth the Lord greatly.

Then the trolls arrived.

WhiteLightPower *Your baking is a mockery of Jesus. You will burn in hell. The only thing of yours I want to eat is you know what.*

She yanked the phone away from her face, her eyes remaining glued to the comment.

What the hell? No! I don't know what! What of mine do you want to—oh.

SumusOmnesPorkHer *Typical woman stays at home and bakes and makes the man do all the real work. Jimmy4Prez!*

She cursed, put down the phone, and returned to her yeast rolls, which seemed much less appealing now.

Ignore the HPV trolls. Everyone has them. They don't mean anything. They just want to make me mad.

She stared down at the rolls and hovered her hands above them, shutting her eyes. Her miracling had improved tremendously over the past few days of practice. Before that, it'd been a while since she'd last performed a miracle of any sort, but it was just like riding a bike—one she didn't necessarily have the ability to steer but stayed upright and kept from going into traffic nonetheless.

She breathed into it and felt the tide of her power flow through her body and down her arms.

Does Jimmy know about these trolls? Does he do anything to stop them? Or does he encourage them?

She felt the energy tug free of her left hand out of sync with her right, pulling her attention back toward the divine task. When she opened her eyes, she groaned.

While they were now gluten-free, her fixation on Jimmy had managed to screw up the batch.

Each image that stared back at her—and some that didn't stare in any particular direction—looked like someone had taken a picture of her when she'd least expected it. On one, she was clearly caught blinking. Another had her mouth lulling open, one eye drooping, and yet another had a chunk of her ash brown hair blowing in front of her face.

And so was the truth of her miracles—focus wasn't a necessary component, but a lack of it usually ended with her looking stupid.

As she scanned the images, not a single one was usable for Instagram, and anger swelled inside her at the waste of an entire batch. Well, she supposed she could still eat them while watching trash TV. Yeah, that would work.

I wonder if Law & Order *is on.*

Of course it was. But TV would come later. For now, there was a singular task she needed to complete, and stat.

(*Law & Order* would still be on whenever she got around to it.)

Grabbing her phone, she scrolled through her list of missed calls until she found the one with the right area code and pressed talk.

There was a single ring, hardly enough time for her to realize this was a terrible idea, before a familiar voice greeted her on the other end of the line.

"Jessica, dear child! What a pleasant surprise to hear from you! How is Austin? I've heard it's a city of sinners."

"Cram it, Jimmy. Are you sending trolls after me online?"

He tsked. "Jessica, daughter of Deus Aper and light in this dark life, I would never send hate to you in any way, shape, or social media form." His voice lowered, growing somber. "But yes, I have heard of the torment you've endured from anonymous accounts claiming to have an affiliation with White Light. It's such a shame."

"I hate you. Just wanted to reiterate that. Also, have you done anything to discourage those people from tormenting me?"

Waiting for a response, all she heard was Jimmy mumbling indistinctly to someone else.

"Wait," she said. "Where are you? You're clearly putting on a show."

Balls, I should have picked up on that sooner. This is Church Jimmy.

"Oh Jessica, the one they call Christ, I'm just sitting here with my friend Leonard Oberhausen, chatting about the book." He chuckled. "I guess I should specify. *My* book, although I can see why you would assume I meant the Good Book. And by the Good Book, I mean *Biblio Deus Aper.*"

As he continued to laugh airily at his stupid comment, Jessica struggled to recall where she knew that name from. Leonard Oberhausen ... It was like she could hear someone saying it. Leonard himself, maybe. Yeah. She could imagine someone saying, "I'm Leonard Oberhausen."

Oh crap.

"You're giving an interview right now?!"

"Oh yes, this is all on camera, though I suspect they'll only include snippets of it." He whispered, clearly not to her, "She's a little camera shy for obvious reasons, but she says hello."

"Call off the dogs, Jimmy. At the very least you're allowing the trolls to multiply. You might even be working with them. I don't know. But make it stop. I know you can do that."

"And then what, dear child?"

"What do you mean ...?" She struggled to read between the lines. Jimmy couldn't be regular awful Jimmy when he was on camera, but he was obviously trying to communicate a regular-awful-Jimmy message to her none-theless. He wasn't stupid, so he'd know she wouldn't answer the phone if he called back later.

And then what? Ah. He wanted to know what she'd do for him. That wasn't a huge breakthrough, since he *always* wanted to know that.

"And then we'll see. Just do it, Jimmy. For the love of my father, just do the right thing for once in your stupid, dumb life."

He laughed. "Oh Jessica, you're such a joker. Yes, I love you back. Tell your promiscuous mother hello for me and that I'm praying for her every night."

And then a click.

She stared at the screen for a moment before carefully and cautiously setting her phone down on the counter—the only other alternative was to throw it against a wall, and she didn't need to add another big purchase to her credit card. She clutched the lip of the marble countertops, and leaned forward, trying to breathe deeply so she didn't pass out.

Her phone dinged at her and without a thought, she did what Apple had trained her to do so well, and checked her notifications.

More trolls.

"RAAAAAAAH!" She grabbed a botched roll and threw it across the room. When it caused minimal damage and felt incredibly gratifying, she grabbed another and repeated the process, over and over again, shouting and throwing until only one roll with a burnt image of the back of her head remained on the tray and the rest were in odd locations around the condo.

A knock on the front door jolted her out of her rage.

Who was that? She wasn't expecting anyone. Oh no, was it one of Jimmy's white-clad freaks? Was it Eugene Thornton? No, that was unthinkable. Her eyes darted around, clarity sinking in. Rolls lay helter-skelter around her living room, or rather, the living room of whoever had offered her free room and board. And here she was ransacking it with baked goods.

Pull it together, Jess. You're an adult now.

She tiptoed over to the door, looked out the peephole and spotted Jeremy.

"Oh boy..." She cracked open the door and tried to smile, but it didn't work, and she was forced to quickly erase the snarl from her face when he jumped back a half step upon seeing it. "Hi, Jeremy."

"Hi. Um. I just wanted to come check on you. I heard the distinct sounds of unbridled rage, and ... well, everything in my brain told me to let it be, but you're my neighbor. So here I am."

It struck her as funny, so she laughed. And laughed.

And Jeremy giggled nervously along as she opened the door a little farther. "Yeah, I'm fine. Just ruined the rolls I was baking."

His eyes darted to something behind her. "Is that why there's one in that house plant? And one on the couch? Oh, and one on the window sill?"

She composed herself and nodded. "Yes. That's why there are rolls everywhere."

"Ah, okay." He folded his arms high across his chest, pausing to rub the afternoon stubble on his chin. "Well, maybe next time you get that angry, you should ... slow your roll, eh?" His serious expression broke, and he grinned at her. "Eh?"

She groaned, wiping a hand over her face but smiling all the same. "Jesus ..."

"As long as you're okay, though, I'll leave you to it." He stepped back to leave.

"Wait, Jeremy. Can I ask you something?"

"Of course."

What was it that made her think he might be a good person to ask about this? Was it his lame jokes? The fact that she never saw other people coming in and out of his condo? Or maybe that his preferred daily wear was leather flip-flops, cargo shorts, and a black T-shirt with the name of some metal band blazing across the front in jagged lettering? Yes, it was probably all those things. "Do you ever have to deal with trolls?"

He squinted at her, confused. "Now did you *mean* to say trolls or are we still talking about rolls?"

"What? No. Trolls. Like internet trolls."

"Oh. Okay. Um, no. I don't get on social media. You really shouldn't either, Jessica." He stared at her gravely, his expression darkening.

She chuckled morosely, trying to lighten the mood. "Tell me about it."

He nodded curtly. "Okay. The government is tracking each and every person who logs into any of the major social networks. But that's not even the worst part. They're working with the corporations, programming you to use the platforms as your main means of communication, then when corporations play the 'private company' card and start slowly restricting your freedom of speech, you begin to tolerate and accept that act of first-amendment suppression as okay, eventually creating enough space for the federal government to pass the constitutional amendment banning anti-government speech that they've been trying to impose for literally centuries now."

Jessica and Jeremy stared at each other in silence.

He clasped his hands together and grinned. "Well, good luck with the baking." With a quick wave, he turned and headed the short distance across the hall to his front door.

"Thanks," Jessica replied, watching him go and deciding that she needed to talk to someone sane, and soon.

The sun set over the patio of the Chews, Stews, and Brews Bar & Grill as Jessica took the first sip of her beer and tried to enjoy it despite the day of failures. None of that mattered now, she reminded herself. All that mattered was that she had a crisp beer, a nice breeze was moving in, and her best friend had shown up at a moment's notice.

Judging by the frizzy state of Miranda's french braids, she hadn't yet showered after softball practice, but she'd at least changed her clothes to avoid standing out.

"Despite the roll snafu and your neighbor being a strangely empathetic and kind-hearted psychopath, I actually envy you a little bit," Miranda said before casually tossing back a queso-covered chip.

Jessica tried not to throw shade at her best friend in the

whole world who, up until three seconds ago, she'd relied on as a constant source of common sense.

Miranda had the life Jessica had wanted since they were young, the life Jessica could've worked for and possibly attained had her father simply been a spoiled lacrosse player, like Miranda's, rather than The Almighty Spoiler. "Why the hell would *you* envy *me?*"

Miranda casually spooned more queso onto a tortilla chip and then popped it into her mouth. "You're out of school, you have a plan, and you're working toward it. I'm a year away from graduating with a bachelor's in psychology and four years of Division I softball under my belt. Considering there's no professional softball league and a psychology degree is useless unless it's a PhD, I don't even have a semblance of a plan for what I'm going to do next."

"Must be nice." Jessica sipped her beer, inspecting Miranda carefully. "You can do whatever you want. Like, anything. In the world. No one expects you to do a specific thing. The world is yours."

Miranda rolled her eyes. "Says the daughter of the one who created the world."

Their server, who'd introduced himself as Racer earlier —or at least that's what Jessica swore she heard him say— approached the table with a small bowl of guacamole. He stared down at Jessica and winked. "For you, Ms. McCloud. On me."

Jessica smiled kindly and thanked him. But as soon as he left, she turned to Miranda. "Don't eat that."

"Wasn't planning on it. Honestly, I'm surprised you

even let other people prepare your food with the kind of social media shit you deal with on a daily basis."

Miranda had a point, one Jessica had long since dismissed with logic that, when applied to anyone else was actually illogic. But when applied to Jessica, it made perfect sense.

And since she happened to love guacamole, she applied it to this scenario, scooping some onto a chip and popping it into her mouth. "Unless my entire existence is a result of some weird vendetta against the Avocado Farmers of America, God won't let someone poison me with guacamole."

"But would He let you get a raging case of the shits?"

Jessica paused, another guacamole chip only inches away from her lips. She stared down at it. "I know from past experience that he would." She set the chip down on her appetizer plate and stared forlornly at it before deciding, what the hell, and tossing it back anyway.

"Suit yourself," Miranda said. "How's the loan process coming?"

"Hmm?"

"The loan process so you can open the bakery." She narrowed her eyes at Jessica, tapping a fingertip to her lips. "You weren't aware you had to get a loan, were you?"

"Of course I know I had to do that! I just, uh, didn't know what specifically you were talking about. And I haven't really gotten to that part yet." She decided not to elaborate on her strategy of ignoring all business aspects and hoping someone else—namely Dr. Bell or another financially inclined angel—would swoop in and do it for her.

Opening a bakery had seemed so simple when she was learning the basics in her business classes, but once she stepped off campus and into her life in Austin, all useful knowledge and confidence had vanished into thin air. "I'm still working on my recipes, and clearly that's not going great, so I don't want to spread myself too thin."

Miranda leaned back in her cast-iron patio chair. "Girl, you know I love you and support whatever you do, but you have got to get your ass in gear on this."

Jessica frowned and hung her head. "Yeah, Jesus said the same thing."

"What? Jesus told you to get your ass in gear and you're not listening? I know your respect for him isn't tip-top, but has he ever led you astray?"

"I know you both have a point, but—" But what? An underlying issue had been nagging at her, a despair she hadn't articulated even to herself. But as soon as she searched for the answer, it surfaced like it'd been anxiously awaiting a summons. "Part of me wonders why I should keep pressing forward when I know Jimmy is just going to find a way to ruin it all."

"Uh-uh. No, no, no, nope." Miranda leaned forward over the table. "You are *not* using Jimmy as an excuse. The man is a megadouche, and if you live your life trying to anticipate the next move of megadouches, you'll never get anywhere."

"Miranda, you've seen what he does. You were there at

White Light when he faked his resurrection—he always wins! And now this book. In the foreword, he claims—"

"I know what he claims in the foreword, because I read the book in the first forty-eight hours after its release so that *at least* one of us would have an idea what we're up against. Therefore, when I say he's a megadouche, part of that is informed by his awful memoir, which I assume you haven't finished yet."

Jess's mouth fell open, so she exploited that to shovel guacamole into her gullet and buy herself additional time to brainstorm a response to Miranda's spot on—though still slightly offensive—assumption.

"Don't worry," Miranda added, "I downloaded a pirated copy so he didn't get a cent."

"You read the whole book already?"

"Yeah, girl. It's not that long." Miranda didn't bother disguising her judgment. "It's like, two hundred pages. You could finish it in a single sitting." She shook her head, changing direction. "Doesn't matter. The point is that I finished it and however bad you think it is, it's worse. Because, believe it or not, he actually comes off as a normal human being in it. Well, not *normal* normal, but not the piece of crap we both know him to be. Maybe a little full of himself, but not more than any other politician or megachurch leader." She downed a queso chip with a sip of her beer. "I can see a lot of people suddenly liking him because of it, which is just balls-out infuriating."

"How could Jimmy seem likable?"

"Enough about him, okay? You really need to stop

focusing on that ass munch and start focusing on your *plan*."

But Jessica wasn't yet ready to let it go. How could Miranda not see what a big factor Jimmy was in Jessica's everyday life? Miranda was there when Jimmy faked his resurrection, and she'd heard all the stories of his shenanigans in San Marcos and back in Midland. Hell, she'd even read his book, which should have made her *more* informed on the subject. So, Jess continued to plead her case. "But what if I start working on the plan, and it works and I'm successful and Jimmy ruins it again like he always does?"

Miranda rolled her shoulders and sighed heavily. "I'd say that's still better than moping around until Jimmy figures out how to make things worse anyway."

Dammit. I hate Jimmy. "Yeah, I guess you're right."

"Duh. Now what's the next step? You obviously need to master chocolate-filled cupcakes, but what about the business side?"

"I guess I need to get approved for a loan, but I don't know how."

"That's no big deal."

"No?"

"Of course not. You don't have to know how to do everything, Jess. You just have to know people who know how to do things. What about that professor of yours? You hit her up lately?"

Guilt pulsed through Jessica's gut. Or maybe it was the guacamole. "No, not lately." She stared down at her pint, which she rotated slowly on the table. "Add that to the list of people I haven't kept up with."

Miranda reached across the table and set a hand on Jessica's elbow. "Hey, I don't mean to get down on you. Moving to a big city is hard, starting a business is hard, long distance relationships are hard. To do all that while a silver-tongued fanatic with more personality disorders than even *I* can name tries to pilfer the power God gave you is more than any one person should have to deal with. And you have to deal with it anyway." She grabbed her pint and raised it. "How about we talk about something else for the next hour?"

Jessica raised her glass and nodded. "Sounds good."

As she allowed herself a lungful of humid evening air, Miranda changed the subject with, "Do you think Quentin and Chris have an unhealthy bromance going on?"

"Probably. Why?"

A crease formed between Miranda's brows. "Because I accidentally saw a message from Chris on Quentin's phone the other day, and he called him 'angel bro,' which seems a little homoerotic, even for Chris." She laughed. "I dunno with those two sometimes."

Jessica forced a laugh. "Ha! Yeah, crazy."

Oh boy. Miranda still didn't know about Quentin.

Note to self: don't out him.

Another note to self: urge Quentin to come out so you don't accidentally out him first.

Most important note to self: remind Chris not to accidentally out Quentin.

"How are things with Chris? You two talk about what happens once he graduates?"

Jessica tucked away her mental notepad, which was quickly filling up, and refocused on the physical world. "Huh? What do you mean?"

"I mean, you know. Have y'all talked moving in together? Marriage?"

Jessica's mouth fell open but she was quicker about filling it with guacamole this time. "No, we haven't talked about ... that. Marriage."

Miranda eyed her skeptically. "I figured it'd be the first thing y'all talked about when you got back together, seeing as how it's your ticket to sex."

Jess shook her head vaguely. "Just because we're back together doesn't mean we have to get married now. Plus, dream sex is pretty great."

"Oh right. I forget y'all have that. Man, I wish Quentin and I could try that sometime, but alas, neither of us are demigods. Just two boring, fully human people."

Jessica stared off to her right, avoiding Miranda's eye. "Yep. So human ..."

Either guilt or guac jabbed at her gut—perhaps in an hour she'd know for sure which, though she suspected it was a little of each.

Chapter Four

Bat-Ass Brew was unusually quiet for a Friday morning. Considering it was the first week of the fall semester at UT, the lack of warm, over-caffeinated bodies was difficult to attribute to anything short of good luck … which always made Jessica nervous, because luck was even more unreliable than her Father, who could, if nothing else, be relied upon to show up when she least wanted him.

"Hey, welcome to Bat-Ass Brew. How's your day going?"

"Hi, Rebel," she said, turning her attention to the menu.

Despite their many encounters over the past month, he said, "You know my name?"

"Yep." She leaned forward to get a good look at the daily specials scribbled onto a small chalkboard on the counter. "What's in the Dark Knight?"

"It's just black coffee. With dark chocolate."

"Then why isn't it called the Mocha Dark Knight?"

Rebel blinked slowly, possibly even higher than she'd seen him on her many recent visits. "Because that doesn't make any sense."

"Okay, you know what? Just get me a Lugosi rabid. Actually, an extra shot of rabies."

"Wait, you want the Rabies Shot?"

"No, I want the Lugosi with two shots of rabies."

He chuckled. "Right on. Hey, back to you knowing my name, though. I feel like we've met, but I can't remember you. Did we bone?"

"Ew. No, I promise we never did."

He nodded slowly, a lecherous grin sneaking onto his plump lips while his gaze ran up and down her torso. "Then why am I having such an easy time imagining you naked?"

"Dude. Just put in the order." She flicked her credit card at him and turned her back to the counter, scanning the tables again to make sure she hadn't overlooked Dr. Bell.

Once her drink was up, she grabbed it without a word to Rebel and hurried over to an open table before the bro in flip-flops and a neon sleeveless tank, who was clearly scoping it out, could beat her to it.

THIS MEETING DOES NOT NEED TO BE.

Yes, it does.

She set her tote and notebook on the table by her drink, spreading out as much as possible to avoid any lunatic asking to share the table.

YOU NEEDN'T RELY ON BANKS TO GIVE YOU MONEY.

Yes, I do.

WHY EVEN HAVE A CHILD IF SHE WILL NOT ALLOW ME TO BESTOW FINANCIAL BLESSINGS UPON HER?

I cannot stress enough how unnerving it is when you ask hypothetical questions. But also, I have a literal answer to that: you shouldn't have had me.

YOU MUST LEARN TO ACCEPT HELP, CHILD.

What do you think I'm doing here? I'm asking for financial help. Just not from you. Or anyone I know personally.

THE LORD GIVES HELP WHEN ASKED WITHOUT EXPECTING IN RETURN.

How am I ever supposed to learn how to live my own life if I just run back to daddy every time I need a couple hundred thousand dollars?

WRONG QUESTION. LIVING YOUR OWN LIFE IS NOT NECESSARY. YOU ALREADY HAVE YOUR PATH LAID OUT BEFORE YOU.

Dr. Victoria Bell appeared in the doorway of the cafe, and Jessica set down her coffee and waved.

As Dr. Bell headed over, another woman, in her early fifties judging by her frizzy hairsprayed bun and conservative floral blouse, followed shortly behind, and Jessica was spared guessing when Bell introduced the two. "Jessica, this is Blanche Gowan-Saunders. Blanche, this is Jessica McCloud."

They shook, Blanche grinning widely, her tongue

pressing against her teeth, the pink of it visible through the various misalignments. "I forget your last name is actually McCloud."

Jessica looked at Dr. Bell, who maintained a poker face. Jessica remembered what they'd discussed on the phone the day before: whatever happens, take it and keep sucking up. Blanche was Jessica's foot in the credit union door.

And as obnoxious as Blanche's fangirling might be, it boded well for Jessica getting a loan.

"I can hold the table if you two want to get some coffee," Jessica offered.

"Oh, I'll get it," Blanche said. "You two catch up." Once Dr. Bell relayed her order, Blanch approached the counter where Rebel was hard at work doing nothing but staring straight ahead.

Dr. Bell cut right to it. "Relax. You're all tense and that's not endearing. Humble but confident, like we talked about. She loves you and she can make things happen at the credit union. You got this."

"How did you meet her again?"

Bell waved her off. "Queer thing. Doesn't matter. One more bit you should know"—Dr. Bell checked over Jessica's shoulder to make sure Blanche wasn't coming back yet —"she's an angel and she doesn't know it."

"What? But she's *old*."

Bell nodded enthusiastically. "I know. I don't understand it either, but she's made it work with a weird mixture of religion and superstition that's handcrafted to justify the strange urges of being an angel. Which means she's drawn to you and doesn't understand why. She'll believe whatever she has to believe to make the impulses fit into her beliefs. So, like I said, you're a shoo-in with her."

Jessica nodded, feeling much lighter. "Great."

Dr. Bell raised her voice slightly. "So I said to Dean Halifax, 'If you want to create a class on Freakanomics, that's fine, but I'm not building a syllabus around pop culture."

Jessica jerked her head back. "Huh?"

Blanche sat down between Jessica and Dr. Bell a moment later, and the pieces came together.

"Colleges cater to pop culture far too often," Blanche crooned. "You were wise to stand up to the dean like that, Vicky."

"Thank you. And thank you for the coffee. Now should we get down to brass tacks?"

"I do admire that about you," Blanche said. "And yes." She turned in her chair to face Jessica, who felt it appropriate to also turn in her chair so the two of them faced each other directly. Jessica instantly knew this was too much, but she wasn't going to back down. "I understand you are attempting to bring a little light to this world, Jessica, and part of that requires opening a business not much unlike the one we're in right now that will serve as a meeting place for the community—only hopefully *your* employees won't feel the need to abuse drugs and harass women." She shot a cruel look back toward the service counter. Rebel nodded back, smirking and clearly misinterpreting the intention behind Blanche's glare.

"I will absolutely not hire someone like him," Jessica assured her.

With a small humph, Blanche turned back around to face Jessica directly. "Good. Now for you to hire anyone at all, or even have cause for it, you need money."

"Yes, ma'am."

"I understand that God provides, but everyone knows that's never meant cash raining from the sky."

ONCE IT DID.

Jessica swallowed hard against the mental distraction, leaning closer toward Blanche and tilting her head slightly, hoping to play off the gesture as intense interest rather than a vain struggle to suppress the words of God.

"Instead, God inspires His mortal pawns to extend help to those He loves most. In this case, Ms. McCloud, I am his mortal pawn." She smiled humbly, despite the inherent self-importance of her words. "I would love to help you with this, but I do have a handful of provisions that go along with it ..."

BUT THE CASH WAS COVERED IN POISON IVY.

What the shit?

HE HAD IT COMING.

You know, most people would find it incredibly horrifying to hear that God talks like a damn mob boss.

THEN KEEP YOUR MOUTH SHUT AND NO ONE GETS HURT.

Again, mob boss. Also, was that a threat?

I SIMPLY MEAN IT WOULD HURT PEOPLE'S HEARTS TO HEAR YOU TALK ILL OF THE LORD.

O-kay. While this is all quite riveting and terrifying, I'm trying to focus here.

"... But as long as you can promise me those five specific things, I have no qualms with throwing my weight around at the credit union to make it happen for you."

Shitballs.

Jessica plastered on a smile, nodded slowly, and looked to Dr. Bell for assistance.

Bell, who was out of Blanche's line of sight, nodded vigorously.

So Jessica said, "Yes, Ms. Gowan-Saunders—"

"Call me Blanche, please."

"Blanche. Yes, I can absolutely promise that what you asked for will be the case."

"Mph!" Blanche sat up straighter in her chair, a self-satisfied smirk resting beneath her turned-up nose, and cautiously sipped her hot tea. "Then I don't see how anyone can *really* argue with a solid business plan and a clear sign from God that He backs the loan one hundred percent, including accrued interest."

Jessica's eyes popped open, and she risked a glance at Bell, who seemed just as surprised as Jessica. "Right. So, uh, remind me what sign from God you need?"

Blanche chuckled and swatted playfully at Jessica's arm. "Oh, I wouldn't flatter myself to tell God how to express Himself. Anything will do, so long as it's obvious enough." She nodded her head to punctuate the statement, then folded her hands in her lap and waited.

But for what?

Oh no, does she expect a sign from God right now?

It sure looked like she did.

"Oh, okay. Yeah, let me just, um ..." Jessica looked around, trying to concoct some crazy scheme that might look like a God act. Could she smite something? That seems like the most obvious solution. But also that seemed like a terrible solution that could go wrong in an instant.

YOU CAN JUST ASK ME FOR A SIGN.

I already know you'll never let me live it down.

HOW BADLY DO YOU WANT IT?

Fine. Just this once.

TELL HER FERGUSON SAYS MEOW.

What the actual fu—

STOP QUESTIONING THE LORD.

Blanche shifted, the first signs of impatience surfacing in her tense lips and arched brows. She didn't seem like a woman Jessica wanted to annoy, even if she *weren't* relying on her for a fat loan.

"Ferguson says meow," Jess mumbled.

Blanche grasped her chest and gasped then began coughing as her eyes turned red and watery. "Ferguson? You mean ... he's in Heaven?"

"Yes," Jessica supplied, struggling to sound confident. Just because God knew about Blanche's apparently dead cat didn't mean the cat was in heaven, but whatever, because it seemed to be working.

Blanche dabbed at the corners of her eyes with a crooked knuckle. "That sounds just like something he'd say, too."

Do cats go to heaven?

I GET WHY YOU'RE ASKING, BUT YOU SHOULD KNOW FERGUSON IS NOT A CAT.

Huh?

"Thank you, God, for giving me such a clear sign!" Blanche proclaimed to the ceiling, drawing the attention of a couple around Jessica's age a table over, who'd previously busied themselves with shameless erotic touching and sharing of a bran muffin.

Blanche returned her attention to Jessica. "I'm sorry I'm so emotional. It's just that, well, Ferguson and I had something very special. Long nights of purring and sharpening claws ..."

Ferguson isn't a cat?

NOPE.

"Lapping milk from our bowl."

Our?

IF YOU WANT THE MISSING PUZZLE PIECE HERE, THE LORD SHALL PROVIDE.

Thou shalt not *provide.*

OOO, LOOK WHO'S FEELING BOSSY.

Blanche stood suddenly. "I'm sorry, I just need some time to regroup. But it was great meeting you, Jessica, and I'll let you know once I get a meeting set up with the right people at the credit union."

Jessica stood and offered her hand, but Blanche

lunged forward and pulled Jessica into a tight hug instead.

The woman smelled like cats, leaving Jessica further confused.

Bell cleared her throat once Blanche was out of sight. "That went well."

Plopping back down into her seat, Jessica felt energy drain from her muscles. "Did it?"

"I thought so." Bell returned to her seat as well, sipping her drink. "Ferguson isn't a cat, you know."

"Yeah, I'm aware."

"I'm gonna go out on a limb here and say you don't have a business plan written yet."

"Wha— of course I—" Dr. Bell's unyielding skepticism stopped her in her tracks. "Okay, yeah, I don't even know what a business plan looks like."

"Well, fortunately"—the professor reached into her bag and pulled out a manila folder—"I do. Here." She scooted it across the table. "That's for you. I didn't know all the details, so some of it's guessing. You just have to go back through and tweak it as it fits your purpose. The finances should be close, though."

Jessica opened the folder and flipped through the pages, pausing when she came to the expense spreadsheet. "Whoa, you did all this?"

"I made sure it got done, which is slightly different and involves an air of authority established through years of hard work and a couple adjunct professors desperate to advance, but yes, I suppose I deserve the credit." She smiled quickly, then pointed at a line. "That's the amount I told Blanche you needed to start."

"Whoa. That's ... will she really be able to pull in a quarter of a million?"

"If she can wrangle a dollar, she can wrangle a million. I figure we shoot for the amount you need to open your dream bakery—or something close to it—while we're already relying on a hope and, literally, a prayer. If anyone can get us that amount when you have no actual credit history and no savings to your name, Blanche can. Don't let the church lady demeanor fool you—she's a bit ... domineering."

Jessica held up a palm. "Say no more. Please. This is amazing, Dr. Bell."

"I know. Now listen up. You're having a little trouble transitioning to this new phase of life, that's obvious, so I've done most of the groundwork here. But now it's yours. You have to do the rest of it. I'll answer your questions and put you in contact with people I know, but this is your launch pad, and if you don't do the rest, you won't feel the accomplishment of being a business owner and your business will flat-out fail. I mean, unless you ask your Father to bail you out, which clearly you're not doing or else you'd already have a bakery and we would've been spared Blanche's emotional display at the memory of her former lover."

"Ugh. Was hoping we wouldn't go back to that."

"Do you hear what I'm saying, Jessica? Not the part about kitten play, but the other stuff."

"Kitten what?"

"Focus."

"I'm trying."

"Do you understand what I'm saying about you doing the rest on your own?"

Jessica sighed, staring down at the mug between her hands. "Yes. I get it."

The idea wasn't her favorite, but she knew her old professor was right.

It was time she stopped messing around and started getting down to business. Now all she had to do was figure out what the hell that meant.

Chapter Five

"It's Dr. Bell again," Chris said from the passenger's seat of his F-350. "Should I answer?"

"What is there to say?" Jessica snapped, white-knuckling the steering wheel. "We're getting there as quickly as we can."

Chris answered the phone anyway. "Hello. Yes, Dr. Bell. We're doing our best. I know. Yes, she's aware. I guess just keep stalling and we'll be there as soon as we can. Uh-huh. See ya." He hung up the phone. "Are you sure you don't want me to drive?"

"No!" Jessica spat. "You drive too slow."

"Well," Chris said, gesturing to the cars on all sides, "it's not like I could do any slower than this crawl. I'm just saying, you're a little stressed, and I don't want to end up in an accident or—"

"Please stop talking."

"I'm not saying you're a bad driver. Normally, you're great at it."

The middle lane began to move, and Jessica went for it, using the size of Chris's truck to bully a Kia out of the way so she could change into the faster lane. She'd heard this strategy never worked over the long haul, but it sure *felt* good. "If you must know, God doesn't let me get in accidents."

"Oh. I guess that makes sense." He leaned his head back against the seat, relaxing for a split second before he bolted up straight again and pointed at her. "What about the one that killed Mrs. Wurst? He let you get into that one!"

"Shit, I forgot about that," she mumbled. "Okay, fine. He's never said anything about protecting me from car accidents. I just wanted you to relax because you're seriously stressing me out."

Chris shot her a mean look for the lie but relented, turning his attention back toward the road. "I guess what's the worst that could happen going five miles an hour, right?"

Jessica's eyes shot open, blood pulsing aggressively through her temples as she rounded on him. "Why would you say that? *Why?* We're practically asking for it now. A crane falling over or discarded metal from the space station falling on us."

"Whoa. Take a deep breath, Jess. You don't want to show up all stressed out."

She growled slightly, but he was right, so she inhaled

deeply against her tense muscles, and when traffic in the middle lane came to a complete standstill, she allowed herself a moment to shut her eyes and think about something that would calm her.

I'm surrounded by a lounging tower of Namibian giraffes, a tangle of knobby legs all around me as we watch the sun go down after a long day of grazing from treetops and Sir David Attenborough summarizes our small victories and the challenges we face in the coming days ...

She'd waited all week for this meeting, chipping away at the business plan and generally feeling more productive than she had in months. What Dr. Bell said was right: doing it herself was important. It felt good, and her vision for the bakery was starting to come together.

Now all she needed was to get to this damn meeting at the credit union, presumably sign a contract, and then it would be smooth sailing until she opened the doors of her bakery, sometime early next year.

Assuming she could make it to the meeting before everyone left. How was traffic so insane?

"Did you know it was a festival weekend?" she asked her moral support.

"Nope. You know I don't care about music."

"And that's one of the things I love about you, Chris." She adjusted the AC vents, hoping in vain that she wouldn't arrive at the meeting drenched in sweat after an hour in direct late-August sunlight. "What's our ETA?"

He glanced at his phone again. "Um ... you're not going to like it."

"What is it?"

"Five minutes later than the last time you asked."

"Shit, shit, shit, shit, shit!"

The car ahead of her began pulling forward, and before she could do the same, another car inserted itself in the tiny space.

"NO!" Jessica pounded the steering wheel with her palms. "Why?! Why would you change lanes?! We're not even near an exit."

Chris glanced timidly at her. "Your road rage is a little much, Jess."

"*Your* road rage is a little much, *Christopher*."

When the cars in her lane started to inch forward again, the one directly in front of her stayed where it was, the driver clearly not paying attention.

"Are you kidding me?! Fuck! MOVE!"

She recognized the sensation immediately. It pulsed through her, but this time was stronger than ever, and while part of her was annoyed by this new discovery, mostly she thought, About damn time!

It started with the car ahead of her sliding sideways to the right. Then the car in the far right lane started sliding too, all the way over toward the shoulder until it was only an inch from the concrete half-wall in the construction zone. Then the next car over slid until it was only a couple inches from the one by the wall.

The same thing happened in the left lane, too, cars sliding over, one after another, moving farther and farther up the highway until the middle lane was clear for as far as Jessica could see.

"No way," Chris said once he looked up from the phone. "Did you ...?"

"I think so."

"Did you know you could do that?"

"No," she whispered.

Chris groaned, shifting in his seat. "I want you so bad right now."

Car horns sounding from either side of the clear lane snapped Jessica fully back into reality.

"Why aren't you going?" Chris asked.

"Uh, because as awesome and convenient as this miracle is, it's also kind of a dick move, don't you think?"

"Please don't talk about dicks while I'm this turned on."

She nodded and slowly drove forward between the sea of pissed off drivers. Rolling down the automatic windows, she shouted apologies as frequently as she could, and Chris did the same, except his shouts were of a more impure nature ...

"I get to have dream sex with this woman! Deal with it!"

"Chris, stop. Seriously. This isn't a game."

"If it is a game, we're winning the shit out of it. Look at this douche." He pointed to a yellow Hummer on their right, where the driver was furiously trying to open his car door to no avail.

"Okay," Jessica conceded, "yeah, that guy's definitely a douche."

Chris leaned out his window. "Guess you'll have to find some other way to compensate! Haha!"

"You're enjoying this too much. Plus, you should just be grateful you don't have to compensate."

Chris straightened in his seat. "I am. And if I'm not mistaken, so are you."

"Oh shut it," she said, trying not to grin. She glanced in her rearview mirror, watching as the cars in their wake slid back into place. "Keep it in your pants for just a little longer, Chris. We can celebrate afterward."

The cleared path veered from the middle lane to an off-ramp. "I guess this is our exit," she said, putting on her blinker to avoid being a *complete* asshole.

She inhaled deeply, trying to steady herself. She'd finally discovered a miracle that was exceptionally useful, and now she could make it to the meeting before everyone left. Things were actually looking up. She was so close to opening her bakery, she could practically taste the gluten-free goodness ...

Jessica returned from the ladies room of Pho Show to the intimate table where Chris sat, staring slightly cross-eyed at the menu, making cross-eyed look sexy and intentional. Last week she'd overheard a customer at Bat-Ass Brew use the phrase "modern Asian fusion" in reference to the way his home was decorated, and as soon as Jessica had set foot in this high-priced Vietnamese restaurant, her mind had traveled back to that phrase. Modern Asian fusion. If she had to guess at what that meant, it would be something like Pho Show—shiny white tables with cherry blossoms painted over the tops, metal artwork along the wall implying bamboo shoots but not outright resembling bamboo shoots, red paper lanterns hanging in clusters from the ceiling, and an entirely Hispanic cooking staff working at breakneck speeds on large cast-iron griddles and broth vats in the center of the dining room.

"I ordered us some wine," Chris said as she sat. "I hope you like red." He wiggled his eyebrows seductively.

She sipped from the ice water already at the table. "You know me so well."

Their server, a man not much older than Jessica and with short facial hair that allowed for hygiene while maintaining an air of ruggedness, approached with the wine but paused after pouring a glass for Chris. He stared down Jessica's empty glass with a deep crease between his brows, the corners of his mouth turned down. "I, uh ..."

"I'd like some too," Jessica said, wondering what in her father's name was happening.

The server turned toward her and cringed apologetically. "I don't feel comfortable serving you, Ms. McCloud."

Okay, so he knew who she was. She's almost gotten used to Austinites being either too self-absorbed to notice or too aloof to care, assuming they even *could* recognize her when she donned her genius disguise of sunglasses and a baseball cap. But she hadn't thought those accessories would go well with her satin razorback shirt and slacks, so she'd left them in her bag in Chris's truck when she did a quick wardrobe change after the loan meeting and before celebratory date night.

Before she could ask any questions, Chris took over. "That sounds like a you problem. We're paying customers. Serve the girl some wine."

"I just ... see, I'm Catholic, and she's—"

Chris's exaggerated shrug and slight neck roll could have easily been mistaken for a pre-fight stretch. "*Perfect.* Y'all love wine. Let her at it."

"But she's ..."

"Over twenty-one? Yes."

The waiter was clearly conflicted, grimacing and white-knuckling the wine bottle. But Jessica was still too confused to offer him any calming words. Besides, she wasn't sure if she liked him or not. She was leaning toward not.

The waiter took a half step back from the table. "I don't actually know where we stand on her."

Chris's eyes crossed slightly, but he puffed up his chest confidently anyway. "What do you mean? You can't serve her because you don't know ..." He shook his head to clear it. "What is there to stand ... about?"

"I mean the Vatican hasn't actually addressed the issue of ... her." He nodded at Jessica but kept his focus determinedly on Chris. "What she claims."

Jessica waved her hand between the men. "I'm right

here. And you can call me Jessica, since you clearly know who I am."

Chris motioned with an open palm for her to play it cool. "So when will you know about the Vatican?"

The waiter scrunched up his tiny nose and sucked in air. "It's anybody's guess. A few hundred years?"

"Listen," Jessica said, "you already brought over water while I was in the bathroom. I can just turn this into wine,"—she held up her hand to keep Chris from asking her if she really could do it—"or you can up-sell me to the insanely expensive bottle you're holding and make a little bit better tip. Either way, it's not in your hands"—she squinted at his name tag—"Rogue." *Oh for shit's sake.* "And you'll be long dead and can therefore hardly be held responsible for your transgression by the time the Pope establishes that it is one."

Rogue stared thoughtfully at her glass of water, but eventually nodded and poured her the wine.

Once he was gone, Chris erupted. "Wait, can you really turn water into wine?"

"You know I can't." She lifted her glass for a toast. "To a successful loan meeting."

Chris leaned forward across the small table for two in Pho Show, the tiny candlelight glowing on his face. "What if he goes and tells everyone you can do it?"

She rolled her eyes keeping her glass suspended in the air. "As far as rumors about me go, that's a fairly benign one to worry about."

Shrugging agreement, Chris clinked glasses with her. "This feels so grown up."

"Right?"

"You killed it in that meeting, Jess. Watching you present that business plan, seeing you answer all those questions that dipshit banker dude kept asking you—I could hardly keep it together, especially after that miracle you pulled on I-35 today. All I could think about was what I want to do to you after we fall asleep tonight."

Jessica bit back a grin and raised her glass. "Then we should definitely get started on the sedation process."

As she took her first sip of the Malbec, Chris decided to ruin her night with, "Should we be talking about marriage?"

Jessica continued sipping her wine to buy herself time to think. But after putting away half the glass before the appetizer had even arrived, she figured she should slow down. "Um. Should we?"

He stared down at his napkin still folded like a fan on the table. "I mean, you know what we can do if we get married."

"Yeah, the same thing we already do every night, except with a blander setting and fewer superheroes." She paused. "Actually, I could do with fewer superheroes."

Chris's attention darted up to her, and he whined, "But I thought they were growing on you!"

"I— Fewer, not ... none."

The small concession calmed him, and he chuckled. "Yeah, you're right, though. We really don't need to talk about it yet. We're only twenty-one, and I'm not even out of college."

"I mean, is it something you think about?" she asked quickly.

He didn't meet her eye, staring vaguely at something over her right shoulder instead. "Yeah, I mean, I definitely want to marry you eventually."

Definitely? He was sure about that? Granted, they started dating back in high school, but there was that long break up, and they'd only been back together nine months. Was that enough time to be sure about marriage? And if so, why wasn't she sure about it too? Did that mean she was sure she *didn't* want marriage?

Chris mistook the meaning of her silence and amended his previous declaration with, "And not just so we can have boring sex, but because, well, you know."

"Yeah," she lied, having only a vague idea what he meant.

They each sipped their wine in silence. Part of the reasoning behind trying this restaurant over the pho place down the street was that it advertised as one of the few places in Austin without live music during the current music festival. It had seemed ideal for intimate conversation, maybe some verbal foreplay, a touch of provocative bragging ...

But now Jessica found herself wishing they'd picked somewhere noisier. Discussion of marriage was much less likely when a brood of thirty- and forty-somethings stood on a stage ten feet away with two amps too many covering everyone's least favorite *fan favorites*. Maybe that was why everyone in this town was single. Serious subjects were never broached for purely auditory reasons.

"Here's a question," Chris said. His jaw twitched nervously before he continued. "Do you think we'll still get to have dream sex once we can have plain real-life sex?" His wide eyes reflected the tea light's flickering flame.

"I don't know. I mean, we can definitely try."

"Good." He nodded seriously. "Good."

"I thought we weren't going to worry about that yet."

"Right, right," he said casually, leaning back in his chair. "I mean, we're going to be together forever anyway, so what's the hurry?"

She forced a giggle and flinched when it sounded more like a gag. "Exactly. That's the plan."

Rogue brought out a basket of sweet buns, and Jessica grabbed his arm, feeling slightly less inhibited by the glass of wine she'd essentially chugged. And perhaps part of her desperately needed a diversion. "Do these have gluten in them?"

"Um, yes? Sorry. I didn't know you had an allergy to—" He narrowed his eyes at the buns like they were a puzzle he was starting to figure out.

"My brother's body? No. I don't. Watch this, though." She held her hand over the buns, closed her eyes, and worked her miracle. When she moved her hands, she was pleased to see the three small portraits of her were each flattering in their own way. "Voila!" she said. "Now they're gluten-free."

Rogue stumbled back from the table and scurried off.

Jessica chuckled and watched him go, but when she glanced at Chris to soak up his amusement, she was met with dark concern. "Why did you do that?" he asked.

"What? I was just having a little fun. Don't I get to have a little fun?"

"I guess so." Chris watched Rogue until he disappeared into the back of house.

"Plus, I might have just converted him."

Chris cocking his head to the side, sizing her up. "Okay. To what? You have a religion now?"

She opened her mouth to reply with something witty, but came up short. "Oh. Right. I guess I don't."

"If anything, you just converted him to White Light Church."

"Shitballs. You're right."

"Don't get used to it." He grabbed one of the buns from the basket, turned it to get a good look at Jessica, and then cringed as he pulled the bun apart to butter the halves. "You know, until you start your own religion, it might be in your best interest to leave the Catholics Catholic and the Mormons Mormon and the Baptists Baptist and so on. At least that way they don't follow Jimmy Dickhead."

"Again, you're right." She grabbed a bun and shoved the whole thing into her mouth to avoid catching a glimpse of herself.

"Hey, cheer up." He leaned forward. "I got great news." Chris practically vibrated in his seat, making Jessica wonder if this news was the *actual* reason for the expensive dinner, rather than her business meeting.

"And what's that?"

"Coach Brown says my name has been thrown around in early talk about the Heisman."

"The Heisman?"

"Trophy. Damn, Jess. You're still totally clueless about football?" He sighed. "I guess that's what happens when it comes naturally. The Heisman Trophy. It's a big deal in college football."

"That's great, Chris!"

"Yeah, it is. But it's still early. Mostly it's just commentators and coaches who are bringing it up over beers or whatever. Even if I don't win—"

"Let's not jump there yet. Let's just pretend you're a shoo-in." She flagged down another server, and when the woman approached, Jess ordered another round of wine.

There was no hesitation on the new server's part—either she didn't know who Jessica was, or she didn't care. Either worked.

They celebrated in good form, slurping their pho and gossiping and switching to cocktails for the next round, and when Chris reached for the bill, Jessica stopped him. "No, I got this." She held up her credit card. "What's a little more debt when I'm about to get a two-hundred-and-fifty-thousand-dollar loan?"

Chris giggled, his eyes bloodshot, and Jessica giggled along with him before slipping the card into the check holder.

Apparently Rogue had officially passed the baton to the female server, Sage, who returned shortly with the receipt. It wasn't until Jess went to sign and leave a tip that she realized how much she'd spent. Regardless, though, Wendy had been clear that she was never to tip less than twenty-five percent, so Jessica gritted her teeth, did the math, and signed the damn receipt feeling sobered.

As they stood then weaved through the restaurant, discussing the logistics of taking a ride-share back to Jessica's condo and getting Chris's truck the next day, a familiar face hooked Jessica's attention. She couldn't place it immediately, but then it clicked.

He was sitting at the bar, a martini held loosely in his hands as he stared forward blankly, sipping his drink disinterestedly.

Chris continued pleading his case that he was good to drive, but Jessica had stopped listening. "Is that Mr. Foster?"

"Huh?" Chris turned sharply, tripping slightly over his feet and officially ruining any further arguments of his driving.

Jessica led the way through the crowded restaurant toward the bar, and only after the "mister" was already out of her mouth did she wonder if she should call her former teacher by his first name instead.

"Mr. Brian Foster," she said, which was the worst of both options.

Mr. Brian Foster? What am I, an FBI agent?

He perked up and turned slowly, and when his eyes

landed on her, he reared back. "Jessica! Chris! What a pleasant surprise." They approached and Chris shook Mr. Foster's hand. "Wow ..." said their former college counselor, "you two are actually still together."

"Yep!" Chris said proudly. "She couldn't escape me if she tried."

Mr. Foster glanced concernedly at Jessica, who mouthed, *I'm fine.* Mr. Foster nodded subtly. "You two on your way out?"

"Yeah," Jessica said, "but we're not in a hurry."

"I dunno," Chris said, "I'm getting a little *sleepy.*" He stared at her meaningfully, and while she understood the message, it could wait.

"You'll be fine." She turned to Mr. Foster. "Mind if we join you, Mister—or ..."

"Brian, please. You're adults now, judging by your level of intoxication in a law-abiding private establishment like this. But hey, why don't we head somewhere a little cheaper? First round on me."

"Done!" Chris shouted into Jessica's ear.

Brian tossed cash onto the bar then lead the way out of Pho Show and down the sidewalk, and it wasn't far before he turned into a less-than-reputable establishment called the Grease Trough and ordered a round of Lone Stars for the table.

"How's life?" he asked, addressing Jessica.

"Pretty good," she said distractedly, looking at some of the shadier characters who were eyeing her with what might have been suspicion but could have also been lust. She never was great at discerning the two.

Brian followed her gaze. "Don't worry, they look like rough types, but Austin is a safe city. They see me in here all the time, and despite the fact that I'm clearly the kind of kid they beat up in their school days, they all leave me alone."

"If you say so."

"How's Texas State?" he asked. "You're both in your senior year, right?"

Chris nodded enthusiastically, and Jessica felt a pit form in her stomach. Mr. Foster had worked so hard with her on finding a college. And now she had to break the news to him that she dropped out? How would he take it?

Chris jumped in with an update before she could decide what to say. "I'm starting quarterback, and Jessica dropped out."

Her mouth fell open, and she risked a glance at Mr. Foster, who nodded pensively before turning his attention to her. "And why's that?"

"I'm starting a bakery."

Mr. Foster squeezed his eyes shut and pinched the bridge of his nose. Then he inhaled deeply and said, "That's unexpected."

"Yeah, well, I found a miracle where I can make things gluten-free, so it just seemed like the logical next step."

Mr. Foster chuckled, then he guffawed. "Of course! How logical. And you came to Austin to do it."

She nodded tentatively, struggling to gauge his reaction.

"No, that's actually perfect. I have to say, Jessica, trying to advise you on college was the ultimate exercise in futility. It would have been invigorating were it not so exhausting."

"What do you mean?"

"I mean, and maybe I'm just saying this because I've been mixing liquors since noon, but I've never encountered a student who was on such an obvious path. Now, that doesn't mean I knew what path you were on, and I'm guessing you didn't know either, but it was pretty clear nothing I could say would alter the course of your future. In that way, our meetings were a little bit freeing."

"I don't know about that. I think—"

"I do. I know about it. I could *sense* it, and for those of you playing along at home, I pride myself on doing a stand-up job of dulling my senses. Which only makes it more remarkable when I have any intuition whatsoever."

As Brian's eyes scanned the rest of the dark bar while he swiveled his Lone Star in its can, Jessica caught Chris's eye, mouthed, "Angel?"

Chris pointed to himself and nodded.

Come on, Chris.

She shook her head then jabbed a finger at Mr. Foster.

Chris crinkled his nose but his gaze roamed the air around Mr. Foster's body.

He shook his head decisively.

Brian sighed and slung his arm over the back of the

booth. "Yes, second only to my healthy repulsion to Dolores, my intuition about you was the strongest thing I felt in Mooretown."

"Who's Dolores?" Chris asked. "Your ex-wife?"

Mr. Foster laughed. "Thank god, no. Dolores Thomas. The principal?"

Chris's mouth opened slowly like a drawbridge. He pointed sharply at Mr. Foster. "Wait, you hated her too?"

"I don't know if hate is the right word."

Chris nodded along. "Exactly. I get it, man. I just didn't know anyone else felt that way."

"Wait ..." Mr. Foster's eyes shifted from Chris to Jessica then back again. "You don't like her?"

Chris shot Jessica an apologetic half smile. "Yeeeah, she always kind of terrified me."

Mr. Foster pointed to Jessica. "But you still keep in touch with her?"

It was a painful subject, but Jessica went with honesty. "Not so much lately. I've been meaning to. We just sort of fell out of touch toward the end of college."

"Good riddance," Mr. Foster said quickly.

"That's what I say." Chris held up a palm and Mr. Foster slapped it.

"Maybe she just hates men," Jessica snapped before she could catch herself. "Plenty of women do." An image of Jimmy standing with arms outstretched on stage in White Light Church reared its head in her mind's eye. "Can you really blame us?" She knew immediately this was not her target audience, and both men shrugged noncommittally.

"I guess not," Mr. Foster said.

"What'd *I* do, though?" Chris asked.

The table fell silent and Jessica's anger sizzled inside her. "Nothing, Chris. Don't worry about it. I have to get up early tomorrow to work on a new recipe. We should probably get going."

"It was nice seeing you both," Mr. Foster said hurriedly. His confusion was obvious, but he stood from the table and escorted them out of the bar.

They said their goodbyes on the sidewalk, Chris shaking Brian's hand again and Jessica giving him an awkward one-arm hug with plenty of air between their bodies. "Let's get lunch sometime," he said to them.

Chris nodded enthusiastically. "Yeah, that would be—"

Whatever it *would be* went unsaid, though, as shouting from down the sidewalk interrupted their conversation. Though Chris instinctively sidestepped in front of Jessica, she was still able to see the scene unfold when she leaned slightly to the right.

"You gonna fuck every dick who looks at you?" a bulky man with a shaved head shouted.

A woman was pinned between him and the wall of Grease Trough. "No, Brock!" she sobbed. "I swear, nothing happened! He offered to buy me a drink—"

"Because you fucked him, you whore?"

"No!"

"You did, didn't you? You fucked him!" Brock punched the wall by her head.

Chris grabbed Jessica and shoved her toward Mr. Foster before approaching the scene. "Hey! Dicklips!"

Chris's distraction worked insofar as giving the woman a moment to flee, but it quickly backfired when Brock reached in his belt and pulled out a gun, holding it out at Chris.

"Holy shit," Mr. Foster breathed behind her.

"What'd you call me?" Brock might have been asking in a genuine way, having never heard that particular insult before, but Jessica suspected it was more in a rhetorical way, like how people use it to buy themselves time to think of something more threatening and cool to say.

But Brock bought himself no time whatsoever. Because nobody was allowed to point a gun at God's daughter's boyfriend. Not even Brock Dicklips.

Jessica's instincts took over, and she didn't try to fight them. She was going to smite the everliving shit out of this guy and love every—

Nope, shouldn't do that.

Her conscience interceded at the last moment before the energy tugged free of her fingertips, and she aimed at the next best thing.

The fire hydrant to Brock's right exploded.

A piece of shrapnel flew right into Brock's wrist, causing him to drop the weapon and yelp as the geyser shot into the sky, drawing the attention to the spot outside Grease

Trough. Jessica didn't miss a beat and lunged forward, grabbing Chris by the arm with one hand, Mr. Foster with her other, leading them away from the scene at a dead sprint.

Once they were safely down the block and out of sight of the Grease Trough, Mr. Foster braced his hands on his thighs, catching his breath from the excitement. "Talk about good timing with the hydrant."

Chris and Jessica exchanged a look. Mr. Foster still wasn't convinced, huh?

Chris slapped a shaky hand between Mr. Foster's shoulder blades. "I get it. I didn't believe it the first time I saw a smiting, either." He nodded at Jessica. "But it's arousing every time."

Jessica cringed. "Ew. You were five when you first saw it."

Chris smirked unapologetically. "I was an early bloomer."

"We should call the cops," Mr. Foster said. "Right? That's what people do when they have guns pulled on them?"

Chris ran a large hand over his face. "I guess so. I've never had someone do that before."

As Jessica pulled her phone from her back pocket, Mr. Foster straightened up, looking down the street where they'd come from. "Me neither. I can't believe that just happened. Austin is such a safe city."

When the operator answered, Jessica began to panic. Would she have to give her name? Would the media be able to find out about this? What would Wendy say? She should've called Wendy first.

Shitballs.

She shoved the phone to Chris. "You talk. Don't use my name," she hissed.

It wasn't until later, after they heard the sirens approaching and after Chris and Mr. Foster spoke with the cops while Jessica hid inside Chris's truck and after Chris insisted he was sober enough to drive and Jessica was fine with playing along if it meant they could get home and start to forget all about the altercation, that she realized what her panic actually implied: Wendy Peterman scared her more than a skinhead with a gun.

Chapter Six

"I bet y'all had some freaky dream sex after that," Quentin said.

He was parked on a stool by the kitchen island of his and Miranda's massive penthouse condo, having so selflessly offered to be a taste tester for Jessica's latest patisserie experiments.

The condo was spacious but cozier than Jessica's, with warm colors, no harsh overhead fluorescents—the natural light streaming in was plenty—and more personal touches than Jessica had bothered with in hers, which just meant there *were* personal touches. Jessica had even made the cut in said personal touches, and photos of their high school and college days were framed and sprinkled thoughtfully on the wall around the TV.

"No freakier than usual," Jessica said. "But you'll have to talk to him about that."

"I'd rather talk to you about it, honestly," Quentin said.

"God love that man, but when Chris starts talking about your dream sex, he always asks, 'Isn't that hot?' and when I politely agree, he tells me to back off. No winning that game."

Jessica leaned down to peer through the glass window of the oven. The croissants still needed a few minutes to brown, but they were coming along better than the batch she'd made two days ago—which had turned into crescent bricks—and, fingers-crossed, these wouldn't explode when she miracled them, like yesterday's had. "Sounds like he's never gotten over that fake love affair we had."

"Clearly."

"I wish Quentin and I could have dream sex," Miranda said from the daybed in the adjoining breakfast nook, where she scrolled aimlessly through her Twitter feed on a tablet propped up on her knees. She turned to her boyfriend. "Not that regular sex isn't great, but what idiot would turn down better sex? Plus, I wouldn't mind making the Avengers watch."

"Justice League," both Jessica and Quentin corrected.

"Ah," Jessica said, "I guess he told you about that one, too."

Quentin didn't bother looking properly ashamed. "And clearly you told Miranda."

"Obviously." As she searched around for where she'd set down the oven mitts, she added, "I bet you could make dream sex happen if you tried."

Quentin replied curtly with, "I don't know why you would say that."

"Because it's an an—" She turned and spotted Quentin's serious expression just in time to stop herself before she accidentally outed him. Horror at how close she'd come to bringing the night to an abrupt and unhappy end boiled up her esophagus, and she fought to keep the emotion from her face. "It's just a matter of you really giving it your all. I guess."

"Trust me," Miranda said, still absorbed in her scree, blissfully ignorant of the close call, "if Quentin tried any harder, I might not survive it."

Quentin's shoulders softened, and Jessica grabbed the oven mitt and pulled out the croissants to cool.

"You know, Jess," Miranda said, "I'm super impressed how quickly you've gotten going on this bakery thing. Sure, it took a little urging from Jesus, but you're doing it. And it's only been a handful of months since you decided this was what you were going to do. Most businesses take way longer to get started."

"When can I taste test?" Quentin interrupted.

"Cool your jets," Jessica said. "I haven't even miracled this shit yet."

While Jessica's condo had a nice kitchen, Quentin and Miranda's was superior by a long shot. She often wondered how much Quentin was making at his new job, but she knew better than to ask, concluding it was somewhere between a lot and a shit ton.

While she used their incredible kitchen as her excuse for the occasional visits, she was pretty sure all parties involved knew her real reason for coming over was the company. With Chris still living in San Marcos and training five days a week on top of taking a couple summer school classes, her life had become much more solitary than she liked.

Which was a surprise. After so many years of wishing everyone would just leave her alone, she realized being left *completely* alone wasn't all it was cracked up to be.

Holding her hands over the heat of the pastries, she cleared her mind and let the miracle work through her.

Not only did the croissants refrain from exploding this time, but she was getting better at the superficial element of her miracle. Some of her images even had the hair curled. *Maybe I can do this. Maybe opening this bakery won't be the huge disaster I and everyone else expect it to be.*

"Damn, Jess," said Quentin, "if you don't stop teasing me with that smell, I'm gonna have to ban you from using the kitchen."

"Like I'd let you do that," Miranda said, standing and walking over. "But seriously, when do we get to eat?"

Jessica hurriedly moved each croissant to the plate then brought it over, plopping it down on the island in front of Quentin. "Bon appetit."

They each grabbed one and took a large bite as Jessica watched closely for their initial reactions. Did they like it?

Neither was giving any obvious signs, though. "You know, if you're going to eat of my body," she said, "you should at least compliment the cook."

Quentin was the first to stop chewing and spit out his

mushy lump, but Miranda was quick to follow. "I swear to your father, Jessica," Quentin said, gagging, "if you ever refer to something I'm eating as your body, I'll—"

"Sorry, sorry. I didn't mean it literally, though. Geez."

"Still," Miranda said, "maybe stay away from that in your branding. You'll definitely attract the wrong people with it."

"Ah, true." She nodded. "Cannibals?"

"I was thinking lapsed Catholics. But yeah, maybe cannibals, too."

"Noted."

As Quentin hesitantly nibbled at his croissant, Jessica's phone vibrated in her back pocket. She wiped the crumbs from her hands on a crumpled-up paper towel then slipped the phone from her pocket and opened the push notification for a new email. It was from the credit union, with the subject line, *Regarding Your Loan Application.*

Wow, they'd moved her paperwork through faster than she'd expected. Blanche had forecasted close to four weeks, three if they were feeling feisty, but it'd hardly been a week and a half. It was like as soon as she set her mind on actually getting things done, once she'd broken through that mental wall, everything fell into place for her.

She opened the email.

Ms. McCloud,

We are sorry to inform you that your lack of credit history does not provide the assurance we need to offer you the requested loan at this time. However, building a high credit score will increase your chances of being approved in the future. For tips on how to get started building your credit, please see the links included at the bottom of this email.

Again, thank you for your interest, and we apologize for being unable to offer you financial assistance at this time.

She read the email again but stopped after the first paragraph as a sharp pain radiated behind her eyes and a dull ringing in her ears caused her stomach to churn.

She'd thought it was a done deal. That BDSM psychopath Blanche had assured her she could get the loan. Dr. Bell said the business plan was airtight. The man at the credit union seemed so impressed. What the hell happened?

Maybe God's backing didn't actually matter in the financial world.

Godless bastards!

Although she supposed she'd never officially gotten word from Him that He would insure the loan personally. But still.

Dammit!

"I'm going to eat so many of these when you open shop," Quentin said around a mouthful of croissant.

She looked at Quentin then Miranda and forced a weak smile. "Hey, sorry to leave you with the dishes, but I suddenly don't feel well. I need to head home. Like, now."

Miranda paused in her chewing, tilted her head to the side, her eyes narrow slits. "That was sudden. You gonna make it back okay?"

"Yeah, I'll be fine. I just gotta go now."

"This shits?" Quentin asked sympathetically. "You can just use Miranda's bathroom if it's the shits."

"It's not the shits." Jessica grabbed her purse. "Sorry. I'll talk to y'all later."

She hurried out the door and made it down the elevator and out onto the street before the first hot tear shook loose from her eyes.

"Help a man out?"

She reached in her purse, pulled out a few pennies, and chucked them at the homeless man without looking then slipped on her sunglasses. She needed to get off the streets. Anyone could snap a photo of her crying, and while the shades would cover the initial redness, she had a feeling something much bigger was on its way, something that she would need a ski mask or maybe a burka to hide.

She considered calling Chris to vent but found she had no desire to talk to him about this. Not yet. His disappointment would be too much to bear on top of her own. Or worse yet, he would manage to be optimistic, and there was no place in her life for that at present.

She went through the list of her go-to contacts. Obviously not Quentin or Miranda. That would mean outing her excuse to leave as a lie. Wendy would show no sympathy, which was almost appealing, except her response would undoubtedly be served with a side of why-are-you-calling-me-about-this? and of-course-you-didn't-get-the-loan-if-you-have-no-credit-history. Not only would Dr. Bell be disappointed, she would feel like a failure, and Jessica wasn't looking to pass along blame to someone who had done so much to help. Destinee was a no-go, too. She would ask for the names of the creditors and not stop until Jessica had ratted them out. Maybe Kate or Judith? She hadn't exactly kept in close contact with them over the past couple months like she'd promised she would, and dumping bad news on them didn't seem like a good way to break the silence.

Mrs. Thomas would understand. She'd probably say exactly what Jessica needed to hear to start feeling better, too—she always did. But the span since they'd last spoken was even more embarrassing and shameful than that of Judith and Kate, and Jessica carried too much guilt about it, feeling like in some ways she'd replaced Mrs. Thomas with Dr. Bell. And who did that? Who just replaced mentors like that?

That left her with no one. Or at least no one who would listen and understand and not be too preoccupied with wondering, *Why is she telling me this? Doesn't she have any close friends?*

Then it clicked. When people can't bear to talk to anyone in particular about what's on their mind, where do they turn? How do they vent?

She pulled out her phone, opening up Twitter. She

wanted to talk to somebody but also nobody, which was exactly what Twitter was good for. Plus, Wendy had told her to tweet more.

Bad news. Bakery plans uncertain. Need to find the money somehow. Disappointed.

Even when something seems certain, it's not. Sad.

Credit is a rigged system. You have to be dependent on it before they'll let you become more dependent on it and then your reward is (1/2)

(2/2) to be offered even more possible dependency. You feel like you're winning only when you're losing. NOT COOL.

She jammed her phone back into her purse, having defused her anger and frustration temporarily.

YOU CAN JUST ASK, AND THE LORD SHALL PROVIDE.

Hand-outs? No thanks.

YOU WERE WILLING TO TAKE ONE FROM THE BANK.

I would have to pay them back, so it's not a hand-out.

YOU SHOULD LEARN TO ACCEPT HELP WHEN IT'S OFFERED BY THOSE WHO LOVE YOU.

You should learn to ... shut up.

HARK! WHAT'S THAT ON THE GROUND?

She halted and turned her attention to the sidewalk in front of her.

A scratch-off ticket.

She reached down, picked it up, and inspected it.

Win up to two hundred and fifty thousand? Way to be subtle.

YOU LOVE SCRATCH-OFFS. PULL OUT ONE OF YOUR HOBO PENNIES AND GIVE IT A GO.

No. I know I'll win, and then what?

YOU HAD NO ISSUE WITH THIS IN COLLEGE.

I was young and dumb. Now I want to do things for myself.

EXCEPT BUILD YOUR CREDIT. YOU'RE FINE USING MINE NAME IN LIEU OF THAT.

Look, I'm trying, okay. I'm not perfect yet, but I'm trying.

YOUR NEED FOR INDEPENDENCE FROM ME IS BAFFLING.

Your *need for dependence from me is baffling.*

THOU SHALT IMPROVE THINE COMEBACKS.

Thou shalt improve thine ... boomerangs.

THOU SHALT NOT SLIGHT MINE MOST AWESOME ACHIEVEMENT IN WEAPONRY, CHILD. OOO ... YOU JUST HAVE TO PUSH IT, DON'T YOU?

She had an idea and scanned the street until she found someone who might fit the bill. It was a young couple walking down the sidewalk on the other side of the road, holding hands, the woman extremely pregnant. Jessica pulled off her sunglasses and jogged across the street toward them. "Excuse me."

The man glanced up first and moved slightly to stand between Jessica and the woman he held hands with. "Yes?" Then his head jerked back and Jessica knew she was officially recognized.

"Is that your wife?"

He stepped to the side and nodded, and the woman came forward hesitantly. "Jessica Christ?"

"Eh ... sure, that's what some people call me. Here." She extended the scratch-off toward the woman, who didn't immediately move, pinching her brows together as she puzzled over the gesture. "It's for you." Jess wiggled the ticket and finally the woman took it.

When the husband and wife exchanged uncertain glances, Jessica realized she had nothing left to say. "Uh, bye. Good luck with the kid." And she hurried off.

As awkward as the encounter was, she figured giving an expecting couple two hundred and fifty grand would buy her some goodwill with the media once the word got out, and that did wonders to temper her depression as she rounded the corner onto her street.

NICE TRY.

Huh?

THAT SCRATCH OFF IS A LOSER NOW.

Come again?

FOR YOU IT WOULD BE A WINNER, BUT FOR THOSE TWO? NUH-UH.

What the hell? Why wouldn't you let them win, too? They're expecting a baby!

NOT HIS BABY. BUT YOU'RE WELCOME TO KEEP QUESTIONING THE LORD'S JUDGMENT LEFT AND RIGHT. IT'S NOT LIKE THE LORD HATH ANYTHING BETTER TO DO.

So you're telling me I just startled a young couple to hand them a dud scratch-off ticket?

YES.

That's something a complete lunatic would do.

YES.

Couldn't you have warned me?

OH SORRY. I WAS DISTRACTED FOR A MERE TEN SECONDS WHILE MAKING A SUICIDE BOMBER'S VEST EXPLODE PREMATURELY WITH DEEPLY COMICAL AND IRONIC TIMING.

Ugh. Does everyone's father pull major guilt trips like you do?

MOSTLY.

She reached the condo entrance and buzzed herself in, indulging in the air conditioning like it was the first time she'd ever felt it. It may be September, but it was Texas September, not Pinterest September. There was no need for hot tea and snuggly blankets in a hammock by an outdoor fireplace, no pre-pumpkin-spice-season excitement blown in on a chilly breeze. Instead, the heat radiated down from the sky and up from the city's concrete like a convection oven, serving as yet another reminder of her bakery failure.

As she reached the landing, she saw Jeremy standing by the Coke machine, focusing intently on the selection. "Oh, hi, Jessica," he said when he noticed her. Then his expression darkened, his wide eyes narrowing, his smile wilting. "You look like you've had a day."

"None taken," she said, before realizing he hadn't offered no offense.

He leaned his back against the machine, crossed his arms, and studied her passively. "You want to talk about it?"

She opened her mouth to say no, but instead, something else came pouring out. "I was rejected by the credit union for the loan I needed to start a bakery, and now I'm not sure what to do, and God keeps trying to give me the money, but I don't believe for a second there aren't serious strings attached to his offers, so there's no way I'm taking it, but part of me wants to since I'm already probably going to die in a gruesome display at the end of all this, anyway, so I might as well enjoy some time working at a bakery until then, right?"

Jeremy pouted his lips thoughtfully, two deep dimples appearing along his jaw. Then he bobbed his head gently. "Yeah, that's a trip. I'm sorry you have to deal with that, Jessica."

It was the "I'm sorry," that put her over the edge, and the flimsy levees she'd built with sandbags of anger gave was as the tears broke free.

"Come here," he said, stepping toward her with his arms spread.

She lumbered forward, shoulders slumped, and let her neighbor hug her. Even as her tears continued to soak into the sleeve of his ratty, black, death metal T-shirt, she understood how pathetic this moment was for her.

He patted her awkwardly on the back until she could peel herself away from him again, and as she sniffled and wiped her nose on her own sleeve, Jeremy said, "You probably don't want to hear this yet, but it's for the best."

"I know, I know," she said, waving him off. "I need to figure out how to do this on my own without relying on God's reputation."

"Huh? Oh, no. Not that. I mean it's for the best because now you're not a part of the big banking system. They put everyone in a registry, and most people don't realize it's all run by a secret coalition of neo-Nazi aborigines."

"Did I ... I think I misheard you."

Jeremy smiled kindly, compassionately. "I know, it's weird to hear the first time, but it starts to make sense once you think about it."

She sniffled. If nothing else, the confusion had derailed her downward spiral. "I don't know that it will."

"No, it will." He slugged her playfully on the shoulder.

She stared at him, leaning cautiously away. "Okay ..." Deciding there was no way she would be able to walk away from this conversation and focus on anything else unless she had more information, she risked further investigation. "Where did you hear about that?"

"The only credible news left for the masses. FactWars."

"FactWars?"

He held up a hand and took a step back. "Wait. You're telling me you haven't heard of it? Oh Jessica. You really should check it out. They *love* you."

She had a feeling that wasn't a good thing. "Okay."

He placed a hand on her back and guided her down the hall toward their front doors. "Promise me you'll check it out before you decide to apply for another loan? At least the website."

"Sure." While she had no intention of doing so, it was an easy promise to make. There was no point in applying for another loan if the one place where she had a connection rejected her. Until she could build good credit, that option was clearly off the table.

"Great. Well, I hope your day gets better. Sorry it's been so rough. You deserve a little happiness."

Despite the insane things he'd just said, his words hit her hard, and she hurried inside before he could see her cry again.

But as soon as she shut the door behind her and faced her quiet, aesthetically sterile apartment, her urge to cry was replaced by the urge to sleep. So she kicked off her shoes, tossed her bag on the couch, and headed straight to her large, expensive bed. Well, not *her* bed. The bed of whoever owned this condo, which was a continuing mystery she was trying to solve, one strange artifact at a time. So far, she'd found a Texas A&M koozie in a kitchen drawer and a copy of *Women's Bodies, Women's Wisdom* in the bedside table. The later was shaky evidence, since there was a distinct possibility that Wendy planted it there in a subtle attempt to have Jessica educate herself where her dubious sex education had failed.

She'd just managed to get her phone attached to its charger and let her head hit the pillow when a buzzing on the bedside table drew her attention. She grabbed her phone and checked the caller ID. Wendy. While it was endlessly tempting to let it go to voicemail, Jessica was too scared of the consequences of such an action, so she answered it.

"Let me guess," she said, "you have fantastic news that you just can't wait to share with me."

Wendy shouted, "Are you high? Because that would at least explain your judgment, not that it would make *my* job any easier at this point."

Jessica turned over onto her side in bed, gazing out between the slats of her blinds at the adjacent bar and grill. "No, I'm not high. I wish I were, if that means anything."

"Oh, are we talking wishes right now? Great. Then I *wish* you would use a filter before tweeting your problems to the world. But wishes don't mean squat for publicists, so."

Jessica tried not to take Wendy's chastisement personally—the woman basically worked three full-time jobs between her PR firm, Jessica's pro bono shitstorm, and dating two lawyers. Stress was a natural companion to that. "What'd I do now?"

"Your little Twitter rampage is spreading like wildfire. I assume you haven't checked, or else you would know why I'm calling, but your complaints about money are *not* what people want to hear."

Jessica groaned and pulled the covers up over her head. "But everyone complains about money. I thought you wanted me to be more relatable."

"Relatable but clearly superior. Is that so hard to manage? You've been retweeted tens of thousands of times just over the last half hour. And guess who's having a field day with this?"

She couldn't even begin to guess. The people who wouldn't mind exploiting her words were legion. "Who?"

"Eugene fucking Thornton. He's coined a new term, which is irritatingly catchy and made me immediately cancel my weekend plans to brainstorm a way to defuse it. Want to know what he's calling you?"

"Not even a little bit."

"The Moochsiah. The god blessed Moochsiah! Jessica," she said pleadingly, her voice cracking, "it's so good. I'm worried this might stick."

Damn, she was right. That was good. Maybe she could fix this if she just thought about it hard enough.

But then again, why would she be able to fix it if the woman whose livelihood revolved around fixing the missteps of others was on the verge of a complete meltdown? There was nothing that would indicate she had better problem-solving skills than Wendy in this arena. Or, really, in any arena.

Man, I should probably become good at something.

"You told me to tweet more," was all she could come up with in her own defense.

"Yeah, but not like this, Jess." Wendy's voice thinned to hardly more than a whisper. "Not like this."

"Take a deep breath. I'll try to think of something." But she already knew that was a road to nowhere.

And Wendy clearly knew it too as her heavy sigh crackled the speaker. "I should have known. Twitter is a no-win game. I'm sorry, Jessica. I'll find someone to handle social media for you. I should have done it ages ago, but I figured, 'Hey, she's young. She probably understands the culture of it.' Seems I was wrong."

Jesus. Jessica thought *she* was having a rough day, but by the sound of it, hers had *nothing* on Wendy's. "Don't take it so hard. You couldn't have possibly known how inept I am. It's not your fault."

"But I—"

"It's not your fault. And even if it were,"—should she? Wendy sounded like she could use it—"I forgive you."

There was silence on the other end, and Jessica wondered if the line had gone dead.

"Wendy? You still there?"

"Huh? Oh, yes. I just felt something strange—"

"That was me."

"What do you mean?"

"Like this: I forgive you."

Silence again. Then Wendy spoke in low tones. "I suppose I should thank you for that, but I'm too terrified about what pandemonium will erupt if the public at large finds out you have that ability. Please tell me you hand out forgiveness with the utmost discretion."

"Of course. Only a couple people know I can do that."

"People you can trust?" Wendy said.

She inventoried her memories. There was Chris, of course. Quentin, too.

Oh no. There was also Greg and Sandra. "Of course only people I can trust," she lied. Now was not the time.

"Good." Wendy's usual confidence came creeping back. "Okay. I think there's a way to spin this where I can make Eugene look like the bag of shit he is and also get you the money you need."

"And what's that?"

"Crowdfunding. It's a beautiful thing."

"No," she said immediately. "No way. I'm not taking money from a bunch of strangers."

"You're thinking about it all wrong. Crowdfunding is hip and makes people feel like they're a part of something bigger than themselves. Granted, it's still essentially begging, but it's socially acceptable begging. For whatever reason. If Eugene keeps up the Moochsiah thing after you've launched your page, he'll look like an idiot for calling crowdfunding, which is hot right now, "mooching," and I'm positive you'll hit your goal in a matter of hours. It's brilliant, Wendy! Brilliant!"

Yeah, the publicist was definitely having a breakdown. But rather than comment on her use of her own name, Jessica stood firm on the important issue. "Still no. If you want to shut down Eugene Thornton, be my guest, but no crowdfunding, okay? Owing one bank is stressful enough. I don't want to feel like I owe thousands of people who may or may not be total asswipes."

"Ohhh ... fine. I'll tuck away my twenty years of experience and do it your way. Which, for the record, is not a way because you haven't suggested anything."

"Good?"

"Stay off social media for a while, please, until I can figure out a plan."

That was something Jessica had no problem agreeing to. "Deal."

She hung up and rolled onto her back, staring at the ceiling.

Moochsiah. Damn, that really was catchy.

If she didn't want it to stick, and she couldn't get a bank loan, and refused to crowdfund or accept what her father offered, what was left?

I guess I just have to do it all myself. No help from others, period.

It wouldn't be easy, but there were no other options. Ultimately, funding her dream was her cross to bear.

Chapter Seven

The dry scrub brush on the edge of the Hill Country crunched under Jessica's tennis shoes as she followed Miranda farther and farther away from the car. It had been a harsh summer, and the native life hadn't yet begun to recover, even as the fall threatened to arrive, sending a new batch of seasonal allergies ahead as scouts.

Miranda led the way along a small foot trail down a hill into a shallow valley.

"You know I love a good adventure, Miranda, but you still haven't explained *why* we just drove forty-five minutes and hopped a gate that clearly said *No Trespassing*, and hiked through as obvious a rattlesnake habitat as I've ever seen."

"You'll see," was all Miranda said, and all she'd been saying, since she'd first arrived at Jessica's condo that morning with a to-go cup of coffee in each hand, ordering

Jessica to change into jeans and closed-toed shoes because it was time for a weekend adventure.

That last bit was welcome news, though. After a week of dealing with the fallout from her Twitter rant plus the rejection of her loan application—something she had yet to talk with her closest friends about—coupled with an ongoing battle with her phone's push notifications, or more specifically, with thinking she'd turned them all off only to have more pop up, she was ready for a diversion.

"Some juries might consider this kidnapping, just saying."

"I'm a scrawny educated white girl, so, no, they wouldn't." Miranda planted her feet as she reached the bottom of the valley. "And maybe that's why I didn't bring Quentin along. Doesn't matter. We're here."

Jessica braced her fists on her hips and scanned the surroundings, scrub brush, more scrub brush, and all. "I think I'm missing something, because this is just the middle of nowhere. Wait, is this the *official* middle of nowhere?"

"First of all, no, that's not a thing. This is my mother's cousin's ranch, and I happen to know they're at their vacation home in Myrtle Beach right now. Second of all, how did you not notice the watermelons?"

"The ..." Jess looked around and sure enough, she *had* missed the watermelons, each resting on a stack of cinderblocks in a wide half-circle around where she and Miranda now stood. There was also a small pile of watermelons resting at the end of the semicircle, next to a small mesquite tree. "No, I did not. But now I see them, yet I'm not any *less* confused."

"I follow you on Twitter, Jess. I saw what you tweeted right after you left our place yesterday. I wish you'd just told us what happened. But ... I get it."

Jessica opened her mouth to apologize, knowing Miranda was right, that she should have just told her and Quentin. Maybe then she wouldn't have felt the need to tweet it to the world and ignite a firestorm online and dangerously high blood-pressure in Wendy. Before she could figure out what to say, Miranda jumped in. "It doesn't matter. I'm not mad, but I assume you are."

Jessica nodded noncommittally, kicking at a crumbling, exposed layer of caliche. "Only at Eugene Thornton."

"Bullshit. No one's internet rage is *that* focused. Just admit you're pissed off. You know I'm not going to tell anyone. Well, not on purpose, anyway."

Jessica crossed her arms over her chest, gazing out over the watermelon pedestals. "Okay, yes. I'm pissed at a lot of people. Some I don't even know."

"Perfect. That's why we're here"—she held out her arms and motioned to the array of melons—"at your very own smiting range."

Jessica laughed before realizing that not only was Miranda serious, she was sort of an evil genius. "A smiting ... range?"

"Yeah. Well, I figured if you're going to be pissed off all the time and have the ability to make things go boom, you should probably practice a little bit so that the next time you decide to perform a little vigilante justice outside a bar —Chris told Quentin because he thought it was sexy, then Quentin told me—you can rest assured that you won't hit the wrong target. I mean, I know you've gotten better, but it doesn't hurt to have a little practice outside of the real thing."

As the situation settled in, more questions surfaced than dissolved. "You're not worried I might accidentally smite you out here?"

"Nope. Not at all."

"Huh." She looked around at the setup once more. It was actually brilliant. How had she not thought of it sooner? Sure, she still had a ton of questions, but those could wait. First, she wanted to smite some melons to ... hell?

Sheesh, I hope that's not where I send smote things.

And, god dammit, Miranda had out-friended her once again.

When the hint of annoyance the thought caused reared its ugly head, Jessica used it, focused on one of the watermelons and smote it with all she could muster.

The watermelon two pedestals over from where she'd aimed exploded instead. "Oof. Yeah. I guess practice is a good idea."

Miranda wiped a bit of juice from her arm and grimaced. "Wow, that was *really* bad. How have you not accidentally killed someone yet?"

"I suppose by the grace of God." She met her friend's eye and both chuckled.

"Sure," Miranda said.

"Right? I wish." Jessica focused on the same watermelon and this time it exploded when she threw her wrath its way. The *thunk* immediately preceding the explosion was morbidly gratifying, and as she went down the row, missing a few and taking out a juniper tree then a distant prickly pear—thankfully far enough away that none of the spines made it back to where Miranda and Jessica stood— and finally, much to their chagrin, a small field mouse, Jessica struggled to focus her mind. The temptation to imagine that each watermelon was Eugene's stupid face with his stupid mustache and stupider eyebrows was strong but *did* present a moral question Jessica didn't feel like considering at present. So she put him out of her mind. The whole point of being out there was less thinking and more smiting anyway.

Once the semicircle of watermelon targets had been properly neutralized, Miranda and Jessica headed over to the pile of spare melons and reset the range.

"Hey, do me a favor," Jess began, "and don't tell Chris about this. He has this thing about superheroes, and if he hears I'm doing this kind of training ..." She cringed. "I occasionally need a real night's sleep without sex dreams. And you wanna talk about someone tampering with my food? I'm fairly sure NyQuil will make it into everything I eat around him if he catches so much as a hint of this."

"I don't think you're wrong."

"He brought up marriage the other day." She bit her lips and waited for Miranda's response.

"Cool. And?" She didn't sound nearly as frantic or excited about it as Jess had hoped. Rather, she carefully balanced the last watermelon, stepped back, and pulled her phone from her back pocket to check for notifications as she strolled to the center of the range.

"And we've never talked about it before, so it was kind of weird and unexpected."

Miranda's eyes shot up from her phone, which she tucked away again. "Seriously? Y'all are just now talking about marriage?"

"What do you mean, 'just now'? We've only been together for ten months."

"No, you've been together for years *off and on*. There's a difference. Hell, Quentin and I have been talking about marriage for almost a year now, and we haven't been together nearly as long as you and Chris. To be honest, I'm surprised you're not already married."

Jessica crossed her arms, glaring at Miranda. "You're not helping here. It kinda freaked me out."

"Don't let it. It would be weird if you two weren't talking about it. And just because you're talking about it doesn't mean he's going to propose tomorrow." She looked Jess up and down, a mischievous smirk forming on her lips. "But if he *were* to propose tomorrow, you'd say yes, right?"

Jessica's stomach clenched. "I honestly don't know."

"Oh." Miranda's grin faded. "Oh."

"It's just that I have a lot going on right now. I can only worry about so much at one time. It's not like Chris is going anywhere, so I don't see why we can't deal with this the whole marriage thing once I open the bakery."

"So you're still planning on opening the bakery?"

"Yeah, I guess so. I don't really know what else I would do."

"You're not going to let the money problem stop you cold?"

Jessica turned to face her directly. "No. Should I?"

"Hell no! Who would you even be if you let anything stop you? You've spent your whole life dealing with assclowns set on keeping you from getting what you want." She ran her hand over her sweaty hair where it was pulled back into a high ponytail. "You know, sometimes I get the feeling you're always so busy fighting to push forward, you don't allow yourself a second to see how far you've come. And that's a damn shame, Jess. Because you've overcome a whole hell of a lot. I *know* everything's a struggle for you. I see it. I feel it. But that doesn't mean you're losing all the time. It just means everything in your life has been hard won." She shrugged. "And as long as you don't give up, this bakery *will* happen. You have my word on that."

Jessica nodded along, knowing there was truth to Miranda's words, but that if she thought too much about them, her aggression might melt to the primary emotion driving it, and that would be no good for target practice.

So instead of responding verbally, she inhaled deeply, closed her eyes, imagined two of the targets, and then let loose. The *thunk* was louder this time, and when she opened her eyes, both watermelons had been obliterated.

With Miranda backing her up, maybe it was possible after all. Maybe, just maybe, she didn't have to do it all on her own.

* * *

"You are so totally Jessica McCloud."

Jessica glanced up from her copy of *Railed to the Cross*. The ambient noise of Bat-Ass Brew surfaced in her field of awareness as she was pulled from the pages of Jimmy's annoyingly relatable life story.

The person staring down at her was definitely not what she was expecting, even after Wendy's repeated cryptic warnings of, "I promise they're the best at what they do. I know you're small-town, but treat them with an open mind." And then her further clarification, after Jessica had inquired whether her social media problems *really* necessitated more than one person to handle them, "No, I'm not sending a team. I'm just sending you Cash Monet." And then her even further explanation, once Jessica said she didn't see how a bit of money would fix her publicity issues, "No, Cash is a person. And they're the best there is."

Jessica eventually resigned herself to not understanding what the hell was going on but promised she would get her ass to Bat-Ass Brew by two on Wednesday afternoon regardless.

The face staring down at her *did* begin to answer some of the riddles in a sort of now-this-makes-sense-but-I-still-don't-quite-get-it way. Said face was composed of smooth cream-colored skin, a shaggy blond pixie cut, and crystal blue eyes beneath lashes that might've been completely invisible, were the sunlight not reflecting off them like icicles. "Are you ... Cash?"

"Oh my god, that's such a Jessica McCloud thing to say. Yes. Cash Monet. At your service."

Cash already had his ... her? coffee in hand and made himself ... herself? at home in the chair facing Jessica. Leaning forward, a self-satisfied grin on his or her face, he or she waggled a finger at Jessica and said, "I know that look. Wendy didn't explain." Cash sighed but leaned back in the chair, threw one arm over the back and crossed his or her legs. "It's okay. I can't expect everyone to get it right away, and considering you're from small-town Texas, I have to say, you're handling my very presence admirably. Let's clear the air, shall we? I am a genderless gift from God, which means two things. First, I prefer for people to use gender-neutral pronouns to describe me, which in English means my options are to be called an 'it,' which isn't okay for obvious reasons, or accept the plural of they, their, them and so on. And you wonder why society can't wrap its head around people like me? We don't even have a pronoun for that shit!" They laughed. "Anyway, being referred to in the plural kind of reminds me of being royalty, so *duh*, I'm gonna go with that.

"And the second thing you should know going forward is that if you ask me what's between my legs, I'll tell you the same thing everyone—regardless of gender—should tell

others who ask that, which is 'none of your goddamn business.' You understand?"

Jessica nodded dumbly. Much to her own surprise, she
did understand.

"Is any of that going to be a problem for you?" Cash
asked, raising a mostly transparent eyebrow.

"Nope. I actually prefer not to think about what's
between everyone's legs."

Cash cackled with laughter and leaned over the table,
swatting Jessica on the arm. As they did so, their eyes
landed on the book, and they recoiled. "Oh dear Lord
Almighty! *What* are you doing with that in public?"

"Huh? Just reading it. I'm supposed to read it,
aren't I?"

Cash clutched at their heart, speaking to no one in
particular when they said, "Oh have mercy. She didn't
even take off the dust jacket. Oh hell." Their eyes refocused on her again. "I have my work cut out for me more
than I thought. But that's okay. I like a challenge. And
you're about as challenging as they come. That's why I
jumped at this opportunity to help out. This could launch
my reputation into the stratosphere. I mean, if I can help
Jessica McCloud break a streak of non-stop social media
blunders, I can help anyone. No offense."

"Little taken?"

Cash reached in their bag and pulled out a pen and
notebook, flipped it open to a clean page in the middle, and
clicked the pen before slapping both down on top of *Railed*

to the Cross. "Let's start with you writing down all your social media logins and passwords."

Jessica wracked her brain and came up with them one by one, jotting them down. "There." She slid the pad back over to Cash, who averted their eyes when the cover of *Railed to the Cross* was visible again. "Please put that in your bag." As she did, Cash began tsk-ing across the table from her.

"What? What is it?"

They put their hands over the login info. "Two things. One, you use the same password for every account. It's a *literal* miracle that you haven't been hacked. Second, I just asked you to write your logins and passwords down on a piece of paper without showing you any type of official identification, and you did it. Just like that. I could be *anyone*, forcing me to ask: are you or have you ever been involved in a multi-level marketing scheme?"

"No. I don't think so."

Cash mouthed, *thank you* to the ceiling. "That's yet another miracle, then, because you're gullible as hell. If I didn't know better, I would actually believe you were the daughter of God himself, avoiding so many possibly catastrophes despite your best efforts to trigger said catastrophes with your reckless online behavior."

"Should I take back those logins, then?" she said, reaching for the notepad.

Cash smacked her encroaching hand. "Absolutely not. I need these. From now on, you don't touch Twitter or Instagram or Facebook or Snapchat or Tumblr and *especially* not MySpace, however desperate for social media you become. Instead, you send me updates about where you are and pictures of what you're doing multiple times a day, and I filter those through my much more refined judgment. After a few months without snafus, we might just heal your online image."

"Let me get this straight," Jessica said. "You want me to *not* get on social media?"

"Yuh-huh."

"Not post, not even look at it?"

"That's the deal, yes." They nodded empathetically, offering a gentle frown of commiseration.

"You're telling me I'm not allowed to read the comments and replies and mentions?"

Cash sat up straight, staring firmly at Jessica. "Yes, I know it'll be hard at first, but—"

"You've got yourself a goddamned deal!" She leaned forward, offering her hand to Cash, whose mouth popped open in surprise as they shook.

"I really thought this would be more of a battle," Cash said.

"Nope." Jessica scrubbed her hands together, wiping them clean of her long-dreaded responsibility. "It's all yours, Cash Monet. Enjoy the trolls."

"Really? But won't you have to go through withdrawals?"

"Nope. I hate social media."

Their head rolled forward, their eyes locked onto Jessica's face. "You hate ... But you're young! You can't be a day older than I am."

Jessica reached in her tote and pulled out her sunglasses and cap, sliding them on. "I have literally no idea how old you are, Cash. Not even a guess. But it's all yours. Do with those logins what you will. Meanwhile, here's my first update." She grabbed her large Nosferabrew with rabies and stood. "Even though I'm about to head back home to subject myself to more of Jimmy Dean's mega upsetting bullshit memoir, I'm having a great day, and it's all thanks to you." She punched them playfully on the shoulder, winked, then turned and headed toward the exit.

From behind the counter, Rebel shouted after her, "Offer still stands!"

Jessica shot him with a finger gun, said, "Still not taking you up on it," and walked out into a beautiful September afternoon. Not even Rebel's unnecessary reminder of his lewd comment half an hour earlier could dampen Jessica's spirits today.

She was free. Free of the trolls.

Chapter Eight

Excerpt from Railed to the Cross

Once we were back on our feet again with more of my mother's government money, I was hardly four, my memory beginning to store small but impactful moments, which was unfortunate timing, because that was when Terrance came into our lives. I never needed my mother to tell me what happened between her and Terrance, because he was Lust, and I heard that loud and clear from where I slept in my mother's bedroom closet each night. I dare not tell you about the obscene moans or about the positions I witnessed my mother and Terrance assume through the crack where the shifting foundation of the crumbling house had separated door from frame. Throughout the rest of my childhood, when I learned of Hell on Sundays, saw the illustrations of the damned writhing in agony in the eternal flames of condemnation, my mind returned to my mother and Terrance in their tango of damnation, as if their souls were already set aflame by the Heavenly Father each time they peeled off their dirt-caked clothes and crawled onto my mother's mattress.

In the time between Dale and Terrance, I'd begun sleeping in my mother's bed, seeking the comfort from her warm, unconscious form that was always denied me when she was awake. But after Terrance left, driven away at gunpoint by my wrathful mother upon learning that he would be a father in a few short months and the baby wasn't hers, I never slept on that tainted and god-forsaken mattress again, not even for the maternal warmth my young body so craved.

My mother's wrath didn't subside in the weeks that followed Terrance's departure. It only grew, the fire stoked by the flammability of alcohol that kept it burning hot in her soul. And as flames consume, occasionally forking, fanning out, breaking off, but ultimately uniting again, so did my mother's rage seem to find and combine with Gustav's.

Gustav had lost his home, his family, and his country, and as his boat had approached Ellis Island, Lady Liberty extending long-sought warmth to him that he had come to believe was dead, he began to hope again. Maybe he could rebuild his home. Maybe he could rebuild his family. Maybe America could be his country.

But he was turned away at Ellis Island on suspicion of being a Soviet spy, and the rejection was like a lash across the back of that small body of hope just as it'd clambered to its feet again. The tail of the whip curved around its side, tearing open the hope's flesh, sending all the entrails tumbling out below the ribcage.

Gustav never recovered.

So after paying what little money he had on him to the right man—or wrong man, depending on your view—he smuggled himself aboard a series of ships that eventually landed him in New Orleans, where nobody cared about mere spies among the horde of crazed, sin-drunk locals and their devil-worshipping voodoo priests.

He traveled from town to town, working for next to nothing in each new location until he was inevitably fired for his temper and moved onto the next place. Then one Sunday morning he wandered up the path to my mother's home right after we'd returned from church. Someone in town had told him there was a single mother who might need help tending to things, so that's what he offered us: help in return for room and board.

Gustav was built like a bull, and about as hairy as one. From a distance, he appeared to have the arms of a black man, his hair was so dense. It always disturbed me that he appeared some sort of biracial Frankenstein monster, but at the same time, his monstrous appearance suited him.

My mother accepted his help before he'd even finished presenting his offer in harsh, broken English. I wasn't sure what she thought we'd need help with. Tending to the mud? Running off the occasional gator or moccasin from the backyard?

Turned out, what she needed was a drinking buddy.

Gustav and my mother would down a fifth each for breakfast, and while the vodka mixed poorly with his temper, the beatings were generally short, because if I could wiggle free of his grasp, I could easily outrun him, as he was too out of shape to catch me. The alcohol also spared me the torment of seeing any perversions acted out in my mother's bed at night.

I was four. Yet I learned about the phenomenon of "whiskey dick," as Mother and Gustav called it. She sometimes yelled at him for it, but he was unconscious for most of that, and she usually shouted herself to sleep before long.

However, the fact remained: Gustav's alcohol-induced erectile dysfunction was a divine blessing, and it was through that revelation at such a tender age that I began to recognize the full spectrum of God's many blessings and the diversity of how they often manifested. Sometimes they took the form of a few twenty-dollar bills floating in the wind, sometimes they looked like the shotgun your no-good daddy left behind when he was carted off to jail that your mother would later use to save herself from perversion, and sometimes they looked like the limp genitals of a Soviet defector.

And sometimes they looked like the foam frothing from the mouth of a Soviet defector as he convulsed on his back in the soupy mid-February mud, rain soaking his clothes in big, condensed drops filtering through the thick evergreen trees of the swamp. Sometimes God's blessings sound like a garbled cry for help in harsh, broken English as a man clutches at his heart and his eyes bulge and he reaches out to the six-year-old boy standing over him whose nose is still swollen from the last beating if not from two straight years of similar beatings. And sometimes those same holy blessings feel heavy at first but reveal themselves in time and distance and through the elongation of memory as so obviously sent from the Almighty that one has the impulse to throw back one's head and laugh, to bestow praise to the Merciful Father through jagged, unbridled mirth.

The sin of sloth seems like a minor one on the surface. It is inaction. How can inactivity be as harmful as, say, wrath or greed? It seems almost like a self-contained sin.

And that's why it is the most insidious.

Lazy is annoying. Lazy might also be frustrating. But in comparison to the effects of the other deadly sins and how obvious those are, it can be difficult to build a strong case against a person's character when their fault is not doing enough. Folks like my mother—those practiced in the art of denial and neglect—can let sloth carry on for years before a final straw is tossed on the pile, and Kenny was the master of managing his own sloth.

When those boiling points were near, and Kenny could see it in my mother's eyes, he knew just what piece of action to take, what chore was nagging at her the most, that he could complete to buy himself another month of sitting on his backside on the couch, drinking beer and watching trash shows on the black and white TV Dale had stolen for us years before. When the screen went fuzzy, he'd holler at me until I came, then tell me to adjust the antennae, giving me precise orders to the eighth of an inch that were always wrong. And when they were wrong, he'd lob an empty at me, but he was no Gustav, and his muscles were weak, his vision blurry, and he couldn't hit the broad side of a house with a rock if he were standing three feet away. Sometimes I would wait until I got the signal just perfect, then on my way out of the cramped living room, I'd knock an antenna with my elbow as if by accident, making the image snowier than before I'd begun tinkering.

Kenny was always too lazy to get up and beat me for it, and if he got lucky and actually hit me with one of his bottles or cans, he lacked any real power behind the throw to make the pain from the knock outweigh the satisfaction of having put his mortal sin on such obvious display. The self-righteousness of the sabotage was the only high I ever experienced in those days.

Kenny slept on the couch most nights, and my mother grew tired of him when I was nearing eight years old. Two years of his sloth was enough for her, even with his occasional displays of energy, and when she finally told him to get gone, he didn't put up a fight, just grabbed what he could carry and walked out the front door and down the muddy dirt road until he, I suppose, disappeared from sight. I can't say for sure because neither of us watched him go. Instead, I grabbed a large black trash bag and my mother and I cleaned up the empties he left behind before she grabbed the couch cushions and beat them until her hand was raw. But even so, the imprint of his backside stayed in those cushions until the day when, years later, the house mysteriously burned down. I can close my eyes and vividly imagine the flames licking up around the base of the couch, the dark and stubborn imprint of Kenny's cheeks being the last holdout before the fire is fully satisfied and moves on to the side table, the wood paneling on the wall, the pile of dirty clothes that took up residence in the corner sometime before I was born and remained until the house was no more.

Chapter Nine

When Jessica had suggested Bat-Ass Brew as the meeting place for coffee—more out of lazy habit than good judgment—Mr. Foster had countered with, "That place is too pretentious even for me," and suggested Java Hut instead. It was a bit longer of a walk for her, but as September moved along, a merciful breeze was starting to waft off Lady Bird Lake and cool the streets of downtown Austin.

Java Hut was a much better spot, though as she walked in and inhaled the wholesome smell of freshly baked bread, a sharp sense of failure poked at her between her shoulder blades.

Mr. Foster was already at a table, reading an actual newspaper and sipping his drink from a large mug.

Brian. You have to call him Brian.

It wasn't the most difficult mental transition Jessica had made regarding her former teachers. Mr. Foster was so casual, being on a first name basis with him didn't seem wrong like it did with Mrs. Thomas. Jessica would never feel okay calling her Dolores. For one, Dolores was a pretty awful name, but also, Mrs. Thomas would always be Jessica's superior, whether she was in school or out.

"Hey, Brian."

He glanced up from his read. "Morning, Jessica. Grab yourself something to drink and join me, won't you?"

She nodded and made her way to the counter, waiting awkwardly in line, fixating on the menu to avoid accidental eye contact with Brian. Outside of the phone call to schedule this meet-up, she hadn't spoken to him since he'd witnessed her defensive smiting outside the Grease Trough.

She'd since added a coffee date with Brian to her to-do list, and as she hit a brick wall with the item *get funding for bakery*, she decided not to let that halt her productivity entirely and moved onto the next item, which was this.

"Yes, ma'am," said a tired-faced girl behind the counter when Jessica made it to the front of the line.

"I'll have a—" Oh shit. She'd become such a regular at Bat-Ass Brew that she forgot what normal people called drinks. Ordering a Cherry Oldman or a Soynar would likely not translate.

"Do you need a menu?" the girl asked, pointing to the giant one directly above her.

"No, no. Just a coffee with room for cream."

While the barista got to work, two men in skinny jeans waiting in line behind Jessica continued a loud conversation that seemed more appropriate for the stage than a coffeehouse.

"I totally couldn't believe it," said the tighter-pantsed man with a sleeveless shirt and handlebar mustache. "I was like, 'Oh my god, is that guy *seriously* carjacking her right now?' It was so wild."

The friend, who was sporting a green flannel shirt over a white tee and likely believed he was "rocking" his faux hawk, tsked and shook his head slowly as his friend spoke. Then he added, "See, you never expect something like that to happen in Austin. Part of the reason I moved here last month is that it's such a safe city, you know?"

"For sure."

The barista's cranky voice cut in. "Coffee room for cream for whatever your name was."

Jessica grabbed her drink and shuffled over to the table, careful not to spill. She set it down and then took her seat, and Brian folded up his paper and tossed it onto the ground under his chair.

"I'm glad you could make the time to visit me, Jessica. I'm sure you're busy getting everything ready for the bakery."

"Um ... yeah." The smiting aspect of their last encounter had weighed so heavy on her she'd forgotten that, as far as Brian knew, she got the loan. Might as well pull off the band-aid quickly. "I didn't get the loan like I'd thought, so I've been trying to figure out a plan B."

"Oh." His shoulders slumped and he leaned back. "Well, maybe that's for the best, I mean—"

She held up a hand. "I know, the banking system is controlled by a secret coalition of neo-Nazi aborigines."

Brian froze, his head cocked to the side, eyes locked onto Jessica. He leaned forward stiffly in his seat. "That was not what I was going to say. And I suggest that not be something you say ever again, because that is mentally unwell rambling."

Jessica nodded, breathing a small sigh of relief that someone smart had refuted the conspiracy. A thorough Google search had been far less conclusive on the matter, resulting in little more than a newfound anxiety about ATMs. "Okay, good. I was just testing you. I didn't believe it."

Brian relaxed. "I guess that means you *did* learn some semblance of critical thinking at Mooremont High, despite all odds against it."

She nodded confidently and coolly. "Psh, who would believe such a dumb conspiracy, even for a second? Not me."

"No, what I was going to say is that maybe it's for the best because receiving a big sum of money from a cold credit union devoid of morality can be more of a curse than a blessing, especially when you've never started a business before. There are other ways to amass capital."

"Like?"

He straightened in his chair, wrinkles appearing on his forehead. Had he not expected her to ask? "Well, working for it and saving up. Perhaps even asking friends you trust and who care about you—"

"Absolutely not."

He sipped his coffee. "Hmm."

Ah yes, she'd almost forgotten how nuanced his judgmental looks could be. "What?"

"That's just a strong reaction. Nothing inherently wrong with asking for help, Jessica."

"Yes, there is. I mean, maybe not for you, but for me, yeah. If I ask for anything, I get a target slapped on my back. I assume you're not on Twitter?"

Brian groaned and Jessica took his point.

"Of course not. So let me fill you in. I was upset about not getting the loan, I tweeted about it, and just that simple act of saying I couldn't do something on my own—not even asking for help, just mentioning that I wasn't able to do it *all* myself—got me labeled the Moochsiah."

Brian sucked in air sharply. "Ooo. That's a good one."

"I know."

"I mean, that's really going to stick."

She rolled her eyes. "Yes, *Brian,* I know."

"Sorry. I get your point. And I see why you're sensitive to it, but it doesn't sound like you've actually asked your *friends* to help. Like I said, there's nothing inherently wrong with asking for help, but there are wrong people and institutions to ask for it. But friends, the ones who really care about you, are fine to ask. Evolutionarily speaking, that's why we make friends, so we have help. I mean, you know Chris, poor sucker, would die for you. And I'm sure you made some friends in college who would help out." Judging by the way his vocal pitch raised at the end, he wasn't sure of that, but Jessica nodded begrudging confirmation, and he continued. "See? Just ask those people. Don't ask the masses. Never ask the masses. The masses are composed of decent people who have lost all decency."

"I've missed your practical optimism," she said dryly.

"You've missed my point, I think, too. If you're going to be in debt to anyone, make it the people who you don't mind paying back. If I could afford to help you, for example, I would. Unfortunately, while working in school administration in Austin pays more than it did in Mooretown, cost of living here is an absolute nightmare, and so I find myself living in an apartment that *sometimes* has water that is *occasionally* warm—though I suspect that's more from the sun beating down on the exposed pipes than the work of a functioning water heater. And this small indulgence of a cup of coffee? That's what credit cards are for, I guess."

"Jesus, Brian. They're paying you that little?"

"Oh, it's not so bad. I mean, my student loans eat most of the paycheck right away, then every so often I get hungry, so I quickly find myself running at a deficit. But it's fine. At least my job as college counselor doesn't require motivating the unmotivated and fielding unreasonable demands from parents who think I'm an overpaid babysitter to their child—who is a *legal* adult."

Jessica grimaced. "Maybe if you get a roommate to split the cost—"

"Oh, I have one. His name's Rocket and he's just

lovely. Very generous. When he invites his friends over, he even shares his needles with them.

"Luckily, Austin is a safe city, so I've only had my apartment burglarized once, and whoever it was just came in, took Rocket's weed and left the rest of our belongings alone. Though it might have been nice if whoever it was had taken out the trash while there."

Jessica hoped Brian never found out about her luxurious living situation. "Want to get lunch after this? My treat."

He laughed dryly. "No, no. It's fine. You can't possibly have money anyway."

"True. But I have my Father."

Brian squished up his face as if the mention caused him physical pain. "Yeah, about that. Not to poke holes in your story, but couldn't you just ask God for money?"

"Sure. But talk about a debt I don't want to have. Hey wait." She narrowed her eyes at him. "You're a science guy. You don't believe God's my father."

Brian shifted in his seat. "Well, I don't necessarily *not* believe it."

"Psh. Since when?"

"Oh gee"—he began flinging his hand about dramatically—"maybe since I saw you smite a fire hydrant right in front of me?"

"I thought you assumed that was a coincidence. You acted like—"

"Look, I'm not happy about it. But like you said, I'm a science guy. I believe in the observable. While I can't prove you made that happen, I'm having a damn hard time disproving it, considering the convenient timing. Ergo, I don't necessarily not believe it."

"Sorry," she said, knowing the possibility of God must be shorting out most of his mental functions.

"Just answer me this," he said, "and I'll feel slightly better about it all." He paused and leaned forward, whispering, "Can you control it?"

"I'm learning."

"Have you ever ... you know."

She shook her head vaguely. "I don't."

"Used it on a human?"

"Oh sheesh. No, not yet."

When he rocked back in his seat, recoiling slightly, she realized what she'd just said. "I mean, no. I don't have any plans on doing it, either. That would be ... messy. No. I haven't and I don't want to."

"Okay, good. Now if you could do me a favor and agree we'll never talk about it again."

"Yeah, sure."

When he paused, sipped his coffee, blinked hard a few times, and then nodded, she knew they'd moved on. "You know, Jessica, when I heard you'd dropped out of college, I was a little concerned, but I think you might be all right after all."

"Thanks, Brian. That means a lot."

He shrugged. "It probably shouldn't. What do I know anyway? At least, that's what irate parents say to me a dozen times a week ..."

The conversation remained surface level after that, mostly catching up on where Brian's former students were nowadays—the intel coming from Jessica via Facebook, since Brian didn't do "that social media thing."

Then finally he cut through a momentary pause with, "Well, I should get going. I have a lot of work to do. It is a Saturday, after all."

They parted ways on the sidewalk, forgoing an awkward hug with an even more awkward handshake, and Jessica started the long walk back, pausing right out of the gates to pass along a handful of pennies to a young couple with dreadlocks and two dogs, who were parked on a blanket on the sidewalk, splitting a slice of pizza.

"Hey thanks, miss!" said the man.

The gratitude came as a surprise. He didn't think she was a whore? Wow. Things were looking up today. "You're welcome. I like your dogs."

He nodded. "Neat."

"What're their names?"

"Stalin and Lenin."

"Okay." She forced a smile and scurried off, wishing she'd ended the conversation on the high note of not being shouted at.

Taking a scenic route along the river, she lost herself in one failed plan for amassing capital after another until a voice with a strong African accent pulled her out of her thoughts. "Miss. Can you please help me, miss?"

Instinctively, she reached into her bag for pennies.

When she held out her hand and finally turned her

attention to the speaker, she was surprised by the disparity between who stood before her and who she's expected to stand before her. This man wasn't dirty, and judging by the state of his ornate and colorful robes, he wasn't homeless, either.

"Yes?" she asked cautiously.

"Miss, no one will help me, but I have an amazing opportunity I'm worried I might miss out on."

The gold threads of his long, loose shirt tugged at her attention. "Okay ...?"

"I am heir to quite a great fortune in my homeland of Nigeria, but because of banking regulations, I cannot transfer the funds to my accounts here. But if you will help me, I can have a check mailed to you, and then you deposit it in your account and transfer the funds to me."

"Um. What?"

"For your trouble, miss, I would give you part of my millions. How does two hundred and fifty thousand sound?"

"That sounds—" *Wait a second.* "That sounds like exactly the amount I need. No thanks." She brushed past the African and stomped forward on her route home.

Nice try.

THE CREATOR KNOWS NOT WHAT YOU MEAN, CHILD.

You thought I would fall for the Nigerian prince scam.

IT WAS NOT A SCAM.

You're telling me you sent the one legit Nigerian prince to Austin to trick me?

THE LORD SAYETH NO SUCH THING.

You almost had me, but that amount was a little too on the nose. Ham-fisted, even for you. I can't believe you thought I'd fall for it.

YOU ALMOST DID. AND YOU WOULD BE SURPRISED HOW MANY PEOPLE DO.

She ran over her options again. There was accepting God's hand-out, which was a big fat no. There was aggressively building up her credit over the next couple years then applying for a loan again, which would require her finding a job to pay off her credit card and who knew what else. But the idea of waiting so long before being able to move forward on the bakery made her lightheaded, so that was the last resort. Then there was accepting help from strangers. That was a hell no if she didn't want to be the Moochsiah forever. She might as well call it Moochsiah Bakery.

Damn, that's still good.

The last option, the one Brian had suggested, might be the best she had at the moment, even if it weren't ideal. Could she ask her friends to help her in this way? She already asked so much of her friends. First, she asked them to be friends with her, which was no easy task, she was sure. Then she asked them to publicly acknowledge they were her friends—well, she didn't ask that of them, but they did it—and she was sure that didn't come without its fair share of public shit-talking.

And Miranda. Why was Miranda still her friend? She wasn't an angel. She didn't have to keep coming back. She didn't always have to be there when Jessica was in dark times. Yet she *had* always been there. She was there when Jessica smote the grackle on the playground, there when Jessica's nerves got the best of her at her first state championship game, there to tackle Destinee and take an elbow to the face in White Light Church ...

Maybe in any case other than her own, Brian's advice made sense. But Jessica just couldn't bring herself to ask anything else of her friends who had already done so much for her even as she offered them nothing in return.

There has to be another option that I haven't thought of yet ... I just have to think harder.

Chapter Ten

"I wish there were something I could do for Mr. Foster," Jessica said, stirring her lo mein with her chopsticks as she and Chris lounged on her living room sofa.

"Yeah," he said from beside her, "but you gotta focus on the bakery. Sure, you didn't get a loan the first time you applied, but you can try again! There are more money-lending fish in the sea."

"No, Chris. We had an in with Blanche and I was still rejected. I've only had a credit card for three months and apparently a four-year lucky streak of scratch-offs doesn't count toward my FICO score. No one will lend me two-hundred and fifty thousand dollars."

He sucked in his noodles, chewed a few times, then said, "You don't know that. There's gotta be a Christian credit union or something."

Impatience bubbled in her chest. "Please, Chris. The vast majority of Christians either actively denounce me or just pretend I don't exist so they don't have to take a stand one way or another. I'm not going to change their minds."

"How do you know that? Do I have to remind you that you changed my mind?"

Jessica chuckled. "Well, sure, but that's because you wanted to bang ..."

Chris shook his head adamantly. "I mean, yes, I did want to bang you, but also, I saw what you did on the football field. I couldn't deny what was right in front of my eyes. So maybe that's what you gotta do. Just go into another credit union and *show* them you're the daughter of God."

She pressed her lips together, cutting off at the pass the meaner things that threatened to burst out of her mouth. "Which miracle do you suggest? Should I take them to a football field, kick an eighty yarder then turn to them and say, 'Now you *have* to give me a quarter of a million dollars!' or should I kill and then resurrect one of their interns? Oh! Or I could make bread gluten-free before their very eyes. There's no way they would assume it was just some sleight of hand and whatever poor celiac fool I brought in wasn't in on the trick. Or maybe I could just smite a few of their desk supplies. That definitely wouldn't get security called on me."

Chris listened patiently to her rant, his face pointedly devoid of a reaction. "I sense you don't like my idea."

"No, Chris, I *love* your idea." She flopped back onto the armrest and groaned. "Sorry. Long day. God keeps tempting me with the money I need."

"God?" Chris asked. "That sounds more like something the Devil does."

"Right?"

"Maybe you're misreading it. God just wants to help you."

"Ha! Right. Because that's a thing."

Her phone buzzed on the coffee table and she groaned, leaning forward and opening the text message. Not surprisingly, it was Cash. She'd known it was coming; she couldn't seem to build the habit of texting them regular updates on her life. So she responded to their request for intel with, *Eating lo mein with Chris. Baked cinnamon rolls this afternoon that didn't completely suck.*

Cash quickly replied with, *Pics or it didn't happen.*

"Ugh."

"What is it?" Chris asked.

"Cash. They're insisting I get pics of my day. Smile." She took a quick selfie of them then sent it back.

Cash replied with, *You're one of those girls who doesn't do the makeup thing I guess. What about the cinnamon rolls?*

Damn. She was hoping the selfie would suffice since she'd forgotten to take a picture of the fresh pan.

She set down her lo mein, ran to the kitchen, pulled out one of the leftover rolls from the fridge, and brought it over to Chris. "Pretend you're eating this." She held up her phone for a picture.

"Can I eat it for real?"

"I mean, it's cold, but sure."

Chris opened his mouth wide and held the cinnamon roll up like he was about to bite into it, and Jessica snapped a few photos, sending the best one to Cash.

But when she looked back up from her phone, Chris was setting down the dessert, unbitten, on a napkin on the coffee table.

Something wasn't right. Chris never set aside dessert. Or any food. "Is everything okay?"

"So I have big news, and maybe it'll fix everything," he said.

Why did he sound so nervous? "Okay."

He adjusted on the couch cushion to face her directly, and she knew this was something big. Chris was ignoring both lo mein and a cinnamon roll to relay the news. She tried not to let that rattle her, but regardless, she was shaken.

"It's been a really good season for me, and I've been talking to recruiters from the NFL. I think I might actually get an invite to the combine."

"Wait, *that's* what this is about? That's great, Chris!"

He held up a hand, gesturing for her to reel in the enthusiasm. "It's been my dream, yes, and if I get drafted in the first few rounds, I would have plenty of money to help you with the bakery."

"Then why do you sound so worried?"

"It's the NFL, Jess," he said like that was supposed to mean something to her. "The National Football League."

"I know what it stands—"

"What if I end up being drafted by the Seahawks and have to move across the country?"

Ah. That was a good point.

The Chinese food started to creep back up her esophagus. She grabbed his hand her hers. "I mean, we can think of something. There might be a market for a gluten-free bakery in Sacramento."

He opened his mouth and narrowed his eyes. "Man, you still don't know *anything* about football. Seattle, Jess."

"Sorry."

"And maybe."

"We'll cross that bridge when we come to it, Chris. Maybe you'll be drafted by the Cowboys or Texans and you can stay in Texas."

He nodded sadly. "God willing." He met her gaze. "If I get drafted, though, would you let me help you out with the bakery?"

How could she say no when he was looking at her like that and she wanted to have dream sex with him shortly? The answer was she couldn't. "Of course. But that's a long way off, and with any luck, I'll already have the bakery open by then. So let's not worry about all that yet, okay?"

"Yeah, okay. But maybe once we're both settled at the end of the school year and see where we are," Chris said, "we can think about, you know, our life."

He means marriage, doesn't he? "Sure. Later. I mean, if we're going to spend our lives together, what's the hurry, right?"

Chris turned his attention to the food. "Heh. Totally."

And so she'd bought herself another eight months at least to figure what the hell she wanted. Well, small victories.

"Let's finish up dinner," she suggested, and he seemed more than happy to oblige, grabbing the to-go container and forgoing the chopsticks he could hardly use by tilting it back and sucking in a mouthful of noodles.

Her phone buzzed again.

Cash, apparently, did not approve of Jessica's photography skills: *Um, are you TRYING to turn your boyfriend into a gay icon? Mouth CLOSED for food photos.*

"Chris, do you want to be a gay icon?"

He shrugged. "I got no problem with that."

"That's what I figured."

She texted Cash back. *Chris says he's fine being a gay icon. Send that baby into the blogosphere!*

Cash quickly responded with, *OMG you genuinely think blogs are still a thing. Wendy was right. You're a complete disaster.*

Jessica didn't bother responding, instead turning on the television to ease into her impending food coma. She flipped to the six o'clock news, which was covering a list of the upcoming music festivals in October.

As the anchors rattled them off, Jessica followed Chris's lead, scarfing noodles and lubricating her throat with copious amounts of beer to hurry along the sedation process. No matter how weird Chris's contribution to tonight's sexscape might be, at least she could fall back on their firm rule of no discussing real life in dreams. The diversion was worth whatever new kink she might discover about her boyfriend.

"And here's a bit of fun news," said Magda Masterson, the perky breasted and perkier haired anchor.

"What's that?" asked Steve Solstice, Magda's white-toothed and whiter skinned co-anchor.

"Looks like American Credit Union is hosting a competition next weekend at the UT football game, awarding a quarter of a million dollars to whoever can kick the longest field goal."

"JESS!" Chris shouted pointing at the television. "What are the odds?!"

She sighed. *Oh come on.*

Some powerful-and-all-that beings just couldn't take no for an answer.

Chapter Eleven

"Lo mein was a good choice," Chris said, rolling off of Jessica and falling flat onto his back in their treehouse overlooking a large swath of the Amazon Rainforest. Jessica was covered in a thick sheen of sweat from the humidity, but it wasn't unpleasant. In fact, it had created a useful lubricant between their bodies as they expressed themselves physically in ways that, occasionally, defied physics. "We'll be sleeping for hours."

"Maybe we'll never wake up," Jess said, chuckling but also thinking about the goliath task of starting a bakery that awaited her whenever she next opened her eyes.

"How about round seventeen?"

"I think we're at nineteen, but yes, please."

"Please refrain," said a perturbed male voice, and for a moment, Jessica worried it was from one of the howler monkeys that insisted on watching them and who Jessica definitely hadn't added to this dream and Chris denied wholeheartedly was a flourish of his.

But then a much further evolved primate stepped around the troop of monkey voyeurs and walked along a branch until he reached the bridge of Chris and Jessica's treehouse sex palace. "I've been trying to save this rain-forest for ages, and now you're ruining it for me," Jesus said. "Sort of feels like it should all be control-burned to the ground after the debauchery I just witnessed."

"You were watching?" Jessica demanded. "What the hell?"

Jesus rolled his eyes and his head along with them. "I didn't *want to.* I would have interrupted before you two even got going, but this place is essentially unnavigable, even in your mind."

"Wait," said Chris. "You had to walk here? From where?"

"The temporal lobe."

"Huh?"

Jessica jumped in. "You *still* haven't talked to God about some workaround? It would benefit everyone if you didn't keep walking in on us."

"Ehh," Jesus hedged. "I mean, I thought about it. But He just seems so busy."

Chris grabbed a large leaf and held it over his groin. "You're scared of God?"

"No," Jesus said sharply, then, "although, I mean, can you blame me?"

Chris stared forlornly at his old-school savior. "What happened to you, Jesus? Growing up, I read all these stories about you where you laid a serious verbal smackdown on people and didn't care what anyone thought about you and just kind of owned all the Pharisees until they were hellbent on killing you and even then you just shrugged it off like, 'Come at me, bro.' I always thought that was pretty badass. But now you're just slinking around, creeping on our sex dreams and scared to ask God for anything, and I don't know what to believe anymore."

Jessica squinted at Chris then turned to her half-brother. "Wait, is what he's saying true? You used to be kind of a badass?"

Jesus shifted on his heels and ran a hand up and down his forearm. "I mean, I still am."

"No, you're not," Chris said with conviction. "You've lost it. You gotta get your groove back, Jesus. And I say this from a place of love." He placed a hand over his heart to emphasize the point.

"Obviously," Jesus said. "But let's see you stand up to the entity that hung you up to dry, literally, as part of His plan."

Jessica could commiserate. "Hey, come on now," she said comfortingly, gesturing to an empty plank of wood at their feet. Jesus sat. "You've already been martyred. What's worse than that? It's not like God would get mad at you and send you to hell. Sort of ruin his story."

Jesus placed his hands in his lap and nodded. "Yeah, and He does love His stories."

"God would never cast down someone he loves so much."

"But wait," Chris said, "didn't God cast down Luci—"

"Not helping," Jess mumbled from the corner of her mouth. She placed a hand on Jesus's shoulder. "I know he seems strict, but, um"—she struggled to find something else to say to comfort her half-brother and so resorted to scraping from the bottom of the barrel—"he wants to help. Even if we don't want his help, he always offers it. For example, he keeps trying to help me finance the bakery."

Jesus's drooping head shot up. "Oh. No. Don't let him help you. Trust me. His help comes at a cost. He says it doesn't, but that's just because he has a weird idea of what constitutes a 'cost.' Does it come at a cost for the greater good? No. But at a cost to you the individual? Psh. *Oh* yeah. If you're okay with that, more power to you, but if I could do it all again ... I just don't know. I can't help but think there was a less excruciating way of going about it that would have accomplished the same thing." His attention drifted to the treetops before snapping back again. "But that's not why I'm here." As he stood, he knocked a large beetle from the bottom of his robe. "You have to continue progress with the bakery. It's important."

"For the *big picture*?" Jess asked skeptically.

"Well ... yeah, but, um. Just keep going, okay?"

"I'm trying, but you know the funding fell through."

"I do know that. But think about it. Did I ever have funding from a big bank?"

"Not that I know of."

"You bet your butt I didn't!"

"Yeah!" Chris pumped his fist. "*That's* what I'm talking about! You showed those money changers who's boss!"

Jesus waggled a finger at Chris. "Exactly, Christopher."

Chris whirled around to Jess. "Dude," he said, despite her many requests not to be referred to as such right after sex, "this guy straight up punked those douchebags. Just went, BLAM! and overturned their tables." Chris dropped his leaf to allow himself more freedom of movement as he mimed the act.

Jesus chuckled and adjusted the shoulders of his robe. "Well, someone had to show those meanies God's way."

Jessica wasn't jumping on this bandwagon just yet, though. "So how did you eat? How'd you get around? How'd you feed your donkey or whatever?"

Jesus smiled triumphantly. "All good questions, Jessica. The answer is friends. My friends helped me out, and that's who you should turn to. Your teacher was right about that."

"Hold up." Jessica plucked two large leaves from a nearby tree, using the fronds to cover her modestly, and stood. "*You* are trying to sell me on the idea of relying on friends?"

Jesus nodded, meeting her eye resolutely.

"And I'm supposed to accept that advice from the most famously betrayed-by-his-friend person in history?"

Jesus gestured vaguely with his hands, his gaze wandering around the surrounding foliage. "One might argue that Julius Caesar is more famously betrayed. *Et tu Brute* and all that."

"Uh-huh." She wasn't convinced.

"Okay, so Judas was a meanie. Maybe even the biggest meanie of all time. That doesn't erase the fact that I wouldn't have survived as long as I did—which, by the way, was still fairly long for the life expectancy at the time— were it not for relying on my friends for help."

"Did you ask them to help you avoid being martyred?"

"She's got a point," Chris added. "You did sort of lie to them about what you knew was going down. They would have helped save you if you'd asked them to."

Jesus crossed his arms. "Sure, sure. So I guess ... do as I say not as I do."

"Now wait a second," Jessica said, narrowing her eyes at her half-brother. "You could have avoided being martyred fairly easily and you didn't do what you could?"

"I guess not."

"Could you explain why, exactly?" The thought of Jesus not doing everything he could to keep from being murdered publicly got under her skin.

Jesus raised his hands in a cartoonish shrug. "Seemed like the thing to do."

"But why?"

He paused, screwed up his nose, then said, "You know, I'm a little bit hazy on it. It was a while ago."

Chris offered an answer. "Wasn't it so we could all have our sins forgiven?"

"Eh ..." Jesus said, shaking his head slowly.

"That can't be it," Jessica said.

"Yeah," Jesus seconded, "that doesn't really make any sense. I mean, why would everyone still be sinning and asking for forgiveness if I just knocked it all out in one go?"

"Okay. So maybe just the sins of people already dead?" Chris offered weakly.

Jesus chuckled. "That would hardly be fair, would it? Holding people responsible for doing the wrong thing before I even told them it was the wrong thing or gave them a way to fix their mistakes. No, not even our Dad would be that mean." He turned to Jessica again. "I'm serious, though. You have to rely on your friends here. Not the money changers, not Dad, but the people who want to help you for human reasons. Part of being a good friend is helping your friends, and part of it is allowing your friends to help you. So do it, okay? Don't make me come all the way out here again."

"Oh, don't worry about that," Chris said. "I think we've pretty much banged out all the majesty of this landscape."

Jesus grimaced. "Agreed."

"So if you'd just relied on your friends more," Jessica said, "would you have been martyred?"

"In hindsight, probably not."

"Done!" Jessica said. "You win, Jesus. I'll do literally whatever you didn't do to keep from going out the way you did. Just promise me one thing."

"Yes?"

"You'll talk to God and see about another option for us to have these delightful little chats."

"I've consented to worse," Jesus said, walking away along a thick bough. "Much, much worse."

Chapter Twelve

The honeydew melon exploded in a splatter of seafoam green, sending chunks in all directions over the barren landscape, silencing the nearest cicadas.

"Not bad," Miranda said.

"Not bad?" Jessica replied. "I just smote the shit out of it."

"Yeah, but look at the cactus behind it."

Jessica stepped to the side to peer around the four-foot stack of cinderblocks. "What cactus?" Then, "Oh, was there a cactus before?"

Miranda nodded. "It's okay, though. A honeydew is a much smaller target than you're used to."

"I don't know, a grackle is pretty small, and I managed to explode one when I was a kindergartener." She sighed, her hands on her hips. "I should be much better at this by now."

"Why?"

"Because I've had sixteen years to practice."

"But have you been?"

"Well, no."

Miranda braced her hands on her hips and smirked. "Then there's no reason why you would be better at it. Try with that cantaloupe."

Jessica stared at it, but couldn't stir the emotion. She imagined Eugene Thornton's face, but still not even a slight tingle in her fingers. "I think I need a break."

"Of course. No problem." Miranda reached into the cooler and pulled out two bottles of water, handing one to Jessica. "You're definitely improving, you know."

"And I wouldn't be if you hadn't set this up for me."

"Well, I figured you needed a stress release. Softball has always been that for me, but this is the last year I'll do it competitively, and that got me thinking, what happens afterward? What'll I do to blow off steam when life does what it does best? I still don't know the answer, but it did make me realize you don't have anything and haven't since you graduated high school. So, I thought I'd help." She chugged the rest of her bottle and threw the empty back into the cooler. "And it's actually gratifying as hell to watch you smite the shit out of melons. If I put this on YouTube, it would get fifty million views immediately. Oh man! What if I did it in *slow motion*?"

"Please don't."

"Yeah, I wouldn't."

"Cash would literally have a heart attack."

Miranda nodded understandingly. "I forgot you have that filter now."

"Oh!" Jessica pulled her phone out of her back pocket. "Speaking of which, I should tell them about this."

She texted, *At target practice with Miranda* and sent it away. When she looked up from her phone again, Miranda was squinting at her through the late September dusk.

"Cash knows about the smiting range?"

"Nah. Just mentioned target practice."

"Eek." Miranda grimaced. "You think they'll post about target practice?"

She chuckled. "Oh, not a chance. It's just fun to screw with them."

On cue, Jessica's phone vibrated and she glanced down at Cash's response: *Omg wut? Can't you do normal things? I'm posting that you're at a charity dinner.*

After shoving the phone back in her pocket and finishing off her water, Jess turned again to her best friend. "I know you've already helped out a lot, Miranda, but can I ask for one more thing?"

"Hold up. You're actually *asking* for something?"

Jessica nodded begrudgingly. "Yes."

"You mean I don't have to guess on this one? You'll just tell me what you need?"

"Yeah."

"Then shit yes, you can ask a favor of me. Whatever it is."

Jess inhaled deeply mustering the strength to say what she knew was the right thing but what still felt like a terrible idea for numerous unnameable reasons. "I need help getting money for the bakery. Without the loan, I don't know what I'm going to do, how I'm going to get a quarter of a million dollars. God keeps dangling it in front of my face, but I don't want to take help from him, and Jesus supports that."

"I support that too," Miranda said. "And don't worry, I'm already on it."

Jessica blinked dumbly. "What do you mean, already on it?"

"I mean, I've already started working on that problem. You think I'd hear about you needing money and just sit on my ass and do nothing?"

Jess groaned. "Your mastery of friendship is really starting to piss me off."

Miranda grabbed Jessica's empty water bottle and threw it back into the cooler. "Good. Use that." She pointed over to a cinderblock tower thirty yards away with a personal-size watermelon on top. "If you focus on how I will always out-friend you, maybe you can actually hit your target without blowing up anything else."

"Screw you," Jessica said, then she turned and smote the melon.

Miranda jogged over to it to examine the scene then hollered back. "You got the top cinderblock, too, but otherwise looks good."

When she returned, she added, "You just have to focus a little bit more."

"Sorry. I guess I'm a distracted."

"What now?"

Jessica hadn't had time to process it in the two days since her lo mein date, what with Jesus and browsing the internet for alternative funding options. Or maybe she'd just been avoiding it.

"Chris might be going into the NFL draft. What if he moves across the country? Do I follow? Do we get married? Will we still be able to have dream sex if we get married? Or even worse, what if he gets drafted a thousand miles away but won't go because I'm here?"

Miranda pressed her lips together and waited until Jessica was completely finished before responding. "To that last point, I know Chris loves you obsessively, but I don't think he'd miss an opportunity to live his childhood dream just because you're not in the same city as him. He could've dropped out of college or transferred to UT to live in the same city as you but he didn't. And now y'all have the long-distance relationship thing down, right?"

"No, it's more complicated than that." How could she explain it to Miranda, though? Chris was an angel, and his pull to Jessica was stronger than just a boyfriend wanting to be close to his girlfriend. It was cosmic.

Miranda waited patiently, but her gaze was relentless. "Well, are you going to explain it? We're out in the middle of nowhere, nothing pressing on either of our schedules, and clearly it's bothering you. So, what is it? Do you have something on him? Why wouldn't he be able to leave? Wait, is he gay? Has this been a cover? Are *you* gay?"

Jessica waved her hands in the air to stop her. "You're actually making it *more* complicated than it is."

"Then just tell me."

Would Chris care? Probably not. While Jessica wasn't going to out Quentin, it didn't seem fair for Miranda to be the only one in the small group of friends who didn't know she was among at least one heavenly being. Well, besides Jessica herself.

"Chris is an angel."

Miranda stared blankly, saying nothing.

So she added, "Literally. He's an angel."

"Come again?"

"I don't really understand it, but he's apparently an angel, which doesn't count for much but does mean that he's naturally inclined to, um, serve me."

Miranda pressed her fingertips to her forehead. "So angels exist, Chris is an angel, and he's your ... slave?"

"What? No! He's not a slave."

"Okay, then I'm going to need further explanation."

If only she could provide it. Unfortunately, she didn't quite understand the nuances herself. But she tried to explain what little she did know. "He's more of a guardian. He and the other angels sort of have a magnetic pull toward me. They can resist it, but it's, I dunno, uncomfortable."

"Uh-huh." She squinted toward the horizon, silent for a moment, and Jessica allowed her the space to digest the new information bomb. Finally Miranda turned back toward her. "You mention 'other angels.'" She leaned forward, watching Jessica's face closely. "How many others, and do I know them?"

Jessica rubbed her shoulder and neck. "Um. A bunch, and yes you know some, but I'm not supposed to out them."

"But you outed Chris."

"I don't think he'd care that you know. But other ones might. Don't tell anyone about Chris, though."

"I'll do my best." A silence fell between them again, then Miranda asked, "Would you out one if knowing might affect my life one way or another?"

Oh shit. Does she know? What if she knows about Quentin and this is a friend test?

But Miranda wasn't that kind of a person. She would just come out and say she knew about Quentin.

As much as Jessica wished she could be honest with her best friend, she knew it wasn't up to her to decide when Quentin came out to his girlfriend. "Yeah, if I thought it would negatively affect your life to not know, I would tell you."

Miranda accepted that answer, nodding and turning back toward the range. "So how do you know if someone's an angel?"

"I usually don't, I just have to wait until another angel outs them."

"That sounds frustrating."

"Yeah, it really is. They don't always mention it. Or they mention it offhandedly way after the point where it would be especially useful. I guess they're just so used to it they forget to mention, 'Oh hey, Dr. Bell is an angel, and that could—'" She gasped. "Shit. I didn't say that."

"Ha! Okay. It's good to know, though. It makes me feel a little better that you have plenty of people watching out for you."

"What? I don't need people watching out for me!"

"Yes, you absolutely do."

"Screw you," Jessica said.

Miranda reached into her canvas grocery bag and pulled out a grapefruit then glanced sideways at Jessica. "Good. Harness that. Now you think you can blast this out of the air, you walking disaster?"

"Just throw the damn fruit."

Miranda chuckled confidently. "If you insist." She let loose, putting her softball muscles to work, and the grapefruit was yards away before Jessica could even react, but then she steadied her mind, condensed her aggression into a thick syrupy energy, and shot it from her fingertips in an energy blast.

The grapefruit fell to the ground with a soggy squish, untouched.

Miranda frowned. "Eesh. I guess we still have some work to do."

Chapter Thirteen

"It sure is green everywhere," Destinee said, her head swiveling to take in the trees on all sides of the Greenbelt trail.

"To be fair, everything's green compared to Mooretown."

They were only ten minutes into their hike, and Jessica was already starting to relax like she hadn't done in months. Not only did she never get out of the loud city streets anymore, but the Greenbelt also allowed her to spend much-needed quality time with her mother without fear of aggressive reporters and paparazzi. A week of heavy rain at the end of September had left the woods with a lush ground cover, and Jessica felt confident she'd hear rustling if anyone tried to stalk them. So, while they did occasion-ally pass other people heading in the opposite directions whose dogs were still dripping wet from an impromptu swim, Jessica and Destinee were mostly isolated and able to indulge in conversation without constantly worrying about filtering.

"I know you been working hard lately, baby, so I'm glad you could take a day off for me to visit." Destinee was slightly out of breath already, but grinned despite it.

"I haven't been working *that* hard."

"Bull. You've been baking your ass off. You know I never bothered making shit from scratch. Pillsbury had my back for a lotta years. Still does, to be honest, though now Rex sometimes handles the baking." She wiped sweat from her hairline. "I tell ya, Jess. Feminism is just the gift that keeps on giving. If only your father were a little more feminist from the start, we might all have it made."

I HAVE NO BIAS.

"He says he has no bias," Jessica said.

"That right there's a load of horse shit. He told me the night we met redheads weren't his type. If that ain't bias, I don't know what is."

"Don't worry, Mom, I'm with you on this." They stepped to the side of the path to let a young couple in full hiking gear with two wet golden retrievers pass by.

"Morning."

"Morning."

The couple disappeared and Destinee jumped back into the conversation where they'd left off. "I don't actually know how God could make a single decision if he weren't at all biased. Just don't make sense."

A path split from theirs, and Destinee raised her chin to peer down it. "Sounds like there's water that way." They walked until they reached the edge of the creek, a strong current rushing by them. "Well, I'll be damned if this ain't the prettiest sight I've seen in my whole life."

THOU SHALT REMIND HER WHO MADE IT.

Jessica groaned. "God wants to be sure you remember who's responsible for it."

Destinee met her daughter's eyes and tilted her head dubiously.

Jessica nodded. "I know."

They turned and headed back toward the main trail. "You gotta listen to him bragging all the time?"

"Not all the time. It's worse when you're around."

IT'S LIKE YOU'RE SET ON EMBARRASSING THE LORD.

It would only work if you were prideful, though. Are you prideful?

... NO.

Then I'm gonna keep doing what I'm doing.

"Has he been helping you lately?"

"He's been trying."

OH WOW, LOOK AT THOSE BEAUTIFUL FLOWERS ON YOUR LEFT.

I see them. And they are beautiful, I'll give you that.

MAKE SURE YOUR MOTHER SEES THAT GLORIOUS CREATION.

That's not my responsibility.

TRUE.

Destinee tripped over an exposed root along the trail and caught herself just before she hit the ground. "Shit!

Nearly busted—oh hey, those sure are some pretty flowers."

Jessica cringed at God's satisfaction.

Once Destinee had her feet properly underneath her, she said, "I miss having you at home, baby, but I get why you would want to move away. I been thinking about it myself."

"Really? But you've lived in Mooretown your whole life."

"And a lotta good that did me. Been working at the same damn pharmacy for going on fifteen years and ain't got a single promotion past pharm tech. If the house wasn't already paid off by your grannie, I wouldn't be able to put food in my mouth on what they pay me. Thing is, it's one of the best paying jobs in town for folks like me who only got a GED, which is most of us."

"You don't have to sell me on Mooretown being a dead end, Mom. If you want to move away, you should."

LET HER KNOW I WILL BE WITH HER WHEREVER SHE MAY GO. SHE CANNOT ESCAPE THE GAZE OF THE LORD.

... Said the Divine Stalker. You need serious help talking to women.

Destinee inhaled a lungful of the freshest air within twenty miles. "Driving into Austin got me thinking about moving to a city."

Jessica glanced over at her mother, feeling guilty for what she was about to say but knowing it had to be said. "You wouldn't like a city, Mom. People here wouldn't understand you and you sure as hell wouldn't understand them. And I mean that in the best way."

"Well shit," she said, pushing back a strand of sweaty hair from her face. "Maybe there's some truth to that."

"There is. A couple months ago, I overheard a vegan talking about getting an abortion." If anyone would understand how confused that'd left Jessica, it would be her mother.

"I'm not sure exactly what a vegan is, but doesn't feminism allow for anyone to get abortions whenever the hell they want? Even on, say, a Tuesday?"

"Oh. Um. I honestly don't know. But never mind. Don't worry about it."

"No, no ... don't just brush me off just 'cause I don't know something. I gotta learn too, baby. Vegans ... are those the ones who can't move their arms or legs?"

"Nuh-uh."

"Ohh, right. I'm thinking of vegetarians."

"Vegetables. That's what you're thinking of."

Destinee scrunched up her face, shaking her head minutely, but let it go. "Fine, I'll play along. What's a vegan?"

Jessica was only half certain herself, but she tried to explain. "They don't eat meat—"

"But chicken's okay, right?" she asked quickly.

Not the question Jessica was expecting, but she rolled with it. "Uh, maybe. And I don't think they eat dairy."

Destinee scoffed. "That's probably because nobody eats dairy. They drink it."

"And they definitely don't eat eggs."

Destinee threw her hands into the air. "Who the hell won't eat an egg but'll eat a chicken?! And you say these people live around here?"

"Yeah. They're kind of everywhere in Austin."

Destinee's head swiveled, scanning for the woods for sneaky vegans. She whispered, "I think you'd do best to steer clear of folks like that, Jess. Some gears ain't turning for them, sounds like."

"Don't worry. I do."

Destinee straightened up and continued on down the path. "After what you just described, I almost think vegans should get *extra* abortions. Be bumped up to the front of the line, ya know? I heard about that kinda crazy being passed from one generation to the other. Take Kathy Mae. You remember her and how she was always collecting them aluminum cans?"

"Yeah, she recycles them, right?"

Destinee wagged her finger at her daughter. "That's what we always thought, yeah. But when she passed away —oh, by the way, she passed away last month; I forgot to mention that on our last call—the authorities went into her home and found all them cans from the years. She wasn't recycling them after all. She was just making a can maze in her home or some shit. Turns out, her daughter Jeanne, who was a few years behind me at Mooremont, has started asking people for their cans lately, too. I think Kathy Mae's passed on her sickness."

"I'm so glad I'm not in Mooretown anymore."

"Yeah." Destinee nodded resolutely. "I need to get the hell outta that crazy shithole."

The trail opened up to the wide, shallow creek, and Jess led the way over to the lip of a rock overhanging the water. As they both took a seat, their only company for the moment was a tall, lean man in his early twenties, shirt off, hair pulled back into a sloppy bun as he threw a tennis ball into the creek for his large mutt, over and over again.

"I need to come out here more," Jessica said.

"It sure is peaceful," Destinee agreed.

I THOUGHT SO TOO ... WHEN I MADE IT.

Not so peaceful when you shout shit like that in my skull.

RUDE.

Obnoxious.

"I hate to be the one to bring this up," Destinee said, "but we ain't really talked about it yet, and it seems long overdue."

The muscles in Jessica's abdomen clenched. There were a number of things Destinee could be referring to. The bakery, Rex's clear interest in making an honest woman out of Destinee and her obvious lack of interest in it, or—oh no—had they ever had that sex talk? No, they'd never actually had the sex talk, had they? Would Jess have to listen to her mother describe good sex, undoubtedly in graphic and personal detail?

"I assume you've read Jimmy's book," Destinee said.

That hadn't even made it onto Jessica's list of terrible

things they hadn't yet discussed, but she supposed it should have. "I've read some of it."

Destinee's eyes shot open. "Wait, you haven't read it all the way through?"

"No, but don't worry, I've already been lectured."

Destinee's eyes grew even wider and she leaned back, a flat palm pressed to her chest. "Oh *no,* baby. I ain't here to lecture you on it. I just figured you'd've read it already and want to talk about it. But if you haven't read it, good on you!" She nodded to punctuate the sentiment. "Whole book is full of lies. I could hardly stomach it."

"Wait, *you* read it?"

"Of course I read it! You know Jimmy's a lying sack of shit. I had to know what sorta lies he was telling." She leaned close, mumbling conspiratorially from the corner of her mouth, "Could hardly get through the part about his childhood. Almost made me feel sorry for the fool. If any of it were true, I woulda."

"God says a lot of it is true. Not all, but a lot."

"Huh." Destinee scratched at her sweaty scalp. "The part about the cult leader? That part true?"

"Oh shit, is that a thing?" Destinee nodded. "I haven't gotten to that part. I don't know if it's true."

"No, I mean, ask *him.*" She pointed skyward.

"He's not in the—" But she stopped herself. If the consensus had it, God *was* actually in the sky. And who was she to argue, really? It wasn't like she'd ever asked Him flat out. Maybe someday she could ignore the echoes of His obnoxious voice in her skull long enough to ask. "I can't ask him right now. I told him to leave me alone."

"Ah." She stared at the creek. "How long does that usually last?"

Jessica leaned back on her hands. "Not long enough."

"But you did read the foreword?"

Jessica sighed. "Sure did."

"And did you smite anything?"

"Not right away."

Destinee put her arm around Jessica, pulling her in close. "I'm proud of you, baby. There's a reason God didn't give me the ability to smite."

Jess conceded with a slight nod. It was as good a case as any for Him actually possessing infinite wisdom.

"Oh! I almost forgot." Jessica pulled out her phone from her sports bra and wiped the sweaty screen on her shorts. "We should get a selfie."

"What for? You putting it on Twitter?"

Jessica leaned toward her mother and snapped a pic. "I'm not. I have someone who does that for me."

"Ooo ..." Destinee mocked playfully. "Look at you! So you just send the pictures to her and she posts them? Or is it a him? Are you two friends?"

Jessica considered it and decided upon the most merciful option for everyone, considering how quickly the vegan conversation had been derailed.

Baby steps.

"I'll tell you about them later, Mom."

Destinee grinned mischievously. "Ooo ... you have a

It is Risen

whole team working for you?" She put her arm around her daughter, pulling her close. "Don't let it go to your head, baby."

Jessica resigned herself to her mother's firm hold, relaxing into it. "Don't worry. I won't."

Chapter Fourteen

Excerpt from Railed to the Cross

Then one evening I overheard a wife speaking with Rupert in the small, poorly ventilated kitchen, her voice low as she prattled on hurriedly about two men who had questioned her while she was in town buying groceries for the evening. I peeked around the corner and could see the pastor's expression vividly. His eyes would have seemed more appropriate for a spooked horse, and the reputably docile lover reached forward, grabbed the wife, and shook her, insisting more information and immediately.

The world crumbled quickly from that moment on. We didn't see Pastor Heathrow the next day, as he remained locked in his room until that night's worship. His sermon was disjointed, his glow fractured and subdued. One might assume a speech like that would lodge itself in my young mind, the stark contrast to all previous ones wedging it in painfully between two fonder memories. But I don't recall what he said that night because it made so little sense. All I'm sure of is that it had nothing to do with his message. Much of it seemed contrary to his previously consistent beliefs.

When it came time for him to select a wife for the night, he hurriedly grabbed my mother's hand, then, to my utter amazement, he grabbed mine as well and led us both out of the great room and into his bedchamber.

His sons and daughters were never allowed there, and as I entered, I immediately felt the need to escape. But it seemed I wasn't the only one with that plan in mind.

The room was nearly bare. The bed was made with the prickly colored comforter spread across it, not a wrinkle visible to the eye. The curtains around the four-poster were drawn and tied neatly, and while two chairs and two side tables remained, there was not a single item on them—no clock, no book, no knick-knacks of any sort. As I had no previous example to compare this to, having never been in the room before, I didn't know for certain that this wasn't the usual state of things. Yet, while we practiced an austere lifestyle by most standards, Rupert had never struck me as the type to adhere to it himself. Plus, at the end of the large inviting bed was a heavy wooden trunk, upon which sat two bulging suitcases, shut but threatening to pop open at any moment. The sparse room and the packed bags relayed the truth of the situation.

"We're leaving, Paula," Rupert said. "I'll explain on the

road, but you and Jimmy are the only ones I'm bringing with me."

My mother bobbed her head excitedly, thrilled, no doubt, to be the one among many chosen as his companion.

I've since come to terms with never precisely understanding why Mother and I were the ones Rupert chose, but I do entertain theories. Firstly, she was the only wife with one child. The rest all had three or more. Traveling with a single child would be far less noticeable than with six, like Melissa had, or even four, like Gertrude. The second possibility is that my mother was easily the most lethal of the wives and could fill the role of bodyguard as much as she could wife. It was a twofer. And if she was led to believe Rupert truly loved her, well, all the more deadly for any men in suits who tried to take him from her. I'd never heard her disclose the sordid details of her past relationships to Rupert, but then again, I wasn't there for all those long nights they'd spent together. Looking back on it now, there must have been a great deal of stories shared for him to have bonded so strongly with each of his wives. Women are only ever that loyal to a man if they feel he's not only heard but adequately comprehended the worst things they've ever done. And a man is only as loyal to a woman as Rupert was to my mother if she's able to accomplish incredible physical feats in the bedroom. Which brings me to the third possible reason why my mother was chosen: her time with Terrance had schooled her in the devilish art of lust so that none of the other wives could equal her prowess.

But while my mother was more than happy to flee with Rupert, I was not.

For the first time in my long twelve years, I had a home. I had brothers and sisters. I didn't get beaten. I had a bed to sleep on, regular meals. I even had a father whom I loved. And because I'd witnessed Rupert's connection to the Holy Spirit fade since the two men arrived on our doorstep, as he stood before me in his bedroom, explaining how we would find a new home and start again, this time even better than before, I didn't believe him. I didn't believe he could start again, let along better than before. I despised him for letting his light dim. I detested him for making me choose, for creating a family only to shatter it in such a reckless manner.

I nodded along with his plan, though my mind on the matter was already made. I wouldn't leave with Pastor Heathrow and my mother. But I *would* leave.

Rupert asked me to stay in his room for the night, but I asked if I could sleep in the bunks; that way the others wouldn't become suspicious of our flight the next morning. I promised I could sneak out undetected before breakfast, and perhaps because of his preoccupation with other loose ends (and his own continued survival), he overlooked my obvious lie. Not the sneaking out part—I really was good at that skill—but the motivation behind my request.

He told me to meet him on the front porch at five minutes before sunrise, and I enthusiastically agreed.

I didn't hug my mother before I left Rupert's bedchamber, and I've never regretted that decision.

The next morning, I slipped out of the front door a half hour before sunrise and hid behind one of the large willow trees, out of sight but with a clear view of the heavy front door of the—let's call it what it was—compound.

Ten minutes before sunrise, I saw Rupert and my mother creep from the house, shutting the door slowly and with care, and glance around suspiciously. They carried four large suitcases between the two of them, though I imagine it was all Rupert's belongings since my mother had little more than the clothes on her back and perhaps one or two spare articles. She was anxious; her eyes darted around, skipping right over my hiding spot without a hint of a hitch, the crest of her arched brows approaching the sprigs of bangs from the pixie cut she'd maintained fastidiously since the first day Rupert had complimented it. I lowered the bucket deep into my internal well, attempting to draw forth emotion I should have felt for her. She was my mother. She'd raised me. We'd been through so much together. And this might be the last time I laid eyes on her for the rest of my life.

The well was dry, no sentimentality to be found. Instead, when I brought up the bucket, I found it filled to the brim with a rugged determination that had laid dormant at the bottom of the well for my twelve years of existence and demanding to be released, finally, from its confines.

Rupert checked his watch compulsively like he was addicted to the passage of time. While I didn't own a watch myself, my suspicion has always been that the two most important adults in my life to that point didn't wait until five minutes before sunrise before departing. Or if they did, they certainly didn't wait a moment longer.

He handed two bags to my mother and she nodded, understanding the implication: they were leaving without me.

I watched them go.

They didn't take the shared car but instead went on foot, so deep was Rupert's paranoia of being tracked. Perhaps it was founded. Perhaps not. Perhaps they were eventually caught by whomever sent those men in suits. Or perhaps they escaped. Maybe, as I write this, they're enjoying cocktails on a beach in Mexico. Or maybe they're both in prison. Perhaps both are dead.

To this day, I don't know where they are and I don't wish to know.

I returned home, or the place I had called home once. Not the one Rupert created for us before razing it to the ground with his betrayal, but the one my mother had built for us, just the two of us with the occasional interloper, that held no pretense of security or happiness, that demanded from the moment one set foot in it, "Don't get your hopes up."

It was a long walk and took me nearly all day. I don't know what drew me back. Habit? A desire to pretend the last year of my life was but a dream? Curiosity? The chance my mother and Rupert had stopped there on their escape route and that I might find them and expose them for the horrible people I now *knew* they were?

I think it was none of those options, and by the time I arrived, I had little I desired to be where I was. The house had never looked as sullied, and that was saying something. Four seasons of neglect in the muggy climate was enough, at least, to allow the surrounding nature to assert a slow, crawling reclamation of its territory. The front door was locked, but a window in the back was smashed out, though who knew the cause? Had it been a bird? A brick? It didn't matter. My childhood home wasn't long for the world. God had a plan for it.

I spent one night in that house, alone, not sleeping, not even trying to, just thinking. Praying here and there. I thought about crying, but the tears wouldn't come. So instead, I planned.

When the sun crept above the hollow windowpane at dawn, I rose from my place on the dingy carpet and walked in the familiar woods one last time before striking out on my own, leaving all the ghosts behind.

I can't explain what happened in any scientific or legal terms, but I returned to the house only to discover it afire. Both then and now, I believe it was an act of God. A purification of the ground upon which that festering den stood and a sign that there was no going back for me. Not even God Himself could look upon my childhood home without scorn, so irreparably saturated in sin it was. And just as He burned the sinful brother cities of Sodom and Gomorrah to the ground, so did he set that ramshackle shake ablaze.

Setting my jaw, I watched the flames extend their forked tongues from the windows, licking the exterior bricks unflinchingly. I would make my own home henceforth, one that was clean and pure, blessed by One who, at the time I knew only as God but now know as Deus Aper.

So long as I let Him guide me, I thought, I might finally build the home I deserve—one large enough, pristine enough to house my innate greatness so that others may enter and be purified of their filth.

As you know, I have accomplished such a feat. But humility compels me to honesty: my path was not a straight one, and young Jimmy had many more mistakes to make, many more lessons to learn, many more herculean trials to pass, and many more evils to overcome before he could build that home in Texas.

Chapter Fifteen

"How're you feeling?" Miranda asked from the driver's seat of her Honda Fit. "Less aggro on the whole?"

Jessica laughed. "I'm never aggro, Miranda."

"There's an empty statue pedestal on the Texas State campus that might disagree."

"Point taken. And yes, the morning target practice was a good call. The hike with my mom yesterday reminded me how nice it is to get out of the city. Thanks again for setting this up." She soaked in the natural landscape as it whizzed past, soon to be replaced by subdivisions then shopping centers, and eventually the jutting buildings of downtown Austin. "When are your mom's cousins coming home?"

"Who?" Miranda looked at her like she was talking gibberish.

"Your mom's cousins ... who own the land we're using as my smiting range?"

Quickly Miranda set her eyes back on the road. "Oh. Right. Um. I dunno."

Jessica groaned. "You don't actually know whose land that is, do you?"

"Not personally, no. But I do know no one is living on it *right now*. It's currently for sale."

"So we were trespassing. In Texas."

"Yeah, but it's super low-risk."

"In a state where people can shoot you in the back because you tripped and caught your footing on their property, you think that's super low risk."

Miranda kept her eyes firmly focused on the road. "Smite beats gun, though, right? Plus, God wouldn't let anything happen to you."

"You keep assuming that, but as someone who has to talk to him on a daily basis, I'm *just* not confident about it."

"Well fine," she conceded, "I'll follow your logic: God'll probably try to martyr you, but until that day comes, he's not going to let you die in some dumb way. Like guacamole or a trigger-happy landowner."

"Are you trying to reassure me?"

"Is it working?" Miranda grinned.

"Unfortunately, yes. Except, like with the guacamole poisoning, *you* could still get hurt or killed."

"I guess so, but I bet He knows that wouldn't play well with you."

"You sure have a lot of faith in the goodness of God."

"Is that a bad thing?"

"Not necessarily. But I wouldn't recommend it."

When Miranda pulled up to a light on the edge of downtown, she glanced over at Jessica. "You might want to fix your hair." She reached in the glove box between the seats and pulled out a brush, offering it.

"I'll fix it when I get home."

Miranda shook the brush at her. "Maybe just fix it now?"

Jessica leaned to the right in her seat, giving herself room to look over at her best friend. "Oh, I'm sorry, is my disheveled hair a nuisance to you?" She took the brush and used the sun visor mirror to straighten the part. "What's with you today, Miranda?"

"Promise you won't be mad?"

Jess jerked her head around. "No. I don't promise that. Especially when someone asks me to."

"We're going to brunch. And before you say you don't have the money, I know. It's my treat."

"Oh." Brunch wasn't so bad. After all, she was hungry, and if Miranda was paying... "Why would I be mad? That's no big deal. Cash will be glad to hear it." She pulled out her phone and texted them, letting them know and hoping it would win her some brownie points for once.

They pulled into a parking spot and Miranda said they'd have to hoof it a couple blocks to where she wanted to go. Considering it was a Sunday and Jessica had no plans other than baking the shit out of some sourdough bread, which she'd failed at five days running, she was fine dragging out the more enjoyable parts of her day.

"I hope we're not going somewhere too expensive,"

Jessica said, secretly hoping the opposite. When was the last time she had a nice meal? Probably on a date with Chris, which she hadn't had many of in the past month, now that football season was heating up and Texas State was actually in the running for a bowl game.

When Miranda led the way up to Chez Shea, Jessica celebrated on the inside. She'd had this place recommended to her by no fewer than eleven people, nine of whom she hardly knew. The consensus was that it was the "delicious and upscale in an understated way, but they usually have the AC cranked too high" brunch spot.

Then she caught sight of her reflection in the tinted front windows and grimaced. She was so not dressed for this. And not just because of the AC.

"You look fine," Miranda said, catching sight of Jessica's gaze while she held open the door. "This is Austin. All our naughtiest bits are covered, so nobody cares."

"I know you!" proclaimed the young hostess when Jessica and Miranda approached the stand.

"Yeah, yeah," Miranda said, breezing past her and straight into the bustle of the restaurant. Not in the mood to continue the conversation the hostess had initiated, Jessica followed closely behind her friend, though she was fairly sure this wasn't the way places like Chez Shea operated. It didn't strike her as a self-seating system, especially considering the presence of a hostess stand.

And then Jessica caught sight of a table of familiar faces, and a few things made sense.

It made sense why Miranda and ignored the hostess.

It made sense why Miranda had told Jessica to brush her hair.

It made sense why Miranda had asked if Jessica was feeling less aggro on the whole.

Jessica wasn't and never had been a big fan of surprises, and Miranda knew that.

... Even if the surprise *was* as well-intentioned as this one.

"Hey!" shouted Kate, who stood, holding out her arms for a hug. Judith stood by Kate's side, nodding a hello and suppressing a grin.

How long had it been since she'd talked with these two? Months. They should hate her for being such a bad friend, but here they were, making the drive from San Marcos and seeming in good spirits.

Destinee and Dr. Bell were also at the table but remained sitting and watched as Jessica hugged her two sorority sisters, shot Miranda a grateful yet perturbed look and took a seat at the table between Kate and Miranda.

"Good to see you, Jessica," said Dr. Bell.

"Sorry, baby," Destinee said. "I know you hate surprises, but I figured this would be a good one."

Jess decided to let it go. "Is this the real reason you came into town yesterday, Mom?"

"It was why I chose this particular weekend, but I've wanted to come see your place for a while. Sorry I lied about leaving town at the crack of dawn."

With the shock wearing off, Jessica struggled to stay

annoyed. "Don't worry about it. I'm glad y'all are all here. I don't know what the occasion is, but I'm not complaining."

"Why does there have to be an occasion?" Judith asked. "Can't we all just miss seeing you?" Then she added, "Always so suspicious, that one," as she restrained a stubborn smile.

"What have you two been up to all morning?" asked Kate. "Looks like you've been working out."

Jessica looked to Miranda, who smiled innocently, allowing Jessica to take it whatever direction she wanted. "Yeah, we did a little hike on the Greenbelt today."

"God leave you alone?" Destinee asked. She turned to Dr. Bell. "We went yesterday and God kept bragging about everything."

Bell pressed her lips together and nodded politely.

"Yeah, he didn't bother us."

"Is he here right now?" Destinee said.

"Nope."

Destinee slapped the table top. "Then hot damn! We got us a real ladies brunch!"

Even Judith laughed along with the rest, before saying, "It's kind of like every day in NAO, except I've never contemplated murdering any of you."

Kate turned to her. "Really? You've never contemplated murdering me?"

"Well, not recently."

"How are things going with all that?" Jessica asked, eager to change the subject from fratricide.

Kate hedged for a second. "Good, more or less. We

should have chapters opening at Texas Tech, University of Houston, and Texas A&M–Corpus Christi in the spring."

Jessica shook her head slowly. "I still can't quite believe other people want to, you know ..."

"Worship but also claim to know a female messiah?" Judith supplied. "I sort of understand where you're coming from, but you have to meet these girls. They're rabid for it. It's scary, but the insanity of it is also freaky and kind of awesome. I wish someone would make a shrine about *me*."

"What about that one guy," Kate said. "Keith? Wasn't that his name?"

"Oh, right." Judith shook a finger at her. "I forgot about him. Yeah, he did make a shrine of me." She turned to Jessica. "The cops had to get involved. It was this whole thing." She rolled her eyes.

Kate jumped back in. "Aaanyway, we sort of promised the other campus chapters you'd make an appearance at every new sorority house when it officially opens." She winced, bracing herself for a negative reaction.

Normally, Jessica might have fulfilled that expectation, but whether it was the endorphins from the range or the rush of seeing her favorite people in one place, she couldn't muster even an ounce of annoyance. "That doesn't sound so bad. To be honest, I expected worse duties."

"Yeah," Miranda said, "it's going to be so hard to go from town to town having college girls treat you like a queen."

Judith pointed at Miranda. "She gets it."

Jessica laughed. "Yeah, yeah."

The waiter came around with two pitchers of mimosas, set them down on the table, and scampered off.

"Is that our waiter?" Jessica said, confused. "He didn't even ask if Miranda and I wanted anything besides mimosas."

Bell nodded subtly at Destinee, who said, "Yeah, I might've scared him off earlier with a comment about his tush. Men in this town sure don't know how to take a compliment."

"It's called sexual harassment," Dr. Bell said kindly.

But Destinee wouldn't hear it. "In Mooretown, we call that hospitality. I just thought it'd be such a shame for him to be walking around and not know how much he's rocking those slacks. Plus, it ain't like men haven't said that kinda shit to me all the time when I'm in my scrubs at the pharmacy. It's gotta go both ways because, you know, feminism."

"She's got a point," Judith said. "And he really does have a perfect little ass."

"I thought you were all about the older men, Judith. That kid's *maybe* eighteen," Kate scolded.

"At least eighteen," Miranda said. "He brought us alcohol. Can't do that unless you're eighteen. Fair game, ladies."

Destinee leaned across the table toward Dr. Bell. "You can't say you weren't thinking it, Vicky."

Bell finished pouring herself a tall mimosa and sipped the top to keep it from spilling. "I can. I wasn't thinking it."

Destinee leaned closer. "Not your type?"

"Mom—" Jessica interjected, realizing instantly that the two women were speaking entirely different languages.

Bell shook her head. "Nope. Not even close."

"You like 'em older?"

Bell shrugged. "Sometimes."

"Manlier?"

"More feminine, actually."

Destinee hopped in her seat. "More feminine than that manchild?"

"*Mom.*"

Bell shot a glance at Jessica. "It's fine."

"So like, what, thinner?"

"More like ..." Dr. Bell lifted up in her seat and scanned around. "That one. There."

Destinee turned around, leaning side to side to see around the waitress.

"Not sure—"

"The waitress, Mom." Jessica covered half her face with her hand. "She's pointing at the waitress."

Destinee turned and plopped back down in her seat. "Oh. Ohhh ..." She waggled a finger at Bell. "I catch your drift." She glanced at her daughter. "Hands over ears, baby," then turning back to Bell, "I did that for a little while. Want me to get her number for you?"

Dr. Bell chuckled good-naturedly. "No, no. I'm in a committed relationship already."

Destinee pouted out her lips, considering it with a bob of her head. "I respect that. But there's no harm in looking anyway." Then she flagged down the waitress and Jessica held her breath for whatever mortifying thing was about to happen, but instead, Destinee simply said, "I think we're ready to order, and I scared off that sweet little honey that was waiting on us, so would you mind?"

They ordered their food along with another round of mimosa pitchers, and Jessica felt herself relax, settling into the moment. She hadn't settled into many moments in Austin, she realized. Every time she left her condo, she was slightly on edge, which she knew shouldn't be the case, since it was such a safe city. Yet it *was* the case.

But with her favorite women around her, chatting about things she could never get Chris to pay attention to or understand, she found herself feeling ... understood? No, surely not. Never that.

After the food had arrived and the frenzied pace of eating had slowed and the sparkling wine of the mimosa had dimmed the cares of anyone at the table, Judith said, "Not to bring up a sore subject, but about the bakery. How's it coming?"

Jess tried to glare at her, but her ideal brain chemistry wouldn't quite allow it. "It's not coming."

"Is it just the money that's a problem?"

"Yep." Jessica sipped her drink.

"So if you magically had the money, you'd be ready to get cracking?"

"Yeah, I guess so, but I don't have the money."

Miranda chimed in. "I know you've been baking like a sonofabitch lately. Anyone who follows you on Instagram knows that. You feel pretty good about your recipes?"

Something was up. Jessica screwed up her face, trying to uncover what it could be. As she looked around the table, all eyes were on her. What the hell? "Yeah, my recipes are getting better."

Destinee and Kate exchanged a sneaky glance and when Destinee nodded, Kate reached in her purse and pulled out a small card. "This is for you." She handed it to Jess, who held it and looked around again. Destinee bounced slightly in her seat, and even Judith was grinning unabashedly.

Jessica tore open the envelope and reached in for the card …

"Another round of drinks or dessert for—"

"God dammit, woman!" Destinee shouted at the waitress. "Can't you see we're busy?"

The girl scuttled away, and as Destinee mumbled, "Shit, scared off another," Jessica pulled the card out from the envelope.

On the front was a picture of Jesus, except someone, probably Judith, had pasted a picture of Jessica's head over her half-brother's and put bread stickers in the outstretched hands as he hovered in the air over his tomb. And above the illustration, the word *He* had been scratched out and *It* was written to the side, so that the card proclaimed *It is Risen*. She laughed. "This is pretty fucked up."

"Open it," Judith said. "It gets even better."

When Jessica pulled open the card, the inside was blank except for *Happy Easter*.

But something fell out of the card.

It'd been so long since Jessica had seen a check, she almost didn't know what it was until she held it in her hand and looked down at it.

"Oh ... my ... hell." She brought the check closer to her face to count the zeros. "This is way too much money." She scanned the other faces at the table, all of whom seemed to happily disagree.

"It's not like we're going broke for it, Jessica," said Kate. "We knew if we were going to help, we had to do it without making too much of a personal sacrifice ourselves or else you wouldn't accept it."

"I haven't decided if I *am* going to accept this. Y'all. It's two hundred *thousand* dollars. Where did you even get it?"

Dr. Bell leaned forward. "I have connections, Kate has connections, Judith has connections, Miranda has connections, Destinee ... um."

"I got ways of getting things from people," Destinee finished, folding her hands together on the table.

"The point," said Bell, "is that, like I've told you before, you don't have to do everything yourself. You just have to surround yourself with people who know where to find what you need. And you have. It's the people at this table."

Jessica nodded, feeling emotion knotting in her esophagus. "Thanks. I, um." A terrifying thought leapt into her mind. "Wait, does Wendy know about this?"

"Duh," said Miranda. "I ran it by her before I even approached any of them."

"It's not crowdfunding, is it?"

"No. Well, sort of. But not really. It's a crowd of people you know."

"Does that include people not at this table?"

Miranda sighed. "We did ask others, but only ones we know and trust. Now *you* should trust that we knew how you would want this done and we did it that way, Jess."

"Yeah," Kate added. "We don't want you to be labeled the Moochsiah any more than you do."

"But because we wanted to make sure to do things the way you would want," Miranda added, hesitantly, "we came up a little short on the goal. It should be enough to get you started, at least. And we'll round up the rest later."

Jessica slipped the check back into the card and set it on the table. "Uh, no. You've done way more than I'd ever expect. Fifty thousand is way less daunting. Please just let me take it from here."

"She has a point," Dr. Bell said. "Businesses are far more likely to succeed when the owner has her own hard-earned capital invested. Jess, I can help you go back through the business plan and find ways to cut back. We'll just have to made some concessions. Will that work?"

Jessica nodded. "Yes. That works."

"Oh! And I almost forgot," Kate said, "I told you about my uncle who's a lawyer, right?"

"Yeah?"

"I hope you don't mind, but I chatted with him about you and what you're doing with the bakery, and when he heard you'd hit a snag with funding, he suggested you file for the bakery to be a 501(c)(3)."

"But isn't that only for non-profits?"

"Yeah. You could claim it as a religious institution and—"

"Hell no." She waved her hands in the air. "Nuh-uh, no way."

Kate jerked her head back. "That opposed, eh?"

"Of course! That's something Jimmy would do. No, I want to start a business, not a church."

"A non-profit bakery can totally be a thing," Kate replied, sounding annoyed. "Besides, you're going to start a church eventually, right?"

Jessica laughed and then realized no one else was laughing. "Oh. Um. No, I have no plans for one."

"Listen," Judith said, "I detest organized religion as much as the next bitch, but I feel like you're wasting an opportunity here if you don't at least set down a list of rules for people to follow."

Miranda set a steady hand on Jessica's shoulder. "While you've been focused on the trolls, Jessica, I've been reading the other responses. People do want to hear something from you, anything. And when you don't give them any answers, the next place they land is Jimmy."

"Fucking Jimmy Dean," Destinee murmured, tossing back the dregs of her sixth mimosa.

"So unless you want Jimmy's insane circus-inspired ideas to proliferate as yours," Miranda continued, "you need to step up."

"About that," Judith said, "what the hell was with that

chapter? Did he really travel around with a circus for like, what, two years?"

Jessica turned her attention to Judith. "What are you talking about?"

"*Railed to the Cross.* That chapter. What was it called? 'Life in Tents'?"

Heads nodded around the table. "Yeah, that thing with the prostitute was pretty weird," Kate said.

"I almost felt bad for him," Destinee added. "And that's saying something, because fuuuuck Jimmy."

"She hasn't read it," Miranda said. "Jessica hasn't read the book."

The table fell silent.

Judith chuckled. "Damn, Jess. You're in for a treat."

"I've read some of it," Jessica protested. "Just not all of it."

"Doesn't matter," Judith interrupted. "The point is that people are ready and waiting for a little bit of insight from you, and if you don't give it, Jimmy will."

"And then they'll be burning shit to the ground left and right!" Destinee exclaimed, gesturing wildly before refilling her glass from the carafe.

"I don't have a message," Jessica said louder than she'd meant to. "I don't have a message for anyone. I don't want people to come to me for spiritual answers. I don't want to be special. I just want to open a bakery and—"

"Serve gluten-free treats that you miracled with the power of God," Judith finished for her. "Nothing special, though."

"You can't help it, Jessica," Dr. Bell added. "Everything you do is special because you're God's daughter. The sooner you accept that, the easier your life will be."

"For some reason, I highly doubt that." She placed a hand on the card with her face crudely pasted over Jesus's. "But I guess I'll give it a try."

"Why so grumpy?" Rebel asked from behind the counter of Bat-Ass Brew.

"I'm not grumpy, I'm focused. And I need caffeine," Jessica replied.

There were a million coffee shops in this town, but Jessica always returned to this one for the reason of it having the best coffee and nothing too terrible had happened to her in it yet. Sure, the baristas at Java Hut didn't make inappropriate comments, but they weren't especially nice, and the coffee was just okay. And the last time she'd been—not her coffee date with Brian Foster, but a time after that, when she'd had a sinus headache from hell (maybe literally; she couldn't be sure) and didn't think quality time with Rebel would do much to improve her mood—a band had set up about ten minutes after she got there. No one came to a coffee shop to hear live music. Sometimes Austin made no sense.

But at Bat-Ass Brew, there was never any live music, and no one had asked to take a picture with her, which had happened multiple at Hill of Beans by the Capitol. No one

had spent an hour giving her side-eye, like many had at
Bean There Done That by the UT campus. And no one
had coughed awful accusations at her as they passed her
table (also Bean There Done That). Because the environment of Bat-Ass Brew was overall more conducive to being
God's daughter, she had resigned herself to tolerating or at
least ignoring Rebel's terrible conversational skills and
frequent sexual harassment.

She ordered a simple Milwaukee Protocol and as he
went to pour it, she leaned her back against the counter
and stared out over the silent shop. How did one create an
environment of acceptance or, at the very least, apathy?
This was what she wanted for her bakery, whenever that
day came. A place where people could come together and
mind their own damn business, each person trusting others
would do the same.

Thanks to the money from her friends, which still
made her head spin when she thought too hard about it,
and assuming Dr. Bell could assist her with a plan, that
dream could become reality sooner rather than later.

"You strike me as a girl who likes a little cocoa," Rebel
said. She turned to face him. "So I took the liberty of
adding a sprinkle of cocoa to the top." He winked.

She wanted to snap back with, "I hate cocoa. Fix me a
new one without the cocoa, you presumptuous asswipe."
But unfortunately, she did love a little sprinkle of cocoa on
her coffee, so she pressed her lips together and paid
the man.

How does someone look like they like cocoa? She

refrained from adding it to her lifelong list of reasons to be self-conscious about her appearance, just below "boring hair," "no calves," and "low boobs."

By the time Dr. Bell joined her at the table a few minutes later, Jessica was fairly certain that it was her childlike chubby cheeks that gave away her love for cocoa.

"How are you feeling today?" Dr. Bell asked, coffee in one hand, black binder in another.

"Good. Better now that I have my coffee."

"Ooo, what you got there?" Bell leaned forward and sniffed. "Is that cocoa? I love cocoa."

Data point two. Jessica homed in on all the physical similarities between Bell and herself. They were few and far between, and childlike cheeks did not fall in the overlap of the Venn circles. Bell's cheeks looked like they were chiseled from marble, two long dimples running the length of her jaw. So it must be some other physical characteristic. Jessica would think more on it later. Probably exactly when she was trying to fall asleep tonight, if she was being honest.

"How excited are you?" asked Dr. Bell.

"Very."

"Me too, actually." She scooted her coffee to the side to make room for the binder, which she flipped open. The first page was the budget spreadsheet for Jessica's business proposal. "To sum things up, I was able to go through, cut a few corners, and eliminate twenty-seven grand that you'll need to get started."

Jessica looked up from the spreadsheet that she couldn't make sense of anyway. "That's great!"

"Yes. Of course that budget means you'll have to open without a few of the flashier things, but once money starts coming in, you'll be able to build and scale up."

"Seriously, that's fine. Only one problem."

"I know. You're still twenty-three thousand short. But I have a plan for that, too. Well, a few. Now hear me out. You have three options."

Bell's tone left Jessica on edge. "Okay."

Bell flipped to a page that was titled Option One. Damn, this woman loved business plans. "Option one is you find alternate work to earn the remaining twenty-three thousand dollars. Since your rent is already taken care of, that shouldn't be as tricky, except considering your sparse job history—"

"That's a nice way to put it."

"And the fact that you didn't graduate college, your earning potential isn't particularly high. My estimate based on typical earning potential minus living expenses outside of rent is that, working forty hours a week, it would take you two point three years to save up that amount. If you worked seventy hours a week, it could be just under a year and a half."

"Wow." Jessica leaned back. "That's a long time to wait before opening the bakery."

Bell nodded sympathetically. "I understand. It would be hard to justify dropping out of college before graduation if you took that route. So I don't recommend it. We have other options, though." She flipped to the next page. "Option two is you get the twenty-three thousand donated. Miranda and myself have tapped our resources, but that doesn't meant the font is dry. It just means you would have to get creative. And possibly renegotiate some of your moral objections to certain tactics."

"Obviously not ideal," Jessica replied, "but better than the first option. You have one more, right?"

Bell flipped the page. "Option three. This one's actually my favorite, because it creates a stepping stone for your business so you can truly test out your ideas before jumping straight into it. It's even more effective overall than having personal financial buy in, although, you *will* be earning money for yourself along the way."

"Yes? Care to explain?"

"You invest eighty thousand dollars of the money you currently have into opening a food truck. You use that to create a buzz about your brand, find what recipes sell, what don't, and create a loyal contingent of customers. Yes, you're investing money into it, but you can make money back faster, or at least the money you make is more within your control than working a nine to five. You'll gather useful data on the market, and you won't just be sitting around or working a job unrelated to your future career. You'll be moving in the right direction. Then, when you're within thirty grand of the total money you need to open a brick and mortar, you can sell off the trailer for the remainder. It would position you to start the permanent location with practical knowledge of how to run a business, what foods sell best, and you would already have established your brand within the community."

"That is ..." She thought about it , but it didn't take long. "That is brilliant, Dr. Bell! That's ... wow. And you're saying I could get started on that right away?"

"Absolutely."

Jessica stared at the table, feeling the pieces come together. "I would have to prep the night before, then maybe reheat in an oven in the trailer. And I would need to make a sign of what I have that day ..."

Dr. Bell laughed. "One thing at a time. But yes, why don't we get started now? We can price some Airstreams and start talking about what you would need to outfit it with."

"I can't believe it." Jessica laughed. "Part of me thought I'd never get started on this, and here I am." She stood up, and, feeling entirely unlike herself, ran around the table, and hugged Dr. Bell at an awkward angle.

"Just goes to show," said the professor, once Jessica returned to her seat, "God works in mysterious ways."

"Please don't bring him into this," she said. "One more question."

"Yes?"

"What's an Airstream?"

Chapter Sixteen

The warmth of the oven was divine in the November chill and made up for the Airstream lacking proper heating and cooling. With the lunch rush slowing at the food trailer park, Jessica was able to stand closer to the heat and let it warm her buns while it warmed the buns.

She'd rarely before had occasion to test out the adage of time flying when one was having fun, but over the past whirlwind month and a half of preparation and operation of Jessica's Gluten-Free Treats, she had lost sight of time completely. As it turned out, when one didn't have anything else to do but had a clear goal in mind and process laid out, one could get shit done at an *alarming* pace. Her days were long, but she never realized how long until she checked the bedside clock at the end of each day. She repeatedly found herself wondering where the time had gone while she was busy shopping, baking, serving customers, pointing to the sign that read *photos with Jessica*: $10, taking photos with customers, cleaning, packing up, heading home, and prepping for the next morning.

Taking photos with adoring fans, turned out, was actually not horrific. Perhaps she should have guessed this, but she hadn't. Positive or negative, special attention wasn't her favorite. But when she knew it was part of her business and she was making money from it that could go toward her dream, it seemed much less personal, and she could detach her ego from it. Only occasionally did fans say unintentionally rude things, like calling her "girl Jesus" or "missiah," which was apparently a new and common title for her on Twitter. No one dared mention "moochsiah," though she wasn't sure if that was more a result of common decency (she didn't especially believe this was a thing) or the fact that, with her current business endeavor and a frightening amount of overtime from Cash Monet, she was finally overcoming the label.

Mostly, though, people took their picture, paid their money, and then ordered food from her. The photos felt a little like the world paying penance for how it objectified her and tried to bend her to its desires. And she would happily accept all the penance the world offered.

Part of Dr. Bell's proposed expenses included a car, and while it was nothing special and guzzled oil and coolant like it had a worrisome addiction, it was Jessica's first, and she quickly wondered how she'd managed so long without one. Certainly it would have been impossible to run her business without it, and she was glad her former professor was insistent on her having it, despite her resistance to getting further in the hole by buying it.

As it turned out, being in the hole wasn't as dire as she'd expected. With the added cash from photos, the cheap rent, and the ridiculous food-truck prices people were willing to pay not only for food in general but especially for gluten-free food, she was on track to hit the threshold where she could sell the trailer sometime in January.

It was like Dr. Bell knew what she was doing.

Judith was scheduled to arrive for her shift any minute now, but Jessica still had to finish the hot cross buns before she was free to go—her favorite reporter, Maria Flores, had requested something seasonal they could use for the interview B-roll to sprinkle into the segment, and Jessica figured this would do the trick.

Judith burst in the back door of the Airstream. "Hey, sorry I'm running late. My stupid senior seminar professor started talking about David Foster Wallace, and I should have texted you right then to let you know I would be running late, but I left my phone—"

"Don't worry about it," Jessica said, smiling placidly.

Judith froze midway through tying her apron behind her back. "Oh yeah, I forget you're happy now. Okay, well, I'm here."

Jessica pulled the hot crossed buns from the oven and began plating them. "I think you have a stalker, Judith."

"But Keith is dead."

"Who?"

"Oh, wait. What?"

The women stared silently at one other for a moment before Jessica decided to press the restart button.

"You have a *new* stalker." She nodded behind her toward the service window. "He came by yesterday when you first got in, and he's back again today. He's been sitting at that table all morning, glancing over here. I think he's waiting for you."

"That's ... not creepy." Judith leaned to the side so she could get a glimpse. "Oh. *Ohh.* He's, like, fine as hell." She sounded shocked. "Did he order anything?"

"Yeah, but just a coffee. He asked if I had challah bread, and when I said no, he didn't order anything else. I explained what else I had, but he just looked at me like I was crazy."

"A Jewish gentleman?" she said, grinning crookedly and wiggling an eyebrow. "You know I love me a Jewish man." Jessica did not, in fact, know that, but she didn't feel like now was the time to bring it up. Judith leaned to the side again to sneak another peek. "He's awfully blond for a Jew."

Jessica moved the last bun over to the platter. "You're splitting hairs about that?"

"No, it's just that Jewish tradition is in right now, so maybe he's just a hipster."

"Or maybe he converted," Jessica suggested. "Or maybe he just really likes challah bread."

"And you said he was here yesterday, too?"

"Yeah." Jessica shook her head, huffing in disbelief. "He's so hot. How do you not remember him?"

Judith flipped her long dark hair behind her shoulder. "I was very high, obviously."

Jessica closed her eyes, cleared her mind, and let the miraculous branding flow through her. She looked down at the rolls. All good except for one, where her image was blinking. She snatched it up and turned to Judith. "Are you high today?"

"Psh, hardly."

Jess tossed her the roll and Judith caught it and bit off the top immediately, like she always did to avoid Jessica staring back at her. "Ooo ... delicious."

Jessica grabbed the icing bag and squeezed it onto the rolls, drawing circular frames around the images. "You should go talk to him."

Judith finished off her roll and went to scrub her hands. "I find it interesting that the same guy shows up two days in a row, is staring at you all morning, and you assume he's *my* stalker. Nine out of ten stalkers agree you're way more interesting."

"I just don't get the vibe from him. I mean, sure, he's hot, but when he came up to order? Man. There was just no chemistry. He had to have noticed that, too. It was like talking to my dumb brother or something."

"Wait, you have a brother? I feel like I should've known this ..."

"Only a half brother but he's—Well, you know. I just mean if I *did* have a brother, I *imagine* it would be like that."

Judith nodded. "Speaking as someone who has three brothers, I'm sorry you had to experience that." She peeked through the window again. "He kind of looks like Chris and Jameson Fractal had a baby." Immediately, she gasped and whirled around to Jessica. "Sorry, sorry. I didn't mean to bring him up. I guess I'm higher than I thought."

"It's okay. I've actually wondered what Jameson is doing lately. Like, maybe I'm over the trauma of seeing his face shot to shit?"

"That's great for you," Judith said airily as she stared back out the window. "Yeah, I'm going to say what's up."

"Good luck."

"Don't need it. I'm great with Jewish men. I always remind them of a young, sexy version of their mother."

"But what if he's just a hipster?"

Judith pouted out her lips, staring at Jessica with pity. "Doesn't matter. The same applies."

Once Judith had closed the door behind her, Jessica laid out a tray of refrigerated pigs in a blanket and another tray of ham and cheese kolaches for the afternoon crowd. She'd have to hang around until they were done reheating so she could perform her miracle, but she would be nearby anyway, since Maria was arriving shortly.

Her phone vibrated in her apron pocket, and she reached in and checked the message. It was from Chris: *Hey sexy. How's your day?*

She typed a quick response: *Busy. I'll hit you up later. Miss you.*

Once she sent it away, she paused. How long had it been since she'd last *seen* her boyfriend? With his football and her frenzied business venture, scheduling had become a bit of a nightmare. She stared down at the kolaches. The last thing they did together was a hike around Lady Bird Lake. But wait, that was almost a month ago. Surely they'd seen each other since then ...

As she popped the second tray into the oven, Maria's voice called out, "Hello!" from the service window. Then a minute later, Jessica hugged the reporter behind the Airstream and offered her and her long-time camera-woman, Gabrielle, croissants from that morning's batch.

"Sorry, those are the worst two images," she said. "Just don't put them on camera, please."

Maria and Gabrielle exchanged amused glances.

"I can't tell you how happy it makes me that you've allowed us to cover your amazing story yet again, Jessica," Maria said.

"I can't think of anyone else I would trust for it. Now, before we start, though, I just want to be clear. Your angle is Mooretown Girl Opens Successful Food Truck in Big City, right?"

Maria nodded at Gabrielle, who seemed to take the hint and wandered off with the camera. "I know that's what we'd talked about on the phone, but I'd hoped you'd reconsider. Sure, opening a business in Austin, or even making it out of Mooretown, is a big accomplishment in itself, but"—she tilted her head forward, opening her eyes wide—"we both know the real story isn't that." She let her words hang in the air before continuing. "You're using your miracle to help others. You're God's only begotten daughter! Anyone who recognizes you knows the claim, even if they don't believe it. Don't you think it would be a bit strange for me to do an entire piece on you without mentioning that teeny tiny detail?"

"I know *you* believe it, Maria, but not everyone does. I guess I just want to know that I can run a business based on my own skills rather than, well, you know."

Maria chuckled. "Oh, I know that's what you want this to be. I could tell the moment I heard your dreary business name. You can't get less inspirational than Jessica's Gluten-Free Treats.

"I hope you don't mind my saying so, but you seem to have only one foot in the boat and one still on land. Your entire business is fueled by your ability to perform a specific miracle, yet you want to pretend you're just a regular businesswoman. I don't doubt that you've worked hard to get to where you are, but you're ignoring the fact that if anyone else put in the same amount of work, they would yield lesser results. Because you have something they don't. It's *that*, the something you have, that is the story. You shouldn't feel guilty for having an advantage, but failing to acknowledge it isn't the way to curry favor, either."

Her good mood was rapidly evaporating. "So?"

Maria's intense stare softened. "Jessica, I see the potential in you. I've seen it for years. Plus, I know the media better than most. This story is about exposure, yet you're holding back the one thing you need to show to the world. Quite frankly, I find it baffling."

"What do you suggest, then? That we make the whole story about my miracle? That I stare directly into the camera and say, 'I'm God's daughter, and if you don't like that, you can do what everyone else does and say horrible shit about me on the internet'? Should I perform all of my known miracles on camera for you? I mean, it's almost rush hour, and surely we can find a football field nearby. And killing people isn't that hard to do, apparently. We could knock out all four!"

Maria didn't respond right away as she squinted analytically at Jessica. "All *four*?" she said. "I only know about three. Field goals, resurrection, gluten-free."

"I meant three," Jessica said quickly. "Never mind. The point is that I don't want to have to put on a whole performance for this story. It's not a persuasive piece."

"And my point is that I won't allow your gifts to be the elephant in the room. That's just bad journalism."

Jessica sighed and leaned up against the trailer, folding her arms over her chest. "Did you speak with Wendy about it?"

"Of course. I'm not trying to go rogue here, Jessica. I'm trying to help you and play my part in the bigger strategy. If you want to open a brick and mortar bakery, you need exposure, which can be expensive. I'm offering it to you for free. And this interview will go a lot further toward that goal if you let me cover the full story."

Jessica balled her hands into fists under her armpits. "Fine. It just seems a bit unethical to exploit."

"Ah. You say exploit, I say *showcase*." She reached in her pocket and pulled out a stack of notecards. "Here are my questions so you can think about your answers. I'm going to round up Gabrielle, and I'll see you in five."

It was nearly impossible for Jessica to focus on her prep for the next day knowing Maria's story was broadcasting to Midland and the surrounding markets at that precise moment.

There didn't seem a point to her watching it herself. What was done was done. And while she knew she was generally in good hands with Maria Flores, she couldn't help but feel raw and terrified after being so honest on camera. Would people laugh at her? Would they be upset with her for her using her status as God's daughter to turn a profit?

Thanks to Wendy and Cash, she might never know the answers to her questions. They kept her well insulated from public opinion, and if the shit hit the fan, they generally wanted her as far away from said fan as possible because she was no fan repairwoman, that was for sure.

She glanced over at her television, the screen black. No, she wouldn't give in.

Shit. Did I already add the salt?

She inspected the mixing bowl, stooping over it, moving her head at multiple angles to try to tell if those were all sugar grains or if some of it was salt.

She decided to split the difference and added half of what the recipe called for in salt. She'd find out in the morning if the challah bread was too salty or not salty enough. That was, if she could figure out how to braid dough.

This is what the trailer's for. To test out new recipes.

Would the gorgeous Jewish man be back the next day to see Judith? Far as Jessica could tell, they'd hit it off earlier that afternoon. He'd stared at Judith like she was the most interesting woman he'd ever met, and she'd returned to the trailer giddy. Hopefully it would turn into something. Judith deserved someone who might pull her out of her cynicism and break her streak of dating significantly older men.

When her phone rang, Jessica grabbed a hand towel to wipe off the dough from her kneading and answered on the fourth ring. "Hey, Mom."

Destinee sounded out of breath. "Baby girl! That was incredible! Mind-blowing."

"I really hope you're talking about the news story."

"Of course! I feel like I owe Maria Flores a drink or thirty. Hot damn! It just makes me feel even worse about not making it down to see your truck."

"Don't worry about that, Mom. I know you can't take time off. And hey, save the vacation time for when I open a real bakery. I'll expect you at the soft opening."

There was silence on the other line, then a sniffle.

"Mom, are you ... are you feeling okay?"

Destinee's voice was strained and quiet. "You made it out, Jess. Deep down I always wanted to make it out, but then I had you and all I wanted was for you to make it out. Then you went off to San Marcos, but I know how many kids go right back home after college, so I didn't want to get my hopes up. But now you've gone and done it. You started a business in a real city, and you're not coming back."

Jessica didn't know what to say. She almost felt guilty, but she was fairly certain that wasn't what her mother was going for.

"I may never get out of this town, Jess, but I'm glad you did."

Jessica braced herself on the countertop, staring at an imperfection in the cement floor as her stomach clenched. "Mom. You're only thirty-nine. If you really want to move, just move. You can come live in Austin. We'll make it work."

Destinee sniffled again then pulled herself together. "I couldn't just leave Rex behind. No, it's fine, baby. I'm just so happy for you."

"Rex can get a job in Austin. He led Mooremont to three state championships. You think there aren't schools here that would hire him in a second?"

"Rex is a country boy, though. He'd never move to a big city."

"Rex is your lapdog more than he is a country boy, Mom. You tell him your ring size and the man would move to Oklahoma with you."

"Jessica," Destinee scolded gently, "I love that man. I would never ask him to move to Oklahoma."

"Ask him about Austin then."

Destinee sighed deeply. "Yeah, I think I will."

"Good."

"I'm so proud of you. God made you his daughter, but you made you the girl that got out of Mooretown."

Jessica's eyes settled on the lump of dough sitting neglected. "Thanks, Mom. I gotta go, though. I'm trying to make challah bread for the first time, and it's not going so well."

"Is that a rap thing?"

She paused but decided not to think too hard about it. "Nooo. It's a Jewish thing."

"Huh. Sounds like ... never mind. I'll let you go. And if you get a chance, could you send another goodie box?"

"Only if I don't have to miracle them first."

"How am I supposed to show them off to Mrs. Mathers if they don't have your shining face?"

So she is still alive. That was good to know. But —"Mom! Are you taunting Mrs. Mathers with my cookies?"

Destinee paused just a second too long. "No."

"Mom."

"She won't let it go what happened between me and her son! That's not my fault ..."

"I'll send you some cookies, but they won't be gluten-free."

"Fine, fine. And if you perfect that holler bread, send me a loaf. I'm intrigued."

Chapter Seventeen

The frigid saltwater began seeping under the doors and into the ballroom, and Jessica knew they didn't have much time before the heavy wooden doors gave way and the North Atlantic Ocean rushed in.

Chris grabbed her by the shoulders, spinning her toward him. "We don't have much longer, Rose. If I'm going down with this ship, I want to know I've ravaged you the way you deserve."

She fought back a smile. It was a real shame Chris never got into theater back in high school. He could have beat out Greg for a lead role, and how gratifying would *that* have been?

Focus!

"But we shouldn't, Jack! Happiness is not meant to be for us. It was never meant to be."

He grabbed the neckline of her dress and yanked

outward, splitting it down the front. "Tell that to my boner."

"Chris."

"Too much?" he asked, breaking character.

"Yeah. Jack would never say that."

"Okay, um ..." He pinched his brows together, chewing his lip, then jumped back in. "I don't care what our parents say, Rose. I want to spend my last moments ramming my ship deep into your iceberg."

She placed her hands flat on his chest, pushing him gently away. "Please no."

"What?"

"Jack wouldn't say that either."

The creaking of the wooden door caught her attention. "Okay, whatever, let's do this."

"Now who's breaking char—"

She silenced him with strategic placement of her fingers, and he moaned against her touch as she started to undress him.

As she fumbled with the buttons of his knickers, the ship shuddered around them and Jessica popped up from where she knelt in front of him, sharing a worried expression with her boyfriend. "I don't think we timed this right," she said a moment before the ballroom door flew off the hinges and the ocean exploded into the room.

"Ooo, that's cold!" Chris said, high-stepping as the water rushed up his legs. "Abandon ship!" he said, reaching down to scoop her up in his arms. But the water was coming in too fast, and before he could even cross the expansive room, he was forced to let go of her so he could tread water next to her instead.

"This was not one of our better fantasies," Jessica said between gasps for air as the icy water stabbed at her lungs.

"Agreed," Chris said. "Is that an actual chunk of iceberg?"

Jess paddled herself around to follow his gaze. "Looks like it."

"When do you think we'll wake up?"

"It seems like we should've already woken up, honestly."

"Damn. What do you think—" A wave hit him in the face and he spit it out. "What do you think happens if we die in a sex dream?"

Jessica didn't know, so she didn't bother responding as the water lifted them closer and closer toward the high ceiling. Time was running out. Maybe they woke up if they died in a sex dream. Or maybe the consequences were much direr ...

Then suddenly, Jessica was no longer treading water, but falling, Chris right alongside her. The relief of being out of the cold was enough to make the jolt of hitting the ground worth it. She looked up and struggled to make sense of her surroundings.

A tall wall of water wobbled on either side of where she and Chris sat on the soggy red carpet of the ballroom.

Chris pointed at her. "Did you ..."

"Nope."

"I claim responsibility for this," came a deep male

voice Jessica didn't recognize. She whipped her head around toward the source and saw ...

"You're not Jesus," she said. Although there were distinct similarities between this man and her half-brother, including wardrobe, skin tone, and unkempt facial hair.

"Nope. Seems Jesus went and got himself a promotion, and surprise-surprise, God's having difficulty finding a willing applicant for the job opening. With how much time Jesus spent complaining about the duties to anyone who would listen, it's not surprising no one jumped on this opportunity. Plus, the employment rate in Heaven is always one hundred percent. So God asked me to come out of retirement, just this once."

"Wait a second." She scanned her surroundings again as a chandelier floated by in one of the water walls. "Moses?"

"Took you long enough. And to whom do I owe thanks for concocting a fantasy that could so easily be tweaked such that both of you lovebirds were doused in cold water, thereby sparing me the punishment of laying eyes on your naked, awkwardly writhing bodies?"

Chris finally spoke up. "That was Jessica."

She smacked him on the arm. "You were the one who wanted to watch *Titanic* tonight."

Moses groaned impatiently. "Doesn't matter. I'm not any happier to be here than you are to have me here. And I don't exactly come bringing good tidings. I need you both to wake up, and Jessica, I think you need to head over to your food wagon as soon as possible."

"Truck," she corrected. "And why?"

"How about you go see for yourself?" He turned and let himself out of the ballroom, and a split second later, the walls of water came crashing down.

Jessica startled awake. She was alone in bed with the covers kicked into a ball by her feet. Freezing cold, she grabbed the quilt between her toes and pulled it back up over her, groggily lamenting the unsuccessful attempt with the Titanic role-playing. She'd have to cross that off her list of fantasies since there were obviously too many logistical factors to mentally juggle and—

Wait, Moses? Was Moses in my dream?

Then she remembered what he'd said.

She needed to get to the food truck.

"Shitballs." Did she take the dream seriously and heed its warning, or did she stay in the warm bed? Inertia was winning until someone else dropped in.

RISE AND SHINE.

Dammit. Moses wasn't just a figment of my dream?

YOU KNOW HE WASN'T.

But it's only two a.m. I'll have to go to work on no sleep tomorrow. Today.

THAT SHALL NOT BE AN ISSUE.

Since when? You know I'm terrible without sleep.

YOU SHALL SEE. HURRY.

She crawled out of bed, slipped on sweatpants, a bra,

and a sweatshirt, then grabbed a warm blanket to throw over her shoulders for good measure before shoving her feet into fur-lined boots and heading out the door—after all, it was mid-November, and the nightly temperatures were dipping into the fifties.

She locked the door behind her and turned toward the parking garage entrance, but jumped at the sudden appearance of another person in the hallway.

Jeremy grinned sheepishly at her. "Oh, you're up ... early? Late?"

"I have to get to my food truck."

He paused, chewing thoughtfully on his bottom lip. "Is there ... food in your food truck?"

With the dream still swirling in her head, she struggled to follow along. "Yeah, a little bit in the fridge."

"Food you could reheat in a relatively short amount of time?"

"Yeah, why are you asking?"

"I'm hungry."

She leaned forward, inspecting at his eyes. "Are you drunk?"

"No. I don't drink. Big Alcohol is singlehandedly—"

"Good. I'm too tired to drive myself. Drive me and I'll heat you up something."

He nodded resolutely and followed her down to the parking garage.

As soon as she was in the passenger's seat of his classic VW Beetle, she knew running into Jeremy was a godsend. Well, not literally ... probably.

She struggled to keep her eyes open until they pulled up to the food trailer park, at which point, yeah, her eyes were wide open.

"What the hell!" She jumped out of the passenger's seat before he'd finished parallel parking, tossing her blanket off her shoulders as she sprinted toward the flames.

Jessica's Gluten-Free Treats was the only one on fire. She stood ten yards away, staring in shock. The service window was opened—she suspected by force, since Judith always locked up—and while the whole structure wasn't yet ablaze, through the open window she saw flames licking up toward the ceiling, and a gray cloud billowed out from the oven vent.

Maybe there was still something she could salvage inside. She had to try. Every penny counted.

But she hardly got a step forward before she felt arms wrap around her waist, holding her back.

"Jessica, stop!" Jeremy shouted. "You can't go in there! You're dressed like a goddamn wick!"

"No! Maybe it's not all ruined yet! Let me go!" She struggled against his firm grasp. "God won't let me die! I just need to see what I can save!"

Jeremy continued to hold her, though, and eventually the fire spread to the interior siding of the metal structure, smoke billowing into the night sky against the backdrop of high-rise hotels and condos.

"How could this happen?" she asked weakly as Jeremy loosened his grasp and she slumped into a pile on the trailer park gravel, staring at what would soon be her former business.

Jeremy sat down next to her, pulling his knees up to his chest. "Judging by the spray paint, I'd say arson."

"What spray paint?"

He motioned at the ground between them and the fire, and Jessica crawled to kneeling and tilted her head to get the right angle.

Antichrist.

Wow, it'd been a while since she'd had anyone call her that in earnest. Once White Light had dropped that campaign a few years ago, the term had slowly disappeared from her life. Seeing it again almost made her nostalgic for simpler times.

She flopped back down next to Jeremy and watched her dream continue to burn. "We should call the fire department."

Jeremy nodded, pulled out his cell phone, and dialed 911.

"This is what I get," she mumbled to no one in particular. Not two days after her interview with Maria had aired, and already someone saw fit to burn down her business. This was exactly what she was worried would happen. She'd even said as much to Miranda, hadn't she? Granted, she'd assumed it would be Jimmy Dean who would come through with a well-timed sabotage, not some Austinite with an overdeveloped sense of moral outrage, vigilante justice, and entitlement.

Or maybe Jimmy had something to do with this after

It is Risen

all? The word spraypainted in front of her trailer *was* one of his go-tos for years. But he'd moved on, hadn't he? Wasn't his new ploy that the two of them were coconspirators? That she was not the antichrist, but Jessica Christ?

It was anyone's guess, really. And at the moment, it didn't matter. Her trailer was being reduced to ashes either way.

If this is what happens when I'm open about my life, it might be time to start hiding again. Otherwise, I'll never accomplish anything.

Two car doors slammed behind her, and she assumed the neighborhood was starting to arrive for the show.

"Jessica?"

She twisted around and the chaos of the evening prevented her from making sense of Miranda's sudden appearance. Quentin wasn't far behind, and he stared at the flames openmouthed.

"How are you here?" Jessica asked dumbly as she stood and dusted herself off.

Miranda shook her head vaguely and shrugged. "Quentin had a bad dream or something, and said he needed to come here?" She grimaced apologetically. "So I told him he wasn't going without me." Her eyes moved to the fire. "Jess, this is— Are you okay?"

"No."

Miranda pulled Jessica in for a tight hug.

"She wanted to run in, but I stopped her," Jeremy said from the ground.

Miranda let go of Jess glared sharply at him. "Thanks. And who are you?"

"I've told you about him. He's Jeremy, my neighbor," Jessica said. "He gave me a ride."

Miranda continued eyeing him suspiciously. "Ah. Okay."

Once the firetrucks arrived, the firefighters herded them back to the sidewalk and out of the way. The flames were already dying by then, but containment was probably still a good idea.

"Moses was right!" Chris came jogging up the sidewalk in boxers and a robe, his eyes wide.

Miranda looked to Jessica, presumably for an explanation. "It's just a weird expression he's been using ... I think it's a football thing?"

Chris to swooped in, wrapping his arms around his girlfriend. "I'm so sorry, Jess. I'm so, so sorry."

"If you keep apologizing like that," she spoke into his exposed chest, "I'm going to start wondering if you set the fire."

He jumped back, staring at her face, trying to get a read. "Of course I didn't. You know I was asleep. I heard Moses's warning, too, that's why I'm here."

"Hold up," Quentin said. "He visited y'all, too?" But then his sleepy mind must have caught up with his mouth, and his eyes darted over to Miranda, his face slack.

Jeremy rested his hand under his chin and inspected the conversation thoughtfully, but Miranda didn't remain as passive. "Wait, Moses ... all three of you had a dream about Moses, then you wake up and come out here?"

"No, no," Quentin corrected. "You misunderstood me. I didn't have a dream about Moses. They did." He pointed at Jessica and Chris. "I said, 'y'all two.' He visited the two of them."

"Ah," she said. "That makes more sense." But her frown didn't disappear.

Jeremy bobbed his head and stepped forward. "I know what's going on here. It's the subliminal messages on channel six, isn't it?"

"And who are you?" Chris asked, squinting at Jeremy like he'd only just noticed him, which was probably the case given the narrow scope of Chris's attention at any point in time.

"It's my neighbor, Chris. He gave me a ride."

"Why are you hanging out with your neighbor at two in the morning?"

Jessica rubbed her fingertips over her eyes. "I wasn't. I ran into him in the hall. You know where I was at two a.m., Chris, so reel it in."

"What subliminal messages on channel six?" Miranda asked.

Before Jeremy could explain, Jess jumped in. "None." She turned back toward the fire. "My business just went up in flames and the word *Antichrist* is spray-painted on the ground. I tried, but I just have zero fucks to give for any of y'all's theories and concerns right now."

She started wandering down the sidewalk away from

the fire, unsure what her next move was, but knowing there was no longer a point in standing around.

Quentin caught up to her. "Jess, fake love of my life. Hold up." He stepped in front. "You say someone spray-painted antichrist in front of the trailer?"

"Yeah."

A grin bloomed on his face and then he chuckled. "This is good. It's obviously arson, and more than that, it's such a clear hate crime—"

"As opposed to another kind of arson, Quentin? Have you ever loved something so much you burned it?"

He steadied his expression. "Sorry. I didn't mean to get excited. It's just that whoever did this actually did you a favor with the spray-paint. You'll get insurance. And if you get a good lawyer, you might even collect on pain and suffering."

"Wait. Really?"

"Yes," he said, opening his arms to her.

Appreciating his reassurance and feeling her frustration subside, she walked forward and let him hug her. When she was close against him, he brushed the hair away from her ear and leaned his lips close. "Swear on your life you won't explain the Moses thing to Miranda."

Jess tried to jerk away, but he pulled her close again, whispering, "If she finds out about me, it's over. She wants a normal life, not one with an angel."

Jessica felt his grip loosen and stepped back.

He yanked her close again. "Promise me."

"Yeah, fine. I won't say anything. But you do realize

that while you're over here with me, you've left Chris alone with her to answer whatever questions she might have, right?"

Quentin gasped, shoved Jessica away, and sprinted back toward the others.

* * *

As Wendy paced back and forth across Jessica's living room, Dr. Bell scrolled through her phone, and Jess was allowed to remain on her back on the couch, where she'd spent most of the past twelve hours since returning home from the fire.

"Are you truly set on waiting for her?" Wendy asked for the third time.

"Yes," Jessica said. "She has a stake in this. She should have a say, too."

A knock on the front door announced Judith's arrival, and Wendy was quick across the room to answer it. "You're late."

"I didn't realize we were under a time crunch," Judith said, sauntering in. "Not like the trailer is going to get any more fucked."

Pulling a bar stool around to the living room, Judith sat and looked at Jessica. "How you holding up?"

"Wonderful," Jessica grumbled.

"Such an optimist."

Wendy clapped her hands. "Shall we dive into it

now?" She looked at her watch. "I have a meeting in two hours that's a three-hour drive away."

"Fire whoever does your scheduling," said Judith.

Wendy pressed her lips together firmly, inhaling deeply through her nose. "I've called this emergency meeting because—"

"We know," Judith interrupted. "Some dipshit lit Jessica's business on fire."

Wendy shot daggers at Judith. "Yes. And now we have to come up with a plan for how we address it. So. There are two paths here. Either Jessica gives up on the bakery dream and tries something else, or we bounce back bigger and stronger in the patisserie industry."

Judith groaned. "I was with you on the second option until you used the word patisserie. I'm majoring in English and minoring in French, and even *I* think that's overly pretentious for what Jessica does."

Dr. Bell cleared her throat, drawing all eyes to her before Wendy could respond to the critique. "It's possible that all is not lost."

Jessica rolled her head toward her professor. "Go on."

"Barring any unfortunate turn of events"—she held up a hand before Judith could speak—"more unfortunate than the present one, you'll be receiving quite a bit of insurance money. I looked over your ledger before I came, and it looks like you were only seventeen thousand shy of hitting your target before you could sell the trailer and move to phase two where you open a permanent location."

Jessica threw her arm over her eyes. "Don't remind me. I was only a month or two away."

"Yes, *but* with the insurance money, you'll likely make back that plus more. Insurance doesn't take into account your intent to sell the trailer, so they'll give you enough money to rebuild it and outfit it with all the appliances, which is much more money than you would have gotten selling it used to someone else. Plus, as Wendy and I were discussing earlier, it was technically a hate crime, so there's a civil suit in this along with a criminal investigation."

"Right. Quentin said basically the same. What does that mean, though?"

Dr. Bell wove her fingers together in her lap. "You could make a lot of money off of this, Jessica."

She propped herself up onto her elbows. "Wait. I could make money because someone burned down my trailer? How does that make sense?"

"It doesn't," said Wendy, "so don't bother worrying about it. Also, it's not a done deal. But I'll get to that." She rolled her shoulders and stretched her neck. "The first problem is that there will have to be an investigation, which takes a while, then an insurance claim once the investigation ends, assuming they conclude someone *else* set the fire and it isn't an attempt at insurance fraud." She paused, her hands on her hips as she stared intensely at Jessica. The condo was dead silent.

Why is she looking at me like that?

"Wait, you think I set the fire myself?"

"Well? Did you?"

"No! Are you out of your mind?"

Wendy nodded, apparently taking no offense. "Just had to clear the air. I believe you, Jessica. No one knows better than I how much people hate you. Honestly, I can't believe we haven't encountered arson sooner. Anyway, insurance will take its sweet time on issuing you the check, meaning it could be literally years before you see that money, and I don't think you want to wait that long before getting back in the saddle again."

"Of course not. But what are my options?"

"Well," Wendy said, avoiding Jessica's eye, "we could rustle up some support from social media. After all, everyone loves a victim from afar."

"This sounds a little like exploiting a tragedy," Judith said. "Not that I'm against that. I mean, morally, yes, but everybody's doing it, you know?"

"Yeah," Jessica said, sitting up straight despite her sleep-deprivation headache, "using this to make money is probably the kind of thing police are looking out for in their investigation, right? Like, 'Oh hey, we've narrowed down suspects to the twenty-six thousand Texans who think she's the antichrist, so what now? Look! She's raising money because her trailer burned! And now she's opening up a bigger and better bakery. Maybe we should just investigate her!'"

Wendy leaned forward. "Do you really think that's how the police operate?"

"No?"

Wendy nodded slowly. "No is correct. But I suppose

you do have a point about it looking suspect. Not one that convinces me we shouldn't still do it, but a point nonetheless."

"There are other options," Dr. Bell said, pulling her black binder from underneath her chair and opening it on her lap. "Option one. You still have quite a bit of money left so that you could dip in and open another food trailer while you wait for the investigation and insurance to go through. I suspect that what fans you have would make an extra effort to come by and support your business after the attack, and a benefit day would be easy enough to organize, so you may be able to make up the difference in three to four months. Of course, it would take another couple months before we could open. Longer this time, since we got 'lucky,' as you'd say, with your first trailer having belonged to a bakery, meaning it had most of the set-up we needed"—she tilted her head toward Jessica, who still wouldn't admit that the fortunate find was likely her Father's doing—"so it would be about five to six months if you're lucky."

"And if no one burns down the second trailer," Jessica added.

Dr. Bell cleared her throat. "Yes. That too." She flipped the page. "Option two is that you get a job. Taking into account the loss of the trailer, which we'd planned to sell, and the amount of money you still needed before we were ready to find a permanent location, you would need to earn roughly forty-four thousand dollars. If we want to cut corners, I think I could get it down to thirty-five.

Depending on what job you find, it could take anywhere from one to three years to save that amount, and only if you keep a tight budget."

"What about Judith? I'm her sole source of income, and I need to make sure she has money, too. She's going to school full-time. She has rent to pay."

But her friend waved that off. "Psh. Don't worry about me. If you open up again, I'll come work for you. Otherwise, I'll just do what every English major does and take on crippling student debt then graduate with practically zero earning potential outside of teaching, which, from what I hear, actually comes out to less than minimum wage when you count all the hours spent working that you don't get paid for."

Jessica waited patiently for her to finish before saying, "Judith, that's insane."

"I know, but I don't make the rules. Write to your congressman."

"No, I mean about taking on debt. What if you sublet your apartment and live here with me?"

Judith scanned the apartment. "Is there a bedroom I don't know about? Maybe a murphy bed tucked into one of these concrete sarcophagus walls?"

"You can have my bed and I can sleep on the couch. Or we can get two twins and both sleep in the bedroom."

Judith leaned forward and placed a hand on Jessica's shoulder. "I love you, but that's a hard pass. I know what you and Chris do in your sleep. I think it's beautiful, but I don't want to share a room with it." She sat back on the stool. "Besides, I'm already like a hundred grand in the hole. What's another twenty thousand? Ooo! Or thirty thousand? I could really live it up this semester. Actually ... you want in on this sweet indentured servitude, Jess? I could throw you a cool twenty grand."

"Please," said Dr. Bell, pinching the bridge of her nose. "Please stop the financial irresponsibility. I'm going to be sick."

"There's another thing we need to address," Wendy said.

When she scooted a tree trunk stool over toward the coffee table and sat down on it, Jessica knew they were crossing into serious territory; Wendy never sat down if she could help it. "For this to count as a hate crime, which, trust me, we need it to for strategic reasons, it must be clear what, exactly, the criminal hated about you. Sure, your reputation is far and wide, but any defense attorney worth his weight in retweets will home in on the fact that you don't have a clear message. How can it be a hate crime if it's unclear what you stand for? It holds just enough water that we need to proactively counter it."

"I don't understand."

"Jessica, you *have* to come up with a clear philosophy you can express to the masses. You have to refine your message and step into your role as Jessica Christ, Female Messiah—or 'missiah,' which Cash says is a thing now. I can only keep your reputation afloat for so long when you reject the power of public life. But once you accept the power the mob offers you, once you slip into the stature of *celebrity*, girl, the shit flinging I can defend you from will be epic. You'll become larger than life. I can make it so that you could shoot someone in the middle of Sixth Street and get away with it. Not only that, I could use it to make you more money, gain you more followers. If you shot someone right now though"—she inhaled sharply—"you'd be going straight to jail."

"Good," Jessica said, trying not to sound as horrified as she felt. "I *should* go to jail if I shoot a random, innocent stranger. That's—that's how the world should work. You know, you're really not selling me on your argument. No one should be that powerful."

Wendy didn't appear even the slightest bit cowed as she gently shrugged a shoulder. "Jimmy will be before long." She paused and pressed her lips together, her nostrils flaring wide as she met Jessica's stare. "I still don't know what his next move is, but I know it's going to be big, and I'd put money on it succeeding. And when that happens, you better hope you're in a position of power too."

Goddamn Jimmy Dean.

"You gonna let Jimmy win?" Wendy prodded.

"I didn't know it was a competition," Jessica said morosely.

"You better get wise, because it is a competition, and if you're not competing, Jimmy fucking Dean will win."

Judith gasped excitedly. "She says fuck?" she asked Jessica.

"Only for Jimmy."

"Ah. Makes sense."

Jessica blinked her dry eyes hard, trying to summon moisture to them. "Okay, Wendy. You win. How do I beat Jimmy?"

Wendy stood and ran her palms over her expensive skirt. "First, you come up with a clear set of beliefs. Then, you *tell me what they are.* I can't stress that last part enough. I'll refine the message to something even a simpleton in Oklahoma can understand and pass it along to Cash to start disseminating one hundred and forty characters at a time. Finally, you find a way to open the damn bakery, and this time you don't name it Jessica's Plain Old Stuff. You lean the hell into it. I don't care how you do it, but I suggest you get started two hours ago. You understand?"

Jessica nodded timidly and Wendy turned to Judith, pointing sharply. "You hold her feet to the fire."

Judith sucked in air. "Oof. Too soon."

"What? ... Oh." Wendy grimaced. "Sorry." She grabbed her purse off the table. "You know what I meant, though. Now if you'll excuse me, I have to speed back to Dallas and hope I don't get pulled over by a small-town cop at any point along the way." She reached the door and paused, turning to the others. "To clarify, I mean because my registration is expired. Not because I'm ... But also partly because I'm ... Never mind. Get to work."

Chapter Eighteen

Excerpt from Railed to the Cross

Some of the events you're about to read following my departure from Hawthorn include unholy acts that I would never engage in today and that I advise others to avoid at all costs.

I would be ashamed of the things I did in my years traveling along the railroads of America, except the Lord has since forgiven me, for He understands why I acted out such base behaviors, and I hope that you follow in His divine logic as I further explain my origins to you. After all, I may be a high and holy man, but I am still a man. I hope this aids in your understanding of that crucial concept.

Puberty is a tender age for a young man. He wants so badly to swiftly hurdle it, to find himself on the other side where he is officially a man. Yet the prospect of becoming a man is so mysterious, terrifying even, that he battles against the transformation every single day, struggling to find purchase on the craggy overhang of childhood to avoid falling into that dark abyss of unknown responsibility and societal expectations. And for a boy who doesn't know what it means to be a man, has rarely, if ever, seen it, the fear is yet stronger, more primal. He must hope that his mistakes are small and the wisdom he gleans from each manifold.

As I left the smoldering remains of home behind, bound for the nearest railroad tracks to wait for a train to pass, none of these considerations were on my mind. These are, after all, hindsight musings, not the kind of thing a young man full of budding hormones has the mental bandwidth or perspective to consider. It's possible I felt hints of these things in abstract and they colored my actions, but I hadn't yet formed them into thoughts that could be acted upon in either direction.

My knowledge of the railways of the region was limited, but I was certain that the one by which I sat, just outside of Mobile, with only the clothes on my back and the growing hunger in my belly ran east-west. The eastern route traveled along the gulf coast, eventually arcing upward along the Atlantic, heading for New England. The western route ran northwest to the Mississippi River then crossed over into Arkansas. After that, I wasn't sure. And it didn't matter to me—it could have headed directly off a cliff for all I cared—because my plan was to catch a train and head east. Coastal life was all I knew, and while I was looking for a change in many ways, that was not among them; heading inland held no appeal to me.

It was hours with no sign of a train. Hunger tore at my gut, and that was bad, but what was worse was the doubt that threatened to take hold of my mind if I didn't act upon my plan soon.

Finally, I heard a train in the distance. It was heading west. I considered it briefly. I wanted to head east not west, but since when had life offered me something I wanted? Rarely. And it never ended well. I had wanted a father, and what I got was Rupert. And then he took my mother and left me parentless. Getting what I wanted did not have an appealing track record in my recent memory.

Then there was the possibility that the other wives had begun searching for me. Unlikely, since most of them had enough children to worry about without adding another, and the obvious assumption would be that I took off with my mother and Pastor Heathrow, but the mere thought of returning to anything I'd once experienced was enough to lift me from my tired rear and propel me forward toward the train.

I was ready for my new adventure, no matter where it led.

The train moved at a lolling pace, creeping along the tracks, yet even still, the relentless grinding of the wheels as they carried the heavy cars was terrifying. What if I slipped trying to leap into the boxcar and fell underneath? The leisurely pace of the wheels crushing my body would only serve to prolong the agony as I was slowly, mercilessly bisected. The fear was almost crippling as I jogged slowly next to an open boxcar, building up the courage to grab the metal bar and hoist myself up and into my new life. Perhaps the fear wasn't limited solely to the unlikely possibility of decapitation but also what it would mean for me to board that train, to cross the threshold into a life where I made decisions for myself.

Then the train slowed to a complete stop, and I couldn't have received a clearer more loving and gentle nudge from God if I'd asked for it. The dark open door beckoned me, and I took a deep breath, grabbed the edge, and pulled myself aboard.

As I inhaled deeply, trying to steady myself, my nostrils were greeted by the scent of manure. But not the familiar scent of horse or pig or cow. Something a little earthier, almost sour. Definitely musty. Whatever animal had produced it had done so days earlier. But the heat of the Alabama sun on the roof of the car worked like an oven to create a stifling environment in the container.

Was it a sign that I should leave? That this was the wrong decision?

I chose to believe it wasn't.

Despite the stench, which grew fainter to my senses over the following hours of acclimation, my excitement bloomed. I'd never experienced anything like my time on the boxcar, staring out at the land as I passed it by, watching it change from soggy coastal sludge to the lushness of the Ozarks.

It was a wide freedom as if the narrow path I had

always assumed lay before me had just opened up into an expansive field of wildflowers that stretched to the horizon in every direction except behind me. My future felt unrestrained, even as my stomach growled loudly. It became so obvious just how little the needs of the body mattered when compared to the needs of the soul, and I quickly fell into the rhythm of the wheels over the rails, melted into my surroundings, allowed my legs to dangle out of the car as I leaned against the doorframe, first clutching the metal for dear life, then loosening my grip as I realized I wouldn't fall, that I could manage this small bit of risk. The fear, all of it, melted away in those first hours.

The train made two stops along the route, and though I could hear voices outside while I hid in a dark corner, no one ever came by to check on the car and I was able to continue without issue until we reached Texarkana.

I knew it was the last stop for a while, because the commotion kicked up almost immediately and the sounds of unloading echoed loudly. As did a few other sounds.

Animals. Ones I'd never heard before, and some I'd only heard on the television.

An elephant was among the latter category, and its mighty trumpet sent chills down my spine. I heard its homeland contained in that call, and I wondered if back in Africa, there was another elephant trumpeting in harmony.

I was spotted immediately as I jumped off the train, but the man who saw me didn't seem too concerned. He had a long, scraggly beard down to his nipples—I only knew that for certain because he wore no shirt underneath the suspenders that held his cotton pants up onto his round waist—and his head was shaved bald. His eyes narrowed on me for a second, then he called out, "Hey boy."

The weightless freedom I'd felt on the journey evaporated instantly as my body prepared for some sort of physical punishment for my breaking the rules and hitching a free ride.

But he didn't chastise me. He held a thick rope in his hands that was attached to something in the boxcar, but what it was I couldn't see.

"Crawl in there and give old Bessy a slap on the rear to get her moving," he instructed.

I did as I was told, and crawled into the car, squinting through the dark until my eyes adjusted and I could see who Bessy was. But even as my pupils dilated, I couldn't quite make sense of the huddled mass of legs in front of me. Until she raised her head.

The rope was tied around her long neck that rested on a scattering of hay over the metal floor. Were giraffes dangerous? She seemed docile enough. I approached with caution and she stared at me with tired, glassy eyes. The shape of each rib became pronounced with each of her inhales, but I had little pity to give her, considering my own famished state.

I moved behind her and gave her a rough shove, despite a twinge of pity for her based more on her sheer size in comparison to the space rather than any other struggle of hers. The cramped quarters could be alleviated, however, if I simply got her out, so that's what my goal became, getting the poor beast out of the small car.

She didn't move at first, so I kept at it until she budged, and then slowly, keeping her head lowered, she crawled onto her knees and shimmied neck-first out into the sunlight.

The rope around her neck seemed wholly unnecessary, as she didn't attempt to run or even walk in any particular direction. She blinked into the sun, as did I once I crawled back out again, and the man holding her nodded his approval at me curtly.

"I don't recognize you. When'd you get on?"

He didn't seem angry, only curious, so I replied honestly. "Back in Alabama."

"You must be hungry then. Help unload the rest of these animals, then I'll get you something to eat. Won't taste good, but it'll be something."

It was my first paid job. Certainly, I'd worked odd jobs with Mother before, but the compensation had never gone into my pocket. Not directly anyway. She'd taken it and distributed it as she saw fit, which was usually never the fit way to go about it and left the pantry empty but her moonshine reserves replenished.

A team of men and a few women who appeared at first blush to be men assembled giant steel grates into small cages over in a nearby field. As each new one went up, the man and I added an animal or three to the new-formed enclosures. We didn't put the last animal—a lethargic Bengal tiger—into her cage until the last glow of twilight.

Once we were gathered round the fire the bald man finally bothered himself with a formal introduction. "Crazy Jake," he said, extending his hand, which I shook. "You did a hell of a job today. What are you, eight years old?"

I was offended but savvy enough not to show it to someone named Crazy Jake. "Twelve. And thanks."

"You gotta stop bringing kids around, CJ," said a person who I strongly suspected was a woman. She sat by the fire, stirring a cauldron of what would be our meal. "You know that brings the authorities snooping."

"He ain't gonna be no trouble," Crazy Jake replied before looking down at me. "Right, boy? You ain't gonna be no trouble?"

"No, sir," I said. "I'm real good at hiding, too, if anyone comes looking."

The woman shrugged and kept stirring.

As Crazy Jake took a seat on one of the small makeshift benches by the fire, he went around the circle making introductions. He started with the woman. "That there's Lucy Goosey, then there's Ol' Six Fingers, Jumping Jerry, Sally Q"—a man, in case you're wondering—"Deaf Lenny, Dumb Lenny, and Racist Wallace."

As I'd later find out, about half of those were misnomers.

Chapter Nineteen

Roughly thirty-five thousand dollars and some sort of belief system—that's all Jessica needed to come up with. If she was as special as everyone claimed she was, it shouldn't be *that* hard.

Sure, she had no job, so unless she was going to relapse to her scratch-off habit, it looked like she'd have to earn money the old-fashioned way. And as far as a belief system went, she'd half-assed most of her Intro to Philosophy class, and didn't know much about any particular religion. But she was the God-damned daughter of God, dammit! Philosophy and religion should be second nature to her.

As she sat cross-legged on the expensive gray shag rug in her living room, scribbling down whatever words or phrases came into her head on the legal pad she'd set up on the coffee table, she discovered that, no, this shit did not come naturally. Not even to her. Also, were brain maps ever *actually* helpful? How were a few circled words connected with lines supposed to give her any insight whatsoever? Why was this one of the few skills she remembered from Marymoore and Mooremont? Why had they wasted so much time learning brain maps and spent so little time learning personal finance and how to draft a manifesto?

The fact that your underfunded education didn't prepare you for life in any capacity isn't exactly revelatory. Focus!

But that was increasingly difficult when the buzzer on her intercom wouldn't stop jolting her from her thoughts.

A shudder of rage trickled down her spine. What was that, the fourteenth time he'd buzzed her? The twentieth?

No one ever says he lacks persistence, that's for sure.

She squeezed her eyes shut then opened them again to stare down at her page. At the center of her word web was, *Don't be an asswipe.* If it was in the middle of her map, did that make it worthy of being a central tenet of her belief system? If so, she should probably paraphrase.

The intercom buzzed again.

"*Man,* I hate him." She scribbled *Death to men,* considered it, savoring the sentiment, swishing it around in her mind indulgently. But when an image of Chris surfaced, followed by a parade of the men she didn't wish death upon, she scribbled out the phrase.

The intercom buzzed again.

"Nope. Not a chance in hell."

Branching out from her contender for central tenet

were words like, *free* and *hanging out* and *Sir David Attenborough.*

Yep, I have no clue what I'm doing. I bet Jesus didn't have to do brain maps to figure out his message.

BECAUSE HE LISTENED TO HIS FATHER.

Oh, hello there. So wait, you just fed him his message?

YES.

That sort of makes him your puppet.

I PREFER 'THE LORD'S OBEDIENT SON.'

I can tell. Out of curiosity, what message would you have me spread to the masses?

IT IS NOT A VENEREAL DISEASE; YOU DON'T SPREAD IT, YOU PREACH IT.

Fine, what message would you like me to preach?

OH, YOU KNOW. LOVE. NOT BEING AN ASSWIPE.

Oddly enough, I already have that written down. But it's not exactly revolutionary. Sounds like what you sent Jesus to talk about.

TO BE FAIR, MODERN TECHNOLOGY HAS REMOVED THE NEED FOR MOST OF MY MESSAGE.

Meaning?

HISTORICALLY, MY RULES SERVED AS AN FAQ FOR HUMANITY.

Again: meaning?

I CONSIDER THE MOST FREQUENT PRAYERS OF THE EPOCH AND PRESENT SOLUTIONS.

Okay ...?

BEFORE JESUS—B.J., AS I REFER TO IT IN ENGLISH, THOUGH I COULD NEVER GET THAT TO CATCH ON—PRAYERS WERE ALWAYS, "OH LORD, MINE BROTHER IS POOPING HIMSELF TO DEATH. DEFINITELY TOO LATE FOR HIM, BUT PLEASE DON'T LET ME GO LIKE THAT," OR "HOLY GOD, WHAT ARE THESE BUMPS ON MY SIN BITS THAT BRING WITH THEM FEVER AND VOMITING?"

ERGO, MOST OF THE RULES WERE ABOUT FOOD PREPARATION AND NOT DIPPING ONE'S MANLY STAFF INTO UNCLEAN HOLES.

Okay, so you and Jesus mostly talked about food poisoning and ... sex?

NOT AT ALL. BY THE TIME YOUR BROTHER WAS BORN, MY CHOSEN PEOPLE ALREADY KNEW NOT TO EAT OR PUT THEIR MANHOOD INTO THE MAIN NASTY THINGS.

So what were the prayers then?

"LORD, PLEASE QUICK WASH ME SO I DON'T HAVE TO ENDURE **ANOTHER** TWO-DAY CLEANSING RITUAL BEFORE BED," AND, "OH LORD, MY HUSBAND IS A MEANIE. PLEASE MAKE HIM NOT A MEANIE."

And your response was to have Jesus tell everyone to ... ease up on the OCD and quit being meanies?

NEVER HEARD IT SUMMED UP LIKE THAT, BUT YES.

Suddenly so many things about Jesus make sense. Okay.

I'll play along. What are the frequently asked prayers nowadays?

A loud knock on her front door made her jump.

Had someone let him into the building? Shit.

She stood and scurried over to peer through the peep-hole, but it was just Jeremy, so she opened the door and stuck her head out.

"Hey, Jess. Sorry to bother you. There's a man down at the front door who, I think, is here for you. He keeps shouting your name, at least. I wasn't sure if maybe your buzzer was broken and you didn't know?"

She leaned against the door frame. "No, I know he's there. I just don't want to let him inside. Because he's the devil. Well, not *actually* the devil—I still don't know who the devil is, and quite honestly, my messiah bandwidth is stretched pretty thin at the moment and I'm running out of energy to keep guessing. Plus, I figure, hey, I'll probably find out in the worst possible way regardless, so why worry about it?"

Jeremy grimaced, exposing a sliver of teeth between his thin lips. "Ah, okay."

"Wait. *You* think *I'm* crazy?"

He took a step back and the laugh that followed was obviously forced. "No, no. Not at all. Um, so do you want me to call someone to take care of him? Not anyone from the police state, obviously—two 911 calls in a month gets you put on a registry—but I have some connections in the Heart of Texas Militia."

As tempting as it was to imagine Jimmy Dean facing

off against a redneck with an itchy trigger finger and illegal body armor, Jessica declined. "No, it's fine. I'm hoping he just goes away"—the intercom buzzed again, this time dragging out as Jimmy held down the button—"but maybe that won't be the case."

"You sure you don't want backup? He seems a little unhinged."

Talk about projection.

But also he's right.

"Yeah, I'm fine. Jimmy's a rage-vomit-inducing dumpster fire of a human, but he wouldn't hurt me. I make him too much money."

Jeremy nodded like he understood and backed the rest of the way across the hall to his front door, appearing to take conspicuous pains to keep from putting his back to her. She allowed him to get fully inside and shut the door before making any sudden movements.

Slipping on flip-flops, Jessica trudged downstairs to the condominium foyer. She'd hear Jimmy out, but she sure as shit wasn't letting him anywhere near where she ate, slept, or dream banged. Plus, she had a few questions she might as well ask him while he was around ... not that she expected honest answers.

She spotted his silhouette through the frosted glass of the main entrance as he reached out and jabbed the intercom. She yanked the door open quickly and soaked in the split second of alarm on his face at her sudden appearance.

In the flesh stood Jimmy Dean. Did the man never age?

"Jessica," he crooned, recovering quickly.

His annoyingly white suit appeared much cleaner in person than it had through the smudged intercom camera, but the hooves that dangled on a red cord around his neck looked just as gaudy. He was in full-blown Church Jimmy attire.

Stepping forward, perhaps expecting her to move to the side, he was forced to take a half-step back to avoid being too close for comfort when she wouldn't budge an inch. He played it off, though, straightening out his shoulders. "I assume you were asleep or in the shower or otherwise indisposed, and that's why you left me out here on the streets for so long. By the way, there are a *lot* of homeless that hang out by your building. It's rather suspicious." He leaned forward and whispered, "They could be plotting something."

"Yeah, Jimmy. Plotting how to not be homeless. Or maybe their next fix. Depends on which one you're talking about." She leaned slightly forward on tiptoes, glancing over the reverend's shoulder. "Hey, Earle. How's it going today?"

She cringed, waiting for his response. Earle wasn't her favorite regular, and she was not his favorite benefactor.

"Go to hell, Jessica Cheapskate! Princess of Pennies!"

She grinned at Jimmy. "See? I'm on a first-name basis with Earle, so nothing to worry about. And as for your first assumption, no, I was not indisposed. I just still hate you."

He bowed his head solemnly. "Yes, I understand that you sometimes get in these moods, and it's perfectly understandable, given your sex, but I think you'll change your tune when you see what I've brought, for I come bearing gifts." He made to step past her and into the foyer, but she stuck her arm out, gripping the door frame so he couldn't pass. He cleared his throat. "Okay, then. I'll cut to the chase. I heard the awful news about your food truck being burned to the ground—"

"Which you had something to do with, right?"

He gasped and stumbled back a step. "Jessica! Dear, sweet Jessica! No! Never! I faithfully support small businesses. But also, I would never commit such a heinous act against the one for whom God Himself has asked me to clear the way."

"Okay, I don't know what you mean by that, so how about this: you tell me what you want in the next thirty seconds, or you'll have to hold it inside and if you start buzzing me again, I'll actually take up my neighbor on his offer to have the militia—which I didn't even know was still a thing until a couple minutes ago—come take you out."

Jimmy's smooth, saccharine demeanor steadied, his nostrils flared as if scenting the air for militiamen, and the muscles in his jaw flicked up and down. "Fine. As we both know," he leaned close, and as much as Jessica wanted to move away, she wouldn't give him the satisfaction, "some or all of the foreword of the #1 *New York Times* and *USA Today* Bestseller *Railed to the Cross* was not written by yourself." While his verbal admission shocked her, she steadied herself not to show it. "Frankly, I expected you to sue me, and I was ready to settle out of court. But for whatever reason, you did not do that."

"You expected me to?"

He leaned back. "Oh yes. Of course I did." He chuckled incredulously. "I would have, if the roles were switched. But it doesn't matter, because I had a contingency plan." He paused, smiling, making her wait until he was ready to reveal his plot. "Here's the thing, dear child. You can do whatever you want in life, so long as you can provide something of value to those who would try to stop you. Had you filed a suit, I was ready to offer you more money for damages than you could ever hope for. We would have settled out of court because, had you taken it to court, there was always the chance that I could not only win, but humiliate you on a public stage yet again. Your publicist would have reached that conclusion soon enough. Anywho, that wasn't the path you chose, and for that, I'm proud of you. Perhaps, even though you didn't write the words yourself, you read them and agreed with them anyway."

"Nope."

He waved her off with a quick flutter of his hand. "No need to lie. Here." Then, reaching into the breast pocket of his suit jacket, he pulled out a piece of paper. As he slowly unfolded it, he explained, "As my royalty checks roll in, I've set aside a percentage for you. Originally, this was intended for a settlement, but as you haven't taken that path, it's now available for something vastly more important: helping you achieve your dreams." He held the piece of paper by the top two corners, right on eye level with Jessica, and as he spoke, his voice grew louder, like he was preaching to a congregation. "Because I believe in you, Jessica McCloud. Because you're like the daughter I never had. I know this will be hard for you to believe, but I want you to be happy and to succeed."

Jessica lowered her eyes from Jimmy's lying face to the check.

Five hundred and seventy-five thousand three hundred and eighty-two dollars and sixty cents.

Holy shit.

She swallowed down the lunatic shout that threatened to jump out of her mouth.

I could open the bakery downtown with this kind of money.

She suppressed a groan. "You made that off the book?"

A sly smirk turned the corner of his mouth and he nodded quickly. "Oh yes. And this is just from the first royalty check. There will be more coming my way, and subsequently, more coming *your* way. Since you've obviously read my book—who hasn't at this point?—you understand the pivotal message of hope it delivers. And it seems readers are more than happy to recommend it to their friends, et cetera. Because you've so graciously contributed to that success with your glowing foreword that you definitely wrote in its entirety, based upon your knowledge of it without taking any legal action, I figure you deserve a cut."

It could just be "Jimmy tax." I could just consider it what he owes me for a lifetime of pain and suffering. In fact, it's not even enough. He owes me back taxes …

It was so much money. And there would more where that came from, too, as he got in more royalties. All her financial woes could be solved in an instant if she just snatched the check from his hands and didn't look back. She could even repay those who donated so much money to her endeavor. She would feel in debt to Miranda or Kate or Dr. Bell or ...

No, but only because I owed all my success to Jimmy fucking Dean and his stupid book.

"This is a bribe." She pushed his hands away from her, feeling nausea rising in her stomach. "I won't take a dime from you."

"I will!" Earle yelled from behind them. "This bitch only gives pennies. A dime would be a huge step up!"

"Fine," Jimmy said. "I guess the Lord's calling isn't enough incentive for you to do what it takes." He folded the check and tucked it in his pocket. "That's what separates you and me, Jessica. When I see the path of the Lord laid out before me, I do whatever it takes to stay on course." He patted his breast pocket. "If you change your mind about the money, let me know. It's yours, far as I'm concerned. I won't touch a penny of it."

"Psh. Unlikely. Don't you still owe my mom hundreds of dollars? Why don't you go knock on her door?"

His eyes opened wide and he leaned forward, hissing, "You know she owns guns."

"And I have militia connections. Guess nowhere is safe for God's biggest thorn in my side." She went to shut the door, but Jimmy jammed a shiny white boot in the space before she could, and the door bounced open again.

"Do you have a television?" he asked.

"Of course."

"Then you should watch channel six news at six."

She narrowed her eyes at him. "Why?"

He yanked his foot back and turned on his heel. "God's blessing, my darling Jessica," he yelled over his shoulder, waving with a twiddle of his fingertips.

Earle rattled his Sonic cup at Jimmy as he approached, and a swift flick of Jimmy's left boot knocked the Styrofoam into the air, sending change skipping across the sidewalk.

"Dick!" Earle shouted.

"You're right about that," Jessica said.

As she closed the door, she checked the giant clock on the foyer wall. Though it was made of repurposed scrap metal and car parts and nearly impossible to read, she was pretty sure it was only a few minutes past three.

Still plenty of time to brainstorm her message and revise her business plan before the ax inevitably fell on the six o'clock news.

* * *

Jessica's vision blurred. She combed over the business plan expense sheet for the umpteenth time but was still unable to find another twenty thousand dollars to trim. It didn't help that she couldn't peel her mind's eye from the check

Jimmy had dangled in front of her face just a few hours before.

At least she knew what he was up to, now. She'd have to tell Wendy. But not yet. Everything still felt too fresh. And as long as no one else knew about her turning down the money, there was still the possibility that she could ...

No. Not now, not ever.

She knew on an instinctual level not to take anything he offered. It would be like following a stranger to an unmarked van because he dangled her favorite candy in front of her face and promised, "There's more where that came from in my big murderbus," and then she said, "Yeah, okay. Maybe it's worth it."

But at the same time, five hundred and seventy-five thousand, three hundred and eighty-two dollars, and sixty cents would make her feel a lot better about him faking the foreword, and maybe it *would* be worth it to walk right into his trap. She would probably end up in one of his traps eventually, and she might as well make a cool half mil off of her unfortunate fate.

His offer would mean that rather than poring over spreadsheets for corners to cut, she could be *expanding* her plans for the bakery into something much bigger, more centrally located ...

No, no, no. Absolutely not. If there's not a way to do this without accepting Jimmy's help, then it just doesn't get done.

It also nagged at her that even *Jimmy* had a clear message, and she still didn't. Of course, outside of Jessica being God's daughter, her mother being the embodiment of Original Sin, and her father being some sort of hog deity, Jessica wasn't sure what that message was.

However, the answer to that mystery was sitting on the concrete floor in the corner of her living room where it'd slid to a stop when she'd, once again, thrown it across the room in disgust. Just looking at it caused the first inklings of a tension headache to gather behind her eyes.

She slammed the pen onto her brain map and stomped over to the book, grabbing it, opening it to the table of contents, and jumping ahead to the section called *Life In Tents*, which had been mentioned at her surprise brunch the month before...

We'd unloaded the rusty machinery but not yet the animals, and were sweating like slaves in the dense southern Louisiana air, when Crazy Jake let us know that something was wrong. Usually, it was Racist Wallace who scouted the set-up location first while the rest of us, sans Fish Head Sally, who wasn't much help because—as I mentioned before—she had no legs among a variety of other disabilities. But whenever we traveled this deep in the South—because as anyone from the South knows, there are various rings in which Southern qualities intensify the closer toward the center one travels—we let Racist Wallace stay back with the rest of us to unload and sent Crazy Jake ahead instead. Back then, it simply wouldn't do to send a black man like

Racist Wallace on a scouting mission solo in this neck of the woods.

When Crazy Jake returned, he was visibly upset. "There's already a tent where we was gonna set up! A big one, too!"

"Were there folks in it?" Ol' Six Fingers asked.

"Sure sounded like it. There was whooping and a-hollering like I ain't even heard in our tents. Whatever they got going on must be something special."

With Bennefort and the rest of the talent not slated to arrive for days, it was left up to our band of misfits to problem solve, which never worked out well.

So it was decided that I, being the smallest among the men despite having grown two inches in the past few months, would conduct a reconnaissance mission. No one would suspect a thirteen-year-old boy of being a spy. I could slip in, see what was going on, and hopefully get to the bottom of why another show had settled on our lot.

Crazy Jake provided me basic directions, adding that I "couldn't miss it." And he was right. Even before I could see the top of the tent peeking over the horizon, I heard the voices. They weren't like the ones I heard regularly at Bennefort's shows. This crowd was energized in a way that told me they were not passive observers but a part of whatever excitement was taking place. The moans and cheers were galvanized. The distinct shouts of individual voices rose up like a bubble breaching the surface of a boiling pot of water. The water boiled faster and faster, and I was almost too exhilarated and terrified to tiptoe into the tent once I'd finally reached it.

There were no giraffes, no zebras, no tightrope walkers competing for the crowd's attention. Just one man.

He stood on a raised platform at the back of the tent dressed in a nice cocoa-colored suit as he paced the stage, speaking into a handheld microphone that pumped out his voice from every corner of the standing-room-only tent.

I pushed toward the front, snaking between bodies to get a better view, and the crowd, so focused on this man, paid me no mind. At last, when I was where I could stare up at him on his rickety stage decorated with a mic stand and a single wooden chair, I began to understand why so many people had gathered.

The words "Jesus" and "God" and "miracles" knocked lightly on a door in my mind, behind which I'd hidden away my teachings from Hawthorn First Baptist and Pastor Heathrow. And when this radiant man's words knocked, those memories answered and came flooding out.

He was handsome, tall, almost fully gray in a way that showed wisdom more than age. He paced as he preached, his voice growing from a soft whisper that silenced the audience completely in their desperation not to miss a syllable to righteous shouting, brandishing his fist at the top of the tent and proclaiming his Truth.

"The Lord is not prideful," he said, swiping an arm

through the air. "Only man is prideful. The Lord possesses no ego. Only man possesses ego, and a harmful one at that. But sometimes, the Lord, in all His infinite wisdom, knows that we feeble-minded men must see to believe. And it is for that reason that the Lord is unafraid"—he lowered his voice, leaning toward the crowd as if whispering a secret—"to show off a little."

Shouts of "Praise Jesus" and "Hallelujah" echoed from various corners of the tent, like a heavenly call and respond.

"So now's the time, children of God. Now's the time for your miracles. Those suffering souls of you selected by the ushers: come up here and be healed!"

Jessica's mind was so absorbed in the strange tale, she almost missed the small tapping on her front door.

"Who is it?" she asked, hoping whoever it was didn't require her to get up from where she'd settled on the couch with a soft throw blanket.

"Jeremy. Your neighbor."

"Damn." She dog-eared the page, shut the book, and answered the door.

"Sorry to bug you again," he said, clasping his hands tightly and frowning. "I've been torn between giving you space and checking on you to make sure you were okay after that guy showed up. Checking on you finally won out. I know you said he was harmless, but he is still a man, and all men are dangerous lunatics, no matter what they say." He grinned apologetically.

"Um. That means you're a dangerous lunatic, too, though, right?"

Jeremy straightened up quickly. "Huh?" He pointed at his chest. "Me? Oh, no. Not at all. Not at all."

She decided to let it slide. "Well, you're right to some degree. The Great and Powerful Jimmy is far from harmless. He harms me pretty much constantly; it's just not in a physical sense."

Jeremy nodded along, though his fear didn't appear assuaged. "So ... are you good?"

"Yeah, no need to call the militia," she said, forcing a reassuring grin.

"Oh no," he said, "you can't call them. They don't have phones."

She chuckled before realizing he wasn't joking. "Of course."

Then, as the memory of his comforting hug in the hallway almost three months earlier surfaced, followed closely by the one where he'd held her back from running into her flaming trailer, a strange idea occurred to her: Jeremy was her friend.

If nothing else, he had proximity in his favor, which was more than could be said for all but two of her friends at present. Sure, he was borderline unhinged, likely suffering from a smorgasbord of mental disorders, but when push came to shove, he'd been there for her. Maybe beliefs didn't matter so much as actions.

"Hey, do you want to come in? I was just about to practice my baking, and I need a test subject."

His concern evaporated and he smiled. "Certainly! I love bread!"

Okay then. Let's see how this goes. She stepped to the side and welcomed him into her home.

"I always smell you baking over here," he said, "so I'll be glad to get to try it myself, finally."

"Make yourself at home, then. It'll be nice to have the company." Only as she said it did she realize how much she meant it.

"Ditto. Ooo, what are you reading?" He pointed at the book then grabbed it off the couch and read the cover himself. "Wait, a second. You said the man downstairs was named Jimmy. Was that Jimmy Dean? *The* Jimmy Dean?"

"The one and only," Jess said, preheating the oven.

Jeremy brought the book over to the kitchen island and parked himself on a stool. "I've heard about him. Seen him on the news, too. Didn't know he had a book, though." He glanced up at her. "You wrote the foreword for this?"

"Of course not."

"Good. You shouldn't call yourself Jessica Christ. It's tacky."

She laughed dryly. "I agree."

"You mind if I read this while you bake?"

"Suit yourself. It's just a bunch of lies."

He pressed his lips together, cocking his head to the side and staring at her with what appeared to be pity. "Of course it is. It's a traditionally published book. Everyone knows the big six only publish pro-anti-freedom propaganda from the mainscream media."

She braced herself on the island, inspecting Jeremy as he browsed the copyright page. "I don't think I ever asked you what you do for work," she said. "I assume you work from home?"

"Uh-huh," he said distractedly. "I'm the CEO of a corporation that owns a lot of other corporations. We specialize in financial and media conglomerates." He flapped a hand at her without looking up. "It's all very boring. Basically, Murdock and Buffet wanted some responsibilities off their plate, so I helped them out."

"That sounds like ... a lot. If you don't have the time in the middle of the day to—"

Jeremy glanced up from the book. "Don't worry. I have nothing but time. Everyone says there's no finish line for success, but that's just because they haven't reached it yet. I limit myself to three major business decisions a day, and that seems to do the trick. The rest of the work is done by other people. They do the research, present me the options, explain the pros and cons, then I say, 'that one,' and they make it happen. It's a nice setup. You should consider it." He flipped to the first page of the foreword. "Anyway, I've already made my three decisions for the day, so I'm free until tomorrow. And in case you're wondering, yes, it's as wonderful as it sounds."

"Huh. Yeah, I can't see a drawback, actually." She turned toward the pantry and away from her neighbor so he wouldn't see her expression of utter confusion while she tried to unpack the riddle of Jeremy's life and also gather the ingredients for banana nut muffins.

"Any food allergies?" she asked.

"I stay away from corn."

"Not a problem."

He scoffed. "I wish. It's in everything."

"Well, since I'm making this from scratch and know the ingredients, I feel safe to say there's no corn in banana nut muffins."

He raised his eyebrows. "Whatever you say."

"I'm using wheat flour."

"Exactly."

Maybe company wasn't what she needed, but it didn't matter, because Jeremy quickly focused in on the book, and she lost herself in the familiar flow of baking, tweaking the previous day's recipe to add a little less mushed banana and a little more flour.

As she put the finished product into the oven, she heard Jeremy slam the book shut behind her. "Phew! What a psycho!" he proclaimed.

She closed the oven and set the timer. "Yep. How far are you into it?"

"Done."

She turned around. "Done? Like, finished?"

He nodded cheerily. "Yep. Speed reader. It's the key to much of my success. I've read over a hundred thousand books in my lifetime."

While she would be the first to admit she wasn't a *reader*, that seemed like a lot by anyone's standards. "Traditionally published books?"

He sighed heavily and rolled his eyes. "Unfortunately, yes."

"Was this one as bad as all the others?"

He leaned forward, stressing each word. "*Much* worse."

She grinned. "I knew I liked you."

"How long do the muffins take?"

When she turned to look at the oven timer, her eye instead landed on the clock on the microwave.

Two past six.

"Shit! I'm supposed to watch the news!"

She ran over to the coffee table, grabbed the remote and turned the TV to channel six.

"Good thinking, Jessica. It's always smart to know what the masses are being fed. I appreciate the dedication."

"No, Jimmy told me to watch it today." She parked it on the sofa. "So I apologize if something on it upsets me."

Jeremy strolled over and joined her on the couch. "I'd be worried if you watched an entire newscast without becoming upset by something. Complacency is their end goal, Jessica."

"Whose end goal?"

"Theirs." He nodded at the TV.

That still didn't answer her question, but she dropped it as the commercial ended and Magda Masterson and Steve Solstice appeared at the anchor desk, grinning like someone had slipped a molly in their afternoon coffee.

Steve took the lead, but not before he wiped the grin

from his face and robotically turned down the corners of his mouth, pinching together his botoxed eyebrows as much as his skin's restricted elasticity would allow.

"A shooting in a north Austin gentleman's club has left three dead and seven injured. Authorities say Caesar Gonzalez-Ramirez entered Amor Loco around one a.m. and opened fire, targeting his girlfriend who worked there. Police say other patrons then returned fire, killing Caesar. It's unclear at this point whether it was Caesar or those returning fire who ultimately shot Maria Castillo, the girlfriend of Caesar Gonzalez-Ramirez, but she was hit and died later at the hospital."

Magda shook her head slowly, then turned to the teleprompter and grinned. *"Watch out, ACL! A new music festival is moving to Austin, and this one plans to be the weirdest of all!"*

Steve jumped back in with, *"The Hemp City Organics Keep Austin Weird Like it Used to Be Festival aims to bring in musicians, filmmakers, tech pioneers, and oil investors from around the globe to celebrate what makes Austin special. The council in charge of the festival hopes it can grow into a profitable business over the next five years that will earn enough to help Austin's many victims of gentrification find affordable housing in Bastrop, Dripping Springs, San Marcos, and other surrounding towns well outside Travis County."*

Jeremy elbowed Jessica to get her attention. "Are you upset yet?"

"Yes, greatly."

"Good, good." He paused then, "Oh, I mean, if you're *too* upset, let me know and I can tell Magda to tone it down with the judgmental head shakes."

Jessica slipped him some side eye. "It's not her gestures that I find upsetting." Then her head swiveled around toward him. "Wait. You know Magda?"

"Psh, no. Not personally. But technically the buck stops with me when it comes to her job. So I just have to write up a memo, and then my assistant hands it to his assistant and so on and so forth until Magda gets word."

"No, that's not necessary," Jessica said, unsure what else there was to say.

It wasn't until the news returned from another commercial break that Jessica found out why Jimmy had told her to tune in.

It started with Magda, and Jessica couldn't help but wonder if the woman knew what sort of a lunatic could determine whether she worked another day in the industry she'd probably spent her whole life clawing through. *"As elections for the Texas Railroad Commissioner position loom, one Texan you might recognize has thrown his hat into the ring."*

"That's right, folks," Steve said, *"Midland's own mayor and self-proclaimed voice of the new messiah, Jessica Christ, has decided to run for the coveted position of Railroad Commissioner, as he announced in a press conference early this morning."*

The screen cut to Jimmy standing outside the original White Light Church, which Jessica almost didn't recognize due to a few massive structural add-ons. But one thing that remained from the two times Jessica had visited the grounds was the giant statue of Jimmy, which was visible just over the real Jimmy's right shoulder. He was dressed in the same attire she'd seen him in hours before, except his hair gel seemed to have a much firmer grasp as he addressed the crowd at his press conference. *"I've served Midland the best I know how, and I'm proud to say I'm the best Midland has ever seen. But my quest to put God back in government doesn't stop at the edge of the Midland city limits. That would be unfair to the millions of others who don't benefit from my efforts. It's time to expand the reach of my stewardship, and while many of my esteemed colleagues have encouraged me to run for the governor of this great state, I reject that notion. The office of governor is seductive, make no mistake, but I prayed to God and asked where He wanted me, and He said, 'Jimmy, your entire life has been leading you on a path that does not take you through the Governor's Mansion. Reflect and you will see what path I have laid before you.'*

"So here I am today to announce that I will be running for Texas Railroad Commissioner, and I believe that if you read Railed to the Cross, *you will understand how my whole life has been leading up to this moment and that I'm the absolute best man for the job."*

The screen cut back to the studio. Steve asked, *"Have you read* Railed to the Cross, *Magda?"*

"Not yet, should I?"

"I did and enjoyed it. Great read."

"Alright then!"

Steve straightened the papers on his desk then looked into the camera. *"Look who's back! It's Mr. Swine Flu!"*

Jessica shut off the TV. "What the hell is the Texas Railroad Commission?" This had obviously been Jimmy's play from the start, but why?

Jeremy stared wide-eyed at the black TV screen. "Wow. This is bad."

"Huh? Why?"

"This is really bad."

She shoved him in the shoulder to get his attention. "Why? Why is this really bad?"

He snapped out of his fugue and looked her dead in the eyes. "For years, the Texas Railroad Commission was one of the most powerful groups in the country, not just the state. Once OPEC came around, some of that control was taken out of the hands of the TRC, but it still holds a frightening amount of power." He shook his head. "I should have known this day would come."

"Hey. I have literally no idea what anything you're saying means, but it's freaking me the hell out."

He grabbed her by the shoulders. "It should." He let go and began pacing around the living room. Finally he stopped and turned toward her, a balled fist held anxiously beneath his chin. "Railroads have long since become federally regulated, meaning the TRC has almost nothing to do with them. What it does regulate, though, is the oil and gas industry. It used to be on a much larger scale—they could determine how much was drilled and sold—they essentially controlled the prices. OPEC took that away from them, at least at face value. Then we created three seats as Railroad Commissioner to split the power, but there's still a top dog among the three. So now the Texas Railroad Commission controls oil and natural gas production in Texas but pretends it doesn't."

"Meaning?"

"Do you realize how much money there is in oil?"

"Obviously not, because you seem to and you look like you're on the verge of a nervous breakdown."

"That's because I am," he spat. "Jessica, the most powerful Texan hasn't been the governor for a very long time. The office that holds the most power in this state is the Chairman of the Texas Railroad Commissioners."

"Shit ... balls." She stood from the couch, too, her heart speeding up. "But wait! Jimmy doesn't know anything about oil and natural gas, does he?"

Jeremy shut his eyes and shook his head, swallowing hard before replying. "Not that I saw mentioned in his book, but he does have quite an intimate knowledge of the railroads of America."

"But you said the TRC has nothing to do with railroads! He shouldn't get elected just because it *sounds* like he *kind of* knows what he's talking about!"

"Jessica!" he shouted, wiping a hand over his mouth, "This is politics. That's the only reason anyone gets elected for anything!"

"Calm down!" she shouted. "Just calm down!" They stared at each other for a moment, breathing heavily. She tried to come up with something, anything, that might work in her favor. "What about the campaign, though, huh? Some reporter asks him about how he'll protect the state from another oil bust, and he won't know what to say."

"You're not listening!" Jeremy grabbed her by the shoulders and shook her, and she let him, feeling like she deserved it somehow. "*Nobody* follows state elections. Most people hear Texas Railroad Commissioner and think what you thought, that it's a job about railroads. It's the most dangerous misnomer in the state. Maybe even in the country, outside of Best Buy. Or Burger King. Or Old Navy." He stopped the shaking abruptly, staring vacantly over her shoulder and out the window that overlooked downtown. "Imagine this. People go to the voting booths, having learned nothing about any of the candidates, as people are wont to do. They see the word railroad, and only recognize Jimmy's name, which he's made sure is synonymous with the image of a young boy of good-ol'-days America riding a boxcar into the great unknown like some nineteen-eighties-Spielberg-coming-of-age porn. Then below his name, maybe there's someone named Carolyn Gaylord. You gonna put your money on Carolyn Gaylord winning that race?"

That was a no-brainer. "Fuuuuuck." Jessica plopped down onto the couch. "You're right. Jimmy's going to win. Jimmy's going to become the most powerful politician in Texas."

Chapter Twenty

She was down to her last handful of pennies. Since she refused to touch the two hundred grand in the bank and couldn't use a credit card to buy lotto tickets (which was fine, since she'd quit that cold turkey and resolved not to relapse) her options were to either call Wendy for more, like she usually did, or earn the money herself.

She would go with the latter, assuming her job application would be approved in a timely manner.

First things first, though. She had to submit the application.

After tossing a few pennies to Earle, who immediately called her cheap, she paused and looked down where he sat on a ratty plaid blanket on the chilly cement. "I don't disagree. But is that the only reason why you hate me? You really do seem to hate me."

He pouted his lips and shook his head sharply. "Nah. I don't hate you."

"Then why do you act like it?"

He leaned away from her cautiously. "I dunno. Because giving someone pennies seems like an empty gesture? Or maybe because I do a lot of drugs."

"Are you high right now?"

"Psh. Of course. Wouldn't you be if we switched places?"

She looked up and down the dirty downtown street. It was mostly vacant except for a homeless woman camped a little farther down and a spattering of sleekly dressed professionals either chatting on their phones as they passed or pretending to chat on their phones as they passed so they didn't have to engage with the homeless. "Yeah, probably so. How do you afford the drugs?"

"Not with pennies, that's for damn sure." He glared at her.

"At least I give you something. I don't even have to do that," she reminded him ... and herself.

"Oh sure. And I suppose you think I should just get up and go get myself a job, right?"

"Well, now that you mention it, yes."

"Too bad," said Earle. "I can't."

"Why can't you?"

He shrugged. "I'm a felon."

"From what?"

"My last job."

She made a T with flat palms. "Time out. What was your last job?"

"Selling drugs."

She mimicked slapping herself on the forehead. "Well duh, Earle! That's why you shouldn't sell drugs."

"I didn't have a choice," he croaked.

She braced her hands on her hips, feeling like maybe if she scolded Earle *just* so, he might change his ways. "And why's that?"

"I had to afford drugs."

"Oh, you just had to?"

"Yeah," he said exasperatedly, his mouth hanging open on the end vowel. "Because I'm an *addict*."

Earle was a tough egg to crack. Personal responsibility clearly didn't come naturally to him. "And whose fault is that?" She raised an eyebrow like *checkmate* and waited for him to admit logical defeat.

"I dunno, probably my uncle who used to make me shoot up black tar heroin at knifepoint when I was twelve."

Jessica took a quick half step back. "Oh, holy shit. Earle. That's ..."

"Enough to earn me more than"—he dumped the contents of his cup into his palm—"two cents and a Canadian penny?"

"I swear didn't know it was Canadian," she said. "I would give you a dollar, but I don't have any cash."

"Oh boy," he said, licking his cracked lips. "I could live like a king on a dollar!"

She narrowed her eyes. "Uh, okay, you know what? You're acting a little entitled, and I'm not sure it suits your cause."

"Thanks for the tip. Now I got a tip I'd like to give you." He grabbed the stiff crotch of his pants.

"Ew. I'm sorry your uncle is literally evil, but I got to go." She scurried off.

She had more pressing matters today than conversing with an incredibly difficult homeless man with a horrifically tragic story that, in all honesty warranted her sympathy.

But that last comment. Jesus.

YET AGAIN, COMPREHENDING MULTIPLE EMOTIONS PROVES TOO COMPLICATED FOR THE DAUGHTER OF GOD.

You are not seriously narrating my life to me right now.

AS SHE WALKED DOWN FIFTH STREET, FRESH URINE SOAKING INTO THE TOE OF HER RIGHT BOOT ...

Wait, what?

She glanced down at her foot. "God dammit."

... SHE WONDERED, YET AGAIN, IF SHE WAS MAKING THE RIGHT DECISION THIS MORNING.

Get out of my thoughts, and I already know I'm making the right decision. It couldn't be more obvious. I have to do this for myself.

Something about Jimmy's visit with the check preceding the news that he would very likely end up as one of the most powerful people in the state lit a fire underneath Jessica's ass to get out there and make the money herself. Even if it took a while, she needed to be *doing* something. Inaction was no longer an option. Opening another food truck was likely the smarter route, but until she could ensure that it didn't get burned to the ground, too, she just didn't want to go there. It was too easy to burn a trailer.

When I get my own storefront, I'm gonna install so many cameras, even Magda Masterson's head will spin.

Starting another food truck, though ... no, the grief was still too fresh. It would be a classic case of "fool me once ..."

According to Dr. Bell, the minimum she needed before she could get the ball rolling and shop for locations was thirty-five thousand dollars. That would make for a lean opening, though, so she was shooting for forty-four. The extra nine grand would help her afford a state-of-the-art security system that included floodlights, an alarm system throughout, half a dozen security cameras, and remote control bars that would lower down over the doors and windows with the touch of a button. The bakery would open only once it was equipped to moonlight as a goddamn fortress.

Working at a coffee shop wasn't a far cry from working at a bakery. She intended to serve coffee at her shop, and Bat-Ass Brew always had a few stale bran muffins sitting forlornly in a glass display case.

Since she'd never held a job before, she decided to be realistic about her skills and what level of work she could and couldn't get. She wondered if she could get a job interning in a company that would put her business skills to use, but apparently, no one paid interns, which negated the entire purpose.

Forty-four thousand dollars. It wouldn't be hard, considering she didn't pay rent and could always open another credit card to buy groceries on until her business started making money. Regardless of what Dr. Bell said, Jessica was sure she could find a way to make that in a year, tops. If one job wasn't enough for it, she'd work two.

And by then Jimmy will be in control of the energy sector and who knows what new ways he'll find to ruin my plans.

She couldn't think like that. If she didn't want to wait a year, she'd just have to get a third job. Or become Austin's best barista. And perhaps part of her hoped that God would send in a few incredible tippers, but she refused to fully acknowledge that hope.

As she walked in, the skunky smell of coffee assaulted her, but she leaned into it. This would be her smell for the next year at least. She needed to embrace it.

"Hey, Rebel," she said as she approached the counter.

"Sup, boo."

"I noticed y'all are hiring, and I want to fill out an application."

As his eyes scanned her lecherously from head to toe, he nodded sharply. "Rad. Picking up a second gig?" He reached underneath the counter and pulled out a paper application before grabbing a pen from a coffee mug full of beans and pens, and sliding that and the application toward her.

"No. A first gig."

"But you're always in here working on ... I dunno, sexy

business stuff. You look real serious, like some hot lady boss. Figured you were one of those slacker billionaires."

She blinked to reset her brain. "You thought I was a slacker billionaire who needed a second job?"

He bounced his shoulders. "I don't pretend to understand billionaires. I'm glad you're applying, though. I've been checking you out from afar. It'll be nice to work up close with you."

She paused in writing her street address, seriously reconsidered handing over that sensitive information to someone like Rebel, and glared up at him. "Excuse me?"

"Your energy is just bangin' like nothing I've ever seen." He leaned back, framing her up with his hands, presumably trying to spot the best angle from which to sexually harass her. "You've got a super crazy, reflective aura around you."

"Oh for fuck's sake. *You?*"

"Me what?"

She snatched up the application and pen. "I'm gonna go sit at a table and fill out the rest of this."

She sat and reconsidered whether she wanted to work at a place with an angel who apparently had no filter and was a little dense. If Chris ever met Rebel, she was sure it wouldn't end well.

Wait, did angels fight each other? That didn't seem like a thing.

I bet the Bible talks about this.

Nope, still not reading it.

She filled out the application, waited until Rebel was

busy with a customer, then did a walk-by drop off on her way out.

If Jimmy Dean wasn't going to keep her from reaching her goals, neither was Rebel.

But damn, did she really have to work with that guy? Maybe this wasn't such a good idea after all. Maybe she should just apply for a small loan. Surely forty-four grand wasn't that hard to get. Hell, the federal government had offered her way more for college without her even asking. They'd practically tried to trick her into taking it. Maybe her insistence on earning the rest the hard way was just another self-imposed obstacle to keep from shooting for her dream. After all, failing sucks, but when the people you care most about have scrounged up two hundred thousand dollars for your goal, "suck" doesn't even come close to how failure feels.

Would God let her business fail?

That depends on the point he's trying to prove that day.

The tip of her shoe caught on something on the ground, and she was forced to take a quick, long step to keep from falling face first onto the sidewalk outside Bat-Ass Brew. Looking down at the pavement, she spotted what had caused it: a fat, brown leather wallet, which was now five feet ahead of her. She grabbed it and stared at it for a moment before deciding the temporary breach of privacy would be forgiven if she could find an ID and return it to its owner.

But when she opened the wallet, no ID was immediately visible. In fact, the wallet was empty except for the thick stack of bills tucked inside. She peeked at it and saw that, yes, those were hundred dollar bills. Easily twenty of them. But taking them out to count in the middle of the sidewalk was perhaps the most clear-cut example of "asking for it," that anyone could concoct.

She wasn't a fool. This had God's name written all over it. Well, literally, if she counted His name on the currency. But also figuratively. Although, God was rarely subtle, and had He put this wallet in her path, she would've assumed it contained forty-four thousand dollars in it, not two thousand or so. Was He getting sneakier or was this good luck?

Maybe it *was* a coincidence. And maybe, because there was no way to identify the owner, she had a right to keep it. Two grand was no chump change and might shave a couple weeks off her time working a crappy job for minimum wage.

When she opened the wallet again, using her body to shield it from view of anyone who might walk past, she ran her finger over the edge of the bills and that's when she saw it.

The scratch-off. *The Ultimate Answer! Win up to $42k!*

"Of course." She pulled up the maps on her phone and typed in *police station*. Perhaps the owner of the wallet might find the lotto ticket a dud, but a couple grand cash was a couple grand cash.

The police station was a fifteen-minute walk, but the

early December air wasn't too chilly, and it was a clear day, so she happily started on the route.

The phone buzzed in her hand, and she glanced down to see Chris calling.

"Hey there," she said.

"Hey, *Hermione*. How's your day?" he replied, referencing the previous night's dream in a sad attempt at a British accent.

She giggled. "Oh, fine. Better now that I can hear your voice, Neville." She paused, debating whether to tell him about her job application, but something held her back. "God just tempted me again, so I'm heading to the police station now."

Chris broke character. "You're reporting God to the police?"

"No, I'm ... well, I guess in a way, yeah. I'm returning a lost wallet that I assume he pickpocket-ed from some poor soul. What's up with you?"

"I got big news."

Yeah, that made sense. Chris hated the phone, preferring texting. She should have known something was up. "Spill it."

"I was invited to the NFL combine."

"Wow. I vaguely understand that's a good thing!"

"Jess, it means I'm going to be drafted! I mean, as long as I don't totally screw it up or injure myself or ... oh God, I feel sick."

She tucked the wallet under her armpit as she headed

east toward the station. "Breathe, Chris. Nothing bad is going to happen."

"Did your dad tell you that?"

"Yes," she lied. "Just now. He said he wouldn't let anything ruin your career before it even started. He loves watching you play." She grimaced at her own dishonesty.

Chris sighed heavily. "You always say He's kind of a dick, but I dunno, Jess. He has our back when it counts, you know?"

"Uh, sure."

"Oh! And there's more good news! Both the Cowboys and the Texans are in desperate need of a QB. The Texans are looking for a starter, so I don't know what the odds are of them picking me over, say, Willie Frank Epstein. But the Cowboys are looking for a rookie backup, and I know for a fact I'm their style of QB. In that case, I would make bank *and* get to stay in Texas. Granted, it would be up by Dallas, but I'd take it since it would be an easy weekend trip to come see you."

"And more importantly," she added, "all your child-hood dreams would come true."

"Well, yeah, there's that, too. I mean, the Cowboys, Jessica! America's Team! I'd be following in the footsteps of greats like Troy Aikman, Roger Staubach—"

Ooo! She had this! It was one of the few pro football things she'd learned it through Texan osmosis: "Tony Romo."

"No, no. *Greats*, Jess. But you're getting better at talking football in general."

She turned the corner and spotted the police station across the street. "I'm so happy for you, Chris. When will you know for sure?"

"Not until the actual draft. Things can change, though. I'm trying not to get my hopes up."

"Then there's no point in worrying about it now. We'll cross that bridge when we get to it."

There was silence on the other end, then Chris rasped, "I love you, Jess."

Oh no, was he about to cry?

Change the subject.

"Did you hear about Jimmy's latest move?" she asked.

"No. Douchebag's still not dead yet?"

"Unfortunately no. But he *is* running for Texas Railroad Commissioner."

Chris chuckled. "Great. There are a lot of railroads in this state. Sounds like a boring job to me, but maybe that'll keep him busy and out of your hair."

Damn it. Jeremy was right. No one had a clue. She considered explaining the actual significance of the job to Chris, but decided now wasn't the time. No point putting a crimp in his celebration.

"Yeah, maybe so," she replied. "Hey, I just got to the police station, so I'm gonna return this wallet before someone jumps me."

He laughed. "Right. Gotta watch your back in Austin. You know, because it's so *dangerous.*"

"I know, I know ..." They exchanged sappy goodbyes and then Jess crossed the street toward the station.

The lobby was well lit but sparse. A group of three male officers gathered by a door leading through the glass partition, one talking animatedly and acting out what Jessica assumed was a recent call, while the other two laughed along.

The woman in full police uniform sitting behind the partition looked up from the newspaper sudoku only when Jessica cleared her throat. A small nameplate on the desk indicated she was speaking to Ofc. Tambreshia Valencia.

"Yes, ma'am? Can I help you?"

"I found this wallet on the street and wanted to get it back to its owner." She set the wallet on the counter and slid it in the hollowed out hemisphere beneath the glass.

Without reaching for it, the woman asked, "Did you see an ID in it?"

"No, ma'am. I couldn't find anything to help identify an owner."

Officer Valencia inspected Jessica skeptically, then pulled the wallet out and opened it up. Her tired eyes shot wide. "Oh wow. That's a lot of money."

"Yeah. And there's a lottery ticket, too, but it's probably a dud."

"They usually are," the woman responded offhand-edly. "These things are basically a poor tax. Don't get me started." She set the wallet back down and swiveled in her chair to face a computer to her left. "What's your name?"

"Jessica McCloud."

"Date of birth?"

"July seventh—"

The woman swiveled back quickly, squinting at Jessica's face. "Wait a minute. Don't I know you?"

Jessica searched her memory, but she was pretty sure any encounter with a cop would pop right up, and none did. "Not that I remember."

Officer Valencia pointed at her. "No." She waggled her finger, a grin spreading across her lips. "No, I do know you. My daughter follows you on Twitter. She loves you. Jessica Christ, right? That's your stage name?"

"It's not a stage name, but—"

"Ahh yes, it's all coming back to me. TheRealMcCloud, that's your Twitter handle, right?"

Laughing uncomfortably, Jessica nodded.

"You gonna tweet about this?"

"Well, I don't actually do the—" No, Cash wouldn't be okay with her admitting that. "Yes, I'll probably tweet about it."

When Officer Valencia stared at her patiently and expectantly, Jessica took the hint and pulled out her phone. "Drafting a tweet right now."

She pulled open her ongoing conversation with Cash. The last message was from them and read, *For the love of God, please go do something outdoors and send me a pic.*

She hadn't done that, but maybe a story about returning a found wallet would do. She shot off a message and then looked back up at Tambreshia, who was still waiting patiently.

"All done. So, um, will that wallet make it back to its owner?"

"Oh, heavens no, child." The officer chuckled. "I mean, maybe if someone comes in here looking for a wallet with a bunch of hundred dollar bills and a"—she peeked inside—"an Ultimate Answer scratch-off, we'll be able to make the match, but my guess is that anyone with this many big bills who's also buying tickets isn't the type of person used to getting money in any legal way. Probably someone who doesn't generally see eye-to-eye with the law."

"Ah. Okay." God had done it again. Not only was He offering Jessica a way to her dream, He was also likely taking money from a criminal who had earned it through shady dealings. Probably a human trafficker or something. Damn, He was good at this. She had to hand it to Him, He really was the Ultimate Multitasker.

Officer Valencia leaned forward. "I was wondering why anyone in their right mind would bring in an unidentifiable wallet full of cash, but this makes sense." She fumbled with it and it fell back into the hemisphere drop box. "Oops." She nodded at the computer screen. "I haven't entered in this report yet if you, you know." Her eyes moved to the wallet, now within Jessica's reach.

It took a second, but then it sank in. "Oh. No. No, I really don't want it."

The woman stuck her lips out and nodded slowly, her whole body rocking slightly in her chair. "Nice. Maybe you're the real deal after all. Or at least close enough to call it. Hey, do you mind if I get a picture with you? My daughter thinks I'm a hardass, and it would go a long way if

I could show you and I are, you know, cool with each other."

There was only one possible answer that she could see here. "Yeah, sure."

"Stay there."

Officer Valencia stood from her chair, and a moment later, she appeared at the door leading into the lobby. She motioned for the three male officers to come with her, and soon Jessica found herself surrounded on all sides by the cops. "McCloud, eh?" said a tall, bald man with a round face and squinty eyes. The pin on his chest identified him as *Jones 3624*. "My son has a poster of you up on his wall."

"Eek. There are posters of me?"

Jones chuckled as the desk clerk sidled up beside Jess and threw an arm around her shoulder, handing her phone to a stocky officer named Olivarro 4539.

Jessica smiled and once the photos were taken, Officer Valencia swapped places with Jones 3624. Jessica moved as close as she could to the Jones without the handle of his Taser jabbing into her ribs. His torso had no give and she realized he was wearing a bulletproof vest. "My son's gonna die," he said right before the phone flashed. "I mean, not literally. But you know how the kids say. I'm gonna hang this over his head for a long time."

"Ooo! My turn!" said Montenegro 5518 as he wedged himself between Jones 3624 and Jessica.

Is this my karma? Is this what I get for turning down your assistance, God? An impromptu photo shoot?

Thankfully, she'd put a little effort into her appearance today, since she was going by Bat-Ass Brew to apply. Not that she'd needed to; not even a bad hair day could stop the onslaught of Rebel's compulsive harassment. But it made her feel good and confident, so she'd done it.

And now she was especially glad she had.

She smiled and the phone flashed again.

It wasn't that she didn't like the officers. In fact, she was surprised by how friendly they were. The issue was more that Austin was usually a safe place to exist without people asking for a photo. People didn't expect celebrities of any caliber to be wandering around, for one, and she'd observed a strange phenomenon wherein the city attracted a lot of people who looked vaguely famous—either they were the doppelganger of someone well-known, or they just had that air to them, like one *should* know their name —but were actually just living on a friend's couch. Add that to the stealth of big sunglasses and her Rangers cap, and she was usually able to move around without being recognized. And perhaps it was the desire of people in this town to play it cool that also held the picture requests at bay.

But none of those reasons slowed these officers.

"She just turned in a wallet full of thousands of dollars cash," Officer Valencia informed the others, nodding approvingly and puffing up her chest like a proud mother. "No ID, nothing. She could've made off with it, but she came straight here."

"Impressive," said Jones 3624.

"And, let's be real," added Olivarro 4539, "probably smart for safety reasons."

Jones 3624 nodded wisely. "True. Carrying that much cash on you is, well, kind of asking for it around here."

"Even in a safe city?" Jessica asked.

The officers' heads swiveled around to stare down at her, and the casual conversation stopped. "No," said Montenegro 5518, "Austin is *not* a safe city."

"That's not even a thing," added Officer Valencia, "a safe city."

Jones 3624 rolled back his shoulders, hooking his thumbs into his duty belt. "I've arrested twelve, count 'em, twelve men for aggravated assault with a deadly weapon this week."

Montenegro 5518 nodded. "And I was just telling these guys about the hat trick of transient-related incidents I responded to last night. The last one was a real doozie. Some dumb tourist tried to take a picture of one of their dogs. Well, *obviously* that's going to set her off, so out comes the rusty razor blade."

"Holy crap," Jessica said. "But literally everyone I've talked to has told me this is a safe city."

"Everyone is wrong," Jones 3624 said unblinkingly. "So very wrong."

"Huh." Jessica looked from one officer to the next, but not a single face indicated that this might be elaborate prank like a good part of her hoped it was. "Then what the hell?"

"It's called denial," said Officer Valencia. "Granted, we

might be slightly biased, since our jobs require us to deal exclusively with criminals and victims, but let's just say there are a *lot* of us working in this city, and there's never a dull moment. Hell, I signed up for overtime working this desk just so I could have a dull moment. And then here you come walking in, making it anything but."

Jessica nodded along. "So why does everyone want to pretend there isn't crime when there is?"

"Million dollar question, Ms. McCloud," Olivarro 4539 said, slapping her congenially on the arm. "My guess is that it's the same reason most people do anything: because it *feels* good."

"Stay safe out there," Jones 3624 said as the cops slowly started to peel off. "Just assume everybody's armed to the teeth."

"Because they probably are," added Montenegro 5518 before the four cops headed through the door and into the back of the station, leaving Jessica all alone to face the outside world by herself, totally unarmed.

Well, except for the smiting.

I gotta get back to the range.

Chapter Twenty-One

As Jessica left the police station, zipping up her cotton jacket against the early December wind, she reassured herself that regret for turning in the money was a totally natural thing to feel. That was a lot of cash. What would happen to the money if no one claimed it? It would probably just sit in an evidence locker until someone got smart and skimmed off the top. More power to whoever decided to do that, rather than letting the money sit out of circulation, she supposed.

To alleviate her regret, she decided her good deed, though stupid in hindsight, had at least earned her a real lunch. Tacos would do. Tacos always did.

Her favorite spot was eleven blocks away and just off her route back to the condo, so surely that was a sign. Or at least it would be if she thought God cared enough to give her signs that were actually useful in her daily life, like what to eat for lunch.

She arrived during the rush, sunglasses on to avoid another photo request that might lose her her place in line, and splurged on a crispy taco plate to-go, rice and beans and all.

As she stood against the wall by the Coke machine, waiting for her number to be called, someone said her name. Her initial instinct to ignore it was overridden by recognition. She looked toward the door and almost couldn't believe who was standing there waving.

"Mrs. Thomas?" she said, walking over.

"Jessica! I thought it was you!" Mrs. Thomas wrapped her up in her arms, enveloping her in her soft body.

"What are you doing in Austin?" Jessica asked as she stepped back.

"Just a required TEA workshop I have to attend if I wish to keep my job. Come here every year for it. Incredibly boring stuff. You ordering food?"

"Already did." She held up her ticket at the same time she heard her number called. "That's me."

"Won't you stay and have lunch with me?" Mrs. Thomas asked.

Jessica grinned. "Of course. I'll get us a table."

She grabbed her food and found a booth toward the back that allowed her to face most of the restaurant—Jones 3624's warning about nowhere in the city being safe left Jessica edgy, so until the paranoia subsided, she would take necessary precautions, thank you very much.

Mrs. Thomas slid into the booth a few minutes later,

her taco salad on a tray, and settled in, unwrapping her plastic silverware and saying, "I haven't heard from you in quite a while, Jessica. I hope everything's okay." While there was nothing accusatory about her tone, Mrs. Thomas's words watered the seeds of guilt Jessica had planted long before.

"It's great. I should have emailed you more. I just get caught up in things and forget about everything else."

"Oh, Jessica, it's not a big deal." Mrs. Thomas smiled kindly. "I'm not hurt. I just like to know you're okay. I find myself worrying about you, given your contentious position in this world. Lots of people want to see you fail, and that's a tough position to be in, I imagine."

Jessica nodded. Mrs. Thomas wasn't wrong. However, Jessica's attention had been slowly pulled away from the woman's sympathetic words by a familiar-looking man sitting a few tables over. He stared over at their booth unabashedly, narrowing his eyes with suspicion as he sipped his drink.

Where did she know him from? In another context, she might've said he was her type—slim, athletic build, scruffy blond hair, golden skin, and dark eyelashes she could spot from ten feet away. Even his nose was attractive, straight with delicately sculpted nostrils.

And man, he wouldn't stop giving her the evil eye.

"What is it?" Mrs. Thomas said. Her eyes followed Jessica's as they snuck covert glances at the man, and as Mrs. Thomas started to turn in her seat, Jessica quickly said, "Nothing. Don't look. Just some guy staring at us. I recognize him, but I can't place it yet."

Mrs. Thomas leaned forward mischievously. "Is he checking you out?"

"Uh, no. He's mean mugging me."

Mrs. Thomas leaned back. "Well, sometimes it's hard to tell the difference. Men are terrifying creatures, both simple and indecipherable at once."

Jessica scoffed. "Ain't it the truth."

"Just ignore him. Don't let his issues ruin what is a perfectly serendipitous meeting of old friends."

Jessica nodded and unloaded her to-go bag. "I'm starving anyway."

Mrs. Thomas grinned. "Tell me what you've been up to in Austin. I've heard rumors, but I never give those much credence when it comes to your life. Otherwise, I would have to believe that you're both the messiah and the antichrist at the same time, and that would be especially confusing."

Jessica mashed up her beans and rice. "I'm opening a bakery."

"Pardon?"

"A bakery. I can turn basically anything gluten-free with a wave of my hands." She shrugged apologetically. "I figure I should use that."

"That's fantastic!" Mrs. Thomas said, setting down her fork and clapping excitedly. "When do you open your doors? I'll be the first one in line."

"It'll probably be another year or so before I do."

"Oh," Mrs. Thomas said, reeling in her excitement. "Why's that?"

"Well ..." She wasn't in the mood to bring up money. It was only noon and she was pretty much money-ed out. Her eyes wandered over to the blond, who continued to stare at her, even as he tilted his head to crunch into his crispy taco. She looked away.

"It's money, isn't it?" Mrs. Thomas said. "Starting a business isn't cheap. I get it. How much do you still need?"

"Not that much more. Miranda and some of my friends from college raised most of it for me, but they said they'd exhausted their connections before they could get all of it."

"You are incredibly lucky to have found Miranda. She's an amazing friend. But I do find it strange that this is the first I've heard about fundraising efforts."

"I think they were trying to keep it quiet so the news didn't take it and run with the whole Moochsiah name."

"Moochsiah?"

Jessica waved it off. "Nothing, just a dumb Twitter thing."

"I would have donated in a heartbeat. And I'd still like to. How much more do you need?"

Jessica shifted uncomfortably in the booth, staring down at her taco plate. "Not that much. I can earn the rest myself. And I should." She mustered the courage to meet Mrs. Thomas's eye. "Dr. Bell—she's a professor of mine who's been helping me with the business part—she suggested I have some personal buy-in to increase my chances of the bakery succeeding."

Mrs. Thomas nodded. "Fair enough. She sounds like a smart lady."

"She is."

Mrs. Thomas dug into her food, which allowed Jessica to do the same. After a few minutes, Mrs. Thomas jumped back in. "I hope you will excuse me if I'm wrong, but is your reluctance to accept help on this last hurdle possibly a delaying tactic?" She hitched a thin brow at Jessica. "Because I know you, and I know you don't like the spotlight, and the daughter of the big man himself opening a bakery would be sure to attract media attention, and then suddenly the success of your business is also tied into a large swath of the population's religious beliefs."

Jessica chuckled under her breath. Of course Mrs. Thomas would get at the root of the issue. Despite their time without speaking, Mrs. Thomas seemed to understand Jessica better than almost anyone else. Sometimes even better than she understood herself.

"Maybe," she said sheepishly. Then, "Yeah, you're probably right."

"I propose that risking your reputation is enough of a buy-in to this project to ensure you work your ass off on it. There's a lot at stake already without you having to invest your own money."

Ugh. I hate how right she is.

"Agreed."

"So what about this, Jessica? You tell me how much more you need, I write you a check, and you pay me back as the bakery makes money and you feel like you have wiggle room. It's not a gift, it's just an interest-free loan. Does that sound like a deal you might take?"

Jessica leaned back in the booth, folding her arms across her chest, and staring up at the ceiling to consider it.

On the one hand, she would be taking on debt that she wasn't certain she could repay. That would be stressful for sure. She would feel terrible if she left someone she cared about high and dry because of her inability to keep a small business open in the best possible market for said small business. It was the same basic fear she'd had going into her application at the credit union, except with a more poignant personal shame at stake.

On the other hand, Mrs. Thomas probably understood the risk. The woman was smarter than Jessica by a long shot. And she probably also understood Jessica's fear of being unable to repay on time since she was smarter about Jessica than Jessica was—also by a long shot.

Taking the deal would mean opening the bakery. When? In a few months? In a few weeks? Everything was lined up except that stupid forty-four grand. If she worked at Bat-Ass Brew to earn the rest, her fear and self-doubt would be there once she had the money, it would just be further in the future.

Then a new thought occurred to her. It felt fresh and

invigorating, like a drink of cool water after running circles in the sun for hours.

Mrs. Thomas didn't have to offer, but she did. Maybe I should believe her when she says she wants to help. Maybe Jesus was right. Maybe letting her help me is the mark of a good friend and refusing help makes me selfish, not self-sufficient.

Ugh. Stupid Jesus.

She opened her eyes. "Thirty-five grand."

Mrs. Thomas tilted her head forward. "That's it? You only need thirty-five thousand dollars?"

"Well, I was shooting for forty-four, but I can find some way to earn nine thousand for myself."

Mrs. Thomas held up a hand. "Stop. Stop getting in your own way, Jessica. While education may not be the most lucrative career, let us not forget I'm married to a congressman. We're doing okay for ourselves, is what I'm saying, and we made it clear to Sandra that she has to pay her way through college, so with her out of the house and Fischer too unfocused and rebellious to particulate in any extracurriculars, we're feeling a bit flush." She reached in her large purse and pulled out a checkbook and a pen.

Jessica was almost too stunned to be happy. "That's ... um, thanks. You really don't have to if—"

"Stop it." Mrs. Thomas's sharp tone was one Jessica had witnessed a handful of times but one of which she'd never been on the receiving end. It shut her up immediately.

"Okay," she said meekly.

As Mrs. Thomas wrote out the check, Jessica sucked air into her lungs for the first time since she woke up that morning, resigned to working at Bat-Ass Brew alongside everybody's favorite pervert barista, Rebel.

She was doing it. She was actually going to be able to open the bakery. "I'll pay you back right away, I promise."

Mrs. Thomas laughed patiently. "I know you will, Jessica. I wouldn't offer this to someone I didn't believe in."

"No, but seriously. I want you to hold me accountable for it. Don't say it's a loan and then never expect it back. Hold my feet to the fire on this, or I'll feel guilty forever if I forget and miss a payment."

Mrs. Thomas rolled her eyes as she signed the check. "Fine. Would it make you feel better if we wrote up a quick contract?"

"Yes! Yes, let's do that. I don't have a lawyer, but I know someone who's dating a couple of them, and—oh! My friend Kate's uncle is one, too."

She stopped jabbering when it was clear by Mrs. Thomas's slight grimace that she was going overboard.

Mrs. Thomas cleared her throat gently. "If you want to get lawyers involved, we can. Or we can just keep it simple. I've done this sort of thing quite a bit, so I know how to jot down a simple and binding contract." She held up her hands. "Totally up to you, though."

"No, no," Jessica said. "It's fine. I just got ahead of myself. If you're okay with this, so am I. As long as it means you'll hold me to it."

Mrs. Thomas reached in her purse, pulled out a legal

pad, flipped to a fresh page, and began scribbling out the contract. Trying not to hover, Jessica looked around the taco bar. The blond was still there, but this time he waved to her. Shit. Where did she know him from? It was at the tip of her tongue.

When he motioned with a crooked finger for her to go to him, she cringed and looked away. The cops weren't kidding about everyone in this town being a psychopath.

"There," Mrs. Thomas said. "This says that I'll give you forty-four thousand dollars to do with as you will, and you'll pay me back the forty-four thousand dollars in payments of five hundred a month once your profit from the bakery exceeds ten thousand a month for three months in a row. That way you'll still have plenty to live on and the payments won't be a burden."

"And if I don't pay you back? Is there something in there about that?"

"Yep." Mrs. Thomas grinned. "Right here." She pointed to the words midway down the page and read them aloud. "For each month you fail to pay, I'll receive unlimited baked goods and beverages from your business."

Jessica laughed. "Fair enough. Where do I sign?"

Mrs. Thomas spun the pad around and pointed to the line at the very bottom of the page. "Oh, but please do read it for yourself before you do. I'd hate to teach you a bad habit by encouraging you to sign a contract you haven't read for yourself."

"Good point. Especially if I'm opening a business."

Mrs. Thomas wagged her finger playfully. "Too true."

She grinned back at her former teacher before turning her eyes to the legal pad, hardly focusing as she grinned at her luck. This random encounter with Mrs. Thomas was almost too good to be—

Wait a second.

She glanced up at her former principal. "This is going to sound strange, but why did you decide to come *here* for lunch?"

Mrs. Thomas was clearly taken aback. "You're right, that does sound strange. I came here because it's right near the conference, and I'm lazy and like tacos. Not a terribly interesting reason, I'm afraid."

"There were no, like, weird coincidences that brought you here? Nothing having to do with lottery tickets or ... anything else?"

"Are you feeling all right, Jessica?"

"It's just such a strange coincidence. I guess I've become a little suspicious of good timing." She leaned forward to avoid being overheard. "God keeps trying to trick me into accepting his help, and I won't. I'm absolutely certain his help comes with a price."

Mrs. Thomas nodded slowly like she was starting to understand. "Yes, well, that's why I prefer contracts. Everything comes with a price, so I find it comforting to know exactly what that price is."

"So, you're not another one of God's ploys to help me?"

She chuckled. "I doubt it. I can be a little deaf when it comes to divine signs. Plus, I'd been thinking about this taco salad since before I left Mooretown. Something about the way they cook the beans. I get it every year when I visit."

Jessica smiled, her suspicions dissolving. "I'll have to order it next time." Maybe not every lucky coincidence was God's doing. After all, Original Mistake was still at play in the world, and though it seemed to function on chaos, even a broken clock is right twice a day.

Jessica grabbed the pen and slid the contract where she could sign it.

"Jessica McCloud," said a voice right next to her, making her jump. She looked up and there was the blond, staring down at her with a stern look on his face. "May I bother you for a photograph of us?"

"Um, no, actually. I'm sort of busy."

This is what I get for taking off my sunglasses.

"Just one photograph. I can use my compact communication device for it. It will be quick." He held up his cell phone.

Jessica exchanged glances with Mrs. Thomas who seemed equally skeezed out.

"Have we met?" Jessica asked. Then it clicked. "Wait. I know you. You came to my food truck a couple times. Yeah. You were stalking Judith, right?" She shook her head. "If you wanted a picture with me, you should have gotten it then. I'm eating right now."

"Yes. I visited your food wagon before it was set on fire. But that bears no connection to why I am here."

Mrs. Thomas's eyes shot open with alarm and she gaped at Jessica. "Someone set your food truck on fire?"

Jessica nodded, the memory weighing her body down into the booth. "Right after this interview I did, someone set it on—Hey, wait!" She sat up straight and glared at the blond. "You were creeping around the week of the fire." She let the insinuation hang in the air.

Mrs. Thomas's nostrils flared and she stared daggers at the man. Jessica felt the waves of aggression flow off the woman as she growled, "I think you should keep moving."

The blond didn't seem to follow the conversation's sudden change of direction. "But—"

"Get lost or we call the cops," Mrs. Thomas insisted more firmly.

With a last pleading glance at Jessica, who offered him no backup, the blond huffed then slowly turned and dragged his heels as he slunk off, grumbling under his breath.

"Thanks," she said to Mrs. Thomas. "Do you think that he could have been the one who did it?"

Mrs. Thomas shrugged sympathetically. "Who knows. Like I said, Jessica, you have a lot of people who want to see you fail. Which is partly why I'm so proud of you for accepting help from the few who want to see you succeed." She glanced over her shoulder where the blond had just left the restaurant. "Maybe you should consider hiring bodyguards when you go out in public."

"Sure. Just as soon as I make my first million."

She signed on the dotted line and slid it back toward

Mrs. Thomas, who took a picture of it with her phone, saying, "I'll text you this picture so you can keep it on file." She tucked her phone away again and added, "In the meantime, I believe this is for you." Beaming, she tore the check from her checkbook and handed it to Jessica. "Congratulations, dear. Your bakery is a go."

Chapter Twenty-Two

Colors seemed more vivid than usual as Jessica paused outside Bat-Ass Brew and took in the sights. As of a half hour ago, when Mrs. Thomas had handed over the check, this was officially Jessica's town. She would settle in, start her business, and become a part of this community, whether the community liked it or not.

She couldn't remember the last time she was this happy, and while fear and doubt still poked at her, insisting there were details to iron out and a possibility of failure, the annoyance was drastically dulled, at least for the time being. And that was good enough.

Rebel was still working, and he acted surprised to see her for a second time that day. "Hey lady," he said as she approached the counter. "Couldn't stay away?"

Not even his creepy comments could get her down, though. "I'll take a Nutellaluna with rabies, and I'd like to withdraw my job application."

His cocky grin faded. "Why's that?"

"Oh, you know, just need an extra pop of energy to get on with my afternoon, and I happened to like hazelnut."

"No, I mean the application."

"Obviously you did. It's just none of your business."

He nodded pensively. "Okay, yeah. Could I recommend a tea blend instead? We just got it in, and it's good for cleansing. Your aura seems muddy right now. Probably not good to add caffeine to that."

It was like he was actively trying to burst her bubble. "Nope. Just the Nutellaluna. And if I could *see* you tear up the application, that would be gratifying, too. There might even be an extra tip in it for you." She extended her credit card, which he swiped begrudgingly. Then he reached below the counter, pulled out the application, held it at eye level, and tore it down the middle. He set the halves on the counter. "I'll get started on your drink *right away.*"

But he didn't budge. So she stepped to the side to wait, wondering how long he would drag it out.

As she found a spot against a large bulletin board, the man who'd been waiting behind her in line started to shout. And at first, she commiserated. More than once had she wanted to shout at Rebel for his atrocious customer service.

But then it dawned on her what the man was shouting about.

"I know you did, you son of a bitch!"

She looked over to see the tense exchange unfold.

Rebel hadn't lost his calm, even as he held up his hands defensively and said something Jessica couldn't hear.

Suddenly the customer lunged across the counter, grabbing Rebel by the collar of his plaid shirt. "I know you fucked her! She told me! You're fucking dead!"

Rebel chopped at the customer's arm, trying to free himself of the grip until he gave up, bent forward, and wriggled free of his shirt.

But that only aggravated the man further, and Jessica wondered if she was dreaming when the man reached in his waistband and pulled out a gun.

Does everyone in this town own a gun?

Then she remembered what state she was in.

So where the hell are all the other guns?

She looked around at her fellow customers, as those closest to the door sprinted out while the rest froze in horror at the scene unfolding.

No one was doing anything, even as the man shook the pistol at Rebel's chest and continued to yell himself into a lather.

But I'm not doing anything either.

She felt the wrath gather in her chest. Good. Very good. This was something she could do. She could stop this and save Rebel's life. But as blood rushed to her face, she became keenly aware she was about to cross a big fat line. Her arms pulsed with the energy, and her fingers started to tingle.

"I didn't do it!" Rebel shouted. "I don't even know an Amber!"

The man with the gun hesitated then took a step back. But then, "I never said what her name was, you dumb fuck!"

No, she couldn't. Rebel didn't deserve to die, but she also wasn't ready to dole out ultimate punishment to another human. (And maybe she empathized with his feelings toward Rebel a little.)

Whatever the reason, she took a different approach, running straight for the man, and shouting, "Drop your—"

She didn't get to finish, though, as the man whirled around, his gun extended at arm's length. She'd hardly made it a step before cramps in both her hamstrings took her legs out from under her, causing her to crumple to the ground in a heap. A gunshot echoed through the restaurant a moment before she hit the old wood floors of the coffee shop. When she looked up, she saw the man staring wide-eyed at her, terrified.

Then quickly he turned and fired off five more rounds.

"Stop!" she screamed, trying to scramble to her feet, but Rebel was already shot multiple times through the chest and head, his limp body crashing into the flavored syrup caddy on the back counter. The gunman sprinted from the coffee shop.

Her vision tunneled and she scrambled to her feet and ran around the counter to find Rebel on the ground. Blood pooled underneath him, and a bullet through the nose presented a gory sight.

"Oh ... God. Oh god oh god." She squatted near him but couldn't bring herself to touch him just yet. There was no hurry, really. She grimaced, made a few awkward noises, then peeked her head above the counter to see if anyone else was still around.

Sure enough, those who hadn't initially fled the scene were still there, though a few girls were now sobbing into the bony chests of their boyfriends.

She squatted down next to Rebel and came up with a quick plan of action. Grabbing four napkins off the counter, she sopped up the blood along his neck before placing her fingers on his pulse.

Except there was no pulse.

Thank whoever! He's dead.

This she could work with.

She glanced up at the counter to see two men and a woman—or were they boys and a girl?—leaning over it with their cell phones aimed at her. "Are you *seriously* filming this?"

They didn't respond but kept their phones steady. The girl then turned hers around to face her said, "Oh my god, I think he's dead," before turning the phone back around

Ooo ... I could just—

THOU SHALT NOT SMITE.

I knew you were here! Thanks for the muscle cramps, asshole! I could've stopped this before it escalated.

THE LORD FINDS IT CUTE HOW YOU THINK THAT.

Don't patronize me right now.

THEN STOP SAYING STUPID THINGS. WHAT

IN YOUR LIFE HAS PREPARED YOU TO TAKE ON A GUNMAN?

Adrenaline?

*YOU WOULD HAVE BEEN **SO VERY** SHOT. WASN'T EVEN CLOSE.*

You're telling me not to smite, yet you antagonize. Always with the antagonizing.

FINE. YOU WANT HELP?

The cell phones exploded in the hands of the amateur filmmakers, who yelped and ran out of the coffee shop.

Oh wow. God had actually made Himself useful. What a pleasant surprise amidst the Greatest Shitshow on Earth. The last thing she needed was to have a video of her kneeling by a dead body that would walk and talk (too much) later on.

BAD NEWS. THEY WERE STREAMING LIVE.

Shitballs!

She would never hear the end of this from Cash. But she'd deal with that later. One thing at a time.

She needed to focus. It'd been years since the last time she'd done what she now had to do, and she didn't want to botch it.

Hovering her hands over Rebel's body—one above his bloody chest, one above his smashed in face—Jessica tried hard not to think of the bullet-riddled Zeta writhing around in the driveway of her childhood home or his agonizing screams as she brought his already decaying body back to life.

Rebel was freshly dead. No doubt he would have a

raging headache and be low iron at first, but his body hadn't started rotting.

Why are these things I have to think about in my life? I hate you so much, Dad.

DID YOU JUST CALL ME DAD?

I'm in distress! Leave me alone!

She closed her eyes and lowered her hands, cringing against the squelching and the warm liquid that bubbled out of him when she made contact.

She'd never *almost* smote and performed a miracle in as close a time frame before, and because of that, she'd never realized how different the two experiences felt. Sure, they both started in her chest like an energy building, like water flowing into a hole in the earth until enough had gathered and it could burst forth as a heavenly geyser, flowing out through her arms, shooting from her hands, remnants trickling down the nerves in her legs. But it was the temperature of the water that felt different. Smiting was boiling liquid through her veins, while her miracles felt like a refreshing spring. It reminded her of the only beach trip she'd ever taken, back when she still lived with her mother in Mooretown ... The sun was brutal, reflecting off the sand and water, and she could feel herself getting burned, regardless of the sunscreen Destinee compulsively lathered on her each time she was within arm's reach. But there was a shower head sticking out of the sand to rinse off with, and though it had taken some convincing for Jess to jump under the cold spray, once she did, the refreshment and sense of relief, of refuge from the heat made her never want to leave. And once she was out, all she'd wanted to do was get painfully overheated again so she had another excuse to experience that immense relief.

Miracles ran through her body like that beach shower had run over her skin, both making her shiver pleasantly.

The power tugged free, and a moment later Rebel's limbs began twitching. He seemed to be unconscious though, so she'd count it a win.

She hurried back and stood, watching him closely, waiting until one of the bullets in his ribs popped free of his skin. She glanced around and was perturbed that there were still people sitting around doing nothing. "Raise your hand if you've called the cops." It was more for her own validation that these were garbage people than any useful intel.

Nobody raised a hand. "Going once, going twice? Nobody?"

As people began exchanging judgmental glances with their friends, she yelled, "Then somebody call the cops! Hell, *everybody* call the cops! They have more than one phone line."

Turning her attention back toward Rebel's flopping body, she caught sight of the expelled bullet on the floor. This was going to be a tough one to explain, especially if the witnesses were as unhelpful with the cops as they were with Rebel ...

Jessica was mostly ignored when the first cops arrived. They entered the scene, guns drawn but pointed at the ground until they were sure the threat was over.

"Officer Jones?" Jess said as the fog started to clear from her brain.

"Ms. McCloud." He nodded but that was all the acknowledgment she received until the entire cafe had been cleared of everyone, including herself. Backup arrived shortly after she walked out into the bright afternoon sunlight, and while she waited for someone, anyone, to come speak with her, she entertained herself by watching pedestrians on the sidewalk rubberneck as they passed the scene.

Finally Jones 3624 approached, nodding to her and clasping his hands in front of his sternum. "Ms. McCloud. The other witnesses tell me you're the one to talk to."

"Yep." Here was the moment she'd been dreading, but she knew what she had to do.

"Would you walk me through what happened?"

"I submitted a job application earlier in the day, then changed my mind and came back to withdraw my application and get a Nutellaluna with rabies—which I never got, come to think of it—doesn't matter. A man walked in, accused Rebel of stealing his wife or something. Maybe just sleeping with her, and then he pulled out a gun. I tried to stop him, but, um, I got a leg cramp and fell. He shot at me, but missed, and I dunno, I guess that freaked him out, because he turned around and fired off five or six shots at Rebel."

Jones 3624 nodded empathetically. At least he didn't openly doubt her story. Yet. "Then what happened?"

She took a deep breath. "Then Rebel went to the ground and the shooter ran out, and I went over to check on Rebel."

"And?"

She paused, gritted her teeth, and continued. "And he was shot a few times through the chest and once or twice through the head." She pointed at her nose and made a poor attempt at a gunshot noise. "He was dead."

Jones 3624 leaned forward, his eyes locking onto Jessica's. "You're telling me the victim was shot multiple times and was dead, just so we're clear?"

"Yep." She smiled apologetically.

"When you say Rebel, are you referring to Grover Hofflefrot?"

"Um. Who?"

"Grover Hofflefrot."

"No, I heard you, I just have no idea."

Jones 3624 stepped to the side and pointed toward the ambulance where Rebel was being cleaned up and examined.

"O-kay," she said. "Yeah, I wouldn't have guessed Rebel was a *better* option. But yes, that's who I mean."

"Now, Ms. McCloud, I don't doubt your story—"

"You should."

Jones 3624 jerked his head back. "I should?"

"I mean, it's unbelievable. Here I am telling you the guy sitting right over there, probably thinking about banging that EMT, was shot multiple times in the chest and head. No offense, Officer Jones, but if you didn't doubt my story with that sort of visual evidence saying the contrary, I'd worry about your ability to do your job."

He didn't respond, just leaned back slightly and narrowed his eyes at her.

"It was a miracle," she said. "I performed a miracle on him. He was dead as a doornail, and I sent God powers into him and then his body healed and he is now the Rebel we all know and wish we didn't. I know you're not supposed to lie to the cops, so I'm telling you the truth and hoping you believe me."

"I do believe you."

"You do?"

"Yes, ma'am. I *know* who you are, Ms. McCloud. I know what you do. The problem is that it's not up to me how these things play out after I write the report."

"Oh."

"But I do happen to know that the owner of the store suspected one of his employees was stealing coffee, so he set up a security camera pointing behind the counter. Assuming you're telling the truth, that'll show it."

The female officer who had been first on scene with Jones 3624 walked up and introduced herself and Officer McBride. "Wanted to let you know the paramedics are hopeful for his recovery ... mainly because there was no clear sign of injury, outside of the blood consistent with gunshot wounds." She arched an eyebrow at Jessica and cocked her head to the side slightly.

"That's good," Jessica said.

McBride turned to Jones. "You know, you see this kind of thing again and again, week in and week out, and you think you'll reach a point where there're no more surprises. Then something like this comes along."

Jessica jumped in. "You see this kind of thing often?"

"Oh yeah," McBride said, resting her hands on her belt. "This one will make the news, but most of them don't."

"Really? Why's that?"

McBride shrugged, a single corner of her mouth turning downward. "The victims are poor or it's your garden variety domestic violence or the perps are people the news doesn't want to vilify."

"So Austin truly isn't a safe—"

McBride chuckled. "Oh no, no, no."

A strange question occurred to her, one that probably had no precedent in the United States legal system. "What'll happen to the shooter when you catch him? Will he be charged with murder?"

McBride looked at Jessica like she was crazy before looking over her shoulder at Rebel then back toward Jones.

He held up a hand to let his coworker—"I'll explain later,"—then returned his attention to Jessica. "I doubt it. But we'll have to see what's on that footage. It'll be one hell of a court case, either way. We'll charge him with it, but it might be that we have to stick with aggravated assault with a deadly weapon, or attempted murder."

"You can add a cherry on top of that," McBride said, pointing toward a Gun-Free Zone sign by the front door.

"Oh man," Jones said, sarcasm dripping, "how did that sign not stop it? Color me surprised."

"Huh," said Jessica. "I guess that explains why no one else was armed."

McBride aimed a finger gun at her. "Bingo."

Jessica continued to stare at the gun-free zone sign that looked about as official as the vanity plate she'd had on her tricycle as a child. "So how do you stop this type of thing from happening?" she asked. It was her second gun encounter since she'd moved to Austin, and that seemed like two too many. There was at least one firearm in every home in Mooretown, as far as she knew, and nothing like this ever happened.

Well, outside of Jameson Fractal's brutal assassination, but she'd always assumed the shooter was some city asshole anyway.

"What, people bringing guns places?" McBride asked. "In Texas?"

"Yes."

"Oh honey. You can't stop it."

Jessica cringed. "That's comforting."

Officer McBride reached over and rubbed Jessica's back in a gentle, motherly way. "Don't worry, though, Ms. McCloud. Guns don't kill people ..."

"McBride," Jones 3624 said in a low, warning tone.

She ignored him. "Men do."

Jones rolled his eyes, mumbling, "Always spreading her

damn feminist hate speech ..." and the two officers walked back to their cars, leaving Jessica alone in a crowd of unarmed witnesses.

Unsure what else to do, she pulled out her phone and texted Cash: *I apologize in advance.*

The reply was immediate: *What did you do? WHAT DID YOU DO?*

No point in explaining. They'd find out soon enough.

Chapter Twenty-Three

Jessica finished scribbling a thick set of eyebrows on the watermelon and set it up on the last empty cinderblock before stepping back to admire her work.

Four crudely drawn faces stared back at her, two she hardly knew, two she knew more than she wanted to.

It was the first time she'd made the drive out here without Miranda, and suddenly the issue of whose land it was seemed much less important when compared to her burning and unfulfilled need to smite the hell out of something.

The day had been long, her mind a maelstrom of gore and fear and anger and confusion when she'd arrived back at her condo. Officer Jones had been kind enough to give her a ride over, and just before she entered her front door, she had an idea, turned around, and headed to the parking garage instead.

After a quick trip to the store, she found herself hiking

down into the small, dry valley with a canvas shopping bag full of melons.

She glared at the cartoonish version of the gunman's face staring back at her from the surface of the watermelon. She had by no means captured the essence of him, but it was enough of a framework for her imagination and fresh trauma to fill in the rest.

She did what her body wished she'd done back at the coffee shop and hurled a wad of smite his way. The watermelon popped, sending red juice in all directions. Much like watermelon itself, smiting was a delightful indulgence but only made her crave more of it.

She turned her attention to the next target down the line. This face was even less detailed than the previous one, the memory of the armed man outside the Grease Trough having faded over the months since the encounter.

She blasted him away too, and it was just as gratifying as the last. But a moment later her lust for it resurfaced.

The Sharpie wasn't even dry on Eugene Thornton's thick eyebrows as she tallied up all the wrongs from him, holding back the rage temporarily to allow it to build before she unleashed it.

Not only did the watermelon of his face explode, so too did the cinderblocks holding it up. She whirled away quickly, shielding her face from the bits of concrete shrapnel, and when she turned back, there was a small hole in the earth where the cinderblocks and watermelon had once been.

"Holy shit."

INDEED.

She turned to the last watermelon. The defining characteristics of this face were the lines she'd drawn for the jaw, the small dimple marks that had taunted her so many times, and the big eyes that seemed friendly but never turned out to be. She'd dangled her jumper cables around the melon so that they hung down the front of the stand, and while the vise grips were no hog's hooves, they worked well enough.

The hungry wrath simmered inside her as she looked at the watermelon and tallied up all the wrongs Jimmy Dean had done to her over the years. So many. Countless. Time and again. And it would never stop. He would continue sabotaging her life and convincing everyone else he wasn't. Even if she smote the man herself, she suspected he would find ways to ruin her life from beyond the grave.

She whirled around and, *pop, pop!* Two empty target stands turned into small craters before she sat down on a smooth rock jutting out of the ground and stared at the open land.

This doesn't make me feel better anymore. It only makes me want to smite more.

TRULY? IT MAKES THE LORD FEEL AMAZING.

When was the last time you smote a human, though?

MONDAY.

But today is Monday.

GOOD POINT. IT WAS IN A VASTLY DIFFERENT TIMEZONE, SO IT FEELS LIKE IT WAS

A DIFFERENT DAY. BUT INDEED, BY YOUR TIME STANDARDS, IT WAS TODAY.

In Asia?

I SEE YOU'VE BEEN PAYING ATTENTION.

And it makes you feel better to smite?

MORE LIKE IT IS ONE MORE STEP TOWARD RECTIFYING ORIGINAL MISTAKE.

Shit's really gotten out of hand, hasn't it?

YOU HAVE NO IDEA. THE EARTH IS NOT A SAFE PLACE.

You know, part of me has always thought that if I could just let myself smite things, everything would become easier. As if not smiting people was just some dumb rule that was holding me back and prolonging my troubles. But now that I've been able to come out here and smite as much as I want, I don't know if it's quite the ace in the hole I thought it was. All smiting makes me want to do is smite more, not less.

So maybe I shouldn't do it at all. Because I don't want to spend my life smiting. I want to spend it doing ... well, anything else. Something meaningful, maybe.

She pressed her palms into her tired eyes before looking around at the brown December landscape.

What am I even doing out here? I have a check I need to cash. I need to find a location and order my ovens and tables and display cases. I need to start hiring staff and decorating the interior. I have so much I need to be doing, and all of it will be better than smiting.

She stood up from the rock, feeling more energized than she had in a long time.

Thanks for listening, Dad.

She waited for a snide comment but none came.

Oh damn. When did he split?

Didn't matter. God skedaddling from her brain was just another thing working in her favor.

I can do it now. I can create something. What the hell am I waiting for?

She inhaled the crisp winter air and looked up at the sky where dark clouds were forming.

Fuck you, omen! I won't hear it!

She grabbed the remaining watermelon and jumper cables and headed back to her car. She needed to get home as soon as possible.

She had a bakery to open. But first: an entire watermelon to eat.

Chapter Twenty-Four

Three months had blown by, and without meaning to, Jessica had lost herself so deeply in her preparation for the new bakery that she'd once again neglected all of her friendships. Tonight was a step in the right direction, though. Granted, it'd been Chris's idea, and she suspected it was born from his need to gush about his recent success rather than any concern for Jessica's dwindling social life. But everyone benefitted from the plans, so she wouldn't split hairs.

"You still don't know whose condo this is?" Quentin asked, following Miranda inside, and carrying a stack of pizza boxes.

"No," Jessica said, taking the food from him and setting it on the kitchen island. "I've scoured this place for clues and can't find anything new. I think the trail is cold. So let's just call it *my* condo."

Chris jumped up from the couch, where he'd been

playing on his phone, and ran over to wrap his arms around his former teammate. While the two of them moaned and inhaled each other's scent, Jessica and Miranda stepped into the kitchen and set out plates and napkins.

"I want to hear all about it," Quentin said as the long embrace concluded.

Chris grinned like an idiot. "And you will. Dude, Quentin. Duuuuude! Combine was so sweet! I tore it up!"

"That's what I heard!" They high-fived. "I've been reading about it all week. ESPN won't shut up about you. And you know who they have you going to, right?"

Chris and Quentin shouted it together. "Cowboys!"

As they cackled and slapped at each other, Miranda cleared her throat and Jessica was more than happy to divert her attention from the lovefest. "How you holding up?" Miranda asked.

Jessica shrugged. "I'm tired. Like, all the time. But the good news is that I was officially been cleared in the Bat-Ass Brew shooting a couple days ago, and it looks like I'm on schedule for the soft opening the weekend after next. You?"

Miranda peeked over Jessica's shoulder to check on the men, who were still gushing incoherently and thrashing around. She leaned forward. "Quentin and I went ring shopping this afternoon."

"Oh cool." Jessica almost never wore rings herself, but it was something she considered from time to time. A few solid ring choices could really make a woman's hands look — "Wait. What kind of ring? Like engagement ring?"

Miranda nodded excitedly, her eyes darting over to Quentin and back.

"So, you're engaged?" Jessica whispered, hoping her mixture of emotions was coming off as excitement rather than mind-numbing panic.

"No, not yet. He still has to propose. But I have a general idea what my ring will look like." She nibbled her bottom lip.

"How do you think he'll do it?"

Miranda smiled coyly. "Well, he *did* sort of arrange a trip to Paris for us over spring break."

"Paris?" Jessica said, struggling to sound excited. "Like, Paris, Texas?"

Miranda took a half step back. "Uh, no? Paris, France. You know, as in the place I've always wanted to go."

"Wine." Jess nodded firmly. "We need wine to celebrate." She turned her back on the others and ran into the pantry, flipping on the light and shutting the door halfway behind her.

Do I even have wine?

Yet again, she considered how much easier her half-brother had it. He never would've found himself hiding in a pantry from his best friend for no good reason and *not* have any wine to serve.

YOU SEEM UPSET.

I'm fine.

YOU FORGET I CREATED WOMEN, SO I KNOW THIS TO BE UNTRUE.

Okay. I'm not fine. But I'd rather pretend I am than talk

to you about what's bothering me and have you downplay it or, more likely, rub salt in the wound.

YE OF LITTLE FAITH.

Ye of little sympathy.

THE LORD WILL TAKE A GUESS. YOU ARE IN THIS PANTRY BECAUSE YOU DO NOT WISH TO FACE REALITY.

I don't think someone has to be a god to figure that out.

(THERE IS NO GOD BUT ME.) YOU HAVE NEVER BEEN GIFTED AT RELATIONSHIPS, DAUGHTER.

How is this not *salt in my wound?*

JUST BECAUSE YOU ARE CHOOSING TO IGNORE YOUR RELATIONSHIP WITH CHRISTO-PHER DOES NOT MEAN EVERYONE ELSE HAS FORSAKEN PROGRESS. TIME MARCHES FORWARD.

I know that! And I'm not ignoring anything!

THE TRUTH UPSETS YOU.

No. Your face upsets me.

OH VERY MATURE. BUT I HAVE NO FACE.

Well isn't that just a goddamn nightmare. Thanks.

"Is this what you're looking for?" Miranda's voice said behind her, causing her to jump and turn around.

Miranda dusted off a bottle of red wine.

"Yep. Where'd you find that?"

"On the wine rack?" she pointed vaguely above the fridge.

Oh right. The wine rack she always forgot she had. Well, at least she knew for sure she wasn't an alcoholic ...

"Are you okay, Jessica?" Miranda asked.

Sucking air deep into her lungs, Jessica said on an exhale. "Yeah, I'm fine."

Miranda rolled her eyes. "Please. I know that's bullshit."

"I'm just tired."

Miranda was gracious enough to drop it and they popped open the bottle of wine ("Ooo! Good idea! This'll knock us out hard," Chris said, crossing the room to paw at her), and dug into the pizza. Thankful for the excuse to not speak for a little while, Jessica stacked three pieces on her plate and grabbed a seat in the living room to chow down and hope the grease numbed her brain.

"Jess. Jess."

She looked over at her boyfriend, who stood by the island, mouth overflowing with pizza as he slung an arm around Quentin. "Get a picture of this and send it to Cash. They'll love it."

"I don't know that they will, but okay." She pulled out her phone, snapped a pic, and sent it to Cash with the message, *Chris spending an evening with his closest friend.*

As she awaited Cash's response, she figured this *was* actually the kind of thing she was supposed to be doing, so she rounded up everyone for a selfie.

Before she could type up her message and send the real photo, Cash responded: *As much as I support interracial relationships, just no. I'm not portraying you as a beard.*

A beard? *Must be an autocorrect thing.* She sent him the group selfie and started on another slice.

Chris was ten minutes deep into a play-by-play of the NFL combine's passing drills when a knock on the door gave Jessica a perfectly good excuse to escape the excruciating conversation. So relieved by the break, she didn't think to look through the peephole before opening the door.

Jeremy's frantic eyes darted around, only sometimes landing on her face as he scrubbed his hands together. "Are you watching the news?" He peeked around her. "Oh sorry, am I interrupting?"

"Nope. Come on in."

Jeremy waved awkwardly on his way into the living room. He spun in a tight circle a few times until he found the remote and turned on the TV.

"What's up, Jeremy?" Chris said cautiously.

Her neighbor ignored it. He turned to Channel Six, but when it was commercial, he griped, "Of course!" and then surfed up stations until he landed on one Jessica didn't know existed. "The regular news won't cover this anyway," he said, "but it's important."

He stepped back and Jessica noticed a beet-faced man sitting at a news desk, red, white and blue flashing on the screens behind him and the words FactWars in the bottom left corner of the screen.

Miranda stepped forward. "Um, why are we watching this crap?"

"It's not crap," Jeremy said flatly. "It's the only independent news available anymore."

"He would know," Jessica said. "Apparently he owns most of the news?" She shrugged.

The man on the TV finished his tirade about fluoride suppositories and quickly jumped to a new topic. *"As Jimmy 'Pigeffer' Dean officially wins the Republican primary for Texas Railroad Commissioner this evening, we have to ask ourselves, where is Jessica McCloud? Why would she let something like this happen if she's really the daughter of God?"* He turned to another camera. *"You might be saying, 'Maybe she's not the daughter of God.' Then what about the videos circulating around the Internet?"* The security footage from Bat-Ass Brew began playing, and Jessica gasped.

"How did they get that?! The police said they wouldn't release that."

Jeremy scoffed. "Right. Keep on believing the police state sticks to its word."

The screen then cut to cell phone footage Jessica didn't know existed. A man's voice was yelling in the background, his car off on the shoulder of I-35 as Jessica and Chris drove by in Chris's truck.

"Wait," said Miranda, stepping forward. "What the hell is this?"

"I—uh. I accidentally performed a miracle. I didn't know people were filming."

The beet-faced man appeared again in a close-up shot. *"Clearly something's going on here, and to help us make sense of it, we have a special guest to discuss these events."*

Jessica's stomach dropped, even before the camera zoomed out and she saw the bushy-browed man sitting opposite the host. *"Independent journalist and founder of Thornton News, a website with a similar mission to our own, Eugene Thornton has had more in-person interviews with Jessica McCloud than any other reporter and isn't afraid to tell it like it is."* The camera cut to a medium shot of Eugene, his mustache resting just above a smirk. *"Eugene, what, in your opinion, is happening here?"*

"It's quite simple, Alan. Jessica McCloud and Jimmy Dean have been in cahoots from the beginning. Their conflict was and is a rouse that the public has fallen for again and again, each and every time the mainscream media force-feeds it to them. And this is where it's led. Texas has not had a Democrat railroad commissioner in decades, and I can't imagine we're about to see the tide turn here. With Jimmy Dean all but assured the position, it's not hard to put the pieces together. Jessica McCloud has been working with him on this for years, as the foreword for his quote-unquote memoir shows."

"Now, I have to stop you here, Eugene, because we on FactWars have long held the belief that Jessica McCloud did not write the foreword for Railed to the Cross.*"*

"Thank you!" Jessica yelled, flopping back onto her armchair.

Eugene nodded compassionately and Jessica wanted to throw her shoe at the TV. *"Yes, I know that's long-since been the belief held by independent sources, but new evidence has unfortunately come to light recently. A few anonymous sources have contacted my site with compelling evidence to indicate Jessica McCloud did, in fact, write the foreword."*

"Now this is truly fascinating," Alan said. "That changes so many things."

"Indeed. We now have reason to believe that Jessica is actually the Antichrist."

"God dammit. Not again." Jessica groaned.

Chris bulled forward, snatched the remote from Jeremy where he crouched in front of the TV, shoving him over with a stiff-arm to the head, and turned off the news. "Buncha fucking lies. I can't believe we just watched that shit."

Jeremy pushed himself up into a squat again and turned to Jessica. "FactWars was the last outlet that truly had your back, Jessica. When I read that Eugene Thornton was their guest tonight, I knew it was bad. They're turning on you."

Chris glared down at Jeremy like he might spit on him. "Not exactly the kind of allies we would choose, though."

Jeremy stood. "They're the only media allies she had, Chris. Well, besides me, but I can't exactly act unilaterally. Too suspicious."

Chris took a bold step toward Jeremy. "She doesn't need you. She still has Maria Flores."

Jessica's gaze flickered over to Miranda and Quentin,

who sat stock still on the bar stools by the kitchen island, passively (but alertly) observing the confrontation unfold.

"Riiiight." Jeremy's eyes dashed from Chris to Jessica. "So, tell me again what happened right after your interview with her aired? Did your food truck *not* burn to the ground?"

"I don't know what you're implying," Jessica said, "but I don't think I like it."

"You should leave," Chris said.

Jeremy pressed his lips into a thin line and sighed deeply through his nose. "I'm not saying she knowingly had anything to do with it, but her story did clearly lead to it."

"You don't know that," Jessica responded.

"I'm not trying to upset you. I just want you to see what's going on here." He glanced around the room where hostile faces glared from all sides. "I'll let you folks get back to your visit."

As the front door closed behind him, Jessica put her chin on her hands, staring at the concrete floor a few feet ahead and wishing she could be left alone with the bottle of wine.

After a long silence, Quentin whispered. "Did she part traffic on I-35?"

Chris nodded excitedly. "So hot, right?"

"Totally."

Chris's spine stiffened. "Dude," he said, "back off."

Chapter Twenty-Five

Hundreds of hours of work and hundreds of thousands of dollars had gone into this night.

Naturally, Jessica expected it to be a disaster.

Chris's mind seemed to be somewhere else as he shuffled around the pristine and permanent home of It Is Risen Bakery. The NFL draft was only a couple weeks away, making that a likely culprit for his thousand-mile stare when she asked him to grab more ice from the back and refill the drink station. If she could just get through tonight, though, then she could spend time bridging the distance she felt from Chris. She knew the gulf was a result of their pursuing separate dreams, but it was there all the same.

Thinking about the conversation that needed to happen only made her more anxious.

She checked the large clock above the front door. Seven forty-five. The sun had already set on the short late-

March day, and it occurred to her that she had been awake for fifteen hours already. The party hadn't even started.

THE LORD IS LOOKING FORWARD TO TONIGHT.

No omens. Please, no omens.

YOU BELIEVE THE MERE MENTION OF EXCITEMENT FROM THE LORD IS AN OMEN?

Yes. Absolutely. One hundred percent. Could you do me a huge favor and leave me alone tonight so I can focus? Please?

ONLY BECAUSE YOU ASKED NICELY. ENJOY THE MANY SURPRISES THAT AWAIT YOU TONIGHT, DAUGHTER. THE LORD CERTAINLY SHALL.

Hold up. Many surprises? What surprises?

But there was no response. Shitballs.

She leaned against the counter, next to the long, empty glass display case, and allowed herself a moment to pause, to look around, to appreciate what she'd accomplished with the help of so many others.

While she'd wanted to go full "nature-fusion" in design, Wendy insisted that not only was that not a style, but it didn't jibe with the It is Risen Bakery brand. But for once in her life, Jessica had been adamant. She was constructing her habitat from the ground up, and she would damn well make one hospitable to her particular evolutionary and emotional needs.

So compromises were made.

Wendy wouldn't OK a mural of a lioness hunt on the

east wall; however, one of a baobab tree could easily be spun into a "tree of life" image, which was on-brand enough to work.

When Jessica had found the perfect ceiling fans online with blades that resembled date palm fronds, Wendy had nixed those before Jessica could finish describing them. The eventual compromised resulted in ruddy-sand-colored floor tiles inside and ferns and palm trees planted outside the building where Jessica could spy them through the front windows.

And in a single openly defiant act, Jessica brought in a foot-tall stuffed giraffe to stand by the register and named her Asha. Wendy backed down from that fight only after Jessica took up the last-ditch defense that she was merely doing her part to Keep Austin Weird.

The rest of the interior decorating was a result of hodgepodge teamwork. Rex had built most of the small, round cafe tables himself, and the chairs were courtesy of a concerted effort on the part of the Texas State and Texas Tech chapters of NAO, the latter of which she needed to pay a visit to sometime soon. *Add it to the list.* Each chair was beautifully sanded and stained, and the amount of effort put into them was almost enough to make Jessica cry.

But there was no time to cry. Not tonight.

Dr. Bell had dedicated most of her free time over the past few months to helping Jessica research and order the necessary equipment, and Wendy and Maria had been on real estate duty. Jessica's only job on that front was to say yes or no. While she didn't have the money to buy or rent

downtown, she did settle in a nice up-and-coming neighborhood and was about to afford enough security equipment to rest well at night knowing that her baby was
probably, most likely, almost assuredly not going to be
reduced to ashes while she slept.

"Oh shit." Jessica spotted the chalkboard for daily
specials still leaning up against the wall. She could have
sworn she'd hung it up this morning, but who even knew at
this point? Painted across the top was *It is Risen daily
specials,* and even such a simple phrase left her giddy and
nervous and satisfied. Sure, she hadn't created a clear,
concise message like Wendy had insisted she do, but using
Judith's dumb joke as the name of her bakery seemed like a
step in the right direction. At least she wasn't completely
disassociating herself from anything religious. And in her
own defense, she'd been incredibly busy getting everything
in order in such a short time. Adding "write a manifesto"
on her to-do list was more than she could handle.

"Let me help you with that, baby," Destinee said, scur-
rying over to guide the chalkboard onto the hooks in
the wall.

They stepped back to check the balance, and Destinee
put her arm around her daughter's shoulder. "This is something else, Jess. I'm so damn proud of you."

"Thanks, Mom."

"My daughter's a business owner!"

For reasons Jessica couldn't put words to, Destinee's
pride made her uneasy. "Well, I haven't officially opened
for business *yet*, so let's not count those chickens."

Destinee paused, chewing her bottom lip. "I know you've lived a strange and unfortunate life, baby, but it doesn't hurt to expect the best."

"Agree to disagree. For what it's worth, though, I'm ... cautiously optimistic?"

Destinee patted her on the back. "That's the spirit. So, um, Jessica ..."

Jess turned her head slowly toward her mother. Destinee calling her by her full first name was always foreboding. "Yes?"

"You got a second to have a seat before the guests show up?" Destinee headed toward the nearest table and sat in one of the NAO chairs. Jessica followed and sat opposite her mother.

When Destinee didn't immediately speak, Jessica took her best guess. "You're not pregnant again, right?"

Destinee eyed her skeptically. "That came outta nowhere. And no. Your father seems set on playing birth control for me. And don't get me wrong, I'm okay with that. It's just ... you know. Seems like it should be my choice. But whatever." She waved off the topic. "No, this is good news."

"Okay."

Jessica cringed as she heard something metal topple onto the tile floor in the kitchen, closely followed by Chris cursing, then Rex telling him to watch his language, then Chris loudly asserting that he was a grown man.

Once the ruckus died, Destinee continued. "You know

how you were saying Rex should get a job coaching in Austin?"

"Yeah, I vaguely remember that."

"Well, he did."

SURPRISE!

"Oh." That was quick. "What about you two?"

"Baby! He got a job out in one of those rich suburbs by the lake! He's gonna be making way more than Mooretown would ever pay him. So I'm moving with him. Neighborhood that rich, I bet they have pharmacies on every corner. Surely one will hire me." She filled her lungs with air, a serene smile resting on her lips. "We're gonna get us a house in Austin!" She smacked the table excitedly.

"How ... You've been in town for two full days. You're telling me you managed to hold this in that long?"

"Course not. We just found out this morning."

"Ah. That makes more sense." She let the news settle in. Her mother was moving to Austin. That was good, wasn't it? Everybody loved having their mother live a short drive away, right?

"I thought about telling you this morning, but I didn't want to distract you. I would've waited till after tonight, but I knew Rex wouldn't keep his mouth shut about it around Dolores—he's been dreaming about telling her where to shove her weekly grade checks for years. I wanted you to hear it straight from me."

"That's great, Mom. I'm so happy for y'all."

"Well, we don't move until the summer, so you'll have

a little time to get things up and running before you see my shining face up in this place asking for free shit."

A slight tap on the glass front door pulled Jessica's attention, and she spotted Judith waving from the front step. She wasn't alone.

"Hot damn," Destinee mumbled. "Who is *that* hot piece of man she brought with?"

Jessica squinted through the glare of the glass but tried not to gawk too overtly. "Wait. I know that guy. He was stalking Judith, and then—" She stopped herself before mentioning the strange encounter with Mrs. Thomas.

"Well, I'd say that's about the best-case scenario for a stalker."

Jessica unlocked the door and let them inside. "Hi, Judith! And ...?" She let the sentence hang, and Judith promptly jumped in.

"This is Joshua. You remember him from the food truck?"

Jessica forced a smile. "Sure do." She held out a hand to shake his, and he stared down at it suspiciously. After a silent moment, he extended his hand and gave a limp-fish shake.

Judith sure knew how to pick them. Granted, he *was* pretty hot. And he appeared to be closer to thirty than fifty. So, assuming the asshole hadn't set her trailer on fire, which she moderately suspected, Judith might have found a keeper.

"Come on in."

As the chitchat started between Joshua and Destinee,

Jessica leaned close to Judith and whispered, "I didn't know you two kept in touch."

"Why wouldn't we? You look at that guy?"

"So is it just a physical thing?"

"Actually, no. We haven't ..."

Joshua put his arm around Judith and she stopped herself midsentence, grinning up at him guiltily.

Jessica figured now wasn't the time to bring up the awkward encounter in the taco shop. Would Mrs. Thomas recognize him from that? Probably not. She hoped not. Things were already becoming more socially complicated than she preferred. Hadn't she learned her lesson about worlds colliding back when she invited her high school friends to Mason's show? Worlds didn't collide and *blend*. They just collided and blew each other to shit.

They blended when it was time to raise money. Maybe it's not impossible.

She'd have to hold onto that hope for at least a couple more hours.

Chris charged in from the kitchen and wedged himself between Jessica and Judith, putting his arm around his girlfriend's shoulder. "Who're you?" he said to Joshua.

"Chris, this is Judith's friend Joshua."

Without smiling, Chris offered his hand and Joshua flinched against Chris's strong grip as they shook.

Jessica turned to her boyfriend. "Hey, I need your help for a second."

"What's that?" Chris asked cluelessly.

"Just, um, something heavy in the back."

"Nah, back of house is good to go. Rex is just connecting one last—"

"Excuse us," she said to the others and dragged Chris behind her into the kitchen and out of earshot. Once they were alone, she hissed, "That's the guy."

Chris's eyes shot wide open. "What guy? Did he make a move on you? Do I need to beat him up?"

She placed a soft hand on Chris's chest. "Easy there. No. That's the guy that came around a couple days in a row right before the trailer caught fire and the one that approached Mrs. Thomas and me at lunch, acting all weird."

"I don't think you ever mentioned any of that to me. Wait, when did you have lunch with Mrs. Thomas?"

Oh shit. The tidbit about Mrs. Thomas's assistance was on a need-to-know basis, and thus far, Chris had been so busy with football matters, he hadn't needed to know. When Jessica told him over the phone that she officially had the money to move forward with the business, his response had simply been, "I'm so fucking proud of you, Jess. You're gonna crush it!" The details hadn't been requested, and she'd been happy not to provide.

"Doesn't matter," Jessica said, moving the conversation quickly away from Mrs. Thomas. "I just don't trust him. There's something *off* about him, you know?"

Chris opened his eyes wide and nodded emphatically. "Oh, I know. He's definitely an angel, but his aura isn't like anything I've seen before. Well,"—he squinted, looking Jessica up and down—"no, that's not *entirely* true. Huh."

"Doesn't matter if he's an angel. Will you keep an eye on him?"

Chris's game face surfaced and he nodded. She knew giving him a set task for the night would be good for him, so she was glad to have found one. "Absolutely. I won't let him mess up the love of my life's big night." Chris swooped in, wrapping his arms around her waist, crashing his lips into hers, and shoving her up against a large oven pulled out a few feet from the wall.

"Ow! God dammit!" Rex's head popped up from behind the oven. "Keep it in your pants, kids."

Jessica pushed Chris away from her quickly. "You have a lot of room to talk, Rex. I *still* hear my mom's bedpost tapping away every time I shut my eyes. Like the damn Tell-Tale Heart."

Although, it was probably good that he'd broken up their anxiety-induced love fest. Jessica had pressing hosting duties to consider.

As she left the kitchen, Miranda and Quentin walked through the front door, large metal buckets in each hand. And in each of the buckets, ice and a dozen beer bottles. "Party's here!" Quentin said, strutting toward the counter where he set down his buckets then took Miranda's from her.

The rest of the guests came flooding in shortly after. The majority of the Nu Alpha Omega sisters arrived in a bunch with Kate and Pippa leading the herd.

It was only the founding members who had received the invite, not so much because Jessica wanted to be exclusive, but because she didn't know if she could afford to feed so many people. But also, that meant Courtney wasn't invited. As much as Jessica believed Courtney had turned over a new leaf, she still didn't want to spend time around the Wurst girl.

Jeremy Archer held open the door for Maria Flores and Gabrielle Polaris, who chatted animatedly with him as the three entered the bakery. He smiled sheepishly at her, and she nodded begrudgingly to let him know he was still welcome after their tense encounter in her condo a week and a half before. Judging by the way he related so easily with Maria and Gabrielle, it was entirely possible that she'd overreacted, that he hadn't been implying what she'd thought he was about the reporter.

Or maybe he was just a psycho. There was *definitely* something off about the man, even if he did seem relatively harmless.

As Jessica welcomed the new arrivals, trying not to let the shock at seeing Maria in casual clothes show, Dr. Bell and Mrs. Thomas arrived. Dr. Bell smiled amicably as she held the door for Mrs. Thomas, who nodded her thanks and entered. Jessica's two former teachers parted ways quickly once they were inside, but not before noticeably sizing each other up.

Where Dr. Bell went to greet Jessica's sisters, Mrs. Thomas made a line straight to Jessica, wrapping her up in her arms. Jessica gave into the softness of Mrs. Thomas's plump body, and a second later, the woman pulled back, her hands still on Jessica's shoulders as she took in the sight of her. "I'm so proud of you, Jessica."

She felt Chris's eyes on her from the opposite side of the room where he was sitting with Destinee and Brian Foster, who'd arrive a few minutes prior. "Thanks, Mrs. Thomas. Couldn't have done it without you, obviously."

"Psh! Of course you could have, it would've just taken a little longer. Oh." She leaned forward conspiratorially, so Jessica did the same. "I've been meaning to ask if you ever got the picture of the signed contract. I texted it to you and never got a response."

"Oh, um." Jessica scanned her memory and cringed. "No, I don't remember getting it, actually." *Yet another detail I forgot about.*

Mrs. Thomas nodded. "That's what I was worried about. My phone is a little old. I'll send it to you again right —" She opened her purse and then paused. "Shoot. Looks like I left my phone in my car. I'll go grab it and be right back."

When she turned, Jessica placed a gentle hand on her to stop her. "Don't worry about it, Mrs. Thomas. I'm not. You can do it later."

Chewing her lip, she finally nodded. "Oh, all right. You know—" Her eyes locked onto something behind Jessica that seemed to disturb her greatly. "Is that the man from the restaurant?"

Jess twisted to spot Joshua. "Yeah. I know. He's here with my friend Judith."

Mrs. Thomas's face was dark, her eyebrows low as she

shook her head slowly. "Oh no, no, no. He shouldn't be here, Jessica. If there's even a chance that he had something to do with the fire ..."

"I'm not thrilled with it either, but I've already asked Chris to keep an eye on him."

Mrs. Thomas pursed her lips and sucked in air through wide nostrils. "Whatever you say, Jessica. But I still don't love it. I think I'm going to have a chat with him."

"If that makes you feel better, be my guest."

Mrs. Thomas nodded determinedly and set off to do just that.

While Quentin and Miranda busied themselves handing out drinks, Chris pumped music through the speakers he'd hung earlier that afternoon. Before long, the alcohol worked its miracle, and the initial tentative conversations grew into a loud ruckus with an occasional outburst of laughter.

This was actually going well.

Jessica tried not to let the notion put her on edge. Instead, she hustled into the kitchen and brought out a fresh tray of hot kolaches, each with her image seared onto the top. And while serving such a vain treat to her closest friends and family seemed endlessly tacky to her, no one else seemed to think so.

Instead, it was a hit.

Dammit. I guess I have to go through with this idea after all.

Certainly it was a little too late to back out, now that she'd spent just about every penny she'd been given to get this place ready for its grand opening in three weeks, but that didn't mean her brain wasn't constantly looking for an out, some perfect excuse that would give her permission to retreat back into a safer lifestyle.

Miranda snaked through the crowd and waited patiently for a break in Jessica's forced conversation with Jeremy and Maria, who seemed to be hitting it off. When Maria turned to face Jeremy directly, asking him to clarify what the term "abductionist" meant, Miranda jumped in. "Looks like you're running low on the kolaches. You got anything else back there?"

Chris hustled over, eyes wide. "Okay! Just listened in on a conversation Joshua was having with Natalie, and something weird is definitely going on with that guy. Natalie mentioned something about being crucified over ... I don't know, something with women's rights, and Joshua got all defensive. I think he might be a Jesus freak. Not that there's anything wrong with that. But, you know, like a Jesus freak who doesn't like that you're God's daughter. Maybe even a Catholic."

Miranda hitched a thumb at Chris but addressed Jessica. "What the hell is he talking about?"

"Nothing," Jessica said. "Just wanted him to keep an eye on—" Movement by the front door caught her attention, and she felt her stomach drop down to her feet. "Oh my god."

SURPRISE!

Chris and Miranda both whirled around to see what Jessica was staring at.

Chris said, "You didn't know Wendy was—oh shit."

"Yeah," Jessica said.

Slowly, as guests caught sight of Wendy's date, the chatter of the room took on a hushed but furious tone.

"Damn, he looks even better in person," Miranda said. "How did you never mention that?"

"I guess I was too busy PTSD-ing out. Um. I should go deal with this."

She left Chris and Miranda, making a beeline for the front door, where she was greeted by two beautiful, smiling faces. One was Wendy's, and the other, which looked no worse for wear despite having had a bullet scorch through it four years before, was Jameson Fractal's.

"Jessica," he breathed. "I'm so happy I finally get to see you again." His hazel eyes bore into her with such intensity that she thought she might actually pass out. Ugh, he was dreamy. It was incredibly inconvenient. "Hi, Jameson."

"When he heard about this, he wanted to come," Wendy said like that was an adequate excuse for dropping this bomb on Jessica's psychosexual well-being.

"We should talk," Jameson said, his gaze flickering briefly from her eyes to her lips.

"Yep." She scooted around him and opened the front door, and he took the cue and went right back out from where he'd entered. She glanced over her shoulder at the rest of the party and immediately regretted doing so. Every single guest was staring. Miranda had a strong arm extended in front of Chris's body to hold him steady. The table of NAOs stared hungrily at Jameson, some of them biting their lips, others lifting an eyebrow ever so slightly. Mrs. Thomas wore a similar lecherous expression where she'd paused in her conversation with Quentin.

Joshua was the only one who didn't seem aware he was in the presence of a celebrity, and he turned this way and that in his seat, curiously studying the intense gazes. Had this guy lived under a rock? What the hell?

She was more relieved than nervous to finally shut the door behind her and be alone with Jameson. He walked over to a bench in front of one of the bakery's front-facing windows and sat down, patting the spot next to him.

"No," she said, shooing him off with a flick of her wrist. "Not in front of the window." She scooted him along until they were out of sight of the rest of the party, which left them standing back by the dumpsters that she hadn't yet had occasion to use for anything but packing materials.

"I know you've been avoiding me, Jessica."

With no clear reason to lie, she said, "Yes."

"I don't want it to be this way. You saved my life."

She held up a hand. "Nuh-uh. I didn't save your life. I pulled your hysterical sister off you so you could die. Then I brought you back to life. There's a difference. A big fucking difference."

He folded his arms across his chest, and she tried not to stare at his perfectly sculpted forearms revealed by his rolled-up sweater sleeves. "That must have been hard for you."

She laughed dryly. "Hard for me? You got shot in the face. No, *through* the face." She pointed to her cheek. "It went in here, and then out here." She touched to the exit point, which she was certain she remembered within a millimeter.

"Hey," he said smoothly, and she immediately thought, *I shouldn't be near a wall with him. I know what he does with women and walls. Could I say no?* She had her doubts, even while Chris was within moaning distance.

"It was a bad situation all around," he said. "And I know you blame yourself for it, but that's bullshit, Jessica. You're the real deal. I know that. I'm alive because of that. Even my skeptical sister believes you are who you say you are. I mean, hell, she's letting you live in her home. Granted, she didn't actually want it when I bought it for her, but she could have sold it—"

SURPRISE! MANKIND, AM I ENJOYING THIS!

"Hold. Up. I'm living in your sister's condo? In Dr. Fractal's condo?"

He squinted at her. "Uh, yeah. I told Wendy to let you know that. She had to have told you."

"She didn't. But that makes sense. Well, once the bakery gets up and running, I'll be able to afford somewhere else. Probably not somewhere as nice, but somewhere safe-ish."

"Jessica, stop. You can stay there as long as you want. Why don't you want to take anything from me and my family? Did we do something to you?"

She chewed the inside of her cheek and leaned forward to get a closer look at Jameson's jaw. Not a trace of the fatal injury.

"You can touch it if you want," he said, turning his head and offering his cheek to her.

"No, that's a very bad idea."

"It's fine. Here." He grabbed her hand gently and moved it toward his face.

"I don't think you understand how—" Her fingertips touched his warm skin in the chilly air, and her eyes rolled back into her head as her brain did a quick system overhaul, wiping all discs of anything Chris related.

She swallowed hard and yanked her hand back. "Yeah, I get it. And I don't hate you or Dr. Fractal. I just ... I feel awful. She warned me against getting involved in politics in the capacity I was doing it, and I didn't listen, and it got you killed."

He chuckled. "It got me cast in better roles, is what it got me." He scrunched his nose, grimacing briefly. "Well, once I wasn't terrified to leave the house."

"So what do you want from me?" she asked. "Forgiveness for getting you shot? I don't think I follow."

"Jessica," he placed a hand on her arm and she wondered if he could help being sexy and flirty or if it were a mental tic he had. "I want you to let me help and support you. I want you to stay in my sister's condo for as long as you want. Hell, I'll sign the deed over to you, since she doesn't want it. And I want us"—he waved his hand between them—"to have a relationship."

What she meant to say was, "I have a boyfriend." But as her discs continued to be wiped, she replied, "I need want too for that."

He seemed to understand, nodding his head before holding his arms open to her.

Were they going to make out? What was happening?

She took a single hesitant step forward and he closed the rest of the space, crashing his body into her and hugging her tightly. She used his soft sweater to muffle her whimper and groan of "you smell like heaven" which was simply an illogical thing to say but *felt* as true as anything she'd ever uttered.

"Huh?" he asked, his chin resting on the top of her head.

"Nothing."

He pulled back and looked into her eyes again. "So, are we good?"

"Yeash. Yes. Yeah. We're good."

"And you forgive me for crashing your party?"

His over-the-top puppy eyes cracked her brittle armor, and she chuckled at the absurdity of the situation. "Yes, I forgive you for—"

Those same puppy eyes rolled back into his head as a shiver ran through his body and he moaned.

She gasped and jumped back, cupping a hand over her mouth. "Oh fuck. I'm sorry, Jameson. I didn't mean to ... Um. That was inappropriate and—" His predatory stare cut her words short.

"Was that ... forgiveness?" he asked.

She cringed. "Yes. Sorry."

"Can you forgive me again?"

Shaking her head slowly, she said, "I really shouldn't. I have a boyfriend."

He rolled his shoulders, inhaled deeply, and regained his sexy composure. "I get it. I respect that."

When he didn't immediately make a move to head back inside, she added, "Will you stay for the party?"

"Yeah, I'd love to."

"Cool. Um. Could you do me a favor?"

"Anything."

Whoa. That was a little much. But okay. "Could you take as many selfies as possible with my sorority sisters? I mean, they're going to want a *lot* of them. And then could you send them to me so I can forward them to my social media coordinator? They said they don't do parties 'IRL'? Not sure what that means."

"You don't happen to be talking about Cash Monet, do you?"

She narrowed her eyes, cocked her head to the side. "Uh, yeah, I do happen."

He grinned. "Of course. Figures. Wendy forced me to hire them after I posted a bathroom mirror selfie on Facebook. Social media is hard."

Jessica smiled, though even *she* knew not to post bathroom mirror selfies. "So true."

"Does my hair look alright?"

"It looks like a goddamn angel styled it. Or maybe the patron saint of barbers or something."

Jameson's brows pinched together, which was annoyingly sexy.

"I just mean it looks great. Whatever. Never mind. Let's go back inside before Chris has an aneurysm." She headed around the building and Jameson stayed by her side. "Oh, also, you should probably go talk football with Chris. Do you like football?"

"Of course."

"What team?"

"Cowboys."

"Perfect. Go talk to him about Jason Witten, okay?" They reached the front door and Jameson nodded.

"Whatever you say, Jessica." He grinned at her and she averted her eyes as a defensive measure while Jameson held the door open.

The guests were much friendlier with one another as she entered, even those who had only just met. Thank god for alcohol.

Jameson headed straight over to Chris, introducing himself. When Jessica heard the words "tight end" float over from their conversation and saw her boyfriend's hardened expression soften around the eyes, she knew she was off the hook for her alone time.

Kate approached through the crowd. "Okay, so not mentioning the fact that you just had time alone with Jameson Fractal, which we *will* be talking about later, I think the time is ripe for you to say a few words."

Jessica glanced around. Kate, in all her leadership wisdom, had a point. This was obviously the last ten minutes of the night before everyone crested and then began the inevitable downhill slide to drunkenness. At the moment, though, everyone was at peak sociability and friendliness.

Making her way over to the front counter, Jessica found the nearest glass object (the tip jar) and the nearest metal object (someone's discarded keys) and clanged them together to get the room's attention. Once all eyes were on her, and Quentin hollered, *"That's* where I set them down!" Jessica cleared her throat and tried to remember what she was planning on saying.

She looked out over the faces, some from her childhood, others the few friends and allies she'd picked up along the road since, and she realized, yep, this was a total mistake. She'd never been good at public speaking, and having all the people she cared about in one room left her paranoid. What if someone set the building on fire?

She scanned around until she located Judith's date. He didn't seem to be up to anything at the moment, which was good.

You're being a crazy person. Focus.

She grabbed a beer from the bucket behind her, twisted off the top, and took a long sip. That helped. She hadn't drunk nearly enough over the course of the evening.

"I don't really have anything important to say to y'all except thanks. I guess I've been a little paranoid about accepting help from anyone, for obvious reasons, and I guess I never really thought that the number of people I could rely on would ever be enough to fill a room. So, um, this is cool.

"Oh, also, you guys are all welcome to free coffee anytime you want once the bakery is open."

"Woo!" shouted someone from the NAO section, but Jess missed who it was. The guests laughed, and Jessica figured now was a perfectly suitable time to wrap things up. "There's still beer left, and I have more food in the back I'm about to go grab, so don't be shy. Since I'm not technically open for business, I'm pretty sure we can stay and drink as late as we want tonight." She glanced at Wendy for confirmation, but her PR rep just shrugged. "Okay. Well, uh, that's it! Pigs in a blanket and donuts are next!"

She hurried back into the kitchen, feeling slightly light-headed after all the attention, and as she slipped on the oven mitts, the kitchen door flapped behind her.

She turned and when she saw who it was, she took a quick step back, trying to assess the situation as her mind cataloged every possible exit route.

Joshua closed the space between them.

"What do you need?" she asked, trying to sound calm.

"I need to talk to you."

"Does Judith know you're back here? Why do you need to talk to me?"

He paused a few feet shy of her as she leaned with her back against the warm oven, mitts still on.

"I've been trying to find the perfect moment, to get you alone. I guess now I have it." He puffed up his chest and nodded slightly, grinning. "It's me," he said. "Jessica, I did it. I asked for a promotion and I got it."

Okay. So Joshua was insane. She was trapped in the kitchen with an insane person while everyone else had a blast outside. Would they be able to hear her scream over the music, or would all the people who cared about her find her murdered body after the fact, once Joshua had fled through the back door?

"I don't know what you want from me, but someone could come back here at any moment, so don't try anything." She risked a glance at the countertop and while there was no knife readily available, she saw a metal spatula. It would have to do.

She grabbed it quickly and held it out in front of her, and when Joshua took a quick step forward, she launched it at him, smacking him uselessly on the forehead. "Ow! Jessica ... Sheesh. Why are you being such a meanie?"

Something bristled in the back of her mind. "A ... meanie?" Then the pieces of his odd behavior and what he'd said about a promotion came together to form an entirely different picture in her mind.

"Nooo. You're not ..."

... *SURPRISE!*

"Yes," he said, nodding enthusiastically as he extended his arms outward. "It's me. Jesus."

She flopped back against the oven, groaning. "Oh for fuck's sake. This is just my luck. Are you possessing that body, or what?"

"This old thing?" he glanced down at his front. "No, he was dead. I gave him new life. Or, *more* new life. Newer life?"

She curled a lip, staring at her half-brother while begrudging how hot he was. "You *really* shouldn't refer to a human body as a 'thing.' Doesn't make you super likable."

"I'm not here to make friends, sister. I'm here to help you."

"So Judith is just, what, a beard?" She'd looked up the term a week before, and while she didn't appreciate Cash's previous implication that she might be one for Chris, it seemed appropriate here ... assuming it worked for this incredibly specific context.

He frowned guiltily. "She's kind of a meanie. But I like it. I don't know why."

Jessica held up an oven-mitt-ed hand to stop him. "Okay. This is definitely something we don't need to get into now or ever. Why don't you just tell me what—"

Chris burst through the kitchen door and planted his feet, looking around, fists in front of him. His eyes darted back and forth between Jessica and the man he knew as Joshua.

"What is going on here?" he asked.

"At ease," Jessica said, motioning for him to lower his fists.

"This doucheheap follows you back into the kitchen and I'm supposed to relax?"

"Hello, Christopher," Jesus said, smiling calmly.

"Wha— How do you know my name?"

Jessica jumped in. "Well, you introduced yourself as Chris, and Christopher *is* usually the full version. But also, this is Jesus."

Chris blinked slowly, opened his mouth, then shut it again and blinked a few more times. "Jesus, like ..."

Jessica sighed heavily, wishing there were a faster way through this. "The guy who interrupts our dream sex."

"Interrupted. Past tense," Jesus added. "I followed your advice, pled my case, and now here I am."

Chris wandered over to the ovens to stand next to Jessica, turning his attention toward Jesus. "So this is why Moses showed up the last time?"

"Moses?" Jesus said. "Moses came to you in a dream?"

"Yeah," Jessica replied. "You didn't know about that?"

Jesus shrugged. "Admittedly I'm a little out of the loop now that I'm down here in physical existence."

SO NICE TO HAVE THE FAMILY ALL IN ONE PLACE.

"Ugh," Jessica said, rolling her eyes. "Wait. Can you hear him in your head like I do?"

Jesus nodded. "Oh yes. Wait, can you hear me when I respond to Him?"

Jessica froze. "I don't think so. Can *you* hear *me*?"

Jesus's eyes were two large moons. "I don't know. Say something to Him."

Are you there, God?

OF COURSE. YOU THINK THE LORD WOULD MISS THIS TOUCHING REUNION?

"Could you hear that?" she asked her half-brother.

He shook his head.

"Oh thank ... whoever." The last thing she needed

piled on top of this weirdness was some sort of telepathic connection with Jesus.

THE LORD ADMITS TO HAVING CREATED MANY WEIRD THINGS, LIKE QUASARS AND UVULAS, BUT A PSYCHIC CONNECTION BETWEEN BROTHER AND SISTER WOULD BE A BIT MUCH.

"Agreed," said Jessica and Jesus.

ESPECIALLY GIVEN THE UNIQUELY UPSET-TING THOUGHTS YOU EACH ENTERTAIN.

Please do not elaborate.

Chris rubbed his palms over his eyes then exhaled. "This is so weird. Let me wrap my head around this. Okay. So you are Jesus. And you're dating Judith."

"Judith!" Jessica said. She pointed at Jesus with a mitt. "You have to tell her who you really are."

"Nuh-uh," Jesus said. "I told you, she's a meanie."

"Dude! Seriously?" Chris hollered. "You're scared of her? You apparently stood up to God and asked for a promotion. You've been whipped and crucified and stabbed, right? What's she going to do that's worse than that?"

Jesus cringed. "Break up with me?"

Chris's hard stare melted, and his shoulders softened. "Oh, yeah. That does suck."

Jessica didn't have time for this. "Chris, you make sure he doesn't leave, and I'm calling Judith in here to have a little conversation."

Chris leaned close, whispering. "What do I do if he makes a run for it?"

"Uh, you stop him."

"But he's *Jesus*."

"Yeah, and I'm his sister. Make a decision, Chris." She forcefully handed the mitts to her boyfriend and then grabbed Judith from the front of house with no further explanation than, "I think there's something you should know."

When they entered the kitchen, Chris and Jesus were engaged in a struggle as Jesus tried to push his way to the back door.

"Oh wow. Is this a gay thing?" Judith answered. "Because I *am* a little turned on, and I didn't even think I was into this."

Jesus stopped struggling and turned to face her. "Judith."

"That's my name."

"Yes. I know. And my name—my actual name—is Jesus." He straightened himself up, raising his chin in a dignified manner.

"I don't get it," Judith said, folding her arms over her chest. "That seems like something someone might say ironically, but the tone is all wrong."

"It's Jesus," Jessica said. "As in Jesus Christ."

Judith glanced at her friend, a wrinkle of concern above the bridge of her nose. "No, it's not. Jesus was not blond, despite how desperately the West wants him to be."

"I wasn't blond originally, but I figured I should inhabit

a body to which my sister could easily relate, so I studied the men in whom she maintains the most intense physical interest and found the closest available amalgamation."

"Wait," Chris said. "Is that why you look like me?"

"Indeed. You and Jame—"

"I think we're getting off topic here," Jessica said curtly. "The point is that the person you thought was Joshua is actually Jesus."

Judith rubbed her arm thoughtfully. "I guess that makes sense." She turned to Jesus and grimaced guiltily. "Sorry I was so persistent about the handsy."

"I forgive you," Jesus said.

Judith shivered. "Oh ... hot damn. You"—she waggled a finger at him—"you shouldn't do that if you're not going to put out."

"I don't know what that means," Jesus said, "but I would like to continue our courtship if you're so inclined."

Judith chuckled. "Uh, no. I'm not so inclined." She glanced toward Jessica and pointed over her shoulder back toward the party. "I'm going to go see if that old teacher of yours is down to bang."

"Mr. Foster?!" Chris spat.

Jessica nodded. "I fully support that."

"Bye, Jesus," she said. "Sorry about the harassment, I guess. But also, you should have picked a much less attractive person to wear, so that's kind of on you." Judith turned and strolled out of the kitchen.

Jesus watched her go, and Jessica almost felt sorry for the guy. "You okay?"

"Yes. I've never been romantically rejected before."

Jessica walked over and patted him on the back. "Well, that's what happens when you lie. Now if you don't have anything else pressing, I'm going to bring out food before everyone gets too sloppy drunk. If you want to make yourself useful, you can grab a tray."

He nodded, still clearly dejected, and the three of them carried the next round of food out into the party.

At Jessica's suggestion, Jesus went to play wingman for Jameson over at the NAO table, leaving Chris and Jessica a moment to themselves.

But only a moment.

Dr. Bell came charging in, much less reserved than her normal sober self. "This is wild, Jessica. *Wild!* I've never been around so many angels at once!"

"Yeah, I guess it *is* quite a few," Chris said, staring amusedly at the professor.

Dr. Bell leaned in mischievously. "How many do you think actually know they're angels?"

"No idea," Chris said.

"There *are* a couple that baffle me, though," Dr. Bell continued. "Chris, maybe you can back me up on this. There are a couple auras that don't seem like the usual ones."

Miranda appeared suddenly. "Jessica, I think we're almost out of booze. Quentin and I might head over to the liquor store and get some more. Any preferences?"

"You know I have zero preferences when it comes to alcohol."

"You're just a doll," Dr. Bell said, flopping a hand on Miranda's shoulder. "Jessica is so lucky to have a friend like you."

Looking to Jessica for support, Miranda cringed sympathetically. "Does she have a ride home?"

"We'll find her one," Jessica assured.

"I was just remarking," Dr. Bell continued, grabbing Miranda's shoulder firmly this time, "about all the strange auras we have here, and maybe you can give me your opinion, since you're basically up to your neck in angels all the time, hanging out with this one." She hitched a thumb at Jessica.

"Up to my neck in ... I mean, I know you're an angel," Miranda said. Then she pointed to Chris. "And *you're* an angel."

"You do?" Chris said jerking back. Then he shot Jessica an accusatory glare. "You're outing me now?"

"No, I'm not. I just figured you wouldn't care if Miranda knew."

"*Nuh-uh!*" Dr. Bell said, swaying slightly. "You shouldn't out other angels. Or lesbians. That's a big no-no, *apparently*. But honestly, how was I supposed to know Frida hadn't told her parents?"

"Who's Frida?" Miranda asked.

Jess frowned sympathetically at Dr. Bell. "Did you and Frida break up?"

"Yes."

"When?"

"Yesterday."

Okay, that made sense. Dr. Bell didn't strike Jessica as the type to get hammered at a small party under normal circumstances.

Chris seemed to follow along, too, and ran to grab a tall chair, bringing it over for Bell. The professor complied, tipping back onto it.

"Like I was saying," she continued, "the auras are weird on a couple. Not just powerful, but kinda colored strange." She addressed Miranda didactically. "Okay, Aura 101. Class is in session. I never get to teach humans about this, but since you know about all this heaven and hell and whatever shit, I get to teach you. Isn't this fun? This is so fun. Now, normally, auras sort of just swirl, and they can have different colors, usually you have to squint to make out any definite color or substance to them. But then you got that guy"—she pointed at Jesus—"and he walks in here and it's like *bam!* Just aura in your face, but it's also kinda clearer than most, like the surface of a glacier lake. Kinda like Jessica's, actually. Right, Chris?"

Chris shrugged amicably, but Jessica had a feeling she should nip this conversation in the bud. While Dr. Bell was the one who'd taught Jessica not to out angels, the woman was also not entirely herself at the moment.

"How about some water?" Jessica said. "I think water would be a good idea." She looked meaningfully at Chris who nodded his agreement but didn't take the hint that he'd just been assigned a task.

"That teacher of yours, Jessica. Boy has *she* got a strong aura, sorta cloudy, too. I've been watching it closely, and it's like some of that cloudiness can pass on into other angels' auras."

"Right?" Chris shouted. "It's nuts."

SURPRISE!

"Wait, Mrs. Thomas is an angel?" Jessica asked, forgetting all about the water.

"I guess that makes sense," Miranda said.

Jessica had suspected as much herself since she first learned about angels, and it *was* nice to have a little confirmation. She turned to Chris. "How did you never mention this to me? You've seen her aura this whole time?"

He lurched back defensively, hands up. "I saw it when we were in Mooretown, but I didn't even understand any of this stuff until a little over a year ago. What, am I just supposed to drop everything and catalog every angel I've ever met and then out them to you, one by one?"

Jessica knew Chris was trying to be absurd, but often in her strange life, the absurd proposal was also the most desirable one. "Uh, yes. That would have been mega helpful, Chris. I mean, if I'd *known* she was an angel, I wouldn't have worried so much about taking the money from her."

"Wait," Bell said, shutting her eyes and waving her hands vaguely. "She's the one who cut you that check?"

"Yeah, but like you said, she's an angel, so it's fine."

Dr. Bell hiccuped. "Well, I don't know that you should blindly trust all angels, after all—" She hiccuped again.

"Slow down," Miranda said, "only angels have auras?"

Dr. Bell nodded dramatically. "Well, and Jessica."

"And Jesus, apparently," Jess added.

Miranda squinted at her. "Did you just say Jesus?"

"Oh, yeah, um." She glanced at Dr. Bell. "I'll explain later."

Dr. Bell continued with her lecture. "Now, Chris here has an all-American aura. It's unusually bright, but about as run of the mill as they come in all other respects."

"Thank you," Chris said, puffing out his chest.

Bell turned to Miranda. "Same with yours."

Miranda's jaw fell open. "Mine?"

"Hers?" Jess said.

"Yeah, hers?" Chris echoed. "I don't see one on her."

"No, no, no." Dr. Bell sliced the air with her hands. "Not her. Hers. Like, her boyfriend. That *is* your boyfriend over there, right?"

Before Jessica could shout, "You're mistaken, Dr. Bell. Miranda's dating Quentin. The black guy. And he's not an angel. Let's go get another beer!" Miranda turned slowly toward the rest of the room. "Wait, who do you think is my boyfriend?"

Chris jumped in front of Dr. Bell, shielding her from the rest of the room. "Ha! You think Jeremy is her boyfriend. No, no. Not at all. That's just Jessica's neighbor. Let's get you some water."

"*Jeremy's* an angel?" Jessica said, suddenly distracted. NOT MUCH OF A SURPRISE!

"Duh," Chris said. "I don't think he knows it, though."

"That would make sense," Dr. Bell said, nodding. "I overheard him saying some pretty batty things to Mrs.

Flores. His long-term denial might've left him a little addled." She jabbed at her head with her index finger.

"Nuh-uh!" Miranda demanded. "She wasn't looking anywhere near Jeremy. She was looking straight at Quentin." She leaned forward, bringing her face close to Dr. Bell's. "You mean the black one, right?"

"I don't know that we have to bring *race* into this," Chris said loudly, trying to maneuver Dr. Bell around Miranda. But she was too quick on her feet.

Goddamn athletes.

"Yeah, the one you walked in with," Dr. Bell said, her brows crinkling together. "That's your boyfriend, right?"

"Ha!" Miranda stood up straight. "I *knew* it!" She pointed back and forth between Chris and Jessica. "You two hid it from me. You knew and you hid it from me." She homed in on Jessica. "I even asked you flat out if you would tell me if it might affect my life." Her eyes narrowed and she scoffed, pointing accusingly at Jessica. "You lied straight to my face. I asked *one* thing—" She balled her hand into a fist and pressed her lips together in a thin white line, staring up at the ceiling and grunting.

Dr. Bell gasped belatedly. "Wait, you didn't know? I outed an angel?"

"You serious?" Chris said. "Paging Dr. Drunky— you've been outing angels for the past five minutes."

Miranda's cheeks puffed in and out and her face turned red. "Does he know? He knows, doesn't he?" she demanded, smartly focusing her interrogation on Chris.

"I—I don't know. You'll have to ask him."

A twitch appeared just below her right eye and she took a deep breath, bobbing her head slowly. "Okay, maybe I'm getting ahead of—" Then her eyes shot open and her jaw dropped. "No! That text you sent him! You called him an angel! He knows." Her nostrils flared and her voice lowered. "*He knows.*"

Jess tried to push between Chris and Dr. Bell. "Miranda, wait."

But she was off, making straight for Quentin, and Jessica knew from experience she couldn't catch Miranda if she tried. At least not in a sprint less than ninety feet.

"Fuuuuuck!" Jessica shouted, throwing her hands into the air.

SUR—

Don't you dare.

She jumped up and down, trying to get Quentin's attention to warn him before Miranda could lay into him, but he was too absorbed in conversation with Coach Rex to notice the flailing.

What now? She looked around the room. Maybe she could pull a fire alarm or smite something as a distraction. But the thought of causing any damage to the bakery she'd worked so hard to build caused her stomach to tighten, and she just couldn't do it.

"She would've found out eventually," Chris said, putting his arm around Jessica's waist. "Better now than later?"

"Sure."

"Yeah, he's gonna be pissed."

"Not as pissed as she is."

As Miranda swooped in, grabbed Quentin, and dragged him out of the bakery, Rex and Destinee stood dumbfounded, watching the couple go before looking around. Destinee was the first to spot Jessica and Chris, and she swatted Rex's arm to get his attention before leading him over. "What the hell was that?" Destinee said. "The wrath of God was in that girl. Saw her coming over, thought she was gonna try to tackle me again like we were back in White Light."

"It's a long story," Jessica said.

"Do I need to call the cops?" asked Rex. "I just mean, to assume that women are the sole victims of domestic violence is to paint them as powerless and perpetuate the societal normalization of women as victims."

Chris said, "I think Quentin can handle himself, Coach."

Jessica swallowed hard. "I'm not so sure, actually. She's got quite the throwing arm on her."

As she looked around the room, it was clear they were officially on a downhill slide. At a two-top table in the far corner, Judith was perched on Mr. Foster's lap, the pair perhaps a mere few minutes away from leaving together. At the NAO table, Wendy was struggling to wrest her favorite client from the arms of intoxicated women with their phones out, snapping one questionable selfie with Jameson after another. "You better not post that!" she yelled over and over again as Jameson grinned like an idiot and continued to scoot so he was at least partly visible in every picture.

Jesus and Jeremy stood by the drink fountain, leaning close while Jeremy prattled on conspiratorially—probably literally—about something that necessitated him occasionally stepping back and flinging his right arm in a large circle like a windmill while Jesus hung on to his every word. That couldn't be good.

Mrs. Thomas brought another round of beers over to Maria and Gabrielle who chatted casually with Kate and Natalie by a nearly half-eaten platter of pigs in a blanket, and Jessica wondered if there were a way to end this whole thing immediately.

But she knew better. No matter how great something seemed to be going, everything went south eventually. This party was no different. Her relationships with these people who she cared about more than anything else were likely not exempt either.

It always comes crashing to the ground, no matter how hard I try.

"You put on one hell of a party," Chris said to her right.

She detected no sarcasm whatsoever.

He put a strong arm around her shoulders and she leaned into him. "We ruined two couples, Chris."

"Nuh-uh. *Lies* ruined two couples."

She jerked her head around to look up at him. "Huh. I guess you're right. That's a damn astute observation."

"Yeah, well. Don't get used to it. Also, you should know that I'd never lie to you. You mean too much to me."

He kissed the top of her head. "Oh, and now that I know Jesus won't be interrupting us tonight, there's some freaky stuff I want to try out. You down?"

After an evening of worlds colliding—and no one coming out the better for it—she couldn't think of anything she'd rather do to take her mind off of reality. "Only if we have a safe word."

"How about 'no'?" Chris suggested.

"That makes sense." She looked up at him, admiring the cut of his jaw, his tan skin, his blue eyes. "I'm lucky to have you, Chris."

He nodded coolly. "I know."

Chapter Twenty-Six

Jessica paused in the hallway at the doorstep of her condo, sleepily fumbling through her keys to find the right one. She had more keys—so many more keys—now that she was officially a business owner. There were two keys to the bakery's front door, a separate one for the back door (the discrepancy arose from the heavy-duty locks she had installed, each of which was unique and included keys that couldn't be duplicated without a series of useful criminal connections), one key for the cash register, another for the safe, another for the freezer ...

Was she really a business owner, though? Officially? The grand opening wasn't for another week and a half. She supposed she had all the legal paperwork to qualify, but she hadn't consummated the thing, so to speak.

The door behind her swung open and male voices jabbered excitedly. Did Jeremy have a friend over? Did Jeremy have friends? Well, besides her.

She twisted to look over her shoulder, flashed a smile, turned back toward her door, registered who she'd just seen, then turned her entire body around. "What are *you* doing here?"

"Oh hello, Jessica," Jesus said merrily, still chuckling about some joke or another. He was dressed in dark-wash jeans and a black Journey T-shirt, one Jessica was fairly sure she'd seen on Jeremy. "How are you doing on this fine spring day?"

"What are you doing here?" she repeated.

Jeremy locked the door behind him—first the standard lock, then the two he'd installed himself—and joined the conversation. He donned light-wash jeans and a Black Sabbath T-shirt. They were dressed like two past-their-prime peas in a pod. "He's staying with me for a while," said Jeremy.

Her eyes jumped back and forth between the two men. "Like, a roommate?"

An inquisitive look passed between the two men, then both smiled. Jeremy nodded. "Yeah, I guess like a roommate."

"I was living on the streets before," Jesus explained. "I'd assumed treatment of the homeless would have improved over the last two thousand years as human consciousness evolved and so forth, but I was quite wrong. People are still big meanies to the homeless. They gave me copper coins, which, at first, seemed quite generous, but it turns out those things are worth very little."

Jessica cleared her throat and guiltily turned her eyes up to inspect the recessed lighting along the hallway.

"Joshua is a riot, isn't he?" Jeremy said, chuckling. "He's the only person I've met who hasn't absorbed all the governmental conditioning. He's got a fresh take on everything!" He patted Jesus on the shoulder, and Jesus bowed his head humbly, saying, "I'm just doing my job, adding a new perspective."

"Really?" Jessica said. "Is *that* why you're here? Because I've been wondering about it for the last week and a half."

"Of course. My purpose in this life is reformation."

"Nooo ..." Jessica held up a pointer finger to correct him. "That was your purpose *last time*."

Jeremy jumped in. "Oh wait, is this the Jesus thing?" He turned to Jesus. "Does she know about it?"

Jessica jerked her head back so far, she could feel the triple chin form. "Wait. Do you know about that?"

"I told him," Jesus said casually. "I didn't want another relationship based on a lie. So I told him."

Jeremy grinned and nodded along, then turned to Jessica. "Don't believe a word of it myself. Just seems a little crazy. But hey, I spent two semesters in college fairly convinced I was an angelic soldier of God, so"—he chuckled —"we all believe crazy things about ourselves sometimes. The human need to feel special is just that strong, I guess."

Jesus guffawed and jabbed a thumb at Jeremy like, *don't you love this guy?*

Jeremy shoved his keys into the pocket of his old jeans. "We'd better get going, Joshua. They fill up fast."

As Jeremy took a step toward the parking garage exit, Jessica jumped in front of him. "Who fills up fast?"

He avoided her eyes and rubbed the back of his neck. "Just this little tucked away kosher place for lunch. No big deal."

"Don't worry," she said, "I'm not trying to invite myself. I have a lot of stuff to do today."

Jesus said, "I'll tell you all about it when we get back, *neighbor.*"

She suppressed a groan.

When Jeremy started off again, Jessica grabbed her half-brother's arm to have a private word. "Hey, I'm glad you're happy and have a friend or whatever, but, um"—she scanned him from head to toe—"if you two keep dressing the same and live together, it's going to raise some questions."

"Like?" he said, grinning.

"Um, just that, well, and it's not a bad thing, but that you two are closer than friends."

He leaned forward, his eyes wide with excitement as he whispered, "You mean *best friends?*"

"Eh ... sort of." Jesus wasn't going to take the hint, and Jeremy had paused four doors down the hallway, presumably noticing that "Joshua" wasn't following. "People will assume you're gay. It's not a big deal nowadays—God's even said so—but if you aren't, then people assuming it might not be something you want." She held up her hands defensively. "That's all I'm saying."

Jesus turned his head slightly, inspecting her expression thoughtfully. "But sis, I *am* gay."

She took a step back to brace herself against her front door. "Okay. Nothing wrong with that, but, um ..."

Jesus threw his arms out to the side, grinning like a fool. "I'm so incredibly gay, I can hardly stand it! Ha!" He bounced up and down. "I don't care who knows it, either! I can't remember the last time I've felt this gay."

She pressed her finger to her lips. "Sh-sh-sh. That's great. I'm incredibly happy for you, but—"

"See?" He pointed at her. "It's contagious. Now you're gay as well!"

She quickly scanning the hallway, making sure none of the other neighbors were around to hear. "Whoa, whoa. Rein it in, cowboy. Gay isn't contagious. It's— Oh." She nodded. "You mean happy. You're gay as in happy."

Jesus nodded his head emphatically. "Yuh-huh!"

Jeremy made his way back and grabbed Jesus by the arm. "Yeah, this guy doesn't have a gay bone in his body. Trust me. I'm gay, so I can tell."

"You're gay too?" Jesus exclaimed. "I'm so glad to hear it. Being the only gay one is no fun."

"Agreed," Jeremy said. "Now let's get going."

As soon as the two were out of sight, she decided the best course of action, at least for the time being, was to also put them out of mind.

She found the right key and strolled into her home, going down her mental checklist.

If she wasn't mistaken, everything was ready to go for the grand opening of It is Risen Bakery. That didn't make her any less anxious about leaving town for a week, though. Any number of things could go terribly wrong in a week. How many times had her life taken a turn for the worst in a single day? A single hour? A single second?

I still made it here, though, didn't I? I'm living proof a person can recover.

CREDIT WHERE IT IS DUE.

No. I'm not letting you take this from me.

She parked it on a stool by the island and slipped her phone from her back pocket to check for updates.

A text from Cash included the latest stats of #itisrisen on Twitter, along with a recap of which celebrities were talking about paying her bakery a visit once it opened its doors.

Whatever. It wasn't like she made more money from a celebrity. A croissant and coffee cost the same no matter who bought it. But it was nice to know Cash was having a fun time on the job. They had been riding high since the photos of Jameson Fractal at her grand opening began not *breaking*, per se, but *disrupting* the internet. Word had officially spread about her business plans, and the photo of Chris and Jameson each planting a sloppy kiss on her cheek, one on either side— taken at the butt end of the party, when all inhibitions had had cinderblocks tied to their ankles before being shoved in the figurative Gulf of Mexico—had started a contentious shipper debate. Jessica herself was obviously #teamchris, but Cash wouldn't allow her to weigh in publicly.

And email update from Wendy popped up, but the subject line told Jessica all she needed to know for now: *Paperwork filed.*

She was officially suing Jimmy Dean. Okay. Good to know. Godspeed then, Wendy's remaining lawyer boyfriend. Maybe in the next couple years, Jessica would be a dollar richer for it and be legally and publicly off the hook for that awful foreword. And all without giving Jimmy the pleasure of believing she did it for the money. Maybe she would frame his check for one dollar and zero cents—the total amount she was claiming in the lawsuit—and put it up on the wall in It is Risen.

Eh ... seemed a little petty.

But awesome.

Another email notification popped up. Wendy again. The subject line was, *News Clip Links.*

That would be Maria's exposé. Maybe also the local coverage, courtesy of Magda Masterson and Steve Solstice, but mostly courtesy of Jeremy Archer, who'd exerted his terrifying power over the media as a sign of good faith to Jessica. Aw, how sweet.

Then she remembered he was living with Jesus.

She shook her head to clear it. That was definitely a "later" problem to deal with.

The sound of a toilet flushing within her home made

Jessica drop her phone on the counter and jump up from her seat. Shitballs. She'd completely forgotten.

She pressed a hand to her chest as Destinee emerged from the bathroom, wiping her hands on her jeans. "You're almost out of TP."

"How? I just put some in there."

Destinee held out her arms like, *and?* "Ain't never walked so much, drank so much coffee, and ate so many damn tacos in a single twenty-four hours. What do you want me to say?"

Jessica cringed but conceded with a tilt of her head. "Yeah, my first week here was a little like that, too. Your body will adjust."

"Doesn't your flight leave soon, baby?"

"Oh, right!" She turned in a tight circle, scanning for where she put the bag of new wintery clothes she'd picked up the day before. While Chicago might not be frigid in April, that didn't mean it would be comfortable without gloves, layers, and a scarf.

"You nervous about flying?" Destinee asked.

"No. God won't let me die in a plane crash." She found the bag over by the couch, but it was empty. That was right, she took out the accessories to try them on …

"You definitely seem anxious about something, though. Is it the bakery?"

"A little bit."

"The Draft?"

"A little bit."

"Miranda?"

Jessica peaked out from her bedroom where she'd gone to grab her suitcase. "No. I already told you. She'll come around."

Though honestly, Jessica had her doubts. Miranda might never come around. That'd be understandable, really. The three people she trusted the most had all lied to her, schemed behind her back.

Shit. Why did we do that? Why didn't we just tell her?

And now Jessica was short one best friend for life and Quentin was short one girlfriend and flush one expensive engagement ring. She hadn't properly apologized to him, but she'd lost sleep over the past week and a half brainstorming the best way to do that while they were both up in Chicago.

She pulled up the checklist on her phone and went through the inventory. Everything except her scarf. Where had she put the damn scarf?

Only after three passes through the condo did she remember: her feet. They'd been cold the night before while she and her mother sat on the couch binge watching that true crime documentary series. The throw blanket they shared wasn't enough, so she'd gone to look for socks. All her socks had been either packed or dirty, so she'd had to improvise.

Which meant the scarf was probably between the couch cushions.

She slipped a flat hand in the crevice, feeling around blindly. Her fingertips hit something hard and slick. Not a scarf, obviously. She grunted and maneuvered the object free.

Dammit. Why do I still have this thing?

She tossed the copy of *Railed to the Cross* onto the other end of the couch and dove back into the cushions until her hand found the scarf. As she shook it out, Destinee said, "You ever finish that thing?"

"Hell no. I had better things to do."

"I won't argue with that." Destinee strolled over to the living room and flopped down onto the stiff couch a moment before kicking her feet onto the armrest. She held the book in her hands and stared at the cover. "You ever think about writing a memoir, baby?" She grinned up at her daughter, who stood rolling the scarf into a tight spiral. "I bet you could write one hell of a memoir."

"Again," Jessica said, "I have better things to do."

As she packed the scarf away in her suitcase, she remembered Wendy's warning. Well, to say she remembered it implied that she at some point forgot it, and while it was rarely front and center of her attention, it was always just out of sight, active in the part of her brain where she stored all fear, an instant away from setting off a fight or flight response should it be shaken loose.

Jimmy was going to be powerful. Only power could fight power. Jessica had to become powerful, too.

And she would. She was. Not there yet, but she was moving in that direction. She could feel it. Her bakery was the epicenter of her power, and as soon as it opened ...

Well, she wasn't sure yet what would happen, but

something would, and she thought it would be something in her favor. Cash seemed to think so, at least. And Wendy. And all those other people who had contributed so much for it to happen. Deep down, they must've known, even if they hadn't heard Wendy spell it out.

It had all come together. Sure, her best friend wasn't talking to her, and she hadn't had a conversation with Chris that lasted more than an hour in months, and sure, she was unofficially indebted to a lot of good people and officially indebted to Mrs. Thomas. But it still felt good to build something, and assuming the NFL draft went well, she might shift some of that indebtedness away from all the sundry sources and squarely onto Chris. And being indebted to Chris felt almost natural. Or rather, it felt safer. Indebtedness was vulnerability, and she'd practiced the latter with him countless times and in countless sexy ways.

Would she marry him? Why not? Who else would she marry? Who else would marry her?

No, that isn't a good reason.

She zipped up her suitcase.

I'll come back to the marriage thing. There's no hurry. If Chris was still around after months of neglect while she'd started the business and they'd lived thirty minutes apart, he would be there when she finally made up her mind about marriage. He deserved to marry someone who was sure she wanted to marry him, anyway. She only had his best interest in mind, really.

She lugged the suitcase off the bed and rolled it across

the kitchen and to the front door. "Hey, can I see that?" she said.

Glancing up, Destinee closed the book and held it out to her.

Jessica took it, spared one last look at the cover with *Jessica Christ* emblazoned across it, then opened the book and began tearing out clumps of pages, setting each one down on the island in a small stack. When she was done, she tossed the hollow hardcover into the recycling bin. "There. Problem solved."

Destinee, who'd cautiously stood when the tearing began, looked from Jessica to the stack of papers to the recycling bin and back to Jessica. "What problem?"

"The toilet paper problem. This should last you till I get back." She patted the papers. "Now let's get going so I don't miss my first flight."

Chapter Twenty-Seven

Excerpt from Railed to the Cross

Two summers flew by in Carson City. My life required little speaking, discouraged it, actually, and I was, on the whole, content in my work. The hours outside graves, though, began to wear on me. And my need to follow a great man of God steadily swallowed up my waking moments on the weekends. Eventually, the need overtook my weekdays, too, once I'd finished my work and emerged from the safe earth. Nightmares often colored my sleep, startling me awake in cold sweats. Mostly they were of Joel, his shriveled body, his gaunt, pocked face as he asked me why I left him there in the desert all on his own. I longed for the time when my nightmares predominantly revolved around watching Gustav clutch his chest in the rain, mud soaking his clothes as he thrashed around, begging for my mercy.

When Reverend Joel appeared in my dreams for the seventh day in a row one August, twelve years after his death, I could take no more. I dressed in the small room I rented from an old lady who seemed intent on making pies with rotten fruit, grabbed my water jug that I took with me to work every day and a large black trash bag, and set out in search of the spot where I'd left the reverend over a decade past. I could make things right. I had the means. If I could find the trailer, perhaps I could gather his bones and slip them into a grave at St. Anthony's without a soul knowing. Perhaps then I could bring him peace and in doing so, provide the same for myself.

My recollection was foggy on where I might find him, but I walked in the tepid night air northeast until I found the train tracks. So long as I followed them northwest, away from Las Vegas and toward Reno, I might start to see familiar landmarks. Then I could follow those landmarks until I broke a new horizon and, if all went according to my plan, find what remained of Joel's tomb.

However, in the desert, most everything looks the same. So I began doubting my plan that had seemed fool-proof only hours before, once I hopped the first train heading in the desired direction.

The morning sun beat down on the boxcar, turning it into a microwave despite the cross breeze of the open doors, and when I first saw the smoke in the distance, I wondered if it were really there or if I were hallucinating from the heat.

Deep within my bones, I could feel it. This was a sign

from God. It was just like Joel had taught me. And of course, this was how I would find my way to the man who navigated his life by following such soulful indicators.

I grabbed my jug, which was almost empty, and the garbage bag, then leaped off the train before I could think twice. I hit the ground and rolled, a practiced maneuver, and dusted myself off. I can't explain with words how I knew to follow the smoke, only that every fiber of my corporal form told me to go. Whatever was causing the smoke was beyond the horizon, which meant I had miles to go before I would arrive there. And then there would be miles back. I wasn't sure how I would manage with so little water, but I didn't let it concern me. If a man dies following signs from the creator, a man dies in the best way possible. But if it wasn't my time to die, God would provide a way. My faith, the very one Joel had instilled in me through dishonest means, carried me forward over the dry landscape. One foot in front of the other, I headed toward the promise God had made when He filled me with so much holy spirit that I had no choice but to leap from that moving train.

The sun was on its descent toward the Pacific and the smoke was thin by the time the source was visible to me.

Little remained of the structure, but I knew it by heart. It was as I'd hoped. Joel's trailer.

The reverend's words returned to me as I slowed to a halt ten yards from the burning box. Moses didn't know to look for a burning bush, but he knew the sign when he saw it. I didn't know to look for a burning trailer, but I also knew the sign when I saw it. And after all these years, for the fire to erupt the same day my conscience got the best of me, compelled me to leave the modest comfort of my bed and drove me here—God's hand in this could not have been any plainer. Perhaps Joel hadn't performed a single provable miracle in his life, but God had no qualms being indelicate when He needed to. And it seemed that with me, He needed to.

I understood now. By returning to Joel's final resting place, now armed with the knowledge of how rare of a man he was, his purpose was complete. I'd learned his lesson, though it took a dozen years. And now God thrust His cleansing upon the man, for his work was done. Joel was purified and forgiven by those flames; I understood that in my soul.

My shepherd was gone. It had taken me twelve long years to confront that truth, but here it was. I was a John with no Jesus. Or if it was as Demarcus said, Joel had been *my* John, and now that he was gone, having wasted away in close confinement like John the Baptist had, it was my turn to lead.

That was it, then. I didn't need another leader. I needed to *become* the leader. It was time to stop suppressing my own greatness, passing the years in graves. And while I didn't feel ready, it looked like God left me no other option.

"Fine," I yelled at the smoldering trailer, "I'll do it. But I don't know how. Please give me a sign now!"

I waited but nothing happened, and the flames began

to die in front of me while I watched, embers dancing spirals toward the sky, turning to ash then blowing away in the breeze.

The sun set, and I waited, sitting on the hot, arid ground as I finished the last drop of my water. Would God let me die out here? The idea of it so close to my realization seemed perverse and unholy. God wouldn't orchestrate something so morose.

The sun lit the western horizon in a crimson blaze by the time the rubble of the trailer had stopped glowing hot. It smoked, but I could approach safely. I circled to the back where the window once was. Melted and warped metal crosses poked out of the ashes at awkward angles. I located where the bed would have been then poked through the soot with the toe of my boot, looking for his bones.

But I could find nothing.

Much could have happened between when I left the trailer and when I returned, but the lack of his bones disturbed me and I continued my search for the next hour but to no avail. Where could they be? I had failed in my mission by waiting so long to return. I couldn't collect his remains and properly bury them. I'd ridden all this way for nothing. I'd failed him. Again.

What was next? Where did I go from here? Had I ever felt so forsaken? I think not. The despair consumed me like the fire had consumed Joel's tomb.

I fell to my knees, but still, no tears would come. Agony, though, was plentiful, and as it took root in my gut and crawled upward to wrap around my lungs and heart, I turned my eyes toward the heavens, crying out an incoherent plea. I stared up at the sun in the west and spotted a flock of birds heading my way from the direction of Lake Tahoe. Had birds carried off his bones?

It was while I considered this possibility that I felt something land on my right shoulder, and when I looked down, I discovered, with some manic glee, that a bird had shat on me as the flock passed overhead. I quickly returned my gaze skyward to see what direction they were headed.

Southeast.

The reverend, a master of godly interpretation, a heavenly antenna for divine signs, had himself become a sign. He no longer remained here, and neither should I.

For God's plan had not ended, and while it's possible I had strayed from the path, He had led me back.

Deus Aper had not forsaken me after all.

Had a man ever been so blessed? In my darkest hour, a flock of birds appeared. The Lord, in His infinite wisdom, had known I would need an obvious signal, and so it was that He provided such.

I set off on foot immediately southeast, following the path God's winged messengers had so blatantly indicated.

Chapter Twenty-Eight

In the high-end hotel suite, Chris's confident composure was wearing thin as he stared at himself in the full-length mirror. Only a moment earlier, he'd tried to put his left shoe on his right foot three times before Jessica stepped in and helped. As he fumbled with his tie, tension pursed his lips and his cheeks flushed. His mother stepped in then, trying and failing twice herself, clearly as nervous as her son about the evening's event. As mother and son began to fuss at each other over the matter, Jessica resorted to calling Coach Brown two rooms over to come help.

Chris's college coach had been through all this before with previous players, and while Jessica suspected his calm demeanor was not entirely representative of his emotional state, his quiet composure was exactly what Chris needed to steady himself.

"You may not be picked in the first round, Riley," he said, "but you'll be picked. The Cowboys want you bad.

Their current quarterback is unbelievably accident prone, and their backup can hardly tie his own shoes. You saw both of those things for yourself in the divisional playoff game. As long as the Texans don't scoop you up, you'll be right where you want to be."

"And the Texans aren't a bad place to be either," Jessica reminded. "Houston's actually closer than Dallas."

Coach Brown shot her sharp side-eye. "More importantly, both teams are set up perfectly for a rookie quarterback. The offensive lines are solid, and it would be a great place for you to settle in and make a name for yourself before you're traded."

"One thing at a time," Jessica said. "Let's just focus on the next four years before we talk about him being traded somewhere across the country." She inserted herself between Chris and Coach Brown, straightening Chris's tie unnecessarily and giving him a quick, chaste kiss on the cheek, aware that Mrs. Riley wasn't as loosey-goosey about PDA as Destinee.

"We should get going," Coach Brown said. "Takes quite a bit of time to make it through the media circus to our table."

Jessica pulled out her phone. "I'll let Quentin and Rex know to meet us downstairs."

While exploring Chicago all week—and indeed, leaving Texas for the first time in her life—had been better than she could have imagined, spending time with Quentin without Miranda felt strange and wrong. But Jessica knew she had to get used to this new reality. She couldn't blame Miranda, but she also felt terrible for Quentin. And for herself.

During the past two evenings, when Chris was asked to attend sponsored parties solo, leaving Quentin and Jessica to entertain themselves around the Loop, never once had Quentin blamed her or Chris for what had happened. He didn't even blame Miranda. And that was somehow worse, knowing he only blamed himself.

Granted, it *was* his fault. But she also understood why he would want Miranda to think he was just a regular human. After all, he didn't choose to be an angel. Though at the same time, Miranda had the right to choose a normal life with a normal human.

She'd tried to apologize for her role in outing him, or rather, preventing Dr. Bell from outing him, as they sat at the hotel bar one night, but he wouldn't hear it. All those hours of planning just what she would say were for naught. He wouldn't let her get more than five words of her apology out before he swiftly shut her down with, "If you're my friend, you'll knock that shit off right now."

So she knocked the shit off right then, aware that Quentin had just out-friended her, just like Miranda always did.

As she and Chris made their way down the escalator to the lobby, he leaned close and whispered, "You look incredible tonight, Jess. I can't wait till we get through this and I can have some alone time with you."

She swatted his hand away from her butt. "And how

exactly are you going to pull that off, since you're sharing a room with your mom?"

"*You're* not. You have your own room. I can come over there."

"You don't think your mom would notice you weren't in the twin next to her? Please. We'll just meet up in our dreams."

"But what if I moan in my sleep?"

Quentin and Rex waved from a couch in the lobby.

"Head in the game, Riley," she said before walking over to meet the others.

The hired car fit all six of Chris and his entourage, and Jessica indulged herself in how nice it was not being the center of attention for once. Luxurious.

At least, until they arrived at Grant Park. Apparently, the reporters hadn't gotten the memo that Jessica wasn't the main event.

Chris kept his arm around her waist as he led her down the red carpet toward the tables, and she pointedly ignored phrases like, "Messiah from Texas" and "World record holder for longest field goal." It'd been so long since she'd given up her football days, she'd forgotten she had a legacy of her own with this crowd.

A female reporter leaned past the ropes, holding out her microphone so that it almost clotheslined Chris. "Are you entering the draft, Ms. McCloud?"

"Hell no," she said on impulse, and Chris pushed the microphone out of his way as they continued.

By the time the usher led them to their table, Jessica

was drained and wondered how long this would take. Others were seated around the venue already, but mostly the tables were empty. Jessica and Mrs. Riley sat on either side of Chris, and Quentin took the seat on the other side of Jessica, with the two coaches sitting opposite the prospective rookie. An old-school black telephone was the centerpiece of the round, formally dressed table.

She leaned over to Chris. "Is that for you?"

He nodded quickly, staring reverently at it. "A representative from the team calls the player they want to draft. When that phone rings, you know I've been drafted."

"What if you don't answer?"

Chris whipped his head around, horror in his eyes. "You have to answer the phone."

"No, but I mean, what if you don't? Like, what if it's the Browns or something? Can you just say, 'Sorry, wrong number'?"

Chris shook his head slowly like she'd just blasphemed. "If I don't answer, I don't enter into the NFL and my dream withers away. Jessica, when the call comes, I answer it."

"Okay, okay," she said, looking around to escape his scornful eyes. "Jesus, I was just asking," she grumbled.

As the rest of the tables filled over the next half hour and small salads arrived for each guest, Chris and Quentin leaned over Jessica to animatedly gossip about each new face that arrived.

"Did you see Le'davian Davidson?" Quentin rasped at Chris.

"What are you," Jessica said, "his fangirl or something?"

Quentin turned to her seriously. "Yes. Dude's a beast. He had fifty-two sacks last season for Notre Dame."

"Dude, dude, dude!" Chris said, staring just past Quentin's right arm. "It's Willie Frank Epstein. Should I go introduce myself to him?"

"What? No way!" Quentin said.

"Yeah, that's a serial killer name, Chris," Jessica added. "You should stay away from him."

They ignored her. "He's your rival now," Quentin explained. "Not the time to cozy up to other quarterbacks. Wait until you figure out where you go and where they go, *then* you can decide who to be friends with. I mean, what if he goes to the Eagles, who we all know desperately need a new QB, safely assuming the current one goes to prison, which he *should*,"—Chris nodded—"then you go to the Cowboys. You two can't be friends if you're in the same division."

"Especially not if he's with the Eagles," Chris said.

Quentin pointed at him. "Exactly."

"Yeah, good call."

As Mrs. Riley gently got her son's attention and the two began talking in low tones, Jessica leaned toward Quentin. "So like, I didn't want to ask Chris because I didn't want to freak him out, but is there a difference in pay from round one to round two? Like, what happens if he's not drafted in the first round?"

"Yeah, there's a huge difference, but it's really only a matter of being filthy rich or filthy stinking rich."

"So we should probably hire a financial planner?"

Quentin jerked his head back to get a clearer look at her. "Uh, yeah. God love that boy, but he doesn't know the first thing about money. He'd probably try to give it all to you, and nobody wants to be in the position of turning down millions of dollars each year."

Jessica nearly choked on the ice water she sipped from stemmed glassware. "Wait, millions?"

"Girl, you really didn't look up any of this?"

"I've been busy. Besides, it's not my business."

"If you and Riley are gonna settle down soon, it is."

"Well." She didn't continue. There wasn't anything else to say. Yet, at least. She'd figure out how her life with Chris might look once the draft was over.

"So if he doesn't get picked in the first round," Quentin continued, "we'll all be back here tomorrow for the second round."

"Oh god, that sounds awful."

"Oh yeah," said Quentin. "Let's just hope it doesn't happen." He narrowed his eyes at her calculatingly. "Or maybe ... *pray* it doesn't happen?"

"Yeah, I'm not bringing God into this."

"I mean, I wouldn't blame you if you did. And never a better time than when the future of the man you love hangs in the balance."

Shitballs. Was Quentin *trying* to make her nauseated? "Chris would kill me if he found out, though."

"Then don't tell him."

She arched an eyebrow. "Yeah? Not telling the other person is a good idea? That couldn't possibly blow up in my face later on?"

Quentin deflated. "You have a point, I guess."

Jessica immediately regretted bringing it up. "I'm sorry."

"No, you're right."

The lights dimmed and quiet murmuring washed over the crowd.

And then the fanfare started with lights and music. An announcer's voice booming over it all left Jessica confused for a split second, wondering why God was welcoming everyone to the National Football League draft before she realized the booming voice was, in fact, external.

The New England Patriots were first up after the opening, and Jess sat back while Chris, Quentin, Rex, and Coach Brown each mouthed the name of the shoo-in, who was apparently announced the week prior.

As each team's time expired and a new pick was selected, cameramen circled the tables like sharks, getting reactions from each prospect. Chris managed to play it cool for the first fifteen picks. But as it switched to Detroit for the sixteenth's pick, his composure started to melt away. She couldn't blame him. In less than an hour, they'd make it to the twenty-fourth pick from the Texans and the twenty-fifth pick from the Cowboys. Would he spend the next four years in Texas, or would he have to wait until the next day, and possibly be scooped up by another team in need of a rookie quarterback?

Butterflies began dive-bombing her stomach in earnest when the Miami Dolphins first-round pick and eighteenth overall pick, Hammer Grossburger, stood onstage, grinning like a dumb idiot and holding up a turquoise jersey with Grossburger across the back. The Eagles were up next, and then it was only four more picks until Jessica could start to answer some of the *what-ifs* swirling in her head.

The massive screens on stage changed from Dolphins logos to Eagles.

The phone in the middle of Jessica's table rang.

Everyone turned to it. Chris stared at it like it was a pissed-off rattlesnake. Then his attention darted back and forth between the phone and the on-stage screens where EAGLES was still prominently displayed above a ticking clock.

Cameramen scrambled over to focus on the table. Surrounded on all sides, she struggled to hide her horror and confusion. But she was sure the cameras picked up on it anyway—it was like the things were specially built to catch every glint of horror and confusion.

"You gonna get that?" Coach Brown said finally, nodding.

Chris started breathing again once Rex gruffed, "Game face, Riley."

On the fifth ring, Chris reached forward and answered.

As he held the receiver to his face, nodding along to the

person on the other end, the crease between his brows disappeared and laugh lines formed at the outer edges of his eyes. Then the muscle in his jaw relaxed and the corners of his mouth ticked up.

Then he laughed. He actually laughed.

Jessica turned to Quentin. "Do teams call ahead? Like, could the Cowboys just be calling to let him know he's still their pick?"

Quentin patted her knee and frowned sympathetically. "No," he said curtly. "No one does that."

"So that's the Philadelphia Eagles?" She almost couldn't believe she was saying it. She still didn't know much about football, but NFL 101 was that Eagles were the opposite of Cowboys. She'd known that since she was a child. Even God had shown a distaste for the Eagles. But where was He now? Where the *hell* was her father when she actually needed him? She hadn't heard from him once since she'd arrived in Chicago, and, sure, that had been a huge relief ... until about thirty seconds ago.

There better be a goddamn tsunami happening some-where. God? God?!

No answer.

She leaned over to Quentin again. "And you said he can't refuse an offer and wait for a better one?"

Quentin pressed his lips together tightly and shook his head while staring at Chris, who was now joking around on the phone. Was he hamming it up for the cameras, or was he genuinely enjoying himself amid this nightmarish turn of events?

"On the plus side," Quentin said, speaking into Jessica's ear, "you're now dating a millionaire."

Chris hung up the phone and stood from his chair, the cameras hardly allowing him an inch to maneuver. Mrs. Riley stood as well, and he hugged her first, just like Jessica had coached him to.

Mrs. Riley was ecstatic. She didn't seem to mind that her son was moving across the country.

What's wrong with her?!

Then Chris turned to Jessica, and when their eyes met, she didn't have the heart to be sad. Well, no, she did, but she didn't have the heart to let Chris know, so she forced an awkward smile and let him wrap her up in his arms.

"We'll figure it out," he whispered into her ear before pulling back and giving her a quick kiss on the lips. Then he did the familiar handshake hug thing with Quentin before shaking hands with both of his former coaches and heading out of the dining area to go backstage and prepare for his big reveal.

Jessica watched him go, camera bulbs flashing, Chris looking like the superstar she always knew he was, and all she wanted to do was run after him. But she kept ass in chair, eventually turning back around to the others.

No more cameras remained pointed at their table. Chris had taken those with him to the exit before they'd turned back and began circling other tables with undrafted players.

Jessica was alone.

When Chris appeared onstage a few minutes later,

holding a forest green jersey with RILEY freshly ironed onto the back, two sexy and nameless women standing on either side of him in evening gowns Jessica knew she couldn't pull off even if one of her miracles was looking good in evening gowns, she struggled to keep air moving in and out of her lungs.

After almost a year of worrying about and scraping together money, amassing piles of credit card and personal debt, her money problems were now completely solved. Poof. Just like that. Chris wouldn't take no for an answer when it came to paying off her debts, and it was likely he wouldn't stop there, either. She should be happy. Thrilled, even. This was it.

So why did she sort of want to throw up the fancy mashed potatoes and overcooked steak she'd consumed a half-hour ago?

Because you have a brand new problem now. A worse one. One money can't fix.

Chris waved to her. She waved back, blinking away fresh tears.

I'm such a fucking idiot.

In the beginning, Jessica had been so sure. When she'd dropped out of college, moved to Austin, started on this crazy path toward opening a bakery. Did she have doubts? Duh. But something about it had felt right at a gut level, so much so that she stuck it out through every setback. She rarely stuck out anything. The fact that she managed to persevere had to mean something. It had to mean she was on the right path.

And maybe she was. But Chris was on another path, which had run parallel for so long she's confused the two as one.

Now they diverged. This was the moment. She could feel that, too.

As he strutted off stage, holding his Eagles jersey high like a banner, she had the urge to scramble through the underbrush between trails to emerge by his side. But could she desert her own path for his?

Wait. Who are you, Jimmy Dean? What is all this horseshit about paths? Maybe there is *no path. Or if there is, it's one God chose, not me. And screw that.*

On the screens above the stage, EAGLES changed to TITANS and a phone rang at a table to her left.

I don't have to play that game. If there are no paths, Chris and I aren't on separate ones!

Checkmate, God. Deal with it.

The conviction jammed a stopper into her tear ducts. She would hold tight to it for as long as she could, even though she knew there was no such thing as checkmate when it came to dear old Dad. But she couldn't stand the thought of letting Him win.

However ... while she hadn't learned much about chess during her foray in tenth grade, she *had* learned one thing: the opponent can't win if you flip the whole damn board.

End of Book 5

Keep reading for a free treat from the author.

Acknowledgments

Thanks be to the Collective Task Force, the Sumus Omnes Porcos Facebook group, my beta readers, my fucking incredible editor, and my husband, who will laugh at literally any stupid idea I run by him.

Okay, I did this thing ...

I started writing this one back in April (five months ago). I made it about thirty pages in and was like, "HOLY MOLEY this is crap."

After a few days spent mulling over a career change, I realized what was going on.

I didn't know this story well enough because I didn't understand *Railed to the Cross*.

I knew I would include excerpts, and what was inside Jimmy's memoirs would inform this plot, so until I knew what the hell Jimmy had in his book, I couldn't keep pushing forward and hope for Book 5 to be anything other than boring nonsense.

I spent about a week reading memoirs of all kinds. And when I say a week, I mean it. A full week. I was at a cabin in the middle of Nowhere, Texas, and read non-stop. Some of the memoirs were interesting, and some were so very horrifying (rhymes with *Crate Again*).

Y'all. I read Bill O'Reilly's *Killing Jesus* as the man (O'Reilly, not Jesus) was in the news for being a complete creep. That's fucking dedication. (It's actually an engrossing read if you get past the whole "this is an historical and totally unbiased account based on ... the Bible" claim.)

I read a little bit about personality disorders, too, but I usually do that. Reading about psychopaths is my favorite.

Finally, once I came up for air and had a whole hell of a lot of notes, I was ready to move forward; I was ready to write *Railed to the Cross*.

So I spent one of the weirdest months of my life writing it in its entirety. Even God doesn't want to go inside Jimmy Dean's head, yet there I was. And it was a mindfuck I don't wish to relive.

However, once Jimmy's book was complete, writing *It is Risen* was a breeze. I scrapped the thirty pages from before and started fresh, and it was fun as hell. Almost worth that month of mornings spent locked away in my office, pretending to be a cult leader, emerging for lunch in a daze and telling my husband in subdued tones, "I think this might be the greatest thing I've ever written." Then adding, "And I'm giving it away for free. What's wrong with my brain?"

There is no conclusive answer to the latter question. But yes, I'm giving away the full manuscript of *Railed to the Cross* for free. Mostly because if I posted it on Amazon and someone bought it out of context, that could be disastrous, but also because you've read five books of this series, and that blows my mind. So I thought a gift was in order.

Granted, thrusting *Railed to the Cross* on people might be considered an act of mental abuse. Verdict is still out on that, but I'll let you decide for yourself.

Get your copy of *Railed to the Cross:*

http://www.hclairetaylor.com/railed-to-the-cross

See you at the end of Book 6.
-H. Claire

About the Author

H. CLAIRE TAYLOR has lived in Austin since the eighties (it's her hometown) and hasn't yet found a compelling reason to move away.

After being a Very Good Student™ of creative writing at Texas State University, she worked an assortment of unfulfilling jobs until her inner tortured artist could recover from four soul-crushing years of academia, at which point she held her nose and jumped into the muddy waters of writing comedy full time.

Now she shares a home with her husband and two black-and-white mutts and suffers from an unhealthy dependency on Post-It Notes that she can quit whenever she wants. Really. When she's not working on her novels, she's blogging and recording her comedy podcast, Something Nice to Say.

Casually stalk her:

www.hclairetaylor.com
contact@hclairetaylor.com

Also by H. Claire Taylor

The Jessica Christ Series

The Beginning (Book 1)

A Great Gulf (short story)

And It Was Good (Book 2)

It's a Miracle! (Book 3)

Nu Alpha Omega (Book 4)

Kilhaven Police (w/Brock Bloodworth)

Shift Work (Book 1)

Wimbledon, Kentucky

A Single's Guide to Texas Roadways